Praise for Camilla Läckberg's

THE GOLDEN CAGE

A *Glamour* and *Real Simple* Best Book of the Year

"Ingenious psychological suspense. . . . The lure of *The Golden Cage* lies in the moral ambiguity of its heroine."
—*The Washington Post*

"The doyenne of Swedish crime fiction serves up a propulsive tale. . . . There's enough haute couture, cava, and hot sex to sate a devotee of romance fiction, but the real satisfaction comes in watching our heroine reclaim her fierceness."
—*O, The Oprah Magazine*

"An extremely satisfying thriller from the ever-compelling Camilla Läckberg, *The Golden Cage* . . . soon evolves into one of the most twisted and triumphant revenge thrillers."
—CrimeReads

"Written by European superstar Läckberg, this is a twisty tale set squarely inside the world of the very rich and very fabulous."
—*Glamour*

"One stunningly sexy and over-the-top psychological thriller."
—*Parade*

"At long last, the thriller genre is serving up a novel that truly deserves to be mentioned alongside *Gone Girl*."
—POPSUGAR

CAMILLA LÄCKBERG

THE GOLDEN CAGE

Camilla Läckberg is the prize-winning, bestselling author of the Fjällbacka series, which has sold more than twenty-three million copies worldwide. Her books are sold in more than sixty countries and have been translated into forty-three languages. She lives in Stockholm.

ALSO BY CAMILLA LÄCKBERG

THE GOLDEN CAGE

THE GOLDEN CAGE

CAMILLA LÄCKBERG

Translated from the Swedish by Neil Smith

VINTAGE CRIME/BLACK LIZARD
VINTAGE BOOKS
A Division of Penguin Random House LLC
New York

FIRST VINTAGE CRIME/BLACK LIZARD EDITION, MAY 2021

The Library of Congress has cataloged the Alfred A. Knopf edition as follows:
Names: Läckberg, Camilla, author. | Smith, Neil (Neil Andrew), translator.
Title: The golden cage : a novel / Camilla Läckberg ; translated by Neil Smith.
Other titles: Bur av guld. English
Description: First edition. | New York : Alfred A. Knopf, 2020.
Identifiers: LCCN 2019036697 (print) | LCCN 2019036698 (ebook)
Classification: LCC PT9877.22.A3413 B87 2020 (print) |
LCC PT9877.22.A3413 (ebook) | DDC 839.73/8—dc23
LC record available at https://lccn.loc.gov/2019036697

Vintage Crime/Black Lizard Trade Paperback ISBN: 978-1-9848-9928-6
eBook ISBN: 978-0-525-65798-9

Book design by M. Kristen Bearse

www.blacklizardcrime.com

Printed in the United States of America
10 9 8 7 6 5 4 3 2 1

For Christina

PART ONE

"Couldn't she just be injured?" Faye said.

She looked down at the table, unable to meet their gaze.

A brief moment of hesitation. Then a sympathetic voice.

"There's an awful lot of blood. From such a small body. But I don't want to speculate until a medical examiner has made an evaluation."

Faye nodded. Someone gave her a transparent plastic cup of water; she was shaking so much as she raised it to her lips that a few drops ran down her chin and dripped onto her blouse. The blond policewoman with the kind blue eyes leaned forward and gave her a tissue to dry herself with.

She wiped herself slowly. The water was going to leave nasty blotches on the silk blouse. Not that it mattered anymore.

"There's no doubt, then? None at all?"

The female police officer glanced at her colleague, then shook her head. She chose her words carefully. "Like I said, a doctor needs to reach a verdict based on the evidence at the crime scene. But as things stand, everything points toward the same explanation: that your ex-husband, Jack, has killed your daughter."

Faye closed her eyes and stifled a sob.

Julienne was asleep at last. Her hair was spread out across the pink pillow. Her breathing was calm. Faye stroked her cheek, gently, so she wouldn't wake her.

Jack was coming home from his business trip to London that evening. Or was it Hamburg? Faye couldn't remember. He'd be tired and stressed when he got home, but she'd make sure he managed to relax properly.

She carefully closed the bedroom door, crept into the hall, and checked that the front door was locked. Back in the kitchen she ran her hand along the counter. Ten feet of marble. Carrera, naturally. Unfortunately it was ridiculously impractical; the porous marble absorbed everything like a sponge and already had some ugly stains. But Jack had never even considered choosing something more practical. The kitchen in the apartment on Narvavägen had cost just shy of a million kronor, and absolutely no expense had been spared.

Faye reached for a bottle of Amarone and put a wineglass on the counter. The glass touching the marble, the glug as the wine poured—these sounds were the essence of her evenings at home when Jack was away. She poured the wine carefully so there wouldn't be another red-wine spatter on the white marble, and closed her eyes as she raised the glass to her lips.

She dimmed the lighting, then went out into the hall where

the black-and-white portraits of her, Julienne, and Jack hung. They had been taken by Kate Gabor, the Crown Princess's unofficial court photographer, who every year took a fresh set of enchanting photographs of the royal children playing in the autumn leaves in crisp white outfits. She and Jack had chosen to have their pictures taken in summer. They were standing by the shore in a relaxed, playful pose. Julienne between them, her fair hair lifted by the breeze. White clothes, obviously. She was wearing a simple cotton Armani dress, Jack a shirt and rolled-up trousers from Hugo Boss, and Julienne a lace dress from Stella McCartney's children's collection. They had had a fight minutes before the pictures were taken. She couldn't remember what it had been about, only that it had been her fault. But none of that was evident in the pictures.

Faye went up the stairs. She hesitated outside the door to Jack's study, then pushed it open. The room was situated in a tower, with views in every direction. A unique layout in a unique property, as the real estate agent had put it when he showed them the apartment five years ago. She had been pregnant with Julienne at the time, her head full of bright hopes for the future.

She loved the tower room. The space and all the light from the windows made her feel like she was flying. And now that it was dark outside, the arched walls enveloped her like a warm cocoon.

She had chosen the décor herself, as she had with the rest of the apartment. She had picked the wallpaper, the bookcases, the desk, the photographs and artwork on the walls. And Jack loved what she'd done. He never questioned her taste, and was always incredibly proud whenever guests asked for the number of their interior designer.

In those moments, he let her shine.

While all the other rooms were furnished in a contemporary style, light and airy, Jack's study was more masculine. Heavier. She had put more effort into this room than Julienne's nursery and the rest of the apartment put together. Jack was going to spend so much time in here, making important decisions that would affect their family's future. The least she could do was give him a refuge of his own up here, almost in the clouds.

Faye ran her hand across Jack's desk with satisfaction. It was a Russian desk, she had bought it at an auction at Bukowski's, and it had once belonged to Ingmar Bergman. Jack wasn't much of a Bergman aficionado—action films with Jackie Chan or comedies starring Ben Stiller were more to his taste—but like her he preferred it when furniture came with a bit of history.

When they showed guests around the apartment he always patted the top of the desk with the palm of his hand twice and said, as if in passing, that the fine piece of furniture had once stood in the world-famous director's home. Faye smiled every time he did that, because their eyes usually met as he said it. It was one of the thousand things they shared in their lives. Those covert glances, all the meaningful and meaningless gestures that went to make up a relationship.

She sank onto the chair behind the desk and spun it until she was facing the window. Snow was falling outside, turning to slush as it hit the street far below. When she leaned forward and looked down, she saw a car struggling through the dark February evening. The driver turned onto Banérgatan, toward the city center. For a moment she forgot what she was doing there, why she was sitting in Jack's study. It was far too easy to drift away in the darkness and become hypnotized by the snowflakes pushing slowly through the blackness.

Faye blinked, sat up straight, and rotated the chair so she was facing the large screen of the Mac, then nudged the mouse, and the screen came to life. She wondered what Jack had done with the mouse mat she had given him at Christmas, the one with a photograph of her and Julienne. Instead he was using an ugly blue one from Nordea Bank, a Christmas gift to its private banking clients.

She knew the password: *Julienne2010*. At least he didn't have anything from Nordea as his background, and was still using the picture he had taken of her and Julienne in Marbella. They were lying at the water's edge, Faye holding her daughter up toward the sky. They were both laughing, but Faye's laughter was more sensed than seen as she lay on her back with her hair floating in the water. Julienne's bright blue eyes were looking straight into the camera, right through the lens. Into Jack's eyes, just as blue.

Faye leaned closer, her eyes looking along her own tanned body, shiny with salt and water. Though only a few months had passed since she had given birth, she had been in better shape then than she was now. Her stomach was flat. Her arms thin. Her thighs slim and taut. Now, almost three years later, she weighed at least twenty pounds more than she had in Spain. Thirty, maybe. She hadn't dared weigh herself for a long time.

She tore her eyes from her own image on the screen and opened the browser, clicked to bring up the history, and typed *porn*. Link after link appeared, sorted by date. She had no difficulty at all tracing Jack's sexual fantasies in recent months. It was like a reference book covering his libido. *Sexual Fantasies for Dummies*.

On October 26 he had watched two clips. "Russian teen gets slammed by big cock" and "Skinny teen brutally hammered." You could say what you liked about the porn industry, but the titles of the films were at least direct and to the point. No attempts to prettify or embellish, to lie about what was coming and what the person in front of the screen wanted to see. A straightforward dialogue, open and honest communication.

Jack had looked at porn for as long as she had known him, and sometimes she looked herself, when she was on her own. She was scornful of friends who declared that their husbands would never dream of looking at porn. Talk about repression!

Jack never used to let his consumption of porn influence their sex life. It had never been a matter of either/or. But now he no longer sought comfort from her, despite seeking satisfaction from "Skinny teen brutally hammered."

The knot in her stomach grew bigger with each clip she watched. The girls were young, skinny, submissive. Jack had always liked his women thin and young. It wasn't him who had changed, it was her. And wasn't that how most men wanted their women? In Östermalm there was no room for aging and weight gain. At least not for women.

In the past month Jack had watched one particular video seven or eight times. "Young petite schoolgirl brutally fucked by her teacher." Faye clicked play. A young schoolgirl in a short, checked skirt, white shirt, tie, socks, and Pippi Longstocking pigtails appeared; it seemed she was struggling with her lessons, particularly biology. Informing her that they have arranged for extra tutoring, her conscientious parents go out for the evening, leaving their daughter at home alone. The doorbell rings. A man in his forties, wearing a jacket with patches on the elbows and clutching a briefcase, is at the door. They go into a brightly lit kitchen. The girl gets her homework and opens her books. They go through the muscles of the body.

"When I say a muscle, I want you to show me where on your body it is. Can you do that?" the teacher asks in a deep voice.

The girl opens her eyes wide, nods, and pouts. She manages two muscles. When he says gluteus maximus, the buttock muscle, she pulls up her skirt, revealing the hem of her underpants, and points at the outside of her thigh. The teacher shakes his head with a smile.

"Stand up and I'll show you," he says.

She pushes her chair back and stands up. He places his large hand behind her knee and moves it up her leg, under her skirt. He lifts her skirt higher and pulls her underwear aside. Pushes a finger inside. The girl groans. A perfect porn groan. But with a trace of astonished innocence and guilt. An acknowledgment to the viewer that she knows she shouldn't be doing this. That this is naughty. But she can't help it. The temptation is too great for her to resist.

He pushes his finger in and out a few times. Then bends her over the table and fucks her. She screams, groans, claws at the table. Begs for more. The whole thing reaches a climax when he tells her to put on her glasses—they have fallen off somewhere along the way—before he ejaculates in her face. Her face contorted with pleasure, her mouth half-open, the schoolgirl receives his semen.

Porn films had to be the clearest indication of just how highly men valued their semen. It was bestowed upon breathless, reverential women with their mouths half-open, always half-open, as if it were a precious gift.

Faye put the computer back in sleep mode with a couple of clicks of the mouse on the ugly Nordea mat. If that was what Jack wanted, that was what he would get.

She pushed the chair back from the desk, and it creaked reluctantly as she stood up. It was pitch-black outside now. The light snow had stopped falling. She picked up her wineglass and left the room.

Faye had everything she needed in her walk-in closet. She looked at the time. Half past nine. Jack's plane was about to land; soon he'd be sitting in a taxi. Naturally, he used Arlanda's VIP service, so it wouldn't take him long to get out of the airport.

She had a quick shower and shaved off the light stubble that had grown out above her genitals. She washed herself thoroughly, then put makeup on, not the way she usually did, but a bit carelessly, like someone with less experience. She rubbed in plenty of blush, used far too much mascara, and, as the icing on the cake, applied some bubblegum-pink lipstick she found at the bottom of her makeup box—probably given to her in a goodie bag at some event.

Jack wouldn't be getting her—not Faye, his wife, the mother of his child—but someone younger and more innocent, someone untouched. That was what he needed.

She picked out one of Jack's thin gray ties and knotted it carelessly around her neck. She put on a pair of the reading glasses he was ashamed to wear in public and always hid when they had visitors. Rectangular, black, Dolce & Gabbana. Faye looked at the result in the mirror. She looked ten years younger. Almost like the person she had been when she left Fjällbacka.

She was no one's wife. No one's mother. It was perfect.

Faye crept into Julienne's room to get one of her exercise books and a pink pencil. She froze when Julienne murmured in her sleep. Was she going to wake up? No, she was soon breathing calmly again.

She went into the kitchen to pour herself some more wine but stopped and pulled out a box of Julienne's plastic cups instead. She filled a large Hello Kitty cup with red wine, one with a lid and a straw. Perfect.

When the key turned in the front door she was sitting looking through *The Economist,* which Jack insisted on leaving out on the coffee table. She was the only person in the family who actually read it.

Jack put his case on the floor, took off his shoes, and inserted the cedarwood blocks that kept his soft, handmade Italian leather shoes in shape. Faye sat still. Unlike her usual discreet lip gloss from Lancôme, the pink lipstick felt sticky and smelled faintly synthetic.

Jack opened the fridge carefully. He hadn't spotted her yet. He was moving quietly, probably thought she and Julienne were both asleep.

She watched him from the gloom of the living room. Like a stranger looking through a window, she was able to observe her husband without his knowledge. Jack was always on the alert otherwise. Now, when he thought no one could see him, he moved differently. He was relaxed, almost careless. His usually upright frame was slouching, only slightly, but enough for someone who knew him as well as she did to appreciate the difference. His face was smoother, without the permanent worry line that was always there these days, even on the social occasions that were closely intertwined with his career, with their life, where the laughter and clink of glasses could be transformed into a multimillion-kronor deal the following day.

She remembered what Jack was like as a young man, when they first met. That cheeky look in his eyes, his happy laugh, hands that couldn't stop touching her, that couldn't get enough of her.

The light in the fridge lit up his face and she couldn't take her eyes off him. She loved him. Loved his broad back. Loved his big hands, which were raising a carton of juice to his lips. Soon they would be on her, in her. Dear God, how she longed for that.

Maybe that longing made her body move, because he suddenly turned his face toward the polished oven door and saw her reflection. He started and spun around, his hand clutching the carton of juice, halfway to his mouth.

He put it down on the island.

"Are you still up?" he said, surprised. The line between his neatly shaped eyebrows was back.

Faye didn't answer, she just got to her feet and took a few steps toward him. His eyes roamed across her body. It had been a long time since he had looked at her that way.

"Come here," she said softly, in a high voice.

Jack closed the fridge door and the kitchen receded into darkness again. But the lights of the city outside were bright enough for them to see each other. He walked around the island, wiped his mouth with the back of his hand, and leaned forward to kiss her. But she turned her face aside and pushed him down onto a chair. She was in charge now. When he reached out one hand toward her skirt she batted it away, only to place it behind her knee a moment later. She pulled her skirt up so that he could see her lace underwear, hoping he would recognize it, hoping he would see how similar it was. To hers. The young girl. The innocent student.

His hand wandered upward and she couldn't help letting out

a groan. Instead of pulling her panties aside like in the film, he tore them apart. She groaned again, louder, bent over the table, swaying gently as he unbuttoned his trousers and tugged them down along with his underpants. He grabbed hold of her hair and forced her lower on the table. He leaned over her with all his weight, nipping the back of her neck with his teeth, and she caught the smell of orange juice mixed with whiskey from the flight. He kicked her legs apart forcefully, stood behind her, and pushed his way into her.

Jack fucked her hard and aggressively, and with each thrust the tabletop pressed against her midriff. He was hurting her a bit, but the pain was a liberation, it made her forget everything else so that she could concentrate wholly on the pleasure.

She was his. Her pleasure was his. Her body was his.

"Tell me when you're about to come," she groaned with her cheek against the cold tabletop, now smeared with sticky lipstick.

"Now," Jack gasped.

She got down on her knees in front of him. He was breathing heavily as he pushed his cock into her open mouth. He grabbed the back of her head with both hands and forced it farther in. She fought against her gag reflex and tried not to twist her head away. Just take it. Always, just take it.

The porn scene was playing in Faye's mind, and when Jack ejaculated she took pleasure in seeing the same look on his face as the teacher when he took possession of the innocent young student.

"Welcome home, darling," she said with a forced smile.

That was one of the last times they had sex as a married couple.

THE FIRST WEEKS IN STOCKHOLM had been lonely. Two years after I graduated from high school I left Fjällbacka behind. Both mentally and physically. I couldn't get away from that claustro-phobic little place fast enough. It suffocated me with its pictur-esque cobbled streets and inquisitive people who never left me alone. All I took with me was fifteen thousand kronor and top grades in every subject.

I would have liked to get away sooner. But it had taken lon-ger than I expected to sort out all the practical details. Sell the house, clear it, get rid of all the ghosts that crowded around me. The memories were so painful. When I walked around my child-hood home, I kept seeing them everywhere. My older brother, Sebastian. Mom. And, not least, Dad. There was nothing left for me in Fjällbacka. Just gossip. And death.

No one had been there for me then. And they weren't there now either. So I packed my bags and got on the train to Stock-holm without looking back.

And swore never to return.

At Central Station in Stockholm I stopped by a trash can, opened the back of my phone, and threw the SIM card away. Now none of the shadows of the past would be able to reach me. There was no threat of anyone coming after me.

I rented a room for the summer in an apartment above the

ugly Fältöversten shopping mall, the one the residents of Öster-malm shake their heads at and tut about it being "the Socialists' fault, they couldn't resist ruining our lovely Östermalm." But I didn't know any of that at the time. I was used to Hedemyr's ICA supermarket in Tanumshede and thought Fältöversten was so upmarket.

I loved Stockholm right from the outset. From my window on the seventh floor I could look out across the ornate build-ings around me, the leafy parks, the smart cars, and tell myself that one day I would live in one of those imposing nineteenth-century buildings with my husband, our three perfect children, and a dog.

My husband would be an artist. Or an author. Or a musician. As different from Dad as possible. Sophisticated, intellectual, and worldly. He would smell nice and dress smartly. He would be a bit hard on other people, but never to me, because I would be the only person who understood him.

I spent those first long, light nights wandering the streets of Stockholm. I saw fights in alleyways when the nightclubs closed. Heard the shouting, crying, laughter. The sirens of emergency vehicles, heading into danger to save lives. I stared in amazement at the prostitutes in the city center, in their 1980s makeup and high heels, puffy white skin, and needle tracks on their arms that they tried to cover up with long-sleeved tops and blouses. I asked them for cigarettes and fantasized about their lives. The liberation of finding yourself at rock bottom. No risk of fall-ing any deeper into shit. I toyed with the idea of standing there myself, just to understand what it would be like, who the men were who paid for five minutes of sordid intimacy in their Volvo with a child's seat in the back and extra diapers and wipes in the glove compartment.

That was when my life really started. The past clung to my an-kles like a deadweight. Weighing me down, spoiling things, hold-ing me back. But every cell of my body was alive with curiosity. It was me against the world. Far from home, in a city I had dreamed about my whole life. I hadn't merely wanted to get away. I had been desperate to come *here*. Slowly I made Stockholm my city. It gave me hope that I might be able to heal and forget.

In early July my landlady, a retired teacher, went off to visit her grandchildren in Norrland.

"No visitors," she said sternly before she left.

"No visitors," I repeated obediently.

That evening I put my makeup on and drank her gin and whiskey. Mixed with cherry liqueur and Amarula. It tasted disgusting, but that didn't matter, I wanted to feel that rush, the rush that promised the bliss of forgetting and spread through my body like a warm glow.

When I had drunk enough to feel brave, I put on a cotton dress and walked to Stureplan. After a bit of hesitation, I sat down at a sidewalk bar that looked nice. Famous faces I had only ever seen on television walked past. Laughing, intoxicated by both alcohol and the summer.

At midnight I got in the line outside a nightclub on the other side of the street. The atmosphere was impatient and I wasn't sure if they'd let me in. I tried to imitate the others, act like them. It was only later that I realized they must have been tourists too. As lost as I was, but with courage painted on.

I heard laughter behind me. Two guys the same age as me walked past the line and went up to the bouncers. A nod and a handshake. Everyone was staring at them with jealousy and fascination. Hours of preparation and giggling over glasses of rosé, only to end up shivering behind a rope. When it could all be so simple. If only we had been someone.

Unlike me, these two guys were people who got noticed, they were respected, they belonged. They were Someone. There and then I decided the same thing was going to apply to me.

At that moment one of the guys turned and looked curiously at the crowd. Our eyes met.

I turned away and felt in my bag for a cigarette. I didn't want to look stupid, didn't want to look like what I was—a girl from the country on her first trip to a nightclub in the big city, giddy with stolen gin and Amarula. The next thing I knew, he was standing in front of me. His hair was close-cut, his eyes blue, kind. His ears stuck out slightly. He was wearing a beige shirt and dark jeans.

"What's your name?"

"Matilda," I replied.

The name I hated. The name that belonged to another life, another person. Someone who was no longer me. Someone I had left behind when I got on the train to Stockholm.

"I'm Viktor. Are you here by yourself?"

I didn't answer.

"Go stand next to the bouncer," he said.

"I'm not on the list," I mumbled.

"Me neither."

A sparkling smile. I pushed my way out of the line, the object of envious, longing stares from girls in too few clothes and boys with too much hair gel.

"She's with me."

The meat mountain by the door removed the rope and said, "Welcome."

In the crowd Viktor took my hand, leading me deeper into the darkness. Other people's shadows, flickering lights, all different colors, throbbing bass, entwined bodies dancing. We stopped at the end of a long bar and Viktor said hello to the bartender.

"What would you like to drink?" he asked.

With the cloying taste of sickly liqueur still in my mouth, I said, "Beer."

"Good, I like girls who drink beer. Classy."

"Classy?"

"Yeah. Good. Solid."

He handed me a Heineken. Raised the bottle in a toast. I smiled at him and drank some.

"So, what dreams have you got for your life, Matilda?"

"To be someone," I replied. Without pausing to think.

"You're already someone, aren't you?"

"Someone else."

"I can't see that there's much wrong with you."

Viktor took a few sideways dance steps, swaying in time to the music.

"So what are your dreams?" I asked.

"Me? I just want to make music."

"Are you a musician?" I had to lean closer and raise my voice for him to hear me.

"DJ. But I'm not working tonight. I'm playing tomorrow; I'll be up there then."

I followed his finger. On a small stage over by the wall, behind a turntable, stood the guy Viktor had arrived with, grooving to the music. A little while later he came over to us, and introduced himself as Axel. He seemed nice, unthreatening.

"Good to meet you, Matilda," he said, holding out his hand.

I couldn't help thinking how different they were from the guys back home. Polished. Well-spoken. Axel got a drink, then disappeared. Viktor and I drank another toast. My beer was almost finished.

"We're warming up beforehand with a few friends tomorrow, if you'd like to come along?"

"Maybe," I said, looking at him thoughtfully. "Why did you want me to come in with you?"

I drank the last of my beer demonstratively, hoping he'd order more. He did. One for me, one for him. Then he answered my question. His blue eyes glinted in the dim light.

"Because you're pretty. And you looked lonely. Are you regretting it?"

"No, not at all."

He fished a pack of Marlboros from his back pocket and offered me one. I had nothing against taking it, mine would last longer that way. There wasn't much left from the fifteen thousand I'd gotten from the sale of the house once the mortgage and everything else had been paid off.

Our hands touched as he lit my cigarette. His hand was warm and tanned. I missed his touch the moment it was gone.

"You've got sad eyes. Did you know that?" he said, sucking hard on his cigarette.

"What do you mean?"

"There seems to be some sort of sadness in you. I find that attractive. I'm suspicious of people who go around thinking life's a barrel of laughs the whole time. Life is fun. But not all the time. People who are always happy bore me. We're not supposed to be happy all the time, because then the world would stop."

One of the bouncers was staring pointedly at Viktor, and he shrugged and stubbed his cigarette out after a few quick puffs. I did the same. But I didn't answer. I had a feeling he was making fun of me.

Suddenly my head started to spin from all the drinks. I decided to get a souvenir, leaned forward, put my hand on the back of his head and pulled his face toward mine. A gesture that must have made me seem far more confident than I was. Our lips met. He tasted of beer and Marlboros, and he was a good kisser. Gentle but intense.

"Shall we go back to my place?" he asked.

Jack was sitting at the kitchen table in his dark-blue bathrobe reading *Dagens Industri*. He didn't even look up when Faye came into the kitchen, but she was used to that when he was feeling stressed. And considering all the responsibilities of his work and all the hours he spent in the office, he deserved to be left in peace in the morning on the weekend.

The four-thousand-square-foot apartment, the result of knocking four smaller apartments into one, felt claustrophobic when Jack needed to be left alone. Faye still didn't know how to behave on days like that.

In the car on the way home from Lidingö, where Julienne had gone to play with a friend from preschool, she had been looking forward to spending the morning with Jack. Just the two of them. Curl up in bed, watch a television program that they would both declare stupid and vulgar. Jack would tell her about his week. They'd go for a walk on Djurgården, hand in hand.

Talk, the way they used to.

She cleared away the remains of her and Julienne's breakfast. The cornflakes had gone soggy in the soured milk. She hated the texture of wet cereal and the sour smell, and swallowed the instinct to gag as she wiped the bowls off with a cloth.

There were bread crumbs on the island, and a half-eaten crisp-bread sandwich was balancing on the edge, defying the laws of gravity. The only thing holding it up was the fact that it was lying face-down.

"Can't you at least try to clear up before you go out?" Jack said without looking up from his newspaper. "Surely we shouldn't need help with the housework on weekends as well?"

"Sorry." Faye swallowed the lump in her throat as she wiped the counter with a cloth. "Julienne wanted to get going. She was making such a fuss."

Jack murmured and went on reading. He was freshly showered after his run. He smelled good, Armani Code, the cologne he had used since before they met. Julienne had been disappointed not to see her dad, but he had gone out running before she woke up, and didn't come back until Faye had left with her. It had been a difficult morning. None of the four breakfast options Faye had given Julienne had been acceptable, and getting her dressed had been a painful, sweaty marathon.

But at least the kitchen counter was clean now. The aftermath of the war had been cleared away.

Faye put the dishcloth in the drainer and looked at Jack, sitting there at the kitchen table. Even though he was tall, fit, responsible, prosperous—all the classic attributes of a successful man—he remained a boy in many ways. She was the only person who saw him for what he was.

Faye would always love him, no matter what.

"It'll soon be time for a haircut, darling."

She reached out one hand and managed to touch a few locks of his damp hair before he jerked his head away.

"I haven't got time. This expansion is complicated; I need to stay focused. I can't keep running to have my hair cut every five minutes like you."

Faye sat down on the chair next to him. Put her hands on her lap. Tried to remember when she had last had her hair cut.

"Do you want to talk about it?"

"About what?"

"Compare."

Very slowly, he looked up at Faye from the newspaper. He shook his head and sighed. She regretted saying anything. Regretted she hadn't carried on wiping crumbs from the counter. Nonetheless, she took a deep breath.

"Before, you used to like—"

Jack flinched and lowered the newspaper. His hair, a few millimeters too long, fell across his face and he jerked his head irritably. Why couldn't she let him be? Just carry on with the cleaning. Be thin and beautiful and supportive. He had been at work all week. If she had to guess, he'd soon shut himself away in the tower room and carry on working. For her and Julienne's sake. So that they could have a good life. Because that was *their* goal. Not his. Theirs.

"What good would talking about it do? You don't know anything about business anymore, do you? It's a perishable product. You can't rely on what you used to know."

Faye fingered her wedding ring. Twisted it around, around.

If she hadn't said anything, they could have had the morning she had been dreaming of. But she had thrown all that away with one stupid question. When she already knew better.

"Do you even know the name of the current Swedish finance minister?" he said.

"Mikael Damberg," she replied without thinking. Immediately and correctly.

She regretted it when she saw the look on Jack's face. Why couldn't she just keep quiet?

"Okay. A new law is about to be passed. Do you know what it is?"

She knew. But she shook her head slowly.

"No, of course you don't," Jack said. "It stipulates that we as a company have to remind our customers one month before their subscriptions expire. Before, things would renew automatically. Do you understand what that means?"

She knew all right. She could have given him a systematic breakdown of what it meant for Compare. But she loved him. She sat there in her million-kronor kitchen, with her husband who was a boy in a man's body, a man only she knew, and who she loved above all else. And she shook her head. Instead of saying that Leasando Limited, a small electricity supplier owned by Compare, would lose approximately twenty percent of those customers whose contracts would have been renewed automatically in the past. In round figures, that meant turnover would shrink by five hundred million a year. And profits by two hundred million.

She shook her head.

Fingered her wedding ring.

"You don't know," Jack said after a long pause. "Can you let me read now?"

He raised the newspaper. Went back to the world of numbers, stock valuations, share issues, and company takeovers that she had spent three years studying at the Stockholm School of Economics before she had quit. For Jack's sake. For the business's sake. For their family's sake.

She rinsed the dishcloth under the tap, then scooped up the soggy cornflakes and crumbs from the drainer with her hand and threw them in the trash. She heard the rustle of Jack's newspaper behind her back. She shut the lid quietly so as not to disturb him.

STOCKHOLM, SUMMER 2001

VIKTOR BLOM HAD A PALE-BROWN birthmark on the back of his neck, and his broad back was very suntanned. He was sleeping soundly, giving me all the time in the world to look at both him and the room we were lying in. The windows had no curtains, and apart from the double bed the only furniture was a chair covered with dirty clothes. The sun was forming prisms that danced across the white walls.

My naked legs were wrapped in a damp, dirty sheet. I kicked it off, then wrapped it around me like a towel and carefully opened the bedroom door. The sparsely furnished apartment that Viktor and Axel were renting for the summer occupied the first two floors of a building on Brantingsgatan in Gärdet. There was a small garden outside, with a table, some wooden chairs, and a black domed barbecue. There was an empty Fanta can on the table, crammed with cigarette butts.

The sound of loud snoring was coming from Axel's room. The living room and kitchen were on the ground floor, so I went downstairs, made coffee, and unearthed my cigarettes from my bag, which lay discarded on the hall floor. Then I went outside with my coffee and cigarettes and sat on a chair in the garden.

Tessin Park lay spread out before me. The sun was low in the sky, making me squint.

I didn't want to be clingy and annoying. That business of Viktor saying he'd like me to come to their party was probably just talk. To get me into bed. I'd heard far grander promises in bars in the past. Viktor seemed to have had fun with me. I'd certainly had fun with him. But it was best to leave it at that. I stubbed the cigarette out in the Fanta can and stood up to go and find my clothes. Then the door opened behind me.

"There you are," Viktor said sleepily. "Have you got a cigarette?"

I passed him one. He sat down on the chair I had been sitting in and blinked in the sunlight. I sat down next to him.

"I was about to go," I said.

I was expecting to see a look of relief on his face. Gratitude that I wasn't going to be one of those clingy girls, the sort who didn't understand when it was time to leave.

But Viktor surprised me.

"Go?" he exclaimed. "Why?"

"I don't live here, do I?"

"So?"

"You and Axel won't want me hanging about here, will you? I get that it was a one-off and you've got your own stuff to do. I don't want to be the annoying girl who doesn't know when it's time to leave."

Viktor looked away and gazed out across Tessin Park. I resisted the urge to stroke the stubble on his shaved head. There was a photograph in the bedroom that showed him with thick, curly fair hair. He sat there in silence and for a while I thought I had seen through him. That he was as easy to read as every other guy.

Eventually he said, "I don't know how guys usually treat you, what things are like where you come from, but I think you're great. You're different, genuine. Obviously you can leave if you want to, but I'd really like it if you stayed for a while. I thought I'd go and get us some juice and croissants from the 7-Eleven, then do a bit of sunbathing and order a pizza."

"Okay." My answer came without me having time to think about it.

A wasp flew past my face. I waved it away, although I'd never been frightened of wasps. There were far worse things to be frightened of.

"'Okay'? Seriously, what kind of guys do you normally hook up with?"

"Back home the guys are . . . I don't know. They usually want you to have sex and then leave, pretty much. They have their own stuff to be getting on with the next day."

I didn't mention the way they looked at you. The things they said. The shame I had to carry, even though it belonged to someone else. Giving my body to someone who wanted it counted as nothing compared to all the rest of it.

Viktor shaded his eyes with his hand.

"How long have you lived in Stockholm?"

"One month."

"Welcome."

"Thanks."

. . .

Around seven o'clock people started to show up in the apartment. Most of them were a few years older than me, and I felt a bit out of place at first. Viktor disappeared in the crowd and I ended up by the table in the garden with Axel. I sipped a drink and smoked while he told stories that made me roar with laughter, about his Interrail trip with Viktor the previous summer. Two girls came out, and introduced themselves as Julia and Sara. Julia had long brown hair and green eyes, and was wearing a beautiful, dark-blue dress. Sara had a denim skirt and white vest, and her blond hair was pulled into a loose knot.

"I'm so fucking stressed about the autumn," Julia said, leaning forward. "I want to give up, or at least take a year's sabbatical, but Dad won't let me. He loses it whenever I try to raise the subject. God, I hate Lund."

"You poor thing," Sara said, blowing smoke rings.

"I wish I'd had the grades to get into the School of Economics instead. But what the hell—let's forget all that and have some fun tonight."

Julia straightened up and looked at me as if she'd only just noticed I was there.

"What do you do?"

I cleared my throat. Blew out some smoke. I had no inclination to discuss my plans for the future with someone I'd known all of five minutes.

"I'm not doing much at the moment."

"That sounds good. You want to be a student?"

I had applied to various colleges in Stockholm, so I nodded. And thought about my bank account, which was starting to look alarmingly empty.

"I'm thinking about it. But it's a while before they let you know," I said.

"How do you know Axel?"

This from the other girl, Sara, nodding in his direction.

"I met Viktor, if you know him, at Buddha Bar yesterday."

"Did you sleep here?"

I nodded.

They finished their cigarettes in silence before getting to their feet.

"Julia used to go out with Viktor," Axel said once they had gone.

"Used to?"

"Until about three months ago, something like that. This is the first time they've met since she got home from Lund."

. . .

Julia and Sara came along to Buddha Bar. They stuck close to Viktor and kept glaring sullenly at me. The more alcohol I got inside me, the more irritated I became.

Viktor took a break from his decks and came over to me and Axel. I put my arms around him as I met Julia's narrowed eyes. He kissed me and I bit his bottom lip gently. When it was time for him to go back to the DJ's booth he asked if I wanted to go with him. He led me through the crowd with his arm around my waist. It took a while because people kept stopping him to talk. We got there in the end. Viktor put his headphones on, adjusted some controls, and started to sway in time to the music.

I did the same. Then I took one of his hands, slipped it under my dress, and put it between my legs. I wasn't wearing any underpants.

"Do you want to come back to mine tonight?" he asked.

"Yes. If you'd like me to?"

He gave me an intense look that made any spoken answer unnecessary.

"What are we going to do?" I teased.

Viktor laughed and changed track.

It was a wonderful feeling. I was free. Free to do whatever I wanted. To be whoever I wanted. Without the past messing up everything around me, inside me. Without all the people who had been pulling me down. I was slowly turning myself into someone else, little by little.

I looked out across the dancing throng, shut my eyes, and thought about what life was like in Fjällbacka. All the curious glances that followed me wherever I went, the mixture of fascination and sympathy, sticky, heavy, suffocating. No one knew here. No one stared here. My place was here. In Stockholm.

"I'm going to the bathroom," I yelled.

"Okay. I finish in ten minutes. Shall we meet up by the door?"

I nodded and made my way to the lavatory. I stood in the line, smiling to myself about the fact that Viktor belonged to me, no one else. The music from the dance floor thudded in the distance, making the mirror on the wall vibrate.

I looked at my reflection. My hair was blonder than usual, and I felt tanned and fresh. I thought I looked older than I had only a few weeks ago. By the basins a girl aimed a pink can of hairspray at her head. The sweet scent caught in my nose, a refreshing contrast to the smell of sweat, alcohol, and smoky clothes.

The door opened behind me and the music got briefly louder.

I felt a tap on my shoulder and turned. I caught sight of Julia before the drink came flying at me. An ice cube hit me on the forehead, fell to the floor, and bounced away. My eyes stung and I blinked hard with surprise and pain.

"What the hell are you doing?" I shouted, stepping back.

"You little slut," Julia said before turning on her heel and stalking out.

Some other girls laughed. I wiped myself with a paper towel. I felt the humiliation like insects crawling inside me. I felt like my old self again. The one who shrank away and hid in the shadows. The one who cowered under the weight of far too many secrets.

Then I straightened up and looked at myself in the mirror. Never again.

. . .

One week later I got a letter. I had been accepted to do an MBA at the Stockholm School of Economics. I got a copy of the letter, found out what Julia's address was, bought an envelope, and put the copy of the letter inside with a Polaroid photograph Viktor had taken, of me on all fours and Viktor behind me, his face contorted with pleasure. When I dropped the envelope in Julia's family's mailbox I had only one thought in my head. I was never going to let anyone humiliate me again.

One month later I registered at the School of Economics under my middle name, Faye, after the author of my mom's favorite book. Matilda no longer existed.

A waiter hurried past behind Faye's back, presumably heading toward one of the large-gutted men sitting a few tables away. They always rushed to serve men like that. Which was hardly surprising, given that they all looked like they were one steak away from a heart attack.

She looked at Alice, who had just sat down opposite her. When Faye had first gotten to know her and the upper-class women in her circle, she had called them the geese, because their main purpose was to lay eggs for their men. They were supposed to focus on giving birth to heirs and then protect their pampered offspring under their Gucci-clad wings. Then, when the kids started at their carefully selected preschools, it was time to fill the days with appropriate interests. Yoga. Getting their nails done. Organizing dinner parties. Making sure the maid was doing her job properly. Keeping the flotilla of nannies and babysitters under control. Keeping an eye on their own weight. Or lack thereof. Be wet and horny. And, most crucial: learning to turn a blind eye whenever their husbands came home from a late "business dinner" with their shirts badly tucked in.

At first she had mocked them. For their lack of general knowledge, their lack of interest in the genuinely important things in life, their ambitions, which didn't stretch further than the latest design of Valentino's Rockstud bag and the choice between Saint

Moritz or the Maldives for the half-term holiday. But Jack had wanted her to "maintain good relations" with them. Particularly with Henrik's wife, Alice. So now she met the geese on a regular basis.

Neither Faye nor Alice felt any particular warmth toward the other. But whether they liked it or not they were bound together by their husbands' business. By their husbands' "remarkable friendship," as one business magazine had once described it.

Alice Bergendahl was thirty-one, slightly younger than Faye. She had very prominent cheekbones, the waist of a ten-year-old, and legs like Heidi fucking Klum on stilts. And had also given birth to two beautiful, perfectly formed children. Probably with a smile on her face throughout the births. And between the contractions she had probably kept herself busy knitting a pretty bonnet for the miracle that was splitting her perfumed muff into two perfect parts. Because Alice Bergendahl wasn't just beautiful, girlish, thin, and perfumed. She was creative and artistic as well, she had lovely little exhibitions that all the geese were expected to attend with their husbands, or else they would find themselves on Alice's blacklist. Which was upper-class Stockholm's equivalent of Guantánamo.

Alice had arrived at Riche in the company of another long-legged woman called Iris, who was married to a financier, Jesper, who traded in shares. A pauper in comparison, but a possible up-and-comer, and Iris had some sort of provisional status in Alice's entourage until Jesper's success was assured. Her fate would probably be decided within the next couple of months.

They ordered salad—naturally only a small portion each—and three glasses of cava. They ate in dainty mouthfuls and smiled at one another as they worked their way through their children. Which was the only thing they talked about. Apart from their husbands.

"Jesper's taking the Easter holiday off," Iris said. "Can you imagine? We've been married four years and he's never taken more than a week's holiday per year. But he came home the other day and surprised me by saying he'd booked a trip to the Seychelles."

Faye felt a pang of envy. She swallowed it with a sip of cava.

"That's wonderful," she said.

She wondered quietly to herself what Jesper had done to need to salve his conscience that way.

The restaurant was full. Tourists at the window tables, delighted to have gotten in. Shopping bags stuffed under the tables. They did their best to look nonchalant, but between mouthfuls they stared around them, wide-eyed. If they caught sight of someone noteworthy they leaned over their plates and whispered to one another, impressed by whichever television presenters, artists, and politicians were in the room. They didn't recognize the people with real power. The ones who pulled the strings behind the scenes. But Faye knew exactly who they were.

"The Seychelles are lovely," Alice said. "So exotic, somehow. What's the security situation like now? There's been a bit of . . . trouble there."

"Are the Seychelles in the Middle East?" Iris asked uncertainly as she pushed a piece of avocado around her plate.

Faye drank some cava to stop herself from laughing.

"Somewhere near there, surely? It's probably ISIS and all that."

Alice's nose wrinkled at the bubbling noise coming from Faye's throat.

"It's bound to be fine," Iris said, now pushing half an egg with her fork. "Jesper would never expose me and little Orvar to any danger."

Little Orvar? Why did people give their children names that were more suited to syphilitic pirates in the eighteenth century? Okay, Faye had to admit that Julienne was pretty pretentious. But the name had been Jack's suggestion. It sounded nice and would work internationally. It was vital to establish your child's global currency even when it was in the womb. They seemed to have forgotten that bit with Orvar, but it could always be remedied later. The other month a Sixten at Julienne's preschool had suddenly turned into an Henri. The three-year-old must have been utterly baffled, but you couldn't let yourself be distracted by something like that if you wanted the boy to hold his own in an international context.

Faye drank the last of her wine and discreetly gestured to the waiter for a refill.

"No, obviously he wouldn't put you in any danger," Alice said, chewing seductively on a lettuce leaf.

But because she had read in a health magazine that you should chew each mouthful at least thirty times, the seductive look soon gave way to that of a ruminating cow. Faye looked down at her own plate gloomily. She had devoured her minute portion and was still ravenous. She looked longingly at the food that was being delivered to the next table. Steak. Meatballs. Pasta. The dishes were placed before the portly, besuited gentlemen. The sort who could afford a bit of surplus weight. Poor men were fat, but rich men had substance. She tore her eyes from the meatballs. When you were in Alice's company, you didn't eat meatballs with mashed potatoes and cream sauce.

"Wouldn't it do you good to be kidnapped for a few weeks, Iris?" Faye said. "The diet would be full of super-foods. If you asked them nicely, they could probably get hold of a yoga mat for you too."

She looked at Iris's untouched salad.

"You can't make jokes about a thing like that. That's awful!"

Alice shook her head and Faye sighed.

"The Seychelles are a group of islands in the Indian Ocean. We're closer to the Middle East here than they are."

A silence followed. Iris and Alice concentrated on their salads, Faye on the cava that was in danger of running out again.

"Do you see who that is?" Iris whispered, leaning forward with her eyes on the door.

Faye tried to work out who she meant.

"There. The one who just came in. Talking to the bartender."

Now Faye saw him. The singer, John Descentis. Jack's favorite. He'd been on the ropes for a few years, and nowadays mostly featured in the gossip columns in connection with failed relationships, bankruptcy, and embarrassing B-list parties. He and his partner, a pretty girl in her mid-twenties with a leather jacket and dyed black hair, were shown to a table opposite theirs.

"Two beers," he said to the waiter. "To start with."

Alice and Iris rolled their eyes.

"How has he managed to get a table here?" Alice murmured. "This place is really starting to take risks."

Iris shifted position uncomfortably, and her stiff, gold Cartier bracelets rattled.

Faye looked over at John Descentis. She had been planning Jack's birthday party for a while now, and he'd be delighted if John Descentis performed at it. She stood up. With Alice and Iris looking on in horror, she made her way to the singer's table.

"Sorry to disturb you. My name's Faye."

John Descentis looked her up and down.

"Hello, Faye," he said with a crooked smile. "Don't worry, you're not disturbing us at all."

"It's my husband Jack's birthday on the fourth of May, and I'm organizing a party at Hasselbacken. He worships you. I was wondering if you might be free then and would be interested in coming by to sing a few songs?"

"Jack Adelheim? The entrepreneur?"

The black-haired girl pursed her lips, but John had straightened up.

Faye smiled at him.

"Yes, that's him, he runs a company called Compare."

"I know very well who he is. Sure, no problem. I didn't know he liked my stuff."

"He has ever since he was a teenager. He's got all your albums. On vinyl, no less!"

Faye laughed.

"That's probably not the sort of thing you boast about in interviews with the business press," John said.

The girl sighed audibly, got up from the table, and announced in a monotone that she was going to the bathroom.

Faye sat down on the vacated seat. She was tempted to drink the beer the waiter had just put down on the table, but controlled herself. From the corner of her eye she could see Alice and Iris staring at her.

She couldn't wait to tell Jack. She should probably keep it a secret, make it a surprise, but she knew herself too well to think that was going to happen.

"Can I . . . would it be okay to take your number? Then I can call you about the details. And we can talk about a fee, and so on."

"Sure, tell me your number and I'll send you a text."

He tapped out a message to her and formed his lips into a smile that still had some of his old charm. Rumor had it that he had succumbed to more than just alcohol and had been in rehab several times, but right now he didn't seem to be on anything.

Faye's mobile buzzed. She glanced at the text and saw a winking smile emoji as she returned to her table.

"What did you say to him?" Alice whispered, though she had probably heard every word.

If Faye hadn't known that she'd had Botox injected into her forehead, she could almost have sworn she saw a worried frown there.

"He's going to perform at Jack's birthday party."

"Him?" Alice balked.

"Yes, him. John Descentis. Jack loves him."

"Jack won't like it," Alice said. "There'll be a lot of business contacts there. It won't look good."

"I know what my husband likes and doesn't like, Alice. You take care of your family and I'll take care of mine!"

. . .

Faye clutched her coat more tightly around her when she finally emerged from Riche. Blasts of ice-cold wind were blowing from Nybroviken. The sky was gray. People were hurrying past, hunched over. Schuterman's seventy percent off sale was coming to an end, and the shop was starting to look empty.

She had an hour before she had to be home to relieve the babysitter. She had just set off toward Stureplan when a nail-varnish-red Porsche Boxster braked sharply, making the driver of the Taxi Stockholm cab behind it blow his horn angrily.

The window glided open and Chris Nydahl leaned across the passenger seat with one arm resting on the wheel.

"Can I offer you a lift, darling?" she said with an exaggeratedly sleazy voice.

Jack hated Chris and Faye looked around anxiously. But the Gucci-clad clothes-horses were still in Riche, probably reeling in shock at her behavior, and all of a sudden Faye realized how much she had missed Chris. Her raw sense of humor, her laughter and outrageous anecdotes about meaningless sex and long nights partying. They had been inseparable once upon a time.

Faye opened the door and jumped in. The leather, leopard-skin-patterned seat creaked as she made herself comfortable.

"Nice car," she said. "Very low-key."

Chris gathered together the shopping bags from the passenger footwell and tossed them carelessly into the cramped space behind them. Another car blew its horn.

"Dickhead," Chris said, giving the driver the finger in the rearview mirror before driving off.

Faye shook her head and laughed. She always felt ten years younger when she was with Chris.

"What's the point of having a fuck-load of money if you can never tell people to fuck off?" Chris muttered, glancing in the mirror.

"Where do you get it all from?"

"I heard that particular line in a television program."

She turned to look at Faye, who would rather she kept her eyes on the road.

"How long have you got before you have to get back to your wifely duties and all the other stuff you're going to regret when you're old and incontinent?"

Faye clutched her seat belt in alarm when Chris appeared not to notice that the lights in front of them had turned red.

"About an hour."

"Great."

Without warning, Chris wrenched the wheel and did a U-turn, narrowly avoiding a head-on collision with a bus. Faye gripped her seat belt even tighter.

"We're going to Djurgården," Chris said. It was all Faye could do to nod.

• • •

They found a restaurant that was open and ordered coffee. As usual, Chris seemed completely unconcerned by the looks the other customers were shooting her. Chris had a column in *Elle* where she wrote about female entrepreneurs, and was a regular guest on TV talk shows. Last week she had been on Malou's program on TV4.

After graduation (unlike Faye, she had completed her degree), Chris opened her first hair salon in what would become the Queen group, a hair-care empire built on the idea that all women deserved to feel like royalty. She had originally trained to be a hairstylist, and used that as a way to earn an income while she was studying to become an economist. The first time she met Faye she had declared that she wanted to establish an empire of her own. Five years after she graduated there were ten Queen salons, located in some of the biggest cities in Scandinavia. But she had earned most of her money from the products she had developed. They were ecologically sound, top quality, and beautifully packaged, and—thanks to Chris's winning personality as a saleswoman—could now be found in major retailers throughout Europe. She had recently started to dip her toes in the lucrative U.S. market.

"I don't understand how you can bear to have lunch with that desiccated mummy and her funeral cortege every week."

"Alice? She's not that bad . . ."

Faye knew that Chris knew she was lying. But Jack would never forgive her if she took Chris's side against Alice.

While she was a student Chris had had a brief but intense fling with Henrik, Alice's husband. Faye, Jack, Chris, and Henrik had been an inseparable quartet. But one day Chris opened the paper to find a notice announcing Henrik's engagement to Alice. He had chosen breeding, money, and docility over love.

In the years that had passed since then Chris had merely used men as a disposable resource. Faye knew Chris had been deeply hurt, and suspected that she was still mourning the loss of Henrik, even if she would never admit it. But Jack had told Faye about everything that had gone on under the harmonious surface, about Henrik's many dalliances. He had always been shy, but with the passage of time and as his fortune grew, he had become a changed man, and seemed desperate to make up for lost time. Or, as Jack usually put it, "Henrik will fuck anything with a pulse."

"Well, if you say so," Chris said. "But don't you think it's a bit odd?"

"What?"

"That in spite of all the millions Henrik has showered her with, she can't afford to find someone to remove that broom handle from her ass."

Faye sniggered.

"Seriously, though, Faye, I don't understand how you can bear it. I know how big a role you played in setting up Compare, the whole damn idea for it was yours, and you helped Henrik and Jack set up the structure of the company. But that's not what comes across in the business magazines when they're boasting about their success. Their success, not yours. Why should you have to stay at home spending your time . . . well, God knows what you spend your time doing! It's a waste of resources! You're one of the smartest people I've ever met, and that includes all the time I spend with myself."

She smiled, but it was a strained smile. She opened her mouth to go on but Faye interrupted her.

"Stop it. I love my life."

Her throat felt tight with anger, like the reflux she'd suffered during the last months of pregnancy. She adored Chris, but she couldn't stand it when she tried to talk shit about Jack, twisting things to make them look different from reality. Chris didn't appreciate everything Jack did for her and Julienne. She didn't see the sacrifices he made for their sake, all the difficult choices he had to make, all the time he had to devote to the business. And what did it matter if she didn't get credit for the work she had done setting up Compare? Jack knew. So did Henrik. That was enough.

It was better for the company if the myth of Jack and Henrik and their unique partnership became even more established. But Chris didn't have a family, she was too busy jumping from one man to the next. She didn't understand what it was like to be responsible for a whole family. The sacrifices that demanded. Chris never compromised on anything.

"I hope you're right," Chris said. "But what would happen if he left you? Like I said, you're one of the smartest people I know. How could you agree to sign that prenuptial agreement? Tell me at least that you've had it amended since Julienne was born? To give you a bit more security? Just in case?"

Faye smiled. It was actually very sweet of Chris to worry about her like this.

She shook her head. "That was Henrik's idea, not Jack's. Obviously Jack didn't want a prenuptial agreement, but the shareholders demanded it."

"If you get divorced you won't get anything. Nada."

Chris was speaking slowly and clearly. Like she was talking to a child. Who did she think she was? Just because she hadn't managed to find anyone like Jack.

Faye took a couple of deep breaths before responding.

"We're not going to get divorced. We're happier than we've ever been. You're going to have to accept that it's my life and I live it the way I like."

Chris said nothing for a while, then held her hands up disarmingly. "Sorry, you're right, I should keep my big nose out of it!"

She smiled that smile that was impossible to resist. And Faye knew that Chris meant well. She didn't want to fall out with her.

"Let's talk about something fun instead. How about going off somewhere together one weekend? Just you and me?"

"That would be great," Faye said, looking at the time. She needed to get going now. "I'd have to check with Jack first though."

She blew Chris a kiss as she called for a taxi.

As she ran out, she was aware of Chris watching her.

I LAY IN BED writing in my diary, recording all my feelings. It was such a liberation that Matilda no longer existed. No one knew her from before. No one knew anything about what had happened. If anyone asked, I told them that my parents were dead. Car accident. And that I didn't have any brothers or sisters. Which was true enough. I didn't have any brothers or sisters. Not anymore.

But sometimes Sebastian would come to me in my dreams. Always out of reach. Always just beyond my outstretched arms. I could still smell him when I closed my eyes.

I always woke up in a sweat when I'd been dreaming about Sebastian. I could see him so clearly in my mind's eye. His dark hair and clear blue eyes. He looked a lot like Dad even though their personalities were so different. It usually took me a while to get back to sleep again.

But my new identity as Faye gave me strength. For the time being I was keeping it secret from Viktor. I wasn't sure he'd understand. But everyone else got to meet my new, confident self, who had nothing in common with Matilda. My chief concern had been that the letters from prison could no longer reach me. I'd never opened a single one. But I remembered the terror I felt when I saw Dad's handwriting on the envelopes. Now he no longer knew where I was, he couldn't contact me. He no longer existed. He belonged to Matilda's world.

I reached for my handbag, tucked my diary in the inside pocket, and zipped it closed.

If it wasn't for the dreams, I might have been able to believe my own lie about the past being dead and buried. Sebastian came to me at night. Alive to start with, with those penetrating eyes that could see so deep. Then dangling from the rope.

Sunday morning. Faye was hurrying to clear up after Julienne's breakfast so that Jack didn't have to see the chaos left in her wake. Okay, she might not actually turn the kitchen into Pearl Harbor, but Faye could see what Jack meant about it not being pleasant to walk into a messy kitchen in the morning.

She had decided not to trouble Jack with the idea of going away for a weekend with Chris. It would only lead to irritation and arguing.

Though she hadn't wanted to admit it to Chris, she and Jack were going through a rough patch. The same thing happened to all couples. Jack's work made such colossal demands of him, and she was hardly the first woman in the world to feel that her husband's job got the best of him. Obviously she wished he had more time and energy. Both for her and for Julienne. But she quickly shrugged off such thoughts. She belonged to the upper echelon of what was arguably the most well-off country in the world. She didn't have to work, didn't have to worry about the bills, or preschool pickup times, or tiresome chores—there was an army of nannies and maids ready to help with everything. She could shop till she dropped and then have her purchases delivered by courier so she wouldn't have to carry them.

Jack, on the other hand, had a huge number of responsibilities, responsibilities that sometimes made him curt and cold.

Toward her, anyway. But she knew it was only temporary. In a few years they'd have more time for each other. They'd be free to make the most of life, go traveling. Fulfill their dreams.

"Do you think I enjoy having to work this hard?" he would say. "Of course I'd rather be at home with you and Julienne, never having to worry about how to pay the bills. But soon it'll be you and me, darling."

It may have been a while since he had last said that. But the promise was there. She believed him.

Julienne was lying on the sofa with her iPad on her lap. Faye had connected the wireless headphones so she wouldn't disturb Jack. He never slept very soundly, so Faye had taught their daughter to be as quiet as possible in the morning.

She settled down on the sofa next to her daughter and brushed a strand of hair from her face, noting without surprise that Julienne was watching *Frozen* for the thousandth time. She turned the television on to watch breakfast news, with the volume turned down low. She liked feeling Julienne's warm body against her, the closeness between them.

The bedroom door opened and Faye heard Jack walking toward the kitchen. She listened carefully to his steps, trying to gauge what sort of mood he was in. She held her breath.

Jack cleared his throat.

"Can you come here?" he said in his groggy just-woken-up voice.

Faye hurried into the kitchen. Smiled at him.

"What's this?" he said, gesturing with his hand.

"What?"

She hated not understanding, the sense that they were failing to communicate. It had always been *Jack and Faye*. Equals. A team, who knew each other inside out.

"This isn't the sort of counter you can make a sandwich on," Jack said, running his hand over the marble. "Not me, anyway!"

He held his hand up. A few crumbs were stuck to his palm.

How could she be so stupid? So careless. She knew better than that.

Faye grabbed the dishcloth. Her heart was beating so hard that it was pulsing in her ears. She wiped away the remaining crumbs, caught them in her other hand, and threw them in the drainer. After a quick glance at Jack she turned the tap on and rinsed the drainer with the dish brush.

She hung the dishcloth up and put the dish brush in the stylish silver holder.

Jack hadn't moved.

"Would you like coffee, darling?" she asked.

She opened the cupboard containing the Nespresso capsules and automatically took out two of the purple ones, Jack's favorites. One lungo, one espresso in the same cup, with a dash of frothed milk. Jack liked his coffee strong.

He turned his head and looked into the living room.

"Every time I see her she's crouched over a screen. You need to make more of an effort. Read to her, play with her."

A few drops of coffee ran down the white cup. Faye wiped them off with her finger and put the cup in Jack's hand. He barely seemed to notice.

"You know what Henrik told me? Saga and Carl aren't allowed to use their iPads more than an hour a day. Instead they go to museums, have piano lessons, tennis coaching, read books. Saga goes to ballet as well, three times a week, at Anneli Alhanko's School of Dance."

"Julienne wants to play soccer," Faye said.

"Out of the question. Have you seen the legs of girls who play soccer? Like tree trunks. And do you want her playing with a load of kids from the suburbs, with dads yelling all sorts of foul language at the referee?"

"Okay."

"Okay what?"

"Julienne won't play soccer."

Faye put her hand on his chest and pressed herself against him. She ran her hand down his stomach, toward his groin.

Jack looked at her in surprise.

"Stop it."

In the shiny glass of the oven door she saw the outline of her pale, pudgy arm. No wonder Jack didn't want to touch her. She had let herself go for far too long.

Faye went and locked herself in the bathroom. She took all her clothes off and inspected her body from different angles. Her breasts looked depressing. Like tulips that had drooped in a vase. Should she talk to Jack about breast enlargement? She knew Alice had had it done. It was all a matter of doing it tastefully. Not tacky. No beach balls.

It had been a long time since her stomach had been flat, and her legs were wobbly and pale. When she tensed her buttocks, little pits appeared on her skin. Like the surface of the moon.

She raised her eyes. Her face looked hollow-eyed and greasy. There was no glow to her skin or hair, and she couldn't be said to have an actual hairstyle anymore. When she looked closer at the mirror she noticed a few coarse gray hairs. She quickly plucked them out and flushed them away.

As long as he hadn't already started to feel ashamed of her. Did he complain to his friends? Had they been teasing him? From now on she was going to eat healthily and exercise once—no, twice a day. No more wine, no fancy dinners, no snacks in the evening while she waited for Jack to come home.

He knocked on the door.

"Are you coming out anytime soon?"

She started.

"In a moment, darling," she croaked in a thick voice.

He didn't move, and she began to feel nervous.

"I know I've been busy lately," he said. "What do you say to going out for dinner on Wednesday? Just you and me?"

Faye's eyes filled with tears as she stood there naked in the bathroom. She quickly put her clothes back on. Her Jack. Her beloved, darling Jack.

She unlocked the door.

"I'd love to, darling."

...

Two hours later Faye was standing in front of the meat counter in the ICA supermarket at Karlaplan, looking for something nice for lunch. Everything was the same as usual. The inflated prices. The yelling children and endless rumbling of the chiller units' fans. The smell of expensive jackets and real fur coats, no politically correct synthetics. The only synthetic things anyone around here might consent to wear would be something by Stella McCartney. If it was expensive enough.

Faye picked up a pack of duck breasts and headed toward the registers. She picked the one where Max was working. He usually worked Sundays.

She looked at Max's muscular arms as he scanned the shopping of the people ahead of her in the line. He must have felt her staring at him, because he suddenly turned and smiled at her.

When it was Faye's turn his smile grew broader. His eyes sparkled.

"And how's the most beautiful woman in Stockholm today?"

Faye's cheeks flushed. She understood that he said the same thing to most of his female customers, but still. He *saw* her.

She walked out of the shop with a lighter step.

When she got home she quickly put the food away. It was never a good idea to leave it out for long.

"Did you go out like that?"

Faye turned. Jack was standing in the doorway. He was frowning.

"What do you mean?"

Jack gestured toward her clothes.

"You can't go out shopping in the clothes you wear at home. What if you ran into someone we know?"

Faye shut the fridge door.

"Max at the checkout seemed to like it. He said I was the most beautiful woman in Stockholm."

Jack's jaw tensed. Faye realized she'd made a mistake. She ought to know she shouldn't joke with Jack about that sort of thing.

"You flirt with people working at cash registers?"

"No, I don't flirt. I love you, Jack, you know that, but I can hardly help it if someone gives me a compliment."

Jack snorted.

Faye watched as he walked stiffly in the direction of his study. Despite the knot in her stomach, she felt oddly pleased at his outburst. He cares, she thought. He really does care.

• • •

Julienne was asleep. Faye and Jack were lying in bed. He had his laptop on his stomach and she was watching a repeat on Channel 5.

"Do you want me to turn it down?"

Jack adjusted his glasses and tilted the screen so he could see the television.

"No, don't bother," he said distractedly.

The female presenter was introducing one of her guests, her hands full of prompt cards.

"Is that Lisa Jakobsson?" he asked.

"Yes."

"She used to be pretty. She's gotten old. And fat."

Jack raised the screen of his laptop again.

After he had fallen asleep Faye cupped her hand around the screen of her iPhone and went onto Wikipedia. Lisa Jakobsson was two years younger than her.

THE INITIATION RITUAL at the School of Economics was a secret, no one was allowed to tell any of the staff how the first-years were humiliated and loaded with drink. Participation was voluntary, but there wasn't any choice for me. I had made up my mind to do whatever it took to be accepted as one of the gang, to belong. And now that I was a blank slate, I finally had the chance to do that.

There were fifteen of us, all girls, gathered on a small meadow beside the water in Haga Park. Roughly the same number of second-years had made their way there. All of them boys. They had several large IKEA bags with them, full of props. They lined us up and inspected each of us thoroughly. Told us to take off everything except our underwear and gave us black garbage bags with arm and neck holes to pull over our heads. Then we had to drink two shots of vodka. Beside me stood a tall, curvy girl with freckles and unbrushed red hair.

"Down on your knees!" called the unofficial leader of the second-years, Mikael, son of a famous property magnate.

He had a blond bob and piggy eyes, and seemed accustomed to being obeyed. We hurried to do as he said.

"Good," he said. He held up a brown egg. "The egg yolk is to be passed from mouth to mouth, along the line, then back again.

And when it gets back to the first person, she has to swallow it. That's you. What's your name?"

Everyone in the line turned to see who had drawn the short straw.

"Chris," the girl next to me said.

Mikael cracked the egg on his knee, tipped the white onto the grass, and held the shell containing the yolk out to Chris. She took it, tipped the yolk into her mouth without hesitation, and leaned toward me. Our lips met and the boys cheered. The yolk was transferred and I tried to stop myself gagging. I turned to my left and repeated the procedure with the next girl.

"Are you really going to swallow it?" I asked Chris.

She shrugged.

"I'm from Sollentuna. I've swallowed worse."

I giggled. Her face remained impassive.

"Are you going to the party?"

"Yes. Despite the fact I can't stand these power-crazed, spoiled little boys. They're just making the most of their opportunity to exploit nervous, impressionable girls. These geniuses are the dregs of the school. That's why this initiation's taking place so early in the term, before we have time to see what losers they are. Two weeks from now none of these girls will even look at them."

"So why are you here?"

"I want to sort the wheat from the chaff, so I know who they are and can avoid them," she said bluntly. "You've got nice lips, by the way. If I get drunk later and can't find anyone to make out with, I'll come and find you."

I found myself hoping she would.

The rest of the afternoon passed in a variety of alcohol-fueled activities that all seemed designed to get the guys horny. They tipped fermented herring juice on our hair so we had to go into the water in our underwear. They drew big zeroes on the foreheads of girls who lost games, and the drunkest girls were given the honor of having the boys autograph their breasts, lower back, and buttocks. More and more of us stumbled off to throw up, but they kept plying us with drinks.

We only stopped when it got dark. We took one last dip, and our clothes were given back. They'd gotten hold of an old bus to drive us to the actual party, it was already half full of first-years who'd refused to take part in the initiation.

When we got on they held their noses. We stank of vomit, seawater, and fermented herring. And alcohol. Two of the girls had to be carried on board and were laid out on the floor in the aisle. One girl's bra had slipped down, revealing a chalk-white breast and dark nipple. The boys laughed and pointed. One of them leaped out of his seat, clutching a digital camera. Chris reacted like lightning. She shot her arm out, blocking his path, then stood up to stop him.

"And where do you think you're going, little fellow?"

"She won't care," he slurred. "She's asleep. Get out of the way."

Chris folded her arms and snorted. I noticed that she had seaweed in her hair, but she had an air of obvious authority. She stood there as solid as a tree even though the bus was lurching and bouncing. As if her feet had grown into the floor of the bus. The guy, who was a head taller than her, started to look uncertain.

"Don't be such a bore, it's only a fucking joke. What are you, some sort of feminist?" he said, spitting the word *feminist* like it was an obscenity and grinning at her.

Chris didn't move. Everyone was staring at them now.

"Fine, I won't bother."

He laughed and tried to pretend he hadn't just gone one round against a girl and lost.

"Where are you going?" Chris called after him as he started to lumber back down the bus.

I held my breath. Wasn't she finished with him yet?

"To sit down," he said uncertainly.

"Forget it. Come back here."

He turned and took a few unwilling steps toward her.

"Take your top off," Chris said.

"What?" The guy's eyes opened wide. "I'm not going to do that."

He looked around for support, but everyone was too busy enjoying the confrontation.

"Take your ugly little top off—polo shirts are so 1990—and give it to me. Hurry up, can't you see she's freezing?"

He gave up and did as she asked, then shook his head and went back to his seat. His pink polo shirt had been hiding a pale, pudgy torso and a pair of man boobs, and he didn't look at all comfortable.

Chris woke the girl, pulled her arms up, and carefully put the top on her.

"Give me that," she said when she sat back down next to me. She drank several gulps of beer.

"Good work," I whispered, tucking the bottle between my legs.

"Thanks. But it was practically an assault to make the poor thing wear such a hideous top," she muttered.

After she dropped Julienne off at preschool, Faye wandered aim-lessly around Östermalm. No more spending the day sitting at home. She would make sure she kept moving. Burning fat and getting thin. The decay had to be stopped at all costs.

Her stomach was rumbling unhappily. All she'd had for breakfast was a cup of unsweetened black coffee, so she'd burn more calories during the walk. Images of food flashed through her head like a gastronomic kaleidoscope. If she went home, she wouldn't be able to resist the temptation to raid the pantry and stuff herself. She speeded up. She was heading along Karlavägen toward Humlegården. She grimaced when her back started to feel horrible and sweaty. She couldn't stand perspiration. But, as Alice often said, "Sweat's just fat crying." Not that she'd ever seen the tiniest bead of sweat on Alice.

The nineteenth-century buildings loomed above her, steadfast and immovable. The sky was bright blue and the sun glinted off the freshly fallen snow that hadn't yet had time to turn gray. In spite of the sweat, she felt more positive than she had for months. Jack's sudden invitation to go on a date was a turning point. And she was going to make sure it really *was* a turning point.

She bore so much of the responsibility for the stagnation of their relationship. It was time to get back to being the person he wanted her to be. This was the dawn of a new era in their marriage.

She made up her mind once and for all to turn down Chris's suggestion of a trip together. She was needed at home, and it would be selfish to go off for a pointless weekend away. She was avoiding Chris's calls, aware of how Chris would react and what she'd say.

Faye quickened her pace. She thought she could feel the pounds falling off her, step by step, ounce by ounce. The horrible sweat was soaked up by her clothes.

A group of pupils from Östra Real School were smoking furtively by the wine-red wall. Two girls and two boys. Gray smoke trailed from their mouths and noses when they laughed. They didn't seem to have a single worry in the world. A few years ago, in a different time, a different life, that could easily have been her, Jack, Henrik, and Chris.

Jack, the easygoing joker. The carefree golden boy who always had some party invitation burning a hole in his pocket. A black belt in social activities and making people laugh. Henrik was the strategist and thinker. He came from straitened circumstances in one of Stockholm's suburbs and had his head for learning to thank for the fact that he had gotten out of there. He had studied industrial economics at the Royal Institute of Technology while simultaneously studying at the School of Economics.

Faye walked past Tösse's. Pastries, tarts, cinnamon buns, piles of them in the windows. Her mouth started to water and she forced herself to look away. She speeded up. Fled. She took a brief pause at Nybrogatan. Opened the door to Café Mocco and ordered green tea. No sugar. It tasted disgusting and bitter without anything to sweeten it, but she drank it nevertheless because she had read somewhere that green tea helped burn calories. She looked through a pile of magazines and found last week's *Dagens Industri* weekend supplement, with Henrik and Jack on the cover.

It was a fancy photo shoot. They were sitting on an old-fashioned motorbike and sidecar. Sunglasses and leather jackets. Jack on the bike, Henrik in the sidecar with a vintage leather pilot's cap on his head. Broad smiles, happy expressions.

THE BILLION-KRONOR EMPIRE STRIKES BACK was the headline. Faye opened the paper and leafed through to the interview. The reporter, Ivan Uggla, had spent a whole day following them around. It was odd that Jack hadn't mentioned anything about it to her. He gave a lot of interviews, but rarely on this scale.

The article opened with Jack in their office on Blasieholmen. He told a story about all the hard work he'd put in to get the company off the ground. He said he had been living in Bergshamra, studying during the day and working on his business plan at night. At first the idea was for Compare to be a voracious telemarketing operation.

"If we were going to succeed, I knew I would have to sacrifice everything for the business and Henrik. There was no time, no money for anything but work, work, and more work, both with Compare, and to earn a living. If you want to win big, you have to play for high stakes."

The truth was that Jack hadn't had to work at all except on Compare, because she had abandoned her studies to support him, and spent her days wiping tables at the Café Madeleine. But they had come up with this PR strategy together. For the good of the business.

The interview went on in much the same vein. In 2005 Compare switched from being the country's most successful telemarketing business to an investment company. They bought smaller businesses, made them more efficient, and sold them for huge profits. Often they broke them up and sold the parts for more than the whole was worth. That meant they had trodden on a fair few toes over the years, but their profits spoke for themselves, and in a world where results were the only thing that mattered,

Jack Adelheim and Henrik Bergendahl were declared geniuses by a unanimous business community.

Some time later they sold off almost everything in order to invest in electricity suppliers and businesses in the service sector: private homes for the elderly, sheltered housing, and schools. With the same result. Everything Jack and Henrik touched seemed to turn to gold, and everyone wanted to be associated with the young Midases. They kept the name from the early years, the one Faye had come up with. You didn't change the basics when the dice kept landing on six.

Those early years, when Faye had supported Jack while simultaneously helping lay the foundations for Compare, had been erased. Sometimes she wondered if Jack and Henrik even remembered that, or if they had come to believe in their revised version of the past. Her part in the story didn't fit the media image of the two young, daring, indomitable entrepreneurs, Jack and Henrik. The backstory dynamic was also so perfect that she had actually pointed it out at the time. Jack with his aristocratic pedigree, his good looks, and his dandyish style, Henrik from a working-class family in the suburbs, handsome in a rougher way, the personification of a man who had worked his way to the top. The perfect combination. It made sense for Faye to stay in the background. So as not to complicate the simple media message.

The reporter had gone for a morning run on Djurgården with Jack. Ivan Uggla gave an enthusiastic account of how many miles they had run. And as they ran Jack had laughed off speculation that Compare was about to have an initial public offering.

The last page had a picture of Jack taken in the office. He was bent over his desk, deep in conversation, as he pointed to a document. Beside him, closest to the camera, stood Ylva Lehndorf, dressed in a pale-blue pencil skirt, her hair pulled into a tight ponytail.

Ylva had made her name in publishing. She'd managed to turn

figures that were deeply in the red back to black. She had made the business more efficient, had come up with new solutions, had challenged those who insisted "but this is what we've always done." She changed structures and broke down walls. Faye had met her at a party three years ago and Ylva had mentioned that she was looking for a fresh challenge. Her ambition and quick wits had impressed Faye, and two weeks later, on Faye's recommendation, Jack had offered her a job. One year later she had been appointed finance director of Compare. It looked good to have a woman in senior management, as Faye had pointed out to Jack. It couldn't be her, because they had made the joint decision that she should stay at home with Julienne for those first few years.

Faye ran her finger across the picture, along Ylva's figure, down her spine, her backside, her thin, suntanned legs, all the way down to her black pumps. She was everything Faye had dreamed of becoming. The age gap separating them was only five years, but it might as well have been twenty. And instead of being in the heat of the action in an office, beautiful and successful, here she was sitting in Mocco, drinking unpleasant green tea and dreaming about the Danish pastries on the counter. She closed the newspaper unhappily. She had made her choice. For Jack. For their family.

. . .

Faye was lying on a yoga mat in a set of new exercise clothes doing the pissing dog in front of the television when Jack came home. He tossed his briefcase aside and stopped behind her. The room filled with the smell of cologne and alcohol. Faye finished her exercise, got to her feet, and walked up to him. When she tried to give him a kiss he turned his head away.

"Did you have a good time?" she said. The knot in her stomach was back.

Jack snatched the remote from the coffee table and switched off the television, and the YouTube video of yoga for beginners disappeared.

"Did you ask John Descentis to play at my party?" he said.

"I thought—"

"He's a drunk, Faye. This isn't my graduation party you're organizing. There are going to be clients there. Investors. Relatives who have looked down on me as a loser all my life because of my father. This is the night when they're finally going to see how far I've come. See that I'm nothing like my useless father!"

He was breathing hard, and his voice had risen to a falsetto.

"And you go and invite John Descentis to provide the entertainment. Like we were some sort of fucking white trash."

Faye backed away a few steps.

"You're always listening to him. You've got all his albums. I thought you'd—"

"How would it look if John Descentis played at my party? We don't want to be associated with people like him. He's a drunk. Just like my father."

He sank onto the sofa and let out a loud sigh.

"It's my fault," he said. "I should never have allowed you to take charge of the party. For God's sake, you let Julienne have her party at McDonald's!"

Faye wanted to say that that was what Julienne had wanted, and that all the children had loved it, but her eyes were pricking with tears as Jack snorted.

"How could I ever have thought you were capable of organizing a party for three hundred people at Hasselbacken?"

"I can do it, Jack, you know that. Let's not bother with John Descentis. I haven't called him yet. Let me do this for you. I want you to have a really great evening, the sort of evening you've always dreamed of having."

"It's too late."

"What do you mean?"

"I've contacted an events company, they're going to organize everything. You can go back to your . . . your exercising."

He gestured toward her clothes. The knot in her stomach grew.

Jack went over to the stereo, pulled out some CDs, went into the kitchen, and threw them in the trash.

She didn't need to guess what the CDs were.

Faye ran her hands over her face. How could she have been so stupid? Why hadn't she realized that this could damage Jack? She should have thought it through. After all, she knew him better than anyone.

She rolled the yoga mat up and turned the light out. Jack was already asleep as she washed her face and brushed her teeth. He was lying with his back to her, on the far side of the bed, facing the window. She crept as close to him as she dared without risking waking him. Breathing in his scent.

It was a long time before she managed to get to sleep.

. . .

The atmosphere between them was still frosty the next day. Jack sat and worked in the kitchen while Faye lay on the sofa watching a reality show.

The phone in the hall started to ring shrilly, but for once Faye chose to ignore it. She heard a sigh from the kitchen followed by irritated footsteps, and the ringing stopped.

A few minutes later Jack was standing in front of her with a sullen look on his face.

"It's for you," he said.

Faye held out her hand, but Jack ignored it and put the phone on the table, then went back to the kitchen. She raised the phone to her ear, feeling like a fifteen-year-old again.

"You never got back to me about our trip," Chris said. "Have you talked to Jack?"

"Oh, hi. Hang on."

Faye got up from the sofa and went into the bathroom. Locked the door.

"Hello?"

She sat down on the closed toilet lid.

"Now isn't a good time," she said. "I've got my hands full with everything here at home, and I've got to organize Jack's party. Maybe we could do it next summer?"

Chris sighed.

"Faye, I . . . I heard from someone I know who works in PR that they've been asked to arrange Jack's party."

Faye nudged the scale out from under the sink with her foot. Got on. No change. She was doomed to be fat forever.

"Well, I felt I didn't have time to do it properly. You'll have to excuse me, but I can't talk now, I've got loads to be getting on with."

"Faye . . . ?" Chris's voice, warm at the other end of the line.

Faye remembered how loudly she had laughed that evening they were out with Jack and Henrik, and Chris suddenly got it into her head that they should dance on the table. Jack had held Faye's hand. Squeezed it tight.

"Yes?"

"Can't we go away anyway, to help you get a bit of perspective on everything? Never mind about Jack's party. I know there isn't an events organizer in the world that could do a better job than you."

Faye pushed the scale back under the sink again and promised herself that she wouldn't look again for a week. So that things had time to change.

"I've been thinking about something," Chris went on. "I could use someone like you in my company. Someone smart, who understands business and knows what women want. Wouldn't it be fun to get out and start working again? Now that Julienne's at nursery?"

Faye closed her eyes. Couldn't bear to see her own reflection in the mirror.

"Preschool, Chris."

"What?"

"It's called preschool, not nursery. And no, I neither want nor need a job with you. If I wanted a job, don't you think I would have sorted it out for myself?"

"But—"

"Do you know what your problem is, Chris? You think you're better than me. You think everyone wants to live your pointless life, but I can't help thinking it doesn't look that much fun to spend your evenings fucking a twenty-four-year-old personal trainer and getting so drunk that you can't remember anything the next day. It's vulgar and it's embarrassing. Instead of lecturing me you should try to grow up. I love my husband, I love my daughter, I've got a *family*! I want to be with them. And I think you're jealous of me and my life. I think that's what this is all about. And I can see why no man would want to live with you! And—"

Chris had hung up. Faye stared at her own face in the mirror. She no longer knew who the woman looking back at her was.

THE CABIN WHERE THE PARTY was going to take place lay
in a deserted industrial park. A provisional bar had been set up
in one corner. Cheesy pop music was blaring out over the yard.
It wasn't long before people were making out or creeping off in
pairs to the small rooms upstairs.

I had sobered up and raised my eyebrows toward Chris, who
seemed thoroughly bored. I sent Viktor a text, asking what he
was up to. I smiled as I wrote it. The other day we had talked
about me moving into his new apartment in Gärdet, seeing as I
never spent any time in the one-room sublet apartment on Villagatan that I'd just gotten hold of.

"I can't handle another wasted hangover. I'm going into the
city to have some fun instead," Chris said.

I looked around at the student version of Sodom and Gomor-
rah in front of me.

"Can I come?"

"Sure, I'll call a taxi. We can stop off at my place on the way
and sort ourselves out. We stink."

Chris was subletting a single-room apartment at Sankt Eriks-
plan. There were clothes scattered across every one of its four
hundred square feet. The bed was unmade, the walls bare apart
from a shelf from which her course books gazed out at the room.
If I had been wondering how she had gotten into the School of

Economics, the answer was on the table. Tossed nonchalantly among the bills and ads lay the results of her high school exams. She'd gotten 2.0. The highest possible grade. I wasn't surprised.

We showered quickly.

"You've got nice tits," Chris said admiringly when I emerged wearing a pair of her underwear. "And a fucking good body. Nice to see someone who hasn't fallen for that whole anorexic aesthetic."

"Thanks," I said lamely.

It was the first time I had ever received a compliment about my breasts or the rest of my body from another girl.

"Have you got a bra I could borrow? Mine stinks of herring . . ."

I held up my disgusting bra.

"What do you want one for? That's like driving around in a Ferrari with the cover on. Do all the dykes and straight men a favor and set those beauties free."

"Burn my bra?" I grinned.

"Yeah, sister!" Chris cried, picking up her own rancid bra and swinging it above her head.

I laughed and looked at myself in the little mirror leaning against the wall in the hall and shrugged my shoulders. When I looked at myself through Chris's eyes I suddenly liked myself a lot more.

"So where are we going, then?"

"One of the cheap bars near college. That's where the real finds are. Well, maybe not the trust-fund kids and bankers' sons—they're far too inbred now—but the genuinely interesting ones. Here, try this!"

Chris threw me a scrap of gray cloth.

"What is it, a tea towel?" I said skeptically, tentatively holding up the dress, which would barely cover my buttocks.

"Less is more, baby," Chris said as she set about applying a huge quantity of mascara to her eyelashes.

I pulled the dress on. It didn't leave much to the imagination. To say the neckline was low would be an understatement. I turned around. The back was open as well.

"Hot, hot, hot," Chris exclaimed as I posed in front of her. "If you don't get a fuck wearing that, you never will."

"I've got a boyfriend," I said.

"Details," Chris said dismissively. "Now come over here and sit down, and I'll fix your hair. You look like you've just gotten off the bus from Skara."

She waved a pair of scissors and a curling iron in the air.

I was skeptical, but did as she said. You didn't contradict Chris.

. . .

An hour later we pushed through the doorway of the N'See Bar and stepped in. As Chris had predicted, the place was full of older students. I recognized a few faces.

"Find somewhere to sit and I'll get the beers," Chris said, and pushed her way toward the bar.

I felt embarrassed that she had already paid for the taxi as well as the beer, but I couldn't afford to repay the favor. My student grant was barely enough to cover food and rent, with nothing to spare, and I was desperately trying to find part-time work.

I found a table toward the back of the room. "Don't Look Back in Anger" by Oasis was blaring from a speaker that was too close for comfort.

The door to the street was open. The outdoor bar had stopped serving and a few customers were standing out there, apparently hesitating over whether to come inside or not. I checked my phone. No message from Viktor.

Chris put two glasses of foaming beer on the table, dripping with condensation. My head was throbbing with the beginnings of a hangover from all the alcohol I'd drunk that day, but the beer soon remedied that. Chris drew something in the condensation

on my glass with her finger. I turned the glass to see what it was.
A heart.

"Why did you do that?"

"Good luck," Chris said with a shrug.

I wiped it off. Luck hadn't played much of a role in my previous life.

I raised the glass and gulped down most of the cold beer.
Drank myself into forgetfulness. Matilda was gone. Now I was
Faye, no one else. Maybe she'd have more luck? I drew another
heart on my glass.

Chris was busy ranting about how childish the guys at the
initiation had been when two people walked through the door.

"Are you listening?" Chris said, poking me in the arm.

I nodded distractedly. The heart on my glass was still there,
just about. Chris rolled her eyes and turned to see what had
caught my attention.

"Oh!" she muttered.

"What?"

"You don't know who that is?" Chris said, gesturing toward
the door with her thumb.

"No—should I?"

I was longing for another beer, but would have to wait until it
was offered.

"Jack Adelheim," Chris whispered.

The name meant nothing to me. With my finger I wiped away
the heart I had drawn.

The doorbell rang at half past six. It was Johanna, the babysitter Julienne liked best. While Jack was working Faye had put on her best La Perla underwear, changed into the black Dolce & Gabbana dress he loved, and had made herself up carefully.

"You look wonderful," Johanna said as she bent down to take her shoes off.

"Thanks!" Faye said, and did a twirl, which made Julienne giggle happily from the sofa in the living room.

"Date nights are fun," Johanna said. "Where are you going?"

"Teatergrillen."

Faye had booked a table the night before. She loved hearing the change of tone of the maître d' and other staff when she gave her name and said that she and her husband, Jack Adelheim, were planning to pay a visit.

Julienne was watching *Lotta on Troublemaker Street*. Faye sat down beside her, gave her a hug, and explained that Johanna would be putting her to bed and that they'd probably be home late.

Johanna sat down on the other side of Julienne, put her arm around her, and asked how her day had been and what she'd been doing. Julienne leaned back against Johanna and cheerfully started to tell her.

Faye smiled gratefully at Johanna. She and Jack needed this evening.

Faye was looking forward to Jack seeing her outfit, hoping his face would light up the way it had done when they were first together. She went into her walk-in closet and put on her Yves Saint Laurent heels, then walked to the drinks trolley and poured a whiskey. With the glass in her hand she knocked on the door of the study. She breathed in the smell before she opened the door. She liked the smell of whiskey far more than the taste, which was pretty disgusting.

Jack was sitting at his desk, immersed in his computer. The tower room was as quiet and calm as always. The darkness outside the windows looked almost solid.

"What?" he muttered without looking up.

His hair was tousled. As usual, he had been running his hands through it as he worked. Faye put the whiskey down in front of him. Nudged it toward him with two fingers. He looked up in surprise. Bloodshot, tired eyes.

"What is it?"

She backed away and spun around. For the first time in a long time she felt properly attractive.

"I've put on the dress you like. The one you bought me in Milan."

"Faye—"

"Hang on, I haven't shown you the best bit yet," she said, pulling her dress up to show him her black lace underwear.

It had cost over two thousand kronor, and had an incredibly delicate fringe of French lace around the black silk. Medium size. With a bit of hard work she'd soon be able to buy a pair of small ones. Maybe extra small.

"You look lovely."

Jack didn't even look up.

"I've picked out a suit for you. Drink your whiskey, then you can get changed. Drinks at the Grand first, then we've got a table at Teatergrillen. The taxi will be here in half an hour. It would have been nice to walk, but that would be a bit tricky in these shoes . . ."

She showed him her black high heels.

A shadow passed across Jack's face. Faye saw her reflection in the tower room's window. A pathetic figure bound up in black Dolce, high heels, and even higher expectations. He had forgotten this was the night they were going out. Drinking, talking, laughing. To remind him how much he loved spending time with her. Remind him of the nights they had spent in Barcelona, Paris, Madrid, and Rome. During those first months in Stockholm they hadn't been able to keep their hands off each other.

She bit her lip to stop herself bursting into tears. The walls started to close in on her, suffocating her. The darkness beyond the glass was a black hole, sucking the life out of her. The look on Jack's face was growing more and more concerned. She hated it when he felt sorry for her. In his eyes she must look like some panting dog, desperate for affection.

"I'd forgotten all about it. There's so much going on at the moment. You wouldn't believe what Henrik . . ."

She forced herself to smile. Not be a nuisance, not be demanding. To be pleasant, amenable. Not get in the way. But she could see how stiff her smile was in the reflection of the window. A contorted mask.

"I understand, darling. You carry on working. We can do it some other time. It's really not a problem. We've got our whole lives ahead of us."

Jack's face twitched. Tiny spasms, a tic he always got when he was stressed.

"Sorry, I'll make it up to you. I promise."

"I know. Don't worry."

Faye swallowed and turned away before he could see her eyes shimmering. She closed the door to the tower room carefully behind her.

• • •

On the sofa Julienne was trying to braid Johanna's red hair.

"You're very good at this," Johanna murmured.

Faye usually enjoyed chatting with her. But right now she just wanted Johanna gone. She wasn't far from tears, the lump in her throat was growing.

"Mommy taught me," Julienne said.

"That's lovely. What book shall we read tonight?"

"*Maddy*, I think. Or *Pippi*."

After her conversation with Jack the previous week, Faye had bought a copy of every Astrid Lindgren book she could find in Akademibokhandeln.

Faye cleared her throat. Johanna's freckled face peered up above the side of the sofa.

"Are you about to go?" she asked.

"No. Change of plan. We're doing it another time. Work crisis."

Faye tried to laugh, but the darkness inside her was threatening to well up, it kept rising and falling.

Johanna tilted her head.

"That's a shame. When you look so lovely. Would you like me to put Julienne to bed anyway?"

"No, it's fine."

Faye swallowed the lump in her throat as Julienne clung to Johanna's arm. She pulled two five-hundred-kronor notes from her handbag and handed them over. Johanna held her free hand up to stop her.

"There's no need, honestly, I've only been here fifteen minutes or so."

"You've still given up your evening. Take it, and I'll get you a taxi."

Julienne was sniffling and tugging at Johanna's arm.

"I don't want Johanna to go! I want her to stay!"

Johanna bent down and stroked her on the cheek.

"I'll see you the day after tomorrow when I pick you up from preschool. Then I'll read to you when we're on the way home in the taxi."

"Promise!"

"I promise. See you soon, sweetie."

When Faye had shut the door after Johanna she took her heels off, tossing them on the hall floor, and carried Julienne into the bathroom and told her to brush her teeth.

"Spit it all out, then we'll go and read *Maddy*."

"I want Johanna to read to me! She makes it more fun!"

"Johanna isn't here now. You'll have to make do with me."

Faye carried Julienne to her room. She squirmed and wriggled, hard feet hitting Faye's arms. Faye's stomach was aching and the lump in her throat was threatening to suffocate her.

She put Julienne down on the floor and shook her. Hard. Too hard.

"That's enough!"

The crying stopped abruptly.

Julienne was looking up at her in shock. Faye had never lost her temper in front of Julienne, she always smiled at her, caressed her, told her she was the best in the whole world. The darkness inside her shifted. Rumbling from somewhere buried deep within her. A different time. A different life.

Julienne curled up in bed. Faye knew she ought to comfort her, say she was sorry, smooth things over. But she didn't have the words. She felt utterly horrified with herself.

She shut her eyes and tried to find herself again. But the past had caught up with her, showing her how small she was. Who she really was.

"Good night," she said quietly, turned the light out, and left.

. . .

Faye was walking aimlessly through the aisles of NK. The vener-
able old department store was one of the few places that gave
her any peace. Sometimes the feeling of suffocation became so
strong that the only thing that could suppress the itch inside her
was wandering around the air-conditioned boutiques running
her fingers over the beautiful clothes.

The staff recognized her. Young women who formed their
collagen-ruined lips into smiles, women she knew would do anything to swap places with her. In their eyes she had everything.
Millions in the bank, status, a husband who could guarantee her
place in the pecking order.

NK was almost empty. Whenever she reached the Tiger boutique she always thought of the foreign minister Anna Lindh,
and how her killer had fled through the store. One of those sur-
real moments when the breezy superficiality of life crashed into
ugly reality. The world had stopped to stare at Sweden in astonishment. A country that was seen by much of the world as some
sort of dream society, with no problems, no crime, inhabited
solely by leggy, big-chested blondes in bikinis, furnished by IKEA
and echoing to a soundtrack by Abba. An image every bit as false
as her own. As unreal as the sight of Anna Lindh lying wounded
among the gray Tiger suits and non-iron white shirts.

Faye's stomach clenched as she touched a black jumpsuit with
a price tag of almost ten thousand kronor. Instead of eating she
was now only drinking juice she had delivered to the door. Five
bottles a day. Green, yellow, white, and red. According to the ads,
packed with all the nutrients you needed. And tasty. In reality
they tasted terrible. Particularly the green one. She had to hold
her nose when she drank them, and stifle the urge to throw up.
The absence of anything to chew was starting to drive her mad.

She had lived on juice alone for two weeks, only occasionally
letting her hair down and eating some fruit. As well as making
her constantly tired, it had also led to her being short-tempered
toward Julienne and Jack. She had read online that severe mood

swings were a common side effect, but she had been unwilling to believe that. A simple diet shouldn't pose a problem. People were capable of amazing feats. Going to the moon. Defeating Hitler. Building Machu Picchu. Britney Spears resuscitating her career after her 2007 breakdown. So surely Faye could endure a bit of hunger without losing her temper and lashing out at loved ones? Julienne had been fragile and anxious ever since Faye lost her temper the other evening, but she couldn't talk to her daughter about it. She had no idea what to say. Time heals all wounds, she tried to tell herself. That had been the case with her.

As she left the store, thoughts swirling in her head, she almost collided with a woman who gave her a wide smile.

"Hi!" Lisa Jakobsson said. "How lovely to see you again! How's your lovely daughter?"

"Thanks, she's fine," Faye said.

She was searching her memory desperately to remember when she might have met the television presenter without there being a television screen in the way.

"And Jack?" Lisa tilted her head sympathetically. "Poor thing, he really does work far too hard. He's lucky to have someone like you to take care of him."

Lisa went on talking about what a great support Faye was, and soon she felt in a better mood. How starved of compliments was she?

"We should go out for dinner sometime, just the four of us," Lisa said.

Faye remembered that she was going out with a colleague who was responsible for several modestly popular entertainment shows. She and Jack had gotten stuck talking to them for far too long at the premiere of a play.

"We'll have to see," Faye said curtly, and Lisa's smile wavered. "I'm afraid I must dash."

Stockholm was a jungle in which she and a handful of other millionaires' wives were the queens. Faye knew that people analyzed every word, every syllable she uttered, fawning and sim-pering just because she was Jack's wife.

She knew that Lisa wouldn't hesitate to dump her boyfriend for Jack. Or someone like him. Women were drawn to money and power. And fake feminists like Lisa were as susceptible as the rest.

Wealth was the power Faye possessed, and it was so intoxicat-ing that it drowned out the rumble in her stomach. Regardless of how much she despised herself for feeling that way.

She walked away from Lisa and took the escalator down to the perfume department, passing a huge poster of an emaci-ated model with smoky eyes and a half-open mouth. It was yet another reminder of all the pounds she hadn't managed to lose.

Jack hadn't touched her since that evening when he forgot their date, he barely glanced at her when she got into her side of the bed.

Her stomach groaned again.

She took out her mobile and sent him a text.

I love you! She added a heart emoji.

She opened Jack's Facebook page and discovered that he'd changed his profile picture. He used to have a photograph of her, Julienne, and himself standing in front of Drottningholm Palace a year or so ago. The new image was a professional pho-tograph from Compare's website. She brought up the list of likes and clicked on every young woman to check out their profile. They all seemed to have come from the same mold: hungry, eager, hunters. They were all thin and had big, expensive lips and long, perfectly styled hair.

Faye forced herself to put her mobile back in her handbag.

The staff behind the perfume counters followed her with their eyes. She picked up a Gucci bottle and sprayed some of the con-tents into the air. She was on the lookout for a sweeter, slightly more youthful scent. She took a few steps back, and found a pink

YSL bottle that caught her eye. She picked up a sample strip and pressed the nozzle twice. Much better. It reminded her vaguely of something but she couldn't put her finger on what.

The sales assistants had grown tired of watching her and turned away. She picked up a box and put it in her basket. The perfume, naturally. No cheap eau de cologne.

Her mobile buzzed. A reply from Jack at last?

You never got back to me. John Descentis

Faye sighed. She had hoped he would understand the situation when she hadn't called him.

I'm afraid I've booked another act. Maybe some other time.

As she was putting her mobile back in her bag it buzzed again.

Can we meet to talk about it?

Can't, off to the cinema.

The cinema? Where had that come from? She used to love going to the cinema when she was younger. She, Sebastian, and their mom would get dressed up and head off to Grebbestad, where they would have coffee and cake and see two films in the same evening. The two films that the cinema was showing. Sebastian would hold her hand in the darkness. Then they would head home with their stomachs full of popcorn and fizzy drinks, while Mom and Sebastian talked about the films. They didn't stop talking until they crossed the little bridge before Mörhult, where the swans always swam about with their young each year.

Faye shuddered. Her thoughts increasingly seemed to find their way onto dark paths.

Her mobile buzzed in her hand.

Love cinema. Which one?

Rigoletto.

Great. See you there.

Faye shook her head. What was she doing? Why on earth was she going to go to the cinema with John Descentis, of all people?

All the same, it felt nice that someone wanted to see her. Maybe it would help take her mind off Jack and their canceled date night.

When Faye opened the heavy door of the Rigoletto, John Descentis was already sitting on a bench waiting for her. She considered turning and sneaking back out, but was worried he'd spot her.

"So you decided to come after all." His voice was gravelly but cheerful. "Thought it was going to be a repeat of the party."

Faye sat down next to him. Maintaining a certain distance.

John Descentis was dressed in a dark T-shirt and jeans, as usual. He had a dark-brown leather jacket over his arm, and a bucket of popcorn in his hand, the largest they had.

"Like I said, our plans changed."

"Maybe next time he has a birthday," John said, still smiling. He moved closer to her.

"What film are you going to see?"

He smelled faintly of cologne, leather, and flat beer. Her body reacted to the smell in a way that surprised her.

She gestured to the poster, where Bradley Cooper's blue eyes were staring straight into the camera.

"I'd like to see that one," he said.

"Why did you really want to meet?" she said. "What do you want with me?"

"I thought it would be nice to talk," he said, getting to his feet. "You struck me as a real person in Riche. Unlike all the other . . ."

He left the sentence unfinished.

Faye took a deep breath. "Sorry, I didn't mean to sound unfriendly. It's been a rough day."

"We all have those. Everyone has their secrets. And their own crap to deal with. The difference is that mine has been all over the tabloids."

She frowned. What was he getting at? What did he know about her having secrets and her own crap to deal with?

"Like my song," he said, registering her expression. "'Secrets.' You know, 'Everyone has their secrets, and their own crap to deal with.' Those are the lyrics. But maybe you've never heard that one?"

The doors to the theater opened and John nodded toward it. Faye took several deep breaths, imagining Sebastian and her mom laughing at a romantic comedy as they ate popcorn from big paper cones. Free for a short while.

They bought tickets and Faye followed John into the empty auditorium. They sat in the back row and Faye took her mobile out again. Jack still hadn't replied. She was feeling increasingly anxious. Didn't he love her anymore? Did he no longer find her attractive?

During the first few minutes of the film Faye was intensely aware of John looking at her. She didn't know why, but being so close to him was affecting her in a peculiar way. Without making a conscious decision to do it, she put her hand on his trousers. With her eyes glued to the screen and Bradley Cooper's chiseled features, she unbuttoned his fly and noted with surprise that he wasn't wearing any underpants. Neither of them said anything, but she heard him breathing heavily, and it excited her. She bent over and took him in her mouth. She heard his breathing get heavier and heavier, and, absurdly, he carried on stuffing popcorn into his mouth as he groaned. Faye felt herself getting wet, forgot whose cock she was sucking; she was sucking Jack, sucking him so well that he would realize how lucky he was. She shut her eyes and stood up to pull her trousers and panties down. She sat astride his hard cock, John's, Jack's, and sank down. He filled her in ways she had been dreaming of, places she had forgotten, and she kept her eyes closed as she moved faster and faster, murmuring, "Fuck me, Jack, oh, fuck me."

Just as she climaxed John filled her with his warm, sticky seed. He groaned as Bradley Cooper's warm voice filled the cinema.

For a few moments Faye curled up numbly in John Descentis's

arms. Then she stood up. His semen seeped out of her, and what had felt so exciting only minutes before now felt nothing but sordid.

She picked up her bag and left the cinema without looking back.

"WHAT'S SO SPECIAL ABOUT THAT Jack Adel . . . What did you say his name was?" I wondered as Chris put another beer in front of me.

"Adelheim," Chris said, sitting down. "Are you kidding, or what?"

"Okay, apart from the obvious, then. He's handsome. In a fairly stereotypical way."

"Handsome doesn't begin to cover it. He's aristocracy. From a family with a tarnished reputation. Everyone at college wants to be his friend, everything circulates around him. All the girls want him. Even I'd like to fuck him till he passed out," Chris said dryly.

I'd just taken a large gulp of beer and had to clap my hand over my mouth to stop myself spraying it across the table. Chris's remark probably wasn't that funny, but the alcohol was making the room spin, and making everything Chris said extra funny.

At that moment, Jack and his friend appeared. They seemed to be looking for somewhere to sit. We'd taken the last free table, but there were spare chairs.

"What's happening?" Chris whispered. She had her back to them, but had spotted the curious look on my face.

"They're looking for somewhere to sit . . . and . . ."

Chris's eyes opened wide. She clamped her mouth shut.

"They're on their way over," I whispered.

"Fuck! Don't look at them! Stop staring! Laugh instead. Laugh like I've just told you the best joke you've ever heard!"

I leaned back in my chair and pretended to laugh. I felt ridiculous. Chris was laughing as well. A loud, exaggerated laugh that sounded to me like she was on the brink of madness. Jack Adelheim and his friend waited until we finished laughing.

"Is it okay if we sit here?" Jack said. "We promise not to disturb you."

Behind him his friend was holding his beer a little too tightly and was swaying gently as he looked groggily toward us.

"Sure," Chris said flatly, looking up with feigned surprise.

Jack sat down next to me, and his friend settled onto the bench opposite. He reached out his hand unsteadily across the table.

"Henrik."

"Mat . . . Faye," I said, not yet used to my new identity.

It was hard to shed my skin. Harder than I'd expected.

I twisted around and repeated the handshake with Jack. He smiled. A beautiful, open smile. His blue eyes looked straight into mine. He *was* handsome, I couldn't deny that. But I had Viktor, and I wasn't that sort of girl. Besides, Chris would probably smash me in the nose with her beer glass if I made a move on Jack.

"Nice to meet you."

Once everyone had shaken hands Chris leaned forward and asked pointedly what I thought about the new U.S. president, George W. Bush. I rolled my eyes and launched into a short lecture that was basically a summary of the editorial in that morning's *Dagens Nyheter*. Jack and Henrik waded into the debate at once, taking issue with my argument, Jack on my side, Henrik against. The noise level—Bryan Adams singing "Summer of '69"—meant that I only heard fragments of what they said.

After a while I had forgotten everything Chris had told me

about Jack. He was just a nice guy who was easy to talk to. Henrik had bought another round of beers.

"As thanks for letting us sit here," he said, pushing two glasses toward us.

He couldn't take his eyes off Chris. In return, she didn't deign to bestow so much as a single glance on him.

The bartender yelled that there was half an hour until they closed, and that it was last orders. Chris started to shuffle about in her seat.

"I need to go to the bathroom," she said apologetically.

Henrik got up and stood to attention as she squeezed past him. Jack turned toward me.

"What are your plans for the rest of the evening?"

I hesitated. Glanced at my mobile, which still hadn't shown any sign of life from Viktor.

"Oh, I don't know. Chris wanted to go out somewhere, so I'll probably tag along with her for a while. How about you two?"

Jack was so intensely present that it was making me feel slightly uncomfortable. He was having a definite effect on me, somehow managing to get under my skin. I wasn't sure what I thought about that.

Henrik remained standing, looking around the bar.

"We'll probably carry on the party back at Henrik's. You're both welcome to join us if you like."

"Maybe. I'll have to check with Chris first."

"Sure," Jack said, his blue eyes never leaving mine. "What line of work do you do? Or are you a student?"

His dark, thick eyelashes framed his eyes, making their blue color seem even more intense. Beneath the table our thighs bumped against each other's.

"I'm studying at the School of Economics," I said nonchalantly, and took a sip of beer.

I always had trouble hiding my pride at my own achievements. The fact that I had risen above everything that had happened—

getting the necessary grades, doing what plenty of people dreamed about—without the advantages of many of the other students at the Stockholm School of Economics.

"Really? Me too. First year?"

"Yes."

I slowly turned my beer glass. Wondered where Chris had gone.

"What do you think of it? Are you enjoying it?"

He was giving me his full attention, and that made me squirm. I preferred to hide in the shadows. Viktor never looked at me like that. That was one of the reasons I felt so comfortable being with him. He was happy to let my secrets stay secret. But Jack appeared to see straight through me.

"I like it," I said slowly. "Though I've only been there a week. So it's hard to say, really."

Chris came back to the table and sat back down with an air of confidence. She looked at us inquisitively.

"He . . . erm, it's Jack, isn't it?" I said uncertainly and he nodded. "Jack was wondering if we wanted to go back to . . . Henrik's? But we were going out, weren't we?"

I was having trouble concealing what I wanted to do.

Chris's eyes revealed how impressed she was by my industry. But to my surprise she just shrugged.

"Maybe. We'll have to see," she said. "I want to go dancing first."

"We could go to Sturecompagniet," Henrik suggested.

"I can't be bothered to stand in a line," Chris said with a sigh and a toss of her red hair.

"No problem. Jack can get us in," Henrik said. "Can't you, Jack?"

"Sure," he said, without taking his eyes off me. "No worries."

He got to his feet and held his hand out to me. I glanced at my mobile. No messages. Viktor suddenly didn't feel all that important. I dropped my mobile into my bag and took Jack's hand.

• • •

As Jack had promised, we were waved past the line by the bouncers. On the way to the VIP section he was stopped repeatedly
by guys wanting to chat and girls making fools of themselves
batting their eyelashes and pouting. I tried to tell myself that I
was immune to Jack's charms, and that it was merely entertaining to see how everyone, men and women alike, seemed to be so
enchanted by him.

He took a lap in the VIP area, shaking hands as if he were a
president on a state visit. Chris, Henrik, and I waited by the bar as
Jack worked his way around the room. Henrik ordered cocktails
and shots for us all. The level of drunkenness had already hit the
roof inside the club. People were yelling into one another's ears,
spraying saliva. The women were dressed in minuscule dresses or
tiny tops and short skirts. The men in thin, pastel-colored shirts
and jeans or chinos. I was holding my end up pretty well in my
borrowed dress, I could feel people's eyes roaming over my body.
I was being evaluated, judged, but was enjoying the attention. I
could see the way it affected Jack when he slipped into my field of
vision from time to time.

"Does he always disappear like this?" Chris yelled over the
noise at Henrik, who was moving awkwardly in time to the
music.

"Yes. He knows everyone." He sighed then he lit up. "It's great
that you both came along, so I don't have to stand here alone!"

I leaned closer to him to hear better.

"Does everyone else know him, then?" I said.

"No. Sometimes I ask myself if I even know him. And we've
been friends for ages, we're going to set up a business together."
Henrik leaned over the bar and took a few sips of his cocktail.
"No one ever manages to get much of an idea of him, which is
why everyone's so fascinated by him. That's my theory, anyway.
Then there's the whole aristocracy thing combined with his

decadent background. Throw in a bit of juicy—and very public—family conflict and tragedy, and hey presto . . ."

He was slurring now, and sucked some more of his cocktail through its pink straw. Then he straightened up and adjusted his glasses.

Jack had stopped in front of a group of girls at the other end of the bar. They laughed when he made a few jokey dance moves. When he left them they stared hungrily after him.

Jack made his way toward us and put his arms around Chris's and my waists. I felt the warmth of his hand against my skin. He was moving his thumb up and down. A tingle ran through my body.

"Didn't you want to dance?" he asked brightly before turning toward Henrik. "Why haven't you shown them to the dance floor? Do I have to do everything myself?"

Henrik threw his arms out. "You know I'm not a dancer."

"Yes, I'm painfully aware of that. Along with the owner of every nightclub in the city."

Henrik blushed but seemed happy to go along with it. There was no animosity in their relationship.

Jack winked at him. "One last shot, then a dance?"

Henrik was starting to look tired, but nodded. "Sure."

Jack beckoned to the bartender, who leaned forward and shook his hand as they exchanged a few words. Suddenly four shot glasses appeared in front of us.

"On the house," the bartender yelled, and patted Jack on the shoulder before turning to deal with the next customer.

We raised the glasses in a toast, tipped our heads back, swallowed, and grimaced. When Jack had set his glass down he put his arm around my waist and let his hand slip to my stomach. I glanced nervously at Chris. She didn't appear to have noticed anything, and was busy talking to Henrik. They seemed to be getting on well. I found myself with yet another cocktail in my hand, and the alcohol numbed any remaining inhibitions. The only thing that mattered was that Jack's hand, right there, right then, felt warm and comfortable against my stomach.

I still found myself thinking of Viktor. And how inappropriate it was to be standing here like this with a guy I'd only known a few hours. Because I was in love with Viktor, I was sure I was.

And I didn't want to spoil my budding friendship with Chris with meaningless flirting. I worshipped her. Chris was a force of nature. And Jack seemed to be more of interest to her than to me.

But at the same time there was something about Jack that made me feel giddy. His hand had come to a halt with his fingers resting gently on my hip bone. And I wanted him to keep moving down my body. Suddenly I realized that I was going to have to put a stop to this. Before it had even started. I pulled free and noticed that Jack was surprised, though he did his best to hide it.

"I have to go now," I said, putting my half-drunk cocktail back on the bar.

"So soon? But we were going to go back to Henrik's to carry on partying."

"I have to go home," I said firmly. "To my boyfriend."

"Ah, you've got one of those," Jack said with amusement, but I thought I detected a hint of disappointment in him—which could easily have been wishful thinking on my part.

"Yes."

"I think I'll come with you anyway."

"What? Why?"

He pointed to something behind me, and I turned around. Chris and Henrik were locked together, their tongues in each other's mouths. Chris had one hand on the back of his head, pulling him toward her.

I turned back toward Jack.

"I'm going now. See you."

Jack took hold of my arm.

"Hang on. Let me see you home. Where do you live?"

"Gärdet. Well, my boyfriend lives there, and that's where I'm sleeping. Why do you want to come with me? You can have any one of those girls you were talking to earlier. I can't imagine any of them turning you down."

I nodded toward the girls on the dance floor, writhing to the Sugababes' latest hit.

"But that's not what I want. I want to go home with you. You're interesting. And beautiful. You're different."

"Am I?"

I felt a knot in my stomach as I remembered all the times I had been told I was different. In a different way from now. A completely different way.

"Yes," Jack said. "And I like your name. It suits you."

He looked into my eyes, pleading like a little boy. I sighed.

"Okay. But we're going back to my place, then. Villagatan. But you're only coming as far as the door."

Jack brightened up.

It was a warm night. We pushed our way through the semicircle of people crowding outside the club and set off along Sturegatan. Jack lit a cigarette and passed it to me before putting another one in his mouth and lighting it. We hadn't spoken a word to each other since we came outside. Even so, the silence felt comfortable.

A taxi drove past. I glanced at Jack, who smiled back at me. We turned into Humlegården.

"What sort of company are the two of you working on?"

"Nothing so far. We're trying to come up with a good enough idea. But when we do we're going to go for broke, put together a professional business plan, find investors, become millionaires."

"Investors?"

"Yes, we want to manage on our own. My parents aren't an option. My dad . . . I don't have any contact with my dad. And Mom lives in Switzerland with her new husband and sends Christmas cards, but that's all. And we need capital. For offices, staff, marketing, and PR."

A small, almost imperceptible change in tone. I wondered what it meant. Jack's eyes followed a man on the other side of the street. Took a deep drag on his cigarette. It was his third already on our relatively short walk.

"Henrik and I have promised each other that we're going to be independently wealthy by the time we're thirty."

He blew a smoke ring.

"Have you got a name yet? For your nonexistent company . . . ?"

I grinned to show that I was joking.

He responded to my lighthearted question seriously.

"We've had a few ideas, but none of them have really grabbed us. I want the name to indicate that our company is best, that there's no competition."

Jack blew another smoke ring.

"How about Compare?" I said after thinking for a while. "It's a confident name, suggesting that the business isn't afraid of being compared to others?"

Jack stopped and looked at me.

"I like it," he said slowly. "It's got a good feel to it."

"You can thank me if you decide to use it," I said, smiling at him.

We had reached Karlavägen and I was shivering. The evening had grown cooler now and I wasn't wearing any outdoor clothing.

Music was coming from an open window a few feet ahead, and suddenly a door opened in the same building. A man and a woman stumbled out. Jack took a few quick steps and caught the door with his foot before it closed, then held it open and bowed theatrically.

"What are you doing?" I said, wrapping my arms around my chest.

"After-party!"

"Do you know the people who live here?" I said in surprise as I followed him through the door.

"I will soon. So will you. Come on." Jack took my hand and

led me up the wide stone staircase. "We'll have a few drinks and then leave."

"You're kidding, right?" I giggled as I let him pull me along. "You're just going to walk up and ring the bell?"

"Yep."

Jack half-ran up the stairs, pulling me behind him.

"You're crazy."

I laughed.

Jack turned and kissed me quickly, and the light touch was electric.

I had to stop for a moment before following him up to the flat where the music was coming from.

The sign on the door said LINDQVIST. We rang the bell and the door was opened by a woman in her thirties, her cheeks flushed with alcohol. Behind her: music, talking, the clink of glasses, laughter. Jack smiled his best smile as I shrank behind him in embarrassment.

"Hi there!" he said breezily. "We couldn't help hearing that you're having a party and it all sounded so nice! Would it be okay if my girlfriend and I came in to warm up?"

I started when he called me his girlfriend, but managed to keep a straight face. Something shifted in my stomach when he said the word. The woman burst out laughing. She nodded and stepped aside.

"Come in. I'm Charlotte."

We introduced ourselves. All the other guests appeared to have kept their shoes on, so we did the same. Charlotte walked ahead of us into a large room where around forty people in smart clothes were spread out beneath the glow of an immense chandelier. Charlotte stopped right under it and raised her glass.

"Listen up! This is Jack and Faye. They thought we seemed to be having fun and decided to come up and check us out!"

Scattered laughter. Someone called out "Welcome!," someone else "Get them a drink!" Before I knew it, I was standing talking to a Japanese lawyer with a lisp, Julia, around ten years older than me.

They were all happy, open, pleasant, urbane. I soon forgot my shyness—Matilda would have felt completely lost there. Faye loved the people around her, the conversation, the atmosphere, the waves of sound rising and falling beneath the huge chandelier. Faye fit in.

I was also conscious that Jack was nearby. I was safe with him. While I spoke to Julia I was constantly aware of where he was. The room seemed to tilt in his direction. He dazzled them all, went around, laughing, joking, filling empty glasses like it was his party. There was a confidence to everything he did that was bewitching. I had never been near anyone as radiant as Jack Adelheim.

Our eyes met. He winked, smiled, and raised his glass in my direction. The bubbles in the champagne sparkled in the light from the chandelier.

Someone put their hand on his shoulder and Jack turned away. And suddenly I felt I missed him. His glance, our brief moment of understanding, his smile. I turned to listen to what Julia was saying about her impossible working conditions in one of the biggest law firms in Stockholm. The room felt cold behind me now that Jack wasn't looking at me. Someone put a glass of champagne in my hand.

* * *

An hour later the guests began to drift away. It was starting to get lighter outside the windows. We were among the last to leave. Jack pulled out a half-full bottle of wine and put it to his lips.

"One for the road." He grinned.

"Stolen property," I retorted.

"Pah!"

He took a couple more swigs, then passed the bottle to me. I thought of his lips around the mouth of the bottle, and imagined I could taste him, mixed with the tepid white wine.

We didn't stop talking as we strolled through the silent city. I was laughing so much I hardly had time to breathe. Jack related conversations, imitating the party guests with precise mannerisms. I told him about Chris and the guy on the bus.

All too soon we were standing outside my door. Silent at last. All of a sudden it felt unreal and unnatural that I should tap in the code, open the door, and go inside without him.

"Well, then," Jack said, now seeming almost bashful. "See you around."

"Okay."

"So long, Faye," he said, like a line from a cheap Hollywood film, and turned on his heel.

"Wait!"

He stopped midstride, turned, ran his hand through his hair, and looked at me curiously.

"Yes?"

"Oh . . . it was nothing . . ."

He turned around again. Started to walk. Raised the bottle.

I didn't move. Waiting for him to turn. To take one last look at me. Wave. Come rushing back. Kiss me again, properly this time. I could still remember how his lips had felt.

But he just lit a cigarette as he ambled nonchalantly toward Karlavägen. There he turned left. And disappeared.

Faye was holding Julienne with one hand and pushing an empty shopping trolley with the other as they walked through the aisles of the ICA supermarket at Karlaplan. The housekeeper had been ill for two days and Faye was thinking of surprising Jack with a home-cooked meal. Her famous spaghetti bolognese. The secret ingredient was celery. And three different types of onion. And it had to simmer for a very long time.

When they were young and poor she used to make a big pot of it every Monday that would see them through to Thursday. She put red and yellow onions in the trolley, along with some shallots and celery.

"I want to push the trolley," Julienne said.

"Are you sure you can manage it?"

"Yeees," Julienne said, rolling her eyes.

"All right then, darling."

Faye let her take hold of the trolley and stroked her hair, pausing to study her face in the middle of the busy shop. She loved her so much that she sometimes thought her heart would burst.

"Tell me if it gets too heavy," she said, and set off toward the meat counter to get some chopped meat.

Julienne pushed the trolley after her.

They passed an elderly man who was helping a woman the

same age to get a can down from the shelf. Faye couldn't take her eyes off them. He passed the can to the woman, who was leaning heavily on a walker. She patted him on the hand, and her wedding ring glinted in the glare of the fluorescent lighting.

Faye wondered how long they'd been married. Was this what she and Jack would be like together? She had always had such a clear image in her mind. Growing older, inseparable, getting wrinkled and fragile together. Even if they were going through a bit of a rough patch now, that's how things would end up. If she were to ask the couple she was sure they'd be able to tell her about the difficulties along the way. Difficulties that they had overcome.

Julienne looked up.

"Why are you crying, Mommy?"

"Because it's so sweet."

Julienne looked confused.

"What is?"

"That he's . . . oh, it's nothing."

The elderly couple turned into another aisle and disappeared.

Faye found the last things she needed and headed to the registers with Julienne following behind her. The evening papers were trumpeting that they'd cracked the secret to simple and speedy weight loss. She picked up a copy of *Expressen* and checked one last time that she had everything she needed. She had long since abandoned the diet juices, and in three days had regained all the weight she had lost. Plus a bit extra.

She picked the line where a young, rather pretty girl was working quickly and efficiently. A woman put a pack of tampons on the conveyor belt. Just as the cashier was scanning them Faye realized that she was late. Badly late. She should have gotten her period two weeks ago. She pushed any thought of John Descentis from her mind. It was probably because of the diet, but she still felt she ought to make sure.

Then it was their turn.

"Do you have . . . ?" She glanced at Julienne, who was staring at a small poodle by the door. "Pregnancy tests?"

"In the machine over there," the cashier said, pointing.

The people in the line behind them sighed and stared as Faye walked past them. She clicked to get to the pharmacy section, then tapped the screen for pregnancy tests. Julienne was busy looking at the dog. Faye took two kits and returned to the register.

"That's four hundred and eighty-nine kronor," the cashier said once she had scanned them.

Faye took out her personal American Express and paid.

"Sorry," she said, "but you don't happen to know if . . . if Max is off today?"

The cashier raised her eyebrows. Was she smiling?

"Max has been fired. Something about him harassing customers."

"I see," Faye said. "Well, thanks."

She hurried out of the shop, holding Julienne's hand hard.

Jack had gotten Max fired. She was certain of it. And that had to mean that he still cared about her, surely? In spite of everything?

Julienne picked up the newspaper and peered at the pictures on the front.

What would happen if she was pregnant? How would Jack react? When they first met he had said he wanted four children. But once they had Julienne he didn't seem very interested in having any more. They hadn't even talked about it. So what about her, then? Did she want more children? Yes, she did. Especially now. A little brother or sister for Julienne could be the catalyst that brought her and Jack back together again, and finally put an end to the strange limbo they were in.

And it would do Julienne good to have a brother or sister. They could become best friends. She had always wished she'd had a sister. An ally.

Faye quickly brushed the thought away. She had learned to shut down such thoughts, not to let her mind wander. It did no good at all to think about things she couldn't do anything about.

...

When they got back to the apartment Julienne dropped the newspaper and her coat on the hall floor. Faye hung the coat on its hook, carried the bags into the kitchen, and started to unpack. From the corner of her eye she saw Julienne come out from her room with her iPad, then throw herself on the sofa, still with her boots on.

"Take your shoes off before you get on the sofa," Faye said.

No answer. She put the frying pan down and went into the living room. She started to remove Julienne's wet, dirty winter boots.

"I don't want to!"

Julienne kicked out, hitting the sofa with her boots and making dirty, muddy marks. Shit, now she'd have to wash and dry the covers before Jack got home. She grew more heavy-handed. There was mud on the rug as well.

"Don't want to! Don't want to! Don't want to!"

Julienne carried on screaming and kicking out wildly.

Faye managed to get the boots off and lifted Julienne down from the sofa, but she threw herself back on it, still shouting. Faye went into the kitchen and came back with a dishcloth. Maybe she'd be able to wipe the dirt off the fabric if she was quick. She ignored Julienne. To her great relief she managed to get the worst of it off the sofa, and bent down to try to get the carpet clean. Julienne kicked out at her and she managed to catch her leg.

"You don't do that!"

"I do!"

The darkness rolled in. It was simultaneously familiar and

unfamiliar. Faye swallowed hard. Clenched her hands several times.

Julienne must have noticed the difference because she was staring at Faye, sniffling.

Faye wiped the rug with the dishcloth again. Pushed her hair back and turned away from Julienne.

"You're fat," Julienne said.

Faye turned around.

"What did you say?"

Julienne stared at her defiantly.

"Fatty." She pointed at her. "You're a fatty."

Faye took a step toward her. "No, I'm not. You don't say things like that!"

"Yes, you are! Daddy says so!"

"Has Daddy said I'm fat?"

Her voice had become so thin. All of a sudden she didn't know what to do, just stood helpless in the middle of the room. Julienne seemed to realize that she'd gone too far and started to cry.

Faye stumbled away. Everything was spinning. She hardly knew where she was. Behind her she heard Julienne calling to her in between sobs.

She shut herself in the bathroom. Locked the door and leaned her forehead against the door for a few seconds. Let the cool wood soothe her. She took out the pregnancy test. Julienne was standing outside the door, banging and screaming. Faye pulled her trousers and panties down to her ankles. Sat down on the toilet and opened the packet with her teeth. She held the stick between her legs, relaxed, and let the warm urine flow over the stick, not bothered that it was splashing her fingers. Julienne went on shouting outside the door.

I SAT ON THE BUS, watching the cars rushing past outside. The air was humid and warm. The driver had opened the window in the roof to let more air in, but it made very little difference, just a slight breeze on my shoulder. Beside me sat a large, sweaty woman with a crying child on her lap.

We passed Humlegården. Where Jack and I had walked. I had replayed that night in my mind hundreds of times.

Since then I had taken every chance I could get to go to Chinatown—the district between the School of Economics and Norra Real School—in the hope of bumping into Jack. But he hadn't shown up.

Apart from that, life was fun, exciting for the first time. Studying was easy, but it always had been. Ever since I first started school, that had been my refuge, the place where I could excel without effort. The professors were full of praise. The courses were enjoyable and interesting, I was having a great time.

Chris and I spent almost all our free time together. Neither of us needed to study particularly hard. Chris because she was happy to just pass. And in my case because ever since childhood I had only had to read a text a couple of times to remember it in its entirety.

Viktor's starring role in my life had dwindled to a walk-on part. I couldn't quite put my finger on exactly what had changed, but after my encounter with Jack my feelings for Viktor had grown cooler. I kept my distance. Invented nonexistent tests to justify why I didn't have time to see him. I avoided his calls and let days pass before answering them. I delayed the idea of moving in with him until he stopped talking about it.

My coldness changed Viktor, it made him pathetic and insecure. He became more desperate, clingy, as I grew colder. Our relationship was dying, but he clung to me as if he were drowning. He called me at all hours, showered me with gifts and declarations of love, constantly asked where I was and what I was doing. He suddenly started to ask me about my past, my family, my life before him. I refused to answer. What could I say? But my coldness, my reluctance to tell him anything about myself only made him more desperate. I became a code for him to crack. It was as if he thought I'd love him again if only he could break the code.

The worst of it was that there wasn't really anything wrong with Viktor. He was handsome, kind, and ambitious. He treated me like a princess. He was faithful and reliable—unusual qualities in Stockholm's jungle.

But he wasn't Jack Adelheim. And I realized that I was going to have to dump him. I had been putting it off. But I couldn't postpone it any longer.

By the time the bus pulled in at Tessin Park I was in no doubt. Hurting him wasn't going to be pleasant, but I had to put an end to it.

"Excuse me, this is my stop," I said.

The woman with the child stood up with an effort to let me past. She looked tired and fed up. Rolls of fat were clearly visible under her tight white T-shirt, spilling over her jeans. The child was dribbling. Green snot was hanging like bunches of grapes from its nose. Dear God. I was never going to be a mother like that. And my child would always be perfect. Jack's and my child. I flinched, blushing with shame at my embarrassing daydreams.

But all my dreams were about Jack these days. Both while I was asleep and when I was awake. There was no longer any space left for someone like Viktor.

The doors opened with a sigh and I was hit by the blazing sun. Viktor was going to meet me in the middle of Tessin Park, like he usually did. I imagined him walking out of his apartment. Happy, thinking we were going to get pizza together. Then go home and have sex. Watch a film, more sex, then fall asleep together. None of that was going to happen.

I felt sorry for him on an intellectual level, but I didn't *feel* anything. My desire for Jack overshadowed everything else, making me indifferent. And the new version of Viktor irritated me. He had grown up in his protected little bubble, everything had been so easy for him. His naïveté had been the first thing that attracted me to him, but now it just annoyed me. He knew nothing about life, whereas I knew far too much. Viktor had no idea of who I was. Or *what* I was.

He was wearing a denim shirt and pale chinos. He grinned, then leaned forward and kissed me on the cheek.

"I've missed you," he said, putting his arm around me. "You're taking your studies far too seriously. Which pizzeria do you feel like? Valhalla or Theodoras?"

"I need to talk to you," I said. "Let's go and sit down."

I pulled him over to a green bench. Viktor turned to face me and took his sunglasses off. He folded them carefully and put them in his top pocket. His eyes were darting about.

"Has anything happened? Are you okay?" he asked, acting as if he didn't know what I was about to say.

A short distance away a group of alcoholics were playing bocce and drinking wine. Happy, hoarse voices.

"I don't want to go out with you anymore. It's over."

I heard how cold I sounded, and made an effort to seem sad. Viktor was staring blankly ahead of him.

"Okay . . . Is it something I've done?"

He shuffled uncomfortably on the bench. Avoided my gaze. Swallowed. Then swallowed again.

"No. It's nothing you've done."

I was having trouble looking at him, I didn't want my derision to show. So I watched the bocce game instead. They were so drunk that the balls ended up all over the place, but they cheered happily anyway. Behind them a little girl fell over on the gravel. Her mom came running over. Wiped the dirt from her grazed knees, picked her up, hugged her.

"Is there anything I can do differently? Maybe you just need some time?"

His voice was thick. What I had said was starting to sink in, and he wasn't far from tears. I looked around. If he started to cry I would get up and walk away. I couldn't deal with people crying. I'd had enough tears to last a lifetime.

"No. I'm sorry, but I don't love you anymore."

"But I'm so in love with you! You're the best thing that's ever happened to me. The best person I've ever met."

He put his hand on mine. Kneaded it, massaged it. As if that might make me change my mind. As if I was the one who needed comforting, not him.

People's biggest problem, I realized, is that they project their own sorrows onto other people. Try to share them. They imagine that, because we share the same sort of DNA, we will automatically feel sad about the same situations. Sorrow doesn't get easier to deal with simply because you share it. Quite the contrary, it gets heavier. And Viktor had no idea what real sorrow was.

"Okay, I get it," he said, nodding. "But can't you come home with me and we can talk about this quietly? I can't handle sitting here with all these people. Let me have one last evening. Just one more. Then you can disappear from my life, and I'll let you go without any protest. Please . . ."

He was holding my hand so hard it hurt, and I knew I should say no. That it wasn't going to help him at all. But it was the easy way out, and I took it.

During the short walk to his apartment I had time to regret my decision many times, but perhaps the breakup would be easier if I let him get everything off his chest. At the same time I wanted to avoid the difficult conversation that was coming, I didn't want to hear his declarations of love, his reproaches. He needed answers, but I had none to give him. All I knew was that my heart belonged to someone else and that I had to move on.

No sooner had we arrived at his place than I offered to go and get pizza. I had a feeling it was going to be a long evening, and that we could both do with some food. Viktor didn't answer. He was sitting perfectly still on his bed with his shoulders drooping despondently.

"I'll be back soon," I said, avoiding his reproachful gaze.

I got my wallet out of my bag and closed the front door behind me. I can let him have one last evening, I thought. Then I'm free.

I got back twenty minutes later. Viktor looked at me strangely when I put the pizzas down on the table. Almost triumphantly. He was where I'd left him, sitting on the unmade bed, but next to him was something I recognized. My stomach dropped. My diary. Viktor had gone through my bag. My college notepad was there too. The one I made notes in while I studied, and which had recently been filled with childish doodles. Jack's name in a heart. My name with his surname. Silly. Ridiculous. But there was nothing ridiculous about it to Viktor.

"Now I know who you really are," he said calmly.

His voice was toneless. Dead. Something inside him had broken.

"I know who you are. The question is, does *he* know . . . ?"

The word *he* sounded like an accusation. Panic coursed through me. No one could know. My diary described my former life. If the truth came out it would change everything. I would get the same stares I had received back when I was Matilda. I'd be subjected to the same humiliation. No one would look at me the same way again. Especially not Jack.

"You've been unfaithful. You've slept with Jack Adelheim. I've got every right to tell him. Does he know about us? About the fact that you've got a boyfriend?"

I knew there was no point trying to explain. It wouldn't make any difference that we hadn't slept together, that it had only been a quick kiss.

Viktor looked like a wounded animal, his eyes black with hatred and despair. I realized he was capable of doing anything to get me back. Or to get his own back. To make me feel the same pain that was tearing him apart. He would tell the truth about who I really was, not only to Jack but the whole world. And my new life as Faye would be over. Everything would be over.

My panic was replaced by an icy coldness I recognized from before. A peculiar calm settled on me and I realized there was no alternative. I wasn't going to let Viktor stop me.

What I felt as I met his gaze was hatred. I had paid a high price to get where I was, and now he was sitting there like some fucking judge. He knew nothing about the pain I had had to endure, the things I had been forced to do, the sights I had seen that I would have to live with for the rest of my life.

But I held all of this inside me. Men were simple. Men were easy to manipulate and Viktor would be no exception. I had done it before and could do it again.

I sat down beside him. Took his hand in mine. Spoke softly to him, warmly, stroked the back of his hand with my thumb. I felt him relax. Against his will.

"You can do whatever you want. I understand. I understand that you're sad and hurt. But I haven't been unfaithful with Jack, and I don't want us to part on bad terms. Let's do what you wanted. One last evening together. You can have a whole night if you like. A morning. Then you can do whatever you want. Hurt me back if you want to. Tell Jack everything. That's your right. But I want us to have one last night together."

I felt him start to relent. He wanted to believe me. Couldn't turn down one last chance of intimacy. I knew him. I knew men.

We ate pizza and shared two bottles of wine. I only sipped my glass, so Viktor drank most of the wine. We made love on the sofa. He took me hard, roughly. I let him. I closed my eyes and thought of Jack. Conjured up his face in my mind's eye, forced myself out of my body as Viktor thrust into me, whimpering. Afterward he turned his back on me. I got up and washed, grimacing with pain when I tried to wipe myself. When I got back he was asleep. Nothing was going to wake him now.

I went out onto the balcony and lit a cigarette. The lights above the city were twinkling in the summer night, and I could hear voices, music. When I had finished the cigarette I lit another one. I went in to Viktor, who was lying on his back, snoring with his mouth open. I prodded him. No reaction. He was completely wiped out by the wine and the storm of emotions. I laid the cigarette on the bed, by the edge of the pillowcase, then stood and waited to make sure that the cheap, flammable fabric caught fire. At first it only smoldered. Then a flame began to form.

The icy chill I had felt started to fade. Panic crept up on me, hammering at my temples. I turned my back on the flames and hurried to the door. By the time I let it swing shut behind me the bed and curtains were alight.

I felt like I was going to be sick when I emerged into the summer night. The smiling people I passed came far too close, sounded far too loud. I clutched my bag tight. I was free once more and my diary was safely back in my hands.

The pregnancy test had been positive. There was an embryo inside her, a new human being. Half Jack. He had always wanted a son, an heir. Maybe she would be able to give that to him.

Faye ran her hand over her stomach as she sat at the kitchen table, unable to do anything. She realized she hadn't had anything to eat for hours. Her meat sauce stood untouched on the stove because Jack hadn't come home yet. There was nothing to stop her eating now. The child needed nutrients to grow. She stood up and walked over to the stove. Dipped a finger in the sauce and found that it was lukewarm. She ladled some pasta into a dish. Drenched it with sauce and ate the whole lot standing at the island. It tasted divine. She closed her eyes and chewed the food as well-being spread through her and her body relaxed. It was so wonderful to eat at last that tears sprang to her eyes.

She would have to put off worrying about her weight until after the child was born. For the time being, her most important job was making sure she got enough nutrition for two.

Just like last time, she would start exercising straight after the delivery, but she would also follow a strict diet once she'd stopped breastfeeding. She wouldn't let herself be sucked into the baby bubble, and would prioritize Jack and their marriage instead. Their son would be a fresh start, for their relationship and for her as a woman and a wife.

She helped herself to another portion and carried the dish to the table.

An hour later the door opened and Faye felt anticipation fluttering in her stomach. She called out to Jack and he looked into the kitchen. Faye stood up and walked toward him. Soon that little worry line between his eyes would be gone.

"I've got some wonderful news to tell you, darling," she said. "Come and sit down."

Jack sighed. "I'm tired, can't it wait until . . ."

"No, come along."

Faye couldn't wait.

Jack raised his eyebrows but sat down at the kitchen table. She knew he'd be happy when she told him, and ignored the harassed look on his face.

"What?" he said.

Faye smiled at him.

"I'm pregnant, darling. We're going to have another child."

His expression didn't change.

"It could be a boy," she said. "You've always wanted to have a son as well."

Faye stroked her stomach and smiled again. He had always loved her smile, said it was infectious. But now he just rubbed his face wearily with his hand.

"What is it?" Faye said.

The lump in her throat was back.

"Now isn't a good time, Faye. I don't want another child."

"What do you mean?"

What was it with him? Why wasn't he happy?

"I just think that Julienne is enough."

"But . . ."

Her voice was barely audible. She didn't recognize the look in Jack's eyes.

"It's not appropriate. I'm sorry, but you'll have to . . . well, you know . . ."

Faye shook her head.

"You want . . . you want me to have an abortion?"

Jack nodded. "Yes, I know it's a nuisance, but it simply isn't appropriate."

She wanted to throw herself at him. Shake him. But she knew it was her fault. She had caught him by surprise, she needed to let it sink in.

Jack stood up.

"Okay?" he said.

Faye swallowed the lump. He fought so hard for her and Julienne. Did she really have any right to demand more?

"Yes, I understand," she said.

Jack's face softened. He leaned over and kissed her on the forehead.

"I'm going to bed," he said.

On the way to the bedroom he stopped and turned.

"I'll call my doctor tomorrow so we can get it done as soon as possible."

The bedroom door closed and Faye leaped to her feet. She hurried into the bathroom and yanked the toilet lid up. The spaghetti and meat sauce came back up, the taste of tomatoes mingling with the bitter taste of bile. She flushed it away, then rested her head on the cold porcelain and let the tears come.

I HAD BEEN SLEEPING like a log for more than twenty-four hours when I was woken by the shrill sound of the phone. It was Axel. When I heard his broken voice tell me what had happened, that Viktor had died in a fire started by a cigarette in bed, the tears came. I sobbed so hard that my whole body shook.

I had been forced to do what I had done, there hadn't been any choice, but the price was high. The price was always high.

After the call I lay in bed with my knees pulled up to my chest. I concentrated on breathing. In, out.

Viktor's words were still ringing in my ears. *I know who you are. The question is, does* he *know* . . . Viktor would never have been able to keep quiet. If he had lived, Faye would have had to die.

. . .

A few days later large raindrops started to fall outside the window. It was liberating. The rain washed away the stifling heat that had been draped over Stockholm like a blanket of humidity.

Chris had gone away. Her parents had invited her to their apartment in Majorca and I was on my own in Stockholm again. When I sent her a short text to tell her about Viktor she offered to come home, but I assured her I was okay.

I buried myself in microeconomics, macroeconomics, statistics, and financial analysis. College was the only thing that mattered. Succeeding, being the best. It was all down to me, no one else could do the work for me. And I had made up my mind. I was going to create a whole new life for myself. Run a business, travel business class, earn more money than I needed, have a handsome husband (Jack), nice, well-behaved children; I'd own houses and apartments in interesting places I'd read about and seen in films. I wanted it all. I was going to have it all.

My phone, charging beside the bed, rang. Probably Chris, calling to update me on her exploits in Spain. I lay on the bed and checked the screen before I pressed answer. It was a number my phone didn't recognize.

"Yes, hello?"

"Hi!"

"Who is this?" I said, although I recognized the voice at once.

"It's Jack. Jack Adelheim."

I closed my eyes. Didn't want to sound too keen.

"Oh, hi . . ." I said hesitantly.

"Am I disturbing you?"

He sounded excited. Happy. I could hear music in the background.

"Not at all. What's on your mind?"

I was making an effort to sound nonchalant, and rolled onto my back.

"I was thinking of asking if you'd like to go somewhere. Tonight. I need to get away from Henrik."

"Sure. Which bar do you want to meet at?"

"Bar? No, I mean go away somewhere."

I laughed. He was crazy.

"Go away somewhere?"

"Yes, for a couple of days. We'll be back on Sunday. Pack a few clothes and meet me at Central Station, and we'll go to Barcelona."

"Okay." I realized I was holding my breath.

"You want to come?" he said in surprise.

"Yes."

"See you in thirty minutes, then."

I hung up without fully understanding what I had agreed to. Then I leaped out of bed and started to pack.

* * *

We were drunk by the time we landed. We'd started to drink at Arlanda, and continued with cocktails the whole way across Europe. We had to wait a while in the line for a taxi but got one eventually. I was giggly and a bit unsteady on my feet, and very conscious of the blood rushing through every vein, every capillary in my body.

"Hotel Catalonia, por favor," Jack said once we were in the back seat. *"Está en el Born, lo conoce usted?"*

The car started with a jerk and I felt Jack's hand on my thigh, burning my skin.

"I didn't know you spoke Spanish."

"There's a lot you don't know about me," Jack said with a wink.

He moved his hand farther up my thigh and all my blood rushed to my crotch.

"What sort of hotel is it?"

"You won't be disappointed."

I smiled and turned my head away. How could I ever be disappointed in Jack?

The dark September night was hot and humid. People in summer attire strolled the streets in search of somewhere cool, dinner, company. I wound the window down and enjoyed the air on my face. I needed to cool off.

I had never been farther from Sweden than Denmark, where I had once been on a motoring holiday with my family. A holiday that had been abruptly cut short. But I didn't want to think about that now. I let the wind in my face blow away all the memories and told myself that I could replace them with new ones. Every cell in our body gets renewed, replaced. The same ought to be true of memories.

"I love this city. You'll see, it's easier to breathe here," Jack said, closing his eyes.

His long, dark eyelashes looked like little fans against his cheeks.

"You've been here before?"

He opened his eyes and looked at me, the glimmer of the streetlights and neon signs reflected in their deep blue.

"Twice."

I wanted to ask if those had been the same sort of trip. If he had sat in other taxis, with unspoken promises and hands on other women's thighs. Perhaps this was Jack Adelheim's standard maneuver? Maybe he was following his usual seduction tactics? But it didn't matter. Three days in this city together with Jack was far too tempting a prospect for me to waste it on pointless jealousy and unnecessary thinking. I was here now. With Jack's hand on my thigh.

We turned off onto one of the avenues, stopped at a red light, then drove into a very picturesque part of the city. The alleys grew narrower. Cobblestones kissed the rubber tires. We waited for an oncoming car to pass. My armpits were sweaty, but I closed my eyes and let myself be seduced by the sounds. Laughter, the clatter of cutlery, intense conversation, music. Bars everywhere, restaurants, cafés. The sweet smell of hash.

I wanted to take Jack's hand, squeeze it, look into his eyes, and tell him how wonderful he was, how happy I was to be here. But I had made up my mind not to take the initiative. Not to force anything.

"Here it is," Jack said.

A white façade, glass doors. Above them a sign with the hotel's name in large letters, HOTEL CATALONIA BORN. A young porter hurried over, skirted around the car, and opened the door for me.

"*Gracias,*" I said, and smiled. I already missed the heat of Jack's hand as I got out of the car.

"You're a fast learner," Jack called as he paid the driver.

The porter took our bags, we walked in, and Jack started to speak to the receptionist in his rough Spanish. He switched to English when the communication gap grew too big. We filled in some forms and handed over our passports. A photocopier rumbled, then we got them back.

"All sorted," Jack said.

The receptionist called the waiting porter over and we followed him into the elevator that carried us up to the fifth floor. When I walked into the room it turned out that Jack had booked a whole suite. I'd never seen anything like it.

"This is amazing," I said, all my intentions to appear worldly blown away. "God, I could fit my apartment in here ten times over!"

There was a group of sofas in the middle of the large room, in front of a flat-screen TV. Next to it was a well-stocked drinks trolley. The external wall had been replaced by huge panoramic windows with a view that stretched for miles.

I pulled back the thick curtains covering the door to the terrace, opened it, and stepped out. The city twinkled below. Sounds and smells drifted up to me. The heat felt as soft as velvet. Guitar music was coming from a nearby apartment. The sea lay dark and endless beyond the shoreline it was embracing.

"What do you think?" Jack asked.

He stopped behind me, put his arms around me, and rested his head on my shoulder. "I don't know what to say," I replied, spinning around and looking into his eyes. I felt like throwing myself at him, kissing him, tearing our clothes off, straddling him and feeling him inside me.

"I know the hotel's owner," Jack said.

"Swedish?"

"Yes. We're staying here free of charge."

"You're kidding?"

"I never joke about money," Jack said. "Shall we head out and get something to eat?"

. . .

We turned left outside the hotel. My heels caught in the cobbles and I stumbled slightly. Jack caught me by one arm. Before we left the room I had touched up my makeup, changed my under-wear, and put on a black skirt. I felt beautiful. And I didn't need to worry about whether or not Jack wanted me. He kept looking at me hungrily. Part of me would have liked to suggest not both-ering with food and staying in the hotel room to fuck ourselves silly. But I was too curious to see the city.

There were clusters of people standing around the street cor-ners. Hoarse laughter echoed through the alleys. A dark-eyed man in a soccer jersey came up to us.

"Hashish?"

Jack haggled over the price. The man gesticulated. The deal was soon concluded, Jack handed over a few notes and received a small parcel in return. He unwrapped it and took out a brown lump.

"Smell."

I closed my eyes and breathed in the sweet smell. I'd never tried it before. Not hash, in fact nothing stronger than cigarettes and alcohol. But here in Barcelona, with Jack, it felt entirely natural. Jack was a drug, a drug that made me want to try all the other drugs in the world.

He carefully wrapped it again and tucked it into the pocket of his jeans. The music grew louder and we came to a square. Chairs and tables were nestled along the buildings. People were smok-ing, drinking, eating.

"Here?" he said, pointing.

"Sure," I said. I was far too busy soaking up my surroundings to make any sort of decision about where to eat.

We sat down at a table. A waiter in a white shirt and bow tie came over. Jack ordered tapas. Beer for him, a mojito for me.

Our drinks arrived. Jack reached over, took a mint leaf from my glass, and popped it in his mouth.

"So what's the deal with you, Faye?"

"You're probably going to have to be a bit more specific."

"You've got it all. You're beautiful, you drink like one of the guys, and according to the people I've spoken to you're the smartest student in your year. Henrik's talking about making you a partner in the business. There must be something wrong somewhere. Are you a man in disguise? Have you got a club-foot?"

He leaned down and pretended to look under the table.

I laughed and kicked my foot toward him. The table wobbled and he joined in my laughter.

"And you're funny too. Are you glad you're here?" he asked.

A sudden shift in his expression. A hint of seriousness and a trace of what looked like insecurity. His blue eyes were gazing right at me, into me. I trembled. Looked away. I couldn't let him know how crazy I was about him, not yet. Men like Jack needed to fight, to hunt, to make them think it worthwhile. Otherwise they'd disappear.

I also knew that I couldn't let him know anything about Matilda. But that wasn't a problem. With each passing day my memories of the past faded. Now only Sebastian came to me in dreams, but even that was happening less frequently.

"There's nothing wrong with the city, but the company could be better," I said, shooting him a challenging look.

"Really?"

Jack toyed with his beer glass and grinned as he looked at me.

"So what happened to the boyfriend?" he asked curiously.

In my mind's eye I saw Viktor lying in bed as the sheets caught fire.

"It's over," I said curtly.

Jack had never met him, didn't know any details. And I didn't feel like giving him any.

The flame of the candle was reflected in Jack's eyes.

The waiter brought us a plate of air-dried ham and thin, triangular slices of cheese. I picked up a piece of ham, it felt greasy on my fingers but melted in my mouth.

"I like being here. I've never been to Spain before."

"Where have you been, then?"

"Denmark. And Fjällbacka."

"That's where you're from?"

"Yes. Fjällbacka. Not Denmark."

I thought back to that trip to Denmark. Legoland. Which, predictably, had ended in disaster.

"What's it like?"

"The opposite of this," I said, gesturing toward the square. "Empty streets. One single place to go if you want to go out. Everyone knows everything about everyone else."

"Your parents still live there? Brothers and sisters?"

Jack reached for a piece of ham but didn't take his eyes off me.

Sebastian's face appeared in my mind. Badly beaten, that terrible night.

I swallowed a few times.

"My parents are dead. I'm an only child."

The waiter appeared with more food. Potato wedges, garlic prawns in oil, olives, meatballs in tomato sauce.

I raised the cocktail to my mouth. The rum burned my throat. It was a strong mojito. Not like the expensive but miserly ones you got at Stureplan. I realized I probably looked depressed. Made an effort to regain control of my features, but all the alcohol we'd consumed since leaving Stockholm wasn't making it easy. I lit a cigarette to buy some time.

"I'd like to go there with you one day."

Jack didn't ask anything about what I'd said. I loved him even more for that.

"No, you wouldn't."

"Yes, I would. Of course I would. I like seeing new places. I can't get enough of new places."

And women, I thought. But said nothing.

"I've got friends who used to spend the summer in Fjällbacka. It's supposed to be lovely," he said, soaking up the oil from the garlic prawns with a piece of bread.

"So what's *your* secret, Jack?" I said, changing the subject.

I drank some more of the mojito as the stars in the night sky above us came closer.

"My dad's an alcoholic and compulsive gambler," he said quickly. He tore off a bit more bread and dipped it in the oil. "He's a fucking loser who's drunk away a large chunk of his inheritance. The black sheep of the family. But he's never been able to take my surname away from me. And, yes, it opens a lot of doors. But not because of him. I've got the rest of the family and my ancestors to thank for that."

"I had no idea."

"No, it's not the sort of thing you put on your business card. There aren't many people who know. When people ask, I usually say he lives abroad. It's easier that way. But it's no secret in the finer social circles in Stockholm. Everyone knows about my old man."

"What about your mother?"

"Remarried. Her new husband's a bastard as well, but at least he's a sober bastard. She's not great when it comes to picking men. Maybe that's what happens when you pick them according to how much money they've got. They live in Switzerland. I left home when I was sixteen. My uncle Carl got me an apartment and gives me a monthly allowance for rent and food, in exchange for me going to college."

"Brothers and sisters?"

"No. An only child, like you."

Jack ran his hand through his hair but his hair fell back across his forehead at once. A man was going from table to table selling roses. As he approached, Jack shook his head and the man moved on.

"You're very easy to talk to," Jack said. "I'm telling you things I don't usually talk about."

"Funny. I was thinking the same. I wonder why that is?"

It was a lie. There were plenty of things I hadn't told Jack.

"Maybe we're pretty similar." Jack lit a cigarette and inhaled deeply. "Other people probably don't realize how lonely you and I are."

I was fascinated by the fact that he saw himself as lonely. I'd only ever seen Jack surrounded by people.

"What are we like?" I asked curiously.

The fact that he thought we were similar was dizzying.

"We like other people, to a certain extent. We know their game. Play along. Pretend to be like them, pretend to be happy. But the truth is, we're . . ." He fell silent and looked at me intently. "Faye, you're a romantic. You don't think anyone can tell. You pretend to be nonchalant, indifferent. But you want the world to be richer, more beautiful. You're not going to make do with an average, humdrum existence. You want to get to the top, to own the world. You've got ambitions. That's why you didn't stay in Fjällbacka, why you moved to Stockholm. And that's why we're drawn to each other. We're the same. Hungry. But you've got one disadvantage if you want to go up in the world. You're a woman. And this is a man's world."

I wanted to protest, tell him he was wrong. But deep down I agreed with what he said. So I swallowed. Nodded. Opened my mouth to reply but was interrupted by the waiter bringing us more dishes. Our table was soon covered with food. Calamari, fried mushrooms, paella, lamb sausages and aioli. My empty glass was replaced by a large glass of red wine, and Jack got another beer. We threw ourselves at the delicacies, and I realized I hadn't looked at the time since I left my apartment.

We sat there for an hour or so after we'd finished eating. We came nowhere close to finishing it all. We drank wine and beer and talked. I fell deeper in love with each passing moment. My head was spinning, from the wine and all these new impressions. My stomach felt heavy with food and satisfaction. I had never been so happy as I was there and then. The stars had moved into my chest.

I took a drag on my cigarette. Let the smoke rise up toward the night sky.

"Tomorrow we'll go to the beach," Jack said. "Unless you'd rather swim in the pool on the roof of the hotel?"

"Let's take it as it comes."

I couldn't choose. I wanted it all.

"You're right. We'll take it as it comes."

He paid, then led the way back to the hotel. There were fewer people in the narrow alleyways now. I stumbled intentionally on the cobbles to give me an excuse to lean on him.

When we got up to the suite I realized I hadn't yet seen the bedroom. I opened the door and turned the dimmer switch. As in the sitting room, the wall onto the terrace had been replaced by panoramic windows. Modern art on the walls. Two leather armchairs. And an enormous bed. In front of the glass wall was an old-fashioned bathtub on gilded lion's paws.

"Jack! There's a bath in our bedroom!" I called. "Look!"

He appeared behind me.

"I know. One day I'm going to have one just like it."

"Me too," I said.

"Good. Then we're agreed."

"Agreed on what?"

"On how we're going to arrange our home."

I pretended I hadn't heard him. I didn't know him well enough to recognize his games. I didn't know when he was being serious and when he was joking. And I wasn't one of those naïve, privileged upper-class girls who had lived their lives behind tall gates and were used to their horse-riding circle always being neatly raked. I knew that life wasn't a fairy tale with a happy ending. But right now, life *was* a fairy tale. And that went a long way for someone like me.

I went over to the bath, turned the tap on, and felt the water.

"Let's try it!"

"Now?"

"Yes."

I turned away from him, pulled my top over my head, and let my skirt fall. I was still wearing my heels. I felt his eyes burning into my back and enjoyed having him in my power. Slowly I unfastened my bra and took my panties off. Then I kicked off my shoes, leaving me completely naked. In the reflection of the glass I could see him standing there, frozen to the spot. Now I was the one in control.

He sat down on the bed. Started to take off his shoes and trousers. His eyes on me the whole time. I liked having him to myself. In my power.

"Are you coming or do you need help?"

"I probably need help," he said.

I turned around slowly. Felt the wine go to my head. I walked over to him and pulled off his T-shirt and trousers. He had an amazing body. Muscular and tanned. The muscles in his arms and chest rippled under his skin. I stood in front of him. Got down on my knees and looked him in the eye. He leaned down and tried to kiss me, but I moved my head away and took hold of his underpants. He raised his backside so I could pull them off. His cock was standing straight up. I bent over and took him in my mouth. One second. Two. Three. I didn't take my eyes off his. Then I pulled back.

"Now, time for a bath," I said, teasing him and walking back to the bathtub.

He stood up and followed me. The bath was half-full, the water warm, a faint smell of chlorine. Then I felt his hand on the top of my arm. His grip was hard, almost aggressive. He pulled me across the room, back to the bed. He stood me at the foot of the bed and gave me a shove, making me fall forward on my stomach. I wiggled my backside to show that I was as eager as him, that I was the one controlling him. When he pushed into me I gasped. Half a second of pain. But he was careful, and waited for me. I got up on all fours and he slowly began to thrust into me. The terrace door was open and from outside came the sound of music mixed with laughter and talking. A car horn. I had only a vague perception of the sounds, distantly through the roaring in my ears. I felt his hands around my waist as he pushed into me. Dear God, I loved getting fucked by him.

"Harder," I groaned. "Harder!"

He put one hand on the back of my neck and pushed my head down into the pillow and did as I asked. I shuddered as the orgasm spread through my whole body. A moment later Jack came with a loud groan. He threw himself forward, lying on me with his full weight. We lay like that for a while. Silent, absorbed in the intensity of what we had just experienced.

Then we moved across to the bathtub. Jack got the lump of hash and rolled a joint that we kept passing between us.

"You're very, very sexy," Jack said.

"You're okay," I said. "In an emergency."

He splashed water at me and I let out a squeal, but it soon turned to bubbling laughter.

Afterward we slid under the covers naked. He put his arm around me, pulling me closer to him. Let his fingers slide across my body, but avoiding my breasts, backside, and crotch. Whenever he seemed to be heading that way he changed direction. It was frustrating. My breathing was getting heavier. I was no longer in control. My head started to spin when I realized that I had let him take charge. It frightened and excited me at the same time.

"Good night, future wife," he whispered.

A few minutes later I heard him snoring gently.

I was still horny. I put my hand on his cock and felt it swell, crept under the covers, and took it in my mouth. He woke up and threw the covers back. Without saying a word I sat astride him, put my hands on his chest, and leaned back. He folded his hands behind his head and looked at me greedily, but said nothing.

I came again. Let him come inside me.

Then I rolled onto my side.

"That's how we say good night to each other from now on," I said.

Henrik and Alice Bergendahl's home was situated in Gåshaga on Lidingö, and had its own jetty and beach. It would almost have looked more at home in Los Angeles. The seven-thousand-square-foot house contained everything from a private cinema, a gym, and an indoor pool to a wine cellar, billiard room, table-tennis room, and no fewer than five bathrooms. The ceiling in the vast "living room"—you could easily have parked several tractor trailers in there—was thirty feet high.

While Faye, Henrik, Jack, and Alice were eating dinner by candlelight with a view across the water of Höggarnsfjärden, their children were playing with the au pair in a different part of the house. The children's rooms had been placed as far away as possible from the rooms where Alice and Henrik spent most of their time.

A cold wind was blowing outside. Waves were rolling against the beach, fighting their way toward them before giving up and rolling back again.

Alice had ordered the food to be delivered, and a Lebanese buffet had been laid out on the enormous dining table. Faye glanced at Alice. She was wearing a tight red dress, open at the sides, so everyone could see her ribs sticking out like a bicycle rack. She was ignoring the buffet and chewing on a lettuce leaf. It probably wouldn't be long before she switched to merely licking those wretched leaves instead.

Faye was helping herself to the mezze. Drinking the strong Amarone. The child in her stomach was going to end its short life in a metal bucket anyway. Later that night she would be taking the pill she had picked up from the pharmacist. The first of two.

"Is it good?" Alice asked with a smile.

She had been watching every mouthful Faye had eaten. Probably counting the calories in her head. And chalking them up happily against her own negative total.

"Very good," Faye said. "Lebanese was a great choice."

Jack let out a laugh.

"Lebanese or not, you eat everything that's put in front of you," he said. "You just shovel it all in."

Faye looked down at her plate. Was that the image her husband had of her? Someone who gorged herself on anything she could find?

Henrik leaned toward her.

"How are you doing these days?" he said. "You never come up and visit us anymore."

"No, I think it's best to leave you in peace at work. You have so much to do."

"Yes, there is a lot going on. But there's always time for you."

"Thanks, Henrik, but it's best if I leave the two of you to look after yourselves."

Why did they sound like strangers? Like polite acquaintances who were filling a gap with small talk? She, Jack, and Henrik used to have fun together. Talk about proper subjects. She used to be treated as an equal, occasionally their better when she rapped their knuckles about business structure and financial tools. In the end she was actually the person who came up with the business model that Jack and Henrik based Compare on. Now she felt like a child who was being allowed to sit at the grown-ups' table.

"Are you ready, Henrik? The taxi will be here any minute."

Jack stood up, wiping his mouth. He and Henrik were going out to meet some old friends in the city center. They were going to drop her and Julienne off at home on the way. Faye heard her running down the stairs.

"I don't want to go home," Julienne said, looking beseechingly at Jack. "I want to stay here."

"Okay, you can stay here with Mommy, then. You don't mind, do you, Alice?"

Faye bit her lip. She had been looking forward to getting home and curling up on the sofa in some comfortable clothes with a bottle of wine. Drinking away all her worries about the following day.

"Of course, the kids would love that," Alice said.

As usual she lit up when she looked at him. More than when she looked at her husband.

"Great," Jack said, and Julienne rushed back upstairs.

Faye and Alice walked to the door with their husbands.

"Have fun, boys," Alice said, kissing Henrik on the lips.

"The babysitter's coming at nine o'clock tomorrow," Faye said.

"Right. Okay, see you," Jack said, and disappeared.

They loaded the dishwasher and put the leftover food in the fridge.

"Leave the rest," Alice said. "The housekeeper can deal with it tomorrow."

She took out another bottle of wine and they settled down on the sofa in front of the big picture window.

"What are you doing tomorrow?" Alice asked.

"I've got a doctor's appointment, that's all."

"Nothing serious?"

"No, nothing serious."

"It's sweet of Jack to go with you anyway."

Faye just murmured in reply.

Alice, with those big Bambi eyes and perfect skin. Was she happy with her life? Was there anything she felt passionate about? Faye couldn't be bothered to play any more games. They were both trapped in golden cages. Like a couple of peacocks. Even if Faye felt more like one of the scabby pigeons at Hötorget these days. Rats with wings, as Chris usually called them with distaste.

Faye didn't want to talk to a bird in a cage. She wanted to talk to a real person. They drank another couple of glasses.

Alice was telling a fantastically boring story about what her son, Carl, had been getting up to at preschool. Did Alice have anything else in her life apart from Henrik and the children? And the status accorded by their lifestyle? Was there a real person behind all that? Real feelings? Real dreams? Or was there something wrong with Faye, who seemed unable to be content with all this? Most people dreamed of a life like hers. Being able to buy whatever she wanted, not having to work, being successful, having beautiful children, getting invited to the opening of a new Louis Vuitton boutique and being in a position to spend more on a handbag than the average Swede earned in a month.

"What would you have done if you didn't have Henrik?" she asked.

"How do you mean?"

"What sort of job would you have done?"

Alice thought about the question for a long time. As if it was something she had never thought about before. Eventually she shrugged.

"Interior design, I think. I like making homes beautiful."

"Why don't you do it, then?"

Alice hadn't even designed the interior of her own home. That had been done by an expensive and much-hyped designer with a long list of Lidingö villas in his portfolio.

Alice shrugged her shoulders again.

"Then who'd look after the children?"

Faye opened her eyes wide and looked around the living room.

"The same person who does now. The au pair! Honestly, though, don't you ever dream about doing anything else? Doing what you really want, independent of the children and Henrik? Being your own person?"

She was drunk, she knew that, but she couldn't stop herself. She wanted to nudge open the door to Alice's golden cage, if only for a brief moment. Though they seemed to be living the same life, the differences between them were immense. She had an education to fall back on, and she had made a conscious decision, together with Jack, because they both thought it was for the good of their family. Unlike Alice, she wasn't dependent upon her husband.

Faye drank some more wine. At least the child would get one hell of a hangover as a parting gift.

A lump rose to her throat and she let out a cough.

"I am my own person," Alice said. "I don't want to change anything."

She moistened her lips. She really was like something out of a fairy tale. Her peacock's feathers were shimmering.

"You're extremely beautiful," Faye said.

"Thank you."

Alice turned toward her with a smile, but Faye wasn't quite ready to let it go yet.

"Doesn't it bother you that Henrik would never look at you if you weren't? That that's why we're in this house? Because we deserve to be shown off? Like dolls. Well, I used to be worth showing off, anyway."

She poured herself more wine, hadn't even noticed she'd finished the last.

"Stop it. You know very well that that's not the case."

"Yes, it is, it very clearly is."

Alice didn't answer, but held her glass out for Faye to refill it. The calories in wine evidently didn't seem to count in Alice's world.

A silence descended. Faye sighed. From farther inside the house came the sound of children yelling.

"Did you know that I've always envied you?" Alice mumbled.

Faye looked at her in surprise. There was something new, something sad in Alice's eyes. Was this a glimpse of the real Alice?

"No," she said. "I had no idea."

"Henrik always speaks so warmly about you, says you're the smartest woman he's ever met. You understand the things they talk about, you understand the business. You eat what you like, you drink beer, you make them laugh. It's probably that—the fact that you can make Henrik laugh—that I'm most envious of. He . . . well, he respects you."

Faye shifted position. She couldn't help thinking that a lot of what Alice had said was no longer true. She was describing the past. There was nothing left to envy. Nothing to respect. Sometimes she wondered if there ever had been, or if she had simply conjured up her own imagined version of what it had been like.

Sometimes unwelcome fragments of memory popped up. Of all the times she hadn't been able to get hold of Jack when she needed him. Some memories, such as Julienne's birth, were so painful that she daren't go anywhere near them. So she suppressed them. And forgave. Over and over again.

Faye shifted on the sofa. Put the wineglass down on a side table. Julienne came running in to ask if they could go for a swim in the pool.

"Are Carl and Saga going to go swimming too?" Faye asked, glancing at Alice.

"Yes!" Julienne said emphatically, nodding hard.

When Julienne had gone Alice let out a sigh.

"I know Henrik would never have married me if I hadn't had my looks and my background. I'm not naïve. But he makes me happy, and he's kind to me. I know women who are in a far worse position." She raised her glass and took a sip. "As a woman in this damn society you're not allowed to say that you want to be looked after. But that's what I want. I want Henrik to be the man of the house. I don't care if he fucks around from time to time."

She gestured with her arm, almost spilling red wine on the white sofa.

Faye couldn't take her eyes off her.

All of Jack's stories about Henrik's affairs, how had she ever thought they were funny? She had never imagined that Alice knew about them. Poor, beautiful Alice, who had given away her rights.

"Alice, I . . ." Her conscience was throbbing behind her temples.

"Don't. I know what's been going on. And I'm sure you know too." Alice shrugged. "Men are men. But I'm the one he comes home to afterward. The one he sleeps next to, the one he eats breakfast with. Our children are the ones he plays with. I know he loves me. In his own way. I'm the mother of his children. To be honest, it's not a problem for me anymore. I . . . I've gotten used to it."

She looked out through the glass at the dark water.

"I could never manage that," Faye said.

The warmth in her stomach. Jack wasn't like Henrik. And she wasn't like Alice.

Alice turned toward her.

"But, Faye, he . . ."

"Don't say it!" Faye said, so loudly that Alice flinched. "I know that plenty of the men we know are unfaithful. The women too, come to that. If you're okay with that, good for you. But Jack and I are soul mates! We've built up so much together. If you ever try to insinuate otherwise, I'll destroy everything you have! Understand?"

The frightened look in Alice's eyes forced Faye to control her anger. She couldn't let Alice know who she really was. Who she had been.

She got to her feet, swaying badly.

"Thanks for a lovely evening. We're going home now."

When the front door closed behind her and Julienne, Faye turned around and looked through the window beside the door. Alice was still sitting on the sofa, staring out at the water.

STOCKHOLM, SEPTEMBER 2001

IN THE TAXI FROM ARLANDA I prepared myself for the possibility that Jack would disappear and life would go back to normal. Happiness only came to me in small doses. I tried to convince myself that I was satisfied with what I'd had as the taxi raced toward Stockholm.

But Jack took my hand in his as the northern suburbs rushed past outside the windows.

"What are you going to do today?"

"I don't know," I said.

We passed Järva Krog and the taxi slowed down as we hit the city traffic. I didn't care. Quite the reverse.

"Me neither. Shall we go out and grab a beer?"

So we did. And that night I slept in Jack's one-room apartment on Pontonjärgatan on Kungsholmen.

. . .

We spent the whole of the following morning in bed, until lunchtime. Talking, watching films, making love. But that afternoon my conscience got the better of me and I went out onto the balcony to study. The weekend in Barcelona had been wonderful, but I had a lot to catch up on.

Suddenly I heard a cry from the sofa where Jack was watching the news.

"What is it?" I called, but he didn't answer.

I closed my book and went back inside.

Jack was sitting motionless in front of the screen. His face was drained of color.

The images being broadcast on CNN were worse than anything I'd ever seen. The planes. The exploding skyscrapers. Bodies falling hundreds of feet. People jumping. People wandering the streets of Manhattan, bloody and covered with dust.

"What's happening?" I stared at the screen in disbelief.

Jack looked up at me with tears in his eyes.

"A plane flew into the World Trade Center. At first everyone thought it was an accident, then suddenly another plane flew into the other tower. More planes have been hijacked. It looks like a terrorist attack."

"Terrorists?"

"Yes."

The situation in the studio was confused. We sat in front of the TV as if we'd been hypnotized. Numbed by sensory overload, panic. The unknown. The utterly unpredictable.

Jack got up and locked the front door. Fetched a bottle of whiskey and two glasses. When the towers fell, one after the other, we wept. The desolation, all the death, was such a contrast to our own happiness.

Suddenly I knew that I needed to be close to Jack, feel his strength, know that he would protect me. My scars were safe in his hands. He didn't know they were there, but that didn't matter. His presence soothed me anyway. It was as if his own scars fit into mine.

All at once I understood the baby boom of the 1940s. That men and women in times of crisis seek out comfort, they are drawn to instinctive, primal, basic responses. The security of reproduction, the very basis for the survival of the species.

I reached for the remote and muted the sound.

Jack looked at me in surprise.

"What . . . ?"

Something in my eyes silenced him. I pulled him to his feet. Undressed him, one item of clothing at a time, until he stood naked in front of me. Then he undressed me and we lay down on the sofa. When he pushed into me I was filled by a great feeling of security. The only thing that mattered was being able to lie here beneath him with his cock inside me. Inside me like life itself. I saw the images on the television in front of me, flickering on my retinas. Time after time they showed the footage of bodies falling from the burning towers. The smoke and flames as those immense, supposedly untouchable buildings fell.

I cried.

But I needed more. It wasn't enough. Sometimes that worried me. That nothing would ever be enough.

"Harder," I said.

Jack stopped. His heavy breathing calmed down and fell silent. Through the thin wall we heard the neighbors listening to the same news program.

"Fuck me as hard as you can," I whispered. "Hurt me."

I felt his hesitation.

"Why?"

"Don't ask," I replied. "It's what I need right now."

Jack looked into my eyes uncertainly, then did as I wanted. He took a firmer grip of my hips and thrust into me with increasing force. His breathing grew heavier and he tugged at my hair. Without holding back. Without trying to be gentle.

It hurt, but I wanted it to hurt. The pain was familiar. It was like balm to my scars. Made me feel safe. The world was burning, and pain was my anchor.

The eleventh of September.

The date already had a place in my life. It was four years ago that day that Dad was arrested for Mom's murder. A year after Mom had found Sebastian hanging from a rope in his closet.

I was fifteen when he died. Perhaps that was when I became the person I became. Perhaps that was the day I became Faye.

Jack was thrusting with increasing frenzy and I could hear that he was crying too. We were united in sorrow and pain, and when he finally collapsed on top of me I knew that we had shared a moment that neither of us would ever forget.

We sat on the sofa for a long time that afternoon and evening, holding each other's hands as we watched the world burn.

. . .

The year that followed turned out to be the best of my life. The year that laid the foundation for our life and the inseparable ties that bound Jack and me together.

He told me all about his childhood. The insecurity, the fights, the constant lack of money. Christmases without Christmas presents, relatives by turns criticizing or taking pity on his father. How everything fell apart when his mother left the family. The home where everything gradually disappeared, sold or pawned, people turning up at odd hours to demand repayment of debts or to drink with his father. The relief when he had been able to leave that life behind.

I didn't tell him anything. And Jack never brought up the subject of my former life. He had accepted that I was alone in the world. That there was nothing left. In a way I think he liked that. That I was his, and his alone. We had only each other, and he could be my hero.

Jack and I would meet up in the bars around Hantverkargatan or in Chinatown after school, sometimes just the two of us, sometimes with Henrik and Chris, we would talk about life, economics, politics, and dreams. We were all equals, though Chris and I often felt like we were queens in Jack and Henrik's world. Sometimes I noticed Jack staring at me jealously when he saw the way other men looked at me. And he didn't like it when I did things on my own. He always wanted to know where I was, what I was doing. I thought his jealousy was enchanting. I wanted him to own me. And I stopped doing things without him. Chris occasionally protested, but we met so frequently as a foursome that it didn't make much of a difference. I stopped dressing in short skirts and low-cut tops. Except when Jack and I were alone. Then he liked me to dress in clothes that were as tight, short, and low-cut as possible.

"You're not like other women," he often said.

I never asked what he meant. I just soaked it all up. Wanted to be different.

We had sex everywhere. Sometimes we arranged to meet between lectures, giggling as we hurried into the restroom and tore each other's clothes off. We fucked all over Stockholm. At the Central Library, in McDonald's on Sveavägen, in Kronoberg Park, in an empty lecture hall, at Sturecompagniet, East, and Riche, in an empty metro car heading for Ropsten in the middle of the night, at private parties, in Henrik's parents' house and on the balcony. Two or three times a day. Jack couldn't get enough of me. I wouldn't have minded skipping a few, but the sex was good and he made me feel like the most desirable woman who had ever walked the earth. I got excited just from the way he looked at me and knowing how much he wanted me. He didn't like it when I said no, he got grouchy and irritable, so I simply never said no. It was no more complicated than that, to my mind. If he was happy, I was happy.

The Karolinska Hospital. A fan was whirring monotonously. The saggy velour sofas groaned whenever anyone changed position. A cough echoed off the almost bare walls.

Faye was fiddling with her mobile, looking at pictures of her and Jack's wedding. Their tanned, hopeful faces. The stylish, radiant guests. *Expressen* had sent a photographer; he had taken a picture from one of the hotel balconies. She would have preferred a smaller wedding, in Sweden. She would even have considered a registry office. But Jack had insisted on a big wedding in Italy. In a house overlooking Lake Como. Four hundred guests, only a handful of whom she knew. Strangers congratulating and air-kissing her through her veil.

Jack had chosen her dress. A meringue fantasy in silk and tulle, specially made for her by Lars Wallin. It was beautiful, but it wasn't her. If the choice had been left to her, she would have picked something much simpler. But when she saw the look on Jack's face as she walked toward him she was happy she hadn't gone against his wishes.

She put her mobile down. Jack was going to be there any minute. He would run a hand through his hair, sit down, put his arm around her, and apologize for being late. For letting her sit here alone, waiting.

"We will bear happiness and unhappiness together," as he had said in his beautiful speech at the wedding, a speech that made the female guests cry and look enviously at Faye.

She was the oldest of the women waiting, and the only one without a man by her side. Apart from a young girl who looked no older than sixteen at most, who had her mother with her. Boyfriends held their girlfriends, lovingly stroking the backs of their hands. Talking in low voices with somber, attentive expressions. Everyone felt that something extremely private was being exposed to public scrutiny. Wanted to be alone. Without anyone looking on. Without anyone wondering. Every so often a nurse would come out and call someone's name. The rest of them would watch as she walked off.

Faye's name was called and she glanced quickly at her phone again. No text from Jack. No missed call. She did a double-check that she actually had coverage.

She stood up and followed the nurse into a room. As she answered the introductory questions, she wondered if the nurse recognized her. Not that it made any difference. Faye assumed she was under an oath of confidentiality.

"Is anyone coming to pick you up later?" the nurse said.

Faye looked down at the table. She felt embarrassed, without knowing why.

"Yes. My husband."

The fluorescent lights in the ceiling cast a cold light on the paper-covered bed.

"Okay. Some people like to walk around the corridors a bit to speed the process up and keep the pain under control. Just let me know if you need anything and I'll keep an extra eye on you."

"Thanks," Faye said.

She still couldn't look the nurse in the eye. But how could she explain why she was there on her own? She didn't even understand why herself.

"You took the tablet yesterday?"

"Yes."

"Good, here's the second one."

A pill in a plastic cup and a warm hand on her shoulder. She fought against the urge to lay her head in the nurse's lap and cry. Instead she popped the pill into her mouth without looking at it.

"Take these as well," the nurse said, putting some painkillers in front of her.

Faye swallowed them. She was used to swallowing.

* * *

Faye was lying down on a large yellow piece of furniture that resembled an armchair, looking up at the ceiling. At least she hadn't had to lie on the green table and was grateful for the chance to lie undisturbed behind a screen. They had put a pair of diaper-like padded pants on her to catch the blood, and she could already feel herself bleeding. At the ultrasound the nurse had told her how old the embryo was, but she hadn't paid attention to how many weeks, she didn't want to know.

Where are you? she texted Jack.

No answer.

Something must have happened. Had he had an accident? She called the babysitter and asked how Julienne was.

"She's fine, we're watching a film."

"And Jack?" Faye tried to sound unconcerned. Blood was seeping out between her legs as she talked. Soaked up by the diaper. "Has he been in touch?"

"No. I thought he was with you?"

She tried calling Henrik. He didn't answer either. Thoughts were bouncing about in her head. She imagined two stony-faced police officers knocking on the door and apologetically informing her that Jack was dead. What would she do then? A feeling of déjà vu. The same anxiety as when Julienne was born.

Julienne had been expected to arrive in early June. Jack had been very loving throughout the pregnancy, even if he didn't

always have enough time for all the checkups and practical matters involved in a pregnancy. Compare had reached a crucial
stage of development and Faye understood that the company
had to come first now that they were expecting a child and he
was determined to build something up for his family.

Jack had been at the office when the first contractions came. At
first Faye hadn't realized that was what they were, she assumed
they were more of the vague preliminary aches that had come
and gone during the previous month or so. But then they became
so strong that she had to hold on to the kitchen counter to stop
herself from collapsing.

Bent almost double, she had called Jack. The phone rang and
rang until eventually she got his voicemail. She sent a text telling
him to come at once, guessing that he was in a meeting. When
she called Danderyd Hospital they told her she had to come in,
but she didn't want to go without Jack. She had imagined him
helping her into their car, then nervously swearing at the traffic
as they rushed to the maternity unit. Toward their first encounter with their longed-for child.

The contractions got worse with each passing minute but her
phone remained silent. Neither Jack nor Henrik was answering
her calls or texts. In the end she called Chris and asked if she
could go with her and stay until Jack arrived.

Quarter of an hour later Chris rushed into the apartment, out
of breath, in high heels and wearing a leopard-print coat. She
half-dragged, half-carried Faye down the stairs. When they were
sitting in the taxi on the way to Danderyd, Faye realized that she
had forgotten the carefully packed bag that had been standing
ready for the past two months. She ordered the driver to turn
back, but Chris snapped at him to ignore Faye and just drive as
fast as he could. You can always buy replacements for whatever
was in that bag, she said, pointing out that children were born
all the time without great long lists of equipment.

Chris had taken over the job of chasing Jack, and she called and texted him frantically. As the taxi pulled up outside the hospital she put the phone back in her bag.

"He knows where we are," she said. "He knows what's happening. Now we need to focus on getting you into the maternity ward before you give birth here in this taxi, okay?"

Faye nodded numbly. Pain was washing over her like an immense wave, and she couldn't concentrate on anything beyond breathing.

She felt oddly detached as she got out of the car, clutching Chris's arm tightly. In the distance she could hear Chris shouting and ordering the staff around as they entered a corridor. She'd probably have to apologize afterward, but right now Chris's shrill falsetto was the only source of comfort she had.

Julienne arrived five hours later. Five hours of pain that left Faye alternately fearing and longing for death. Chris stayed by her side the whole time. Wiping the sweat from her brow, asking for pain relief, yelling at the midwife, massaging her back, helping her with the gown and keeping track of the contractions. And when Julienne appeared Chris cut the umbilical cord, carefully passed her to Faye, and made sure she was in the right position to suckle. It was the only time Faye had ever seen Chris cry.

Two hours later a shamefaced Jack arrived at the hospital. He was carrying the biggest bouquet of roses Faye had ever seen. One hundred perfect red roses, so many that the staff couldn't find a vase large enough. He stared at his shoes, his hair fell across his face, and Faye felt all her anger and disappointment drain away.

Jack mumbled something about meetings, his phone running out of battery, a whole series of unfortunate circumstances. He seemed crushed, and Faye couldn't help thinking that he was the one who had lost out, when it came down to it. He had missed the birth of the most beautiful baby the world had ever seen.

Very carefully, she handed Julienne over. She was wrapped in a blanket, and was snuffling happily after her first meal outside the womb. Jack sobbed so hard that his shoulders shook, but Chris stood behind him with her arms folded. Faye quickly looked away from her friend and watched her husband instead as he held their newborn daughter in his arms. It was obvious he loved her. No one was perfect.

Faye took a deep breath and forced the memories away. She had made herself suppress the birth, but this situation was far too reminiscent of it. Even if no child was going to be born today. A life was going to be extinguished instead.

Her stomach tensed, then clenched. She bit her lip to stop herself crying. She had to stay strong, both for her own sake and for Julienne's. Jack would be proud of her.

Her forehead felt feverish, sweat was sticking her clothes to her skin. Behind a screen she heard another woman sobbing.

"There, there, darling. It's okay."

Someone was comforting her, holding her.

Her stomach started to cramp. The seconds ticked by. She let out a gasp when it eased. She realized she had been tensing and holding her breath. She wanted to have someone there to comfort her as well. Couldn't stand the loneliness any longer. She took her phone out and called Chris. Wept. Explained where she was. Didn't care if anyone overheard. She let out a groan when another cramp came, and clutched the phone so hard her knuckles turned white.

Sweat was running down her back.

"I'm on my way," Chris said. Like she always did.

"Really?" Faye sniffled.

"Of course I am, darling."

Half an hour later the sound of Chris's heels echoed along the corridor. She leaned over Faye. She stroked her hair with neatly manicured fingers. Wiped her brow with a napkin she took from her YSL Sac de Jour.

"I'm sorry," Faye whispered. "Sorry for everything."

"Don't worry about that, darling. It is what it is. Now let's just get through this and get out of here. Okay?"

Chris's hoarse voice was simultaneously matter-of-fact and sympathetic, in a way that managed to calm Faye down. She had always been able to do that. Faye hadn't realized how much she had missed that until now.

She met her gaze. "I love you."

"And I love you," Chris said. "I was with you when Julienne was born. Of course I'm going to be here now."

Faye grimaced with pain and squeezed her hand. It was the most beautiful hand she had ever seen.

While a life was running out of her, she pressed her cheek against Chris's hand.

WE WERE LIVING IN A three-room apartment in Bergshamra. Jack's uncle had wanted his apartment back when one of his children returned from abroad. It was on the red line of the metro, close to the city, but it was a different world. The neighbors were a mix of ordinary Swedes and migrant families. Chatty, friendly mothers. Children shouting and being noisy in the public spaces, but they were pleasant and well-behaved.

Jack and Henrik had both graduated from the Stockholm School of Economics, Henrik with top grades, Jack with average ones. But neither of them had tried to find work. They spent all their time trying to get Compare off the ground. The business idea was telemarketing, with a commission-based wage structure that was more aggressive than any similar company. Motivation, motivation, motivation, as Jack used to chant. His favorite quote was "Hungry wolves make the best hunters," and the business model I had developed for them suited hungry wolves. More than anything, it suited two men who were as eager for glory as Jack and Henrik.

Our living room was their office. They shared a large desk and worked side by side on a couple of chairs I had found down in the garbage room but told Jack I had inherited from my grandmother.

I admired their intensity, and was convinced they were going to succeed, confident that they were well on their way. As a result I was taken by surprise one afternoon when I got home to find Jack sitting on the sofa, staring into space.

"What's the matter, darling?" I said, sitting down beside him.

"We've run out of money. Henrik's used up all his savings and I've gone cap in hand to try to get more capital, to no avail. I haven't managed to find any investors. We simply weren't good enough."

He ran his hands through his hair.

"Maybe it isn't a complete disaster. We'll both be able to find jobs. Henrik's talking about moving to London and getting a job in the financial sector. Maybe it would be just as well if we gave up these childish dreams and grew up. I'll tell him I want out tomorrow, that would be the best way forward. I could go to London as well, that's where the real money is. Or New York. Wall Street. Maybe I should go to Wall Street."

Jack's speech was intended to convince himself, but I could tell he didn't mean a word of it. He was nowhere close to giving up on his dreams. And the very thought that he might move and leave me on my own again was enough to make me panic.

I couldn't begin to imagine a life without Jack. Anxiety started to well up inside me, but I swallowed the nausea and said as calmly as I could, with my hand on his, "Where's all this coming from? I thought it was going well, you both sounded enthusiastic as recently as last night when we went to bed. I heard you talking on the phone."

"We were convinced we'd found some investors, but today we were informed that they aren't interested after all. So we've got no money, darling. Right now we're surviving on your student grant and that job in the café. I haven't even been able to pay my mobile bill this month."

The hopes of generations lay heavy on his shoulders, and the disappointment was etched in his face. He was the one who was going to put right everything his father had done, and restore the family's honor. But now he was ready to give up his crusade.

I cupped his face with my hands.

"No. I'm not going to let you give up your dream."

"Aren't you listening? We need money. Some sort of income. And you're still at college . . ."

He turned to look at me. His eyes were as deep and wet as a puppy's. Jack needed me, in a way that no one ever had before.

"I can take a year's sabbatical."

"But you love college . . ."

Those blue eyes looked into mine, and I could already see the spark glinting in them, and that he was only raising objections for the sake of it.

"I love you more. And I know that you're going to succeed, as long as you get the chance to do your thing. We're a team, you and I. Jack and Faye. We're going to take over the world, that's what we've always said. I can graduate a year later, and what difference does one year make in the broader scheme of things?"

I shrugged.

"Are you absolutely sure?" Jack said, pulling me toward him.

"Of course I am," I said with a laugh.

Happiness was bubbling inside me like a fizzy drink. I was giving him a gift, and he was accepting it, because he loved me.

"I know you'd have done the same for me. And I believe in Compare, I know we're going to be millionaires. And then you can pay me back!"

"And I will! Everything that's mine is yours, darling. Ours!"

He kissed me, then picked me up and carried me into the bedroom.

One year wasn't so bad. And it meant everything for Compare. Not so much for my education. I found studying so easy, whereas Henrik had to work hard for his grades. Sure, I hated wiping tables, serving coffee, getting my backside pinched by old men who thought the waitress was included in the price of a coffee and pastry. But Jack was the love of my life. My soul mate. We held each other up. Next time it would be Jack volunteering to help me.

I informed the School of Economics of my decision that evening, and called my boss at the Café Madeleine. He was delighted. I knew he had plans to expand, but found it hard to get away from the day-to-day running of the café. There and then he offered me the position of personnel manager. The monthly salary felt dizzyingly large. Twenty-two thousand kronor. I said yes.

The only person who objected to my decision was Chris. She came into Madeleine's at closing time with a black look in her eyes.

"You and I need to talk," she said.

She dragged me across a rainy Stureplan and into a bar. She snapped at the bartender that she wanted two beers, then pushed me into one of the booths.

"I know this isn't what you want to hear, and it might well make you angry with me. Maybe this is the end of our friendship. But someone's got to say it! You're making a mistake."

I sighed. How would Chris be able to understand? What she and Henrik had was nowhere close to what Jack and I had.

"I know you only want what's best for me. But this is something that has to be done. Jack needs to concentrate on Compare if their dream is going to become a reality."

"What about *your* dream, then? Hell, Faye, if Jack and Henrik had half your brains they'd be billionaires by now."

"I'm happy as long as I've got Jack. And his dreams are my dreams."

"Are you worried he'll leave you if you don't do this?"

"No."

I almost started to laugh. The thought was so absurd. Obviously, his talk about London and New York had worried me a bit, but that was all it was: talk. Jack wanted to be with me as much as I wanted to be with him.

Chris gestured irritably to the bartender to bring us another glass each.

"In that case," she muttered, "why can't he put Compare on ice for a year while he works instead? Why are you the one who has to give up college for his sake?"

Chris lit a cigarette with trembling hands.

"It's so fucking typical," she muttered.

I reached for Chris's pack of cigarettes. Jack didn't like me smoking, but I seized the opportunity to have one now. I'd just have to remember to buy some mint chewing gum before I went home.

"One year, Chris. Then I'll be back. By then Jack and Henrik will have Compare up and running."

I blew a perfect smoke ring, which framed Chris's skeptical expression. She dropped the subject, but the look on her face made it abundantly clear what she thought about it.

. . .

Six months later Compare was launched, and became an instant success. Jack and Henrik's young telemarketing team and new way of working hit Sweden like an invading army. They achieved results unmatched by anyone before them. Companies were soon lining up to have Compare take over their own telemarketing operations. Money rained down on us. Just over a year later we were millionaires.

Neither Jack nor I saw any good reason for me to return to my studies. We had already reached our goal. Together. Why should I fight my way through college exams when things were going so well for us?

You studied in order to become successful, and we had done that. The future was so bright, I needed shades.

The crisis was edging closer and closer. Obviously she should have seen the signs. Opened her eyes. They say nothing blinds us like love, but Faye knew that nothing blinds as much as the *dream* of love.

Hope is a powerful drug.

She decided to change tactics. Instead of sitting at home like a sad puppy, waiting for Jack, she would give him the time and space to miss her.

There were two weeks to go until his birthday party. The event organizers had told her when to show up, but that was all. Apart from the instruction that the dress code was "evening dress." She had been contemplating rather more entertaining themes when she was still under the impression that she was going to be organizing her husband's birthday party. The Great Gatsby or Studio 54. But evidently that wasn't what Jack wanted. Sometimes she couldn't help wondering if she had merely imagined that she knew him. She seemed to have the wrong idea about everything these days. At least when it came to Jack, anyway.

Faye knocked on the door of his study in the tower, heard an irritable yes, and walked in.

She put on a smile. Not that it mattered. Jack was staring at the screen.

"Sorry, I don't want to interrupt. I just thought I'd let you know that I'm going away with Julienne for a few days."

He looked up in surprise. His handsome profile stood out against the glass of the window.

"Oh?"

"Yes, you've got so much going on at the moment. And I . . . well, I suppose I don't. I've rented a house in Falsterbo."

She was prepared for Jack to protest, he had never been very enthusiastic about her wanting to do things on her own. But to her surprise he seemed almost relieved.

"That's a great idea. It'll do you good to get away for a while, after, well, all that unpleasantness."

He was avoiding her gaze. When he'd gotten home late the night of the abortion, he had offered a cursory apology about an emergency at work. No more than that. No roses this time. No tears. And she had swallowed once again, accepting what she couldn't change, even if it left a bitter aftertaste. But she could still feel the coolness of Chris's hand against her cheek when she went to bed.

"Do you think so?"

She kept her voice neutral. Keep looking forward. Never back. She could turn this around. She was stronger than Jack realized. She had been playing the weaker sex for a long time now. Because that had been what Jack needed. But now she realized it was time for her to take charge, without Jack noticing. He wasn't the sort of man who liked taking direction.

"Yes, definitely," Jack said, smiling at her.

His face looked more youthful, more at ease. She relaxed. She was on the right track. They just needed a bit of time away from each other.

"It's a good idea to get a bit of mom and daughter time," Jack said. It sounded a little forced, but she was happy to take whatever crumbs she could get. "A girls' trip, or whatever you want to call it. It'll be harder to do that sort of thing once she starts school." He fiddled with a pen and asked nonchalantly, "How long are you planning to be away?"

"I was thinking five nights."

She held one hand out toward him, and he took it, to her surprise. And relief.

"You're sure you don't mind?"

"Of course not! Though I'm obviously going to miss you both."

She blew him a kiss before leaving.

"We'll miss you too," she said.

And she meant it. She was missing him already.

There wasn't much traffic on the E4, mostly tractor trailers. Faye enjoyed driving, and Julienne seemed excited to be going on an adventure.

"Can we go swimming?" she asked.

"The water's going to be very cold. Let's see what you think when you've felt it."

A diplomatic answer. Obviously she knew Julienne would think it was far too cold. It would be several months before the water was anywhere close to warm enough to swim in.

Julienne immersed herself in her iPad. Faye overtook a DHL truck, the driver stared longingly at their Porsche Cayenne as she pulled in front of him.

The phone rang. It was Jack.

"How are you getting on?"

He sounded happy, and Faye couldn't help smiling. It had been a long time since she had heard anything but irritation in his voice.

"Daddy!" Julienne cried.

"Hello, darling! Are you having a good time?"

"Yes! Really good!" Julienne said, then went back to her iPad.

"Where are you?"

"We've just passed Norrköping," Faye said. "Time for a break soon, probably that place with the golden arches . . ."

"McDonald's!" Julienne exclaimed happily.

There was no fooling her.

Jack laughed and Faye felt it sweeping away the bad memories, dissolving them like the dandelion heads she used to blow as a child.

They hung up and she concentrated on driving. There was a long way to go before they got there.

"Mommy, I feel sick."

Faye glanced at Julienne, whose face did indeed have a disconcertingly greenish-white pallor.

"Maybe you could try looking out of the window? I think you might be feeling sick because you've been looking down at a screen."

Faye took her right hand off the wheel and felt Julienne's forehead. It was warm and sweaty.

"Are you hungry? There's an apple in the bag by your feet."

"No. I feel sick."

"We can stop at McDonald's soon, if you like."

Julienne said nothing, her eyes fixed on the road. It'll pass, Faye thought.

A few minutes later Julienne started to cough and Faye pulled over onto the roadside with a grimace. As they came to a stop Julienne threw up all over.

Faye jumped out of the car and hurried around to the passenger side. She lifted Julienne out, and held her hair as she whimpered feebly before being sick again.

A little cloud of steam rose from the warm vomit on the frozen grass.

A truck drove past and the turbulence rocked the car.

Faye put Julienne back in her seat, emptied a bag and put it on her lap. She found a roll of paper towels in the trunk and wiped up the worst of the mess inside the car. The smell turned her stomach and she didn't dare think about what Jack would say when he heard what had happened. The car would have to go in for detailing before she could so much as blink.

"If you have to be sick again, try to do it in the bag."

Faye wound the window down and breathed through her mouth. The stench was terrible as she started the car. Whitney Houston was singing that she would always love you, and Faye turned the volume down. She preferred the original by Dolly Parton.

A few miles farther on they pulled in to a petrol station. Faye perched Julienne on a chair while she bought some disinfectant and a cloth and tried to clean things up, all the while cursing the decision to drive down on her own.

They could have flown, then hired a car at the airport. Why did she always have to complicate things? Jack was right. She was completely useless. As a wife, and as a mother.

Her good mood had vanished altogether.

Faye fetched Julienne, and bought a banana that she ate on the way to the car, then tossed the peel in a can before getting them both back in the car.

"How are you feeling now, darling?"

"I want to go home. Please, can we go home?"

"Try to get some sleep and you'll feel better."

Julienne was too tired to protest. She leaned her head against the door and closed her eyes. Faye put one hand on her thigh and pulled out onto the highway again.

Twenty miles from Jönköping she had had enough of Whitney Houston. Keeping her eyes on the road she felt for her mobile to put a podcast on instead, but couldn't find it. She slowed down and pulled in behind a red Volkswagen Golf, then reached for her handbag, which she had left on the back seat after stopping at the petrol station. As she felt behind her, the car veered slightly. Julienne let out a whimper, sighed groggily, then fell back to sleep again.

Faye stopped. Shivering with cold she felt through her pockets, under the seats. But her phone wasn't there. She realized it could be anywhere, on the roadside where they had stopped, or at the petrol station. She stifled a scream so as not to wake Julienne. She hit the steering wheel with both hands in frustration. Her phone contained the number and address of the neighbor who was going to give them the keys to the house.

Faye turned around on a side road and started to head back toward Stockholm. When she was younger she never gave up, but in recent years she had had a lot of practice at it.

Matilda would never have given up. But Faye knew exactly how it was done.

...

Faye was carrying Julienne in one arm and their luggage in the other. The elevator door closed and she slid the grille across. She looked at her face in the mirror: dark rings under her eyes, puffy, pale skin. Beads of sweat on her forehead and top lip. And a look of resignation.

Julienne opened her eyes.

"Where are we?" she murmured sleepily.

"Home, darling. You weren't feeling well, we can go to Falsterbo another time."

Julienne smiled dully. Nodded.

"I feel sleepy," she whispered.

"I know, sweetheart. You'll soon be back in your own bed."

The elevator stopped with a jolt. Faye opened the grille and hoisted Julienne up onto her hip. The weight was making her arms ache. Julienne had her arms wrapped around her like a little monkey, and protested feebly when she put her down to look for the keys.

Jack hated it if she rang the doorbell and disturbed him.

Eventually she got the door open and they stumbled into the

apartment. She summoned the last of her strength to get Julienne's coat and boots off, carry her to her bed, and kiss her good night. Then she went up into the tower to see if Jack was still working.

The study was empty and smelled stuffy. She opened the window to air it, placing a plant pot in the gap to stop the window from slamming shut.

Jack must be at work, she thought with relief as she headed toward the bedroom to shower and change her clothes. She was glad she had a chance to freshen up before he got home. She felt pathetic, and didn't want him to see her looking like a damp rag.

Faye pulled the bedroom door open and it was as if the room in front of her was suddenly full of water. Everything stopped around her. All she could hear was the sound of her own breathing and a ringing in her ears that grew louder with each passing second.

Jack was standing at the foot of the bed with his back to her. Naked. Faye stared at his backside. Saw the familiar birthmark on his right buttock. The birthmark was moving back and forth as he groaned and thrust his hips. In front of him was a woman on all fours, her back arched, legs wide apart.

Faye staggered and reached out for the doorframe for support.

Everything was happening so slowly. All sound was muffled, subdued. The floor around the bed was littered with clothes, as if they had been in a hurry to get out of them.

She had no idea how long she had been standing there before they noticed her.

Maybe she let out a shriek without being aware of it. Jack turned around, Ylva Lehndorf leaped up and tried in vain to cover herself with a pillow.

"What the hell, I thought you were in Skåne!" Jack yelled. "What are you doing here?"

Faye tried to speak. How could he be angry? With her? She stood there speechless. Then a torrent of words tumbled out, about Julienne, her phone, the drive home. She tried to explain, tried to make excuses. Jack held one hand up and Faye fell silent at once.

Jack gestured to Ylva, his business partner, to put her clothes on, and reached for a bathrobe. He was bound to be frustrated by the fact that he hadn't been able to come. He hated to be interrupted. He used to say that the ruined orgasm stayed in his body all day.

Jack sat down on the edge of the bed. Looked at her with a cold, steady gaze.

"I want a divorce," he said.

The air went out of her.

"No," she said, clutching the doorframe. "No, Jack. I forgive you. We don't have to talk about this again, you made a mistake, that's all. We'll get through this."

The words echoed in her head. Bounced between the two lobes of her brain without finding a foothold. But she heard herself say them. So she must have said them. And meant them.

Jack was shaking his head from side to side. Behind him Ylva had put her underwear on and was staring out of the window.

Jack was looking directly at Faye, studying her from top to toe, and she ran a hand nervously through her hair, all too aware of how she looked. He tied the bathrobe tighter around his waist.

"It's not a mistake. I don't love you anymore, I don't want to live with you."

"We can get through this," Faye repeated.

Her legs were close to giving way. Tears were running down her cheeks. She could hear the desperation in her voice.

"Can't you hear what I'm saying? I don't love you anymore. I . . . I love her."

He nodded toward Ylva, who turned to look at Faye. She was still wearing nothing but her underwear. Gray La Perla. Her taut stomach, perfect breasts, narrow boyish hips, all mocked Faye. She was everything that Faye no longer was.

Jack sighed and Ylva's wary expression turned to derision as Faye sank to her knees in front of Jack. The wooden floor felt hard under her knees. They had had all the floors replaced when they moved in. Faye had wanted them to sand and oil the original floors, she thought they were beautiful, but Jack had snorted at the suggestion. Instead they had imported new floors from Italy, at a cost of several thousand kronor per square foot. But the expensive floor hurt her knees just as much as the old original floor would have. It made no difference to her humiliation.

"Please," she begged. "Give me one more chance. I'll change, I'll be better. I know I've been hard to live with, mean . . . foolish . . . stupid. But I'll make you happy. Please, Jack, give me a chance. You and Julienne are all I've got. You're my life."

Faye tried to take Jack's hand but he pulled it away. He seemed disgusted. And she could understand that. She was disgusted by herself too.

He went over to Ylva, who was now sitting on the bed with one long leg crossed over the other. With a proud air of ownership he stood beside her. Put one hand on her bare shoulder. Ylva put her hand on his. Together they looked at Faye, who was still on her knees on the bespoke Italian wooden floor.

Jack shook his head and said, without the slightest tremble in his voice, "It's over. I want you to go now."

Slowly Faye got up from the floor. She backed out of the bedroom, unable to take her eyes from Jack's hand on Ylva's bare, bony shoulder. She didn't turn around until she had passed Julienne's closed door. She knew she ought to be thinking of her daughter, make some sort of decision, take her, not take her, say something, not say anything. But Julienne was safe and the only thought her brain was capable of formulating was that she had to get out of there. At once.

With the image of Jack's bare backside between Ylva's legs etched on her retinas, she stumbled out of the front door and let it swing closed behind her. Only when she was standing on the landing did she realize she'd forgotten to put any shoes on.

. . .

Faye was sitting on the floor outside Chris's apartment, her body racked with sobs.

Somehow she had managed to hail a taxi, and when he saw the state of her the driver had helped her into the back seat without a word.

She had banged on the door in the vain hope that Chris could save her from everything, but when there was no answer she had collapsed to the floor. Now she didn't know if she was ever going to have the strength to get up again.

"Faye? Christ, what's happened?"

At last.

Faye looked up and saw Chris walking cautiously toward her. Faye reached out to her, now sobbing so hard that she couldn't speak.

"Help me" were the only words she managed to utter.

PART TWO

"How can you be sure that . . . that it was him who did it?"

"I can't go into detail about that at the moment," the policewoman said, without meeting Faye's gaze.

"Please, I've lost my daughter. But the idea that Jack . . . I mean, we've had our problems, but I still can't believe . . . there must be some sort of mistake . . ."

"I really shouldn't . . ."

The policewoman looked around. The other officer had gone to fetch Faye some coffee. She lowered her voice and said, "It's not just the blood we found in the car. The satnav shows that Jack drove to a harbor on the shore of Lake Vättern in the middle of the night. We found a boat there with traces of blood that's probably Julienne's."

Faye nodded, then winced as the movement made the wounds on her face sting. The interview was being taped, so she knew she wasn't going to hear anything they weren't ready to release. They wanted her to trust and form a connection with the woman standing in front of her looking at her sympathetically. They wanted to get her to cooperate. They didn't understand that they didn't have to play any games with her. She was going to cooperate. Jack wasn't going to get away.

"Is there anyone we can call? Anyone you'd like to come over?"

Faye shook her head. She grimaced again with the pain. She had been patched up in the hospital, and now had a number of stitches.

"We can probably leave it there for today. But I'm sure we'll have to come back to ask some more questions."

"You've got my number," Faye mumbled.

"The reverend's on his way. Obviously you can go home if that's what you'd like to do. But I don't know if it's such a good idea for you to be on your own right now."

"The reverend?"

At first Faye didn't understand what the police officer was talking about. What did she want with a reverend?

"Well, people who . . . who have suffered a loss like yours often need comfort, someone to talk to."

Faye looked up and met her gaze.

"People whose children have been killed, you mean?"

The police officer hesitated, then said, "Yes."

A movement on the bed. Someone had sat down on it. Faye forced her eyes open and found herself looking directly into Chris's. They looked simultaneously concerned and firm.

"I love you, Faye, but you've been lying in this bed for two weeks now. As soon as anyone mentions Jack or Julienne you start crying. This can't go on."

She nodded toward the door.

"If you want anything you're going to have to come and find me. If you want food, from now on you're going to have to go to the kitchen and make it yourself. I won't be coming into this room again, even if you swear Denzel Washington is lying naked and tied to the bed."

The next day Faye stumbled into the kitchen, wearing her underpants and a Nirvana T-shirt.

Chris had a cup of coffee in one hand, and *Vanity Fair* lay open on the table in front of her. She looked at Faye over the rim of the cup.

"There's breakfast in the freezer. I'm sticking to the Lindsay Lohan diet."

Faye pulled out a chair and sat down.

"Which is?"

"Coffee, cigarettes, and the morning-after pill."

She smiled ironically.

"Get yourself something to eat. I have to get to work soon. Do you want to come along?"

Faye shook her head.

"Probably better to stay at home. Watch a film, have a cry, feel sorry for yourself. I'm just glad you've emerged from that room. It was starting to smell."

Faye put her hand on Chris's arm and looked her in the eye.

"Thanks," she said. "For everything. For . . . oh, you know."

"Don't mention it. You can stay at casa de Chris until you're back on your feet again. As long as you shower regularly."

Faye nodded. That sounded like a deal she could live with.

. . .

Faye felt wretched. Almost hungover. When Chris had gone she lay on the sofa, took out her mobile, and called Jack. As she had done every day. Obviously because she wanted to talk to Julienne, but perhaps even more because she wanted to hear his voice. Each time she called he sounded more irritated and their conversations grew shorter and shorter. It was like talking to a stranger.

"Yes?" he replied curtly.

"Hi, it's me."

"So I saw. Julienne isn't here right now. They've just left for preschool."

"They?"

Jack cleared his throat. She could hear noises, voices in the background.

"I didn't have time to take Julienne today, there's a lot going on, so Ylva drove her."

Faye couldn't believe it. Only two weeks had passed, and already Ylva and Jack were playing happy families. Faye had been replaced. Exchanged for a newer model. Like any old housekeeper or babysitter.

Not seeing Julienne had been a torment, but up until now she hadn't felt up to it. She had persuaded herself that it was in her daughter's best interests to be in familiar surroundings, and that it would only harm her to see her mom shattered by grief.

"Hello?" Jack said.

"I need to come and get some things," Faye said, forcing her voice to sound normal. "And I want to see Julienne."

"Now isn't a good time."

"For what?"

"For you to come and get your things. Everything's a bit upside down here. We . . . I've bought a house. We're in the middle of moving."

Faye closed her eyes. Focused on her breathing. She mustn't let herself go to pieces.

"Where are you moving?"

"Gåshaga. Close to Henrik and Alice, actually. It wasn't planned, but we . . . well, we saw a wonderful property online."

We. He was talking about them as *we*. Jack and Ylva. Since 2001 it had been Jack and Faye, but now he was *we* with someone else entirely. Faye held the phone away from her ear to stop herself hearing. She had nagged him for years about moving to a house, saying it would be good for Julienne, but he hadn't wanted to. He liked being close to the city and his office. But now evidently he and Ylva had seen a "wonderful property online." Just like that.

". . . text me a list of what you need, and I'll have it couriered over."

"Okay," she said through clenched teeth. "What about Julienne? I need to see her."

"I really think that could wait until you've got yourself somewhere to live, but okay. You can come next week, once the move is over," he declared magnanimously, and ended the call.

In her mind's eye Faye could see Ylva making nice with Julienne, spoiling her, dressing her up, indulging her, watching films, braiding her hair. She was probably an expert at French braids. Even the inverted type Julienne always asked for but Faye had never managed to get right.

And every time she closed her eyes she saw Jack and Ylva in front of her. Ylva with her perfect lips and pert breasts. Jack penetrating her, telling her how beautiful she was, groaning her name when he came.

The biggest irony of all was that Ylva Lehndorf was everything Faye could have been if Jack hadn't said he wanted a housewife who'd be there for him when he needed it. Why had he changed his mind?

He was the one who had transformed her into a different person, after all. Someone she no longer recognized. And if she wasn't Jack Adelheim's wife, who was she? During her years with Jack she had peeled everything else away, layer by layer. There was nothing left.

Faye had borrowed Chris's car. Her hands were shaking so hard that she could barely hold onto the steering wheel. She was going to see Julienne again. At last.

There was hardly any traffic on the road out to Lidingö. The sun was shining, and thin clouds were chasing across the blue sky. She followed the satnav's instructions and stopped in front of a hill. At the top lay a large stone building that looked like a palace. A wonderful property. The sort of house she herself had dreamed of.

Jack's Tesla was parked in the drive. Some men were lifting moving boxes from a large truck.

She rang a bell at the gate, looked into a camera, and had to wait a few seconds before it opened with a gentle rumble. She drove in and parked behind the truck.

A bald foreman yelled at her to move her car so it wasn't in the way. Faye raised her hand apologetically and did as he asked.

Julienne came running out, and Faye undid her belt and jumped from the car. She clutched her daughter to her, breathing in her smell. Tears were burning behind her eyelids despite the promise she'd made to herself that she wasn't going to cry. She would grit her teeth and bear it, no matter what.

Jack came out onto the steps. He was wearing beige chinos

and a green sweater with a pale-blue shirt collar sticking out of it. He was more handsome than ever.

"Darling, I've missed you so much," Faye said, kissing the top of Julienne's head. "I just have to have a little talk with Daddy. Can you go and play, and I'll come and find you?"

Julienne nodded, gave her a kiss on the cheek, then ran back inside the house.

Jack smiled nonchalantly at Faye. She looked in vain for some sign of guilt, but couldn't find anything. Part of her wanted to claw at his face. Another part wanted to fall into his arms and bury her face in his sweater.

"What do you think?" he said, with a broad gesture toward the building behind him.

It was utterly bizarre. He was behaving as if nothing had happened.

"We need to talk," she said curtly.

Adrenaline was coursing through her body, making her rock back and forth on the soles of her feet.

"About what?"

"About what's happened. About . . . well, this."

"You must have seen it coming, though? Dear God, it can hardly have come as a surprise." He sighed. "Okay, you'd better come in, then."

He walked ahead of her into the house. Moving boxes stood stacked in the hall. Two men were carrying a sofa up the stairs.

"Let's go and sit over here," he said, leading her through a sitting room and out onto a glazed veranda looking out over the water.

Faye sat down in a chair she didn't recognize. Ylva must have brought it from her own home. Unless they'd bought everything new. Out with the old. In with the new. Whether it was wives or furniture.

"I need money, Jack. Not much. Just enough until I get back on my feet."

He looked down at his hands and nodded.

"Of course. I'll transfer a hundred thousand kronor."

Faye shivered and Jack raised his eyebrows in surprise.

Behind him she saw the water, the ice starting to melt and break up. Julienne would love being able to run down there to swim in the summer.

"I need to buy an apartment. Surely you want Julienne to be comfortable when she's with me?"

"I can't see that it's my responsibility to provide accommodation for you. That's up to you to sort out. But sure, I understand that my daughter needs to have a certain standard, even if her mother hasn't prioritized having an income of her own. I'll transfer enough money for you to find somewhere to rent. But I recommend that you get yourself a job."

Faye clenched her teeth so hard that they squeaked. It went against the grain to come to him, cap in hand. But all their assets were in Jack's name. She had no savings, no job. And she had to think of Julienne. Motherhood before pride. She needed to sort out cheap temporary accommodations until she got her money from the divorce. She had no idea how much she might get, but surely she ought to get a decent share of Jack's wealth? She had played a large role in its acquisition, after all. He had said that everything he had was hers, that his success was thanks to the two of them. How could Jack suddenly have forgotten that?

She looked at him. His hair was a little shorter than usual. She thought back to when they had first met and she used to cut his hair in the kitchen out in Bergshamra. *No matter how rich I get, you'll always cut my hair, the way you touch me feels so great,* he had said. Yet another promise he had broken. For the past three years he had been going to Marre, the hottest celebrity salon in Stockholm.

"What are we going to do about Julienne?" she asked.

"She'll live here until you've sorted out a proper home,

anything else is out of the question. She and Ylva are getting on really well, so you don't have to worry about that."

Jack smiled contentedly. Outside the window some geese were wandering along the shore. Hope they shit a lot, Faye thought.

She tore her eyes from the birds.

"Have you made your mind up?" she asked in a low voice.

"Made my mind up?"

"About her. That this is what you want?"

Jack scratched his forehead. Stared at her as if he hardly understood the question.

"Isn't that pretty obvious?" he said. "I wasn't happy with you, Faye."

Faye felt a jolt in her chest, as if he'd stuck a knife between her ribs. She wanted to ask how long he'd been having an affair with Ylva Lehndorf, but managed to stop herself. She could only handle one dagger to the heart at a time.

She stood up abruptly and called for Julienne.

"So you'll bring her back at six o'clock this evening?"

"Yes."

Julienne came running in. Faye took her by the hand and led her out of the house. As they drove off Julienne babbled excitedly about her new room. Apparently it was "even nicer than the Barbie Princess's room."

Faye put her foot down on the accelerator.

The weeks passed. Merged into a stagnant fog. Each evening Faye borrowed Chris's car, drove out to Lidingö, and parked a short distance away from the magnificent villa. In the big picture windows she could see her life from outside, like a film, but the difference now was that Faye was no longer playing the central role. And it was no longer her life. Jack and Ylva unpacked their boxes, drank wine, kissed, ate dinner, laughed. Candles flickered in their room, no doubt scented candles from Bibliothèque. "Never anything reduced, only the most expensive," as Jack often used to joke, even though he actually meant it. Sometimes she caught a glimpse of Julienne. Always on her own. Or with the full-time au pair Jack had employed.

She told Chris she was driving around the city, but her friend knew her too well to be fooled. Her grief still overwhelmed her at times, but Faye told herself that it would pass. Jack was her heroin, and once she had gotten through the withdrawal she would get back on her feet, and the pain would fade with time. Just as it had before.

She had a vague memory of once being the strong person in her family. That strength must be hiding in there somewhere. Jack couldn't have stolen that from her as well.

· · ·

Faye was sitting at Chris's kitchen table when Jack called. She'd convinced herself that he was going to say it had all been a big mistake and that he wanted her to come home. Or that the past few weeks had been nothing more than a drawn-out nightmare. She would take him back without a moment's hesitation. She would be as happy as a puppy. Yapping and jumping around him with her tail wagging.

Instead Jack informed her that she wasn't going to be getting any money at all.

"The prenuptial agreement applies," he said at the end of his long explanation. "And you signed that yourself. I thought it was airtight, but I wanted to check with my lawyers first. And sure enough, it is a valid agreement."

Faye stifled her anger as well as she could, but could hear the tension in her voice.

"I gave up my studies at the School of Economics to support you while you and Henrik were getting Compare off the ground. Do you remember? Then when I said I wanted to get a job you told me there was no need and that I shouldn't worry about it. You promised that the prenuptial agreement was merely a formality. For the board. That of course I'd get my share. The whole idea for the structure of the company came from me!"

Jack didn't answer.

"This is her idea, isn't it?" she said.

"I don't know what you mean."

"It's her, Ylva, she doesn't want me to get any money. Don't you think you've humiliated me enough? I've got nothing, Jack. My life is ruined."

"Don't bring Ylva into this. The money's mine, it's what I've earned while you were at home having a nice time. Those long lunches at Riche with the girls didn't exactly bring in any money, did they?" Jack snorted. "You'll just have to go out and get a damn job like everyone else. Try living in the real world for a change. Most people don't get the chance to live life as one long holiday the way you have the past few years. While I've been working hard to support my family."

Faye forced herself to stay calm. Breathed in. Breathed out. Refused to believe that he could simply draw a line under their years together. Under everything they had experienced.

Jack interrupted her thoughts.

"If you carry on fighting, I'll crush you. Leave me and Ylva in peace."

After he hung up Faye sat for a long time with the phone in her hand. Then, to her own surprise, she let out a roar. A primal scream that she hadn't heard for many, many years, in another life. Now it bounced off the walls like a violent echo.

Faye was panting by the time she finally stopped. She threw herself back in her chair. Enjoyed the pain of the hard back of it. Welcomed the anger that surged through her.

She felt the familiar darkness seep through every pore of her body, the darkness she had managed to forget. She had been pretending it had never existed, that it had never been part of her. But now, very slowly, she started to remember who she was, who she had been.

The hatred was familiar, comforting. It embraced her in its warm cocoon, giving her a purpose, giving her a firm footing again. She would show Jack. She was going to get back on her feet.

Faye used the metro for the first time in many years. She got on at Östermalmstorg, traveled out to Norsborg, then came back again. She got off at T-Centralen and wandered across Sergels Torg, where the drug trade was still in full swing, just as it had been when she first arrived in Stockholm thirteen years ago.

But Stockholm felt like a different place. There was so much to see and explore now that she no longer had to worry about what Jack thought was "inappropriate." Faye was thirty-two years old, but felt like she had been born again.

She crossed Sveavägen close to the plaque marking the site where Olof Palme was shot.

A few hardy souls were hunched over their beers, smoking in the spring wind at the outdoor tables beside the church. The poor, the unemployed, the outcasts. Scum, as Jack called them.

Faye opened the door and walked in. The bartender raised his eyebrows as he looked at her obviously expensive coat. At least Jack had let her keep her clothes when he cleared their apartment.

She ordered a beer and sat down in a corner. It tasted bland. Thoughts were swirling through her head. How humiliated had she been? Had everything Jack said been a lie? Was Ylva the only one, or had there been more? Things she hadn't wanted to think about before now. But now she needed to wallow in those thoughts, feed her anger. Of course there had been others. She knew Jack. The way he really was.

She got her mobile out of her bag and brought up Alice's number.

"Have you got a few minutes?" Faye said when Alice eventually answered.

She heard her hesitate.

"I'd like to ask you a few questions. And I want you to answer honestly."

"Hold on . . ."

The sound of a child crying grew louder behind her. Alice called for the au pair, then closed a door and the noise of the crying became more distant.

"Okay, I'm listening," she said.

"You know all about Ylva. I assume it has been going on for a while. I want to know how long, and if there were others."

"Faye, I . . ."

"Skip the bullshit, Alice. I get that you knew all along. That's okay. I'm not looking for a fight. I just want to know the truth."

Alice didn't say anything for a long time. Faye waited patiently. Eventually Alice took a deep breath.

"Jack has been unfaithful to you for as long as I've known Henrik. With everyone, Faye. Jack would fuck anything with a pulse. Sometimes I felt like rubbing your face in it, to pull you down from your high horse where you used to sit and judge Henrik. And me. But I never did. I know how it feels, after all."

Alice fell silent. Presumably aware that she had betrayed her ambivalence over Henrik's affairs. The ambivalence that Faye had never believed, not deep down.

Faye let her words sink in. It didn't hurt as much as she had imagined it would. She almost felt relieved. On some level she had always known.

"I'm sorry," Alice said hesitantly.

"It's okay. I had a feeling."

"You won't mention this conversation to Jack?"

"I promise."

"Thanks."

"You should leave Henrik," Faye went on in a dry, factual voice. "We're too good for this shit, to be trampled on and exploited like this. No doubt you'll realize that one day. It wasn't my choice, but I've gotten there now. And once you emerge on the other side, it's rather a liberating place to be."

"But I'm happy."

"So was I. Or so I thought. But time catches up with us, Alice. Sooner or later you'll end up where I am now, and you know that."

Faye hung up without waiting for Alice to answer. She knew her friend didn't actually have an answer. That nothing she had said came as news to Alice, who probably wrestled with the same thoughts a thousand times each day. That was Alice's problem. Not hers.

She was ready for war now.

Faye knew she had the best weapon in her arsenal—her femininity. It made men underestimate and objectify her, assume she was stupid. There was no way Jack could ever win this fight. She was smarter than him. Always had been. She had just allowed him, and herself, to forget that.

But now she was going to remind him. Remind them both.

To start with, she had to let him go on believing that things were the same as they used to be—that she was the same old, cowed Faye, hopelessly naïve and in love. That was the easy bit. She had played that role for so long that she knew it inside out.

But in the meantime she would secretly build up a business of her own, become rich and finally crush Jack. She didn't yet know exactly how that was going to happen, and there were a number of practical difficulties to deal with before then. First and foremost, she needed somewhere to live. She couldn't go on relying on Chris. She was too poor to live in the center of the city, but she couldn't be too far away from Julienne's preschool. And she also needed to be able to save up a bit of capital, get back in shape, update her knowledge of the financial world, and build up her own network. There were a thousand things to do. A thousand goals to achieve before Jack was ruined. She felt exhilarated.

"Have you got something I could write on?" she asked the bartender. "And a pen."

He put a pen on the bar and pointed to a pile of napkins. Faye wrote a list of things she needed to sort out. When she was finished, she called Jack to negotiate peace. She didn't have a problem with that, it was just an act. An opening move in a game of chess. She needed a cease-fire in order to be able to gather her forces and regroup.

She softened her voice and made sure it sounded rather fragile. The way he remembered it.

"I've been so sad," she said. "That's why I've been behaving so badly toward you. But I'm better now, I realize that you're right about a lot of things. Can you forgive me?"

She took a sip of her beer. It was almost finished and she gestured to the bartender that she'd like another.

"Well, I understand that it's been difficult for you," Jack said with a mixture of surprise and pompous magnanimity.

Faye drank the last of her beer as the fresh glass was placed in front of her. She drew circles in its foamy head. Thought back to the time when Chris had drawn a heart in the condensation on the glass.

"It has been. But that's no excuse. I'm going to pull myself together. For Julienne's sake. And for yours. Your daughter's mother shouldn't behave in an unworthy fashion and keep nagging about money. I don't know what got into me. I . . . I haven't been myself lately."

She fell silent, wondering if she might be overdoing it a bit. But Jack had merely heard her confirm what he had thought all along: that he was right, and she was wrong.

Jack wanted to see himself as the hero, the noble victor. She was offering him a chance to reaffirm that image of himself. The way everyone around him always did.

"That's okay. But try not to be so . . . difficult in the future, that's all," Jack said.

When they had hung up Faye quickly finished her second glass and asked for a third. There was no longer anyone to raise any objections. She started to giggle, and couldn't stop. Intoxicated by alcohol and freedom.

The red, two-story house dated back to the 1920s, and lay in an idyllic residential area in Enskede. Faye opened the green-painted gate, walked through the neatly tended garden, and rang the doorbell.

The woman who answered had high cheekbones and white hair pulled into a bun on top of her head, and was wearing a black collared top. Her posture was upright, almost militaristic. She held out a bony hand.

"Kerstin Tellermark. Come in," she said, stepping aside.

Faye followed her through a hall lined with black-and-white photographs into a comfortably furnished living room. Old paintings of landscapes and maritime subjects adorned the brown wallpaper, there were a couple of rather saggy armchairs and a sofa by one wall, and an old piano in the corner.

"What a lovely room," Faye said. And meant it.

"It's a bit old-fashioned," Kerstin replied apologetically, but Faye could see she was flattered. "Would you like some coffee?"

Faye shook her head.

"In that case . . . so it would be you and your daughter living here?"

"Yes, Julienne. She's four."

"Divorce?"

Faye nodded.

"The good sort?"

"No."

Kerstin raised her eyebrows. "Do you have a job?"

"Not yet. But I'm working on it. I . . . I studied at the School of Economics. I just need to get back on my feet first."

Kerstin stood up and showed Faye up the stairs. The upper floor contained a smaller living room and two bedrooms. It was perfect, exactly what she was looking for.

"Five thousand kronor per month."

"I'll take it."

. . .

Two days later Chris helped her to move in. Kerstin stood on the steps with her arms folded, looking on as they carried in the three boxes that contained everything Faye owned. She had sold most of the clothes from the apartment in one of the smarter second-hand boutiques on Karlavägen. All to get a bit of money.

She no longer wanted Jack to give her anything. She wanted to take it instead. It was more fun that way.

When Chris had gone, Kerstin knocked on the door. Faye was unpacking her clothes as she asked her to come in, but Kerstin stopped in the doorway.

"The daughter you mentioned, where is she?"

"With her dad. She'll be coming later this week," Faye said, holding a blouse up in front of her.

"He left you?"

"Yes."

"Whose fault was it?"

"Whose fault?"

"It's always someone's fault."

"In that case, it was his. He was sticking his cock into anything that moved, and I was too stupid to notice."

Faye flinched when she realized what she'd said, but Kerstin merely nodded.

Faye hung her clothes in the wardrobe, vacuumed, made the bed, and lay down on it with her hands behind her head. She needed to find a way to support herself. Quickly. To start with, just to survive. To pay Kerstin her rent, to buy food, things that Julienne might need. But the work had to be flexible enough for her to be able to work on her business plan at the same time. She couldn't work for someone who was constantly breathing down her neck.

Faye went over to the window. A blond man in his fifties was walking past with a large Rhodesian ridgeback, which seemed to respond to the name Hasse. The dog started, then strained at the leash, leaving the man struggling to keep his balance.

Faye looked on thoughtfully as they passed.

· · ·

Kerstin had made beef patties with potatoes and gravy. There were dishes of lingonberry jam and pickled gherkins laid out on the circular dining table.

"This is lovely," Faye said.

"Thanks."

Kerstin served Faye another helping.

On the windowsill there was a photograph of Kerstin as a young woman. Her hair was brown, cut in a bob, and she was wearing a short white dress.

She saw that Faye was looking at it.

"London in the late sixties. I was an au pair for a family there, and was in love with an Englishman, Lord Kensington. They were good times."

"Why didn't you stay?"

"Because Lord Kensington's mother, Lady Ursula, didn't think it suitable for her only son to live with a Swedish au pair. A few years later he married a society girl called Mary."

"How sad," Faye said.

"It is what it is. I'm not complaining."

"Have you been married?"

"Oh, yes. To Ragnar."

Kerstin turned her head away. Tugged unconsciously at her collar.

Faye watched her, then looked around the room. She couldn't see any pictures of Ragnar. Or of Ragnar and Kerstin together.

There was a clink of cutlery as Kerstin put her knife and fork down. She stood up and left the room, then returned with a photograph. She put it down on the table in front of Faye. It showed a bare-chested man in a pair of white shorts sitting on a lounge chair.

"Ragnar," she said. "Palma, 1981."

"Nice," Faye said. "It must be hard to lose someone you've lived with for so long. How long has it been since he passed away?"

"Passed away?" Kerstin opened her eyes wide and looked at her uncomprehendingly. "No, no. Ragnar's alive. The bastard's in an old people's home on Södermalm, slowly rotting away."

"I don't understand."

"He had a stroke three years ago."

"So you live alone?"

Kerstin nodded.

"Yes. But I'm happy," she said, popping a potato in her mouth. "It's nice and quiet. The only thing that disturbs my peace of mind is the fact that he's still breathing." She looked at the picture. Then she turned it upside down and said, "Help yourself to another patty. Good food's a balm to the soul."

Faye nodded and took the dish from her. It was the first time in ages that food actually tasted of anything.

Faye woke up early the next morning. She was met by the smell of freshly brewed coffee as she went down the creaking stairs.

Kerstin was already up. She was reading *Dagens Nyheter,* and beside her on the table was a folded copy of *Dagens Industri.* The photograph of Ragnar that had been on the kitchen table was gone.

"Good morning," Kerstin said. "Help yourself to coffee."

It was still dark outside, though spring had started its slow advance. Faye sat down at the table and reached for the copy of *Dagens Industri.* She read the editorial, then one of the comment pieces. She turned the page and found herself staring straight into Jack's blue eyes. She started, and briefly considered moving on, but her eyes were automatically drawn to the headline. Fuel. She needed fuel.

ADELHEIM DENIES RUMORS OF INITIAL PUBLIC OFFERING, it read.

Kerstin must have noticed the change in her breathing, because she glanced up from her paper to look at Faye.

"Bad news?" she asked.

"No, it's nothing. Just someone I used to know."

In the article Jack said they weren't planning to put Compare on the stock market. But he confirmed that the company's head of finance, Ylva Lehndorf, would be leaving the business to work for the music giant Musify instead. Jack said it had been a mutual decision, and wished Ylva well in her career. Not a word about the fact that he was living with her. Presumably the paper knew that, but *Dagens Industri* was too polite to mix personal gossip with business.

He's already started to change Ylva, Faye thought. The next step would probably be for her to stop working. Faye wasn't sure how she felt about that. Should she enjoy the schadenfreude? Or feel sorry for her? In a way it would have been easier if she could have believed that Ylva was simply better than her. Smarter, stronger. But now Ylva had begun to subordinate herself. Which made her seem even more like Jack's little whore. Bought off by his money and charm.

Faye scanned through the article a second time before moving on. She didn't yet know what was going to come in useful, she had no clear plan. For the time being she was simply gathering information.

"What are you going to do today?" Kerstin asked.

"I thought I might take a walk. Do you happen to know if there's anywhere nearby where I could get some leaflets printed?"

"Leaflets?"

"I was thinking of setting up a small business."

"Oh?"

Kerstin put the newspaper down and looked at Faye.

"Yes, a dog-walking service. Everyone around here seems to have a dog. I thought I could walk them during the day while I'm figuring out what I'm going to do. To earn a bit of money quickly and easily. Then we'll just have to see what I do after that. It would buy me a bit of time, though."

Kerstin looked at her intently. Then she went back to her paper.

"Try the library in Dalen," she said.

. . .

Faye printed twenty posters and pinned them up in strategic places around Enskede. She imagined what Alice and her friends would have said if they could see her. To her great joy she realized that she didn't care. She couldn't afford a gym membership, and spending her days walking dogs would give her exercise that would help her to lose weight. And at the same time she would earn money, something she desperately needed if she was to make any progress.

Chris would have given her a loan without a moment's hesitation if she had asked. But Chris had done enough. Faye had to fend for herself now, to prove both to herself and everyone else that she could do it. And for the first time in many years she felt ready to fight. Her past had finally turned out to be an advantage, not just something that woke her in a cold sweat with Sebastian's image fixed in her mind. She refused to think about her father. She still had that much power over herself.

She quickened her pace, stopped at a lamppost in front of a yellow villa, and pulled out the roll of tape she had bought at ICA.

Two girls of about the same age as Julienne were bouncing on a trampoline in the garden. They were laughing and yelping.

Faye stood and watched them for a while.

How many times would they be betrayed? Have their dreams crushed? Ahead of them lay a long string of beaded insults doled out by men. The experience of being sidelined, judged on their looks, the struggle to fit in, to please everyone—all the things that had humiliated women of all ages, in all countries, over the years.

And then it hit her like a flash of lightning. There was an army out there, waiting to be set loose. Most women—no matter how rich and successful they might be—had been betrayed by a man. Most of them had that one ex, that unfaithful bastard, that liar, deceiver, the one who broke their heart and stamped on it. That male boss who gave the promotion to a male colleague with worse qualifications and less competence. The comments, the wandering hands at the company's Christmas party. Most women had their own war wounds. One way or another.

But they kept quiet. Gritted their teeth. Responded magnanimously, showing understanding and forgiveness. Comforted the children when he didn't show up like he promised. Smoothed things over when he made patronizing remarks. Carried on inviting his parents to the children's birthday parties even though they took his side in the divorce and kept singing the praises of his new partner. Because that's what women did. They internalized their rage. Turned it against themselves. God forbid they should ever make a fuss or demand justice. Nice girls don't fight. Nice girls don't raise their voices. That's something women were taught from an early age. Women soaked things up, smoothed things over, bore the responsibility for all relationships, swallowed their pride, and subordinated themselves until they all but vanished.

Faye was hardly the first woman in the world to be humiliated by her husband, to be treated like an idiot, to be replaced by a younger model.

Enough of that now, she thought. Together we're strong, and we're not going to stay silent any longer.

Faye barely had time to get back inside the house before her mobile started to ring. That evening she heard from another four dog owners asking if she had time to take their dogs on. Her gut feeling had been right, there was a definite need for this service.

She could hear clattering from the kitchen downstairs. Faye had offered to cook dinner, but Kerstin insisted on doing it. But she had at least agreed to let Faye pay two thousand kronor into a shared grocery pot. That was a solution they were both happy with.

Faye opened her laptop, clicked to bring up Excel, and made a simple schedule for her future activities. The very next day she had two walks booked. She was charging one hundred and twenty kronor per hour. When the spreadsheet was finished she registered a private company in her name. She had already decided on the name in readiness for the day when she turned the business into a corporation.

. . .

The rain was pouring down, creeping under her raincoat, getting in everywhere. Faye couldn't remember the last time she'd been this wet. Zorro and Alfred were tugging at their leashes, the rain didn't seem to bother them.

If anyone had told her a month ago that she'd be celebrating her birthday in the pouring rain with two golden retrievers she'd have thought they were mad.

But life was full of surprises. Faye of all people had learned that lesson.

Her routines had changed entirely over the past few weeks. She got up at five-thirty every morning, showered, ate a breakfast consisting of a boiled egg with smoked fish roe, then headed out. The two dog walks per day had quickly become eight, and some of the dog owners were booking her for two walks a day. Kerstin had no objection to her volunteering to dog sit some evenings as well.

Faye sneezed. She was looking forward to getting home and sinking into a warm bath, like she did every evening after the last walk.

"Okay, that'll have to do, boys," she said as the skies opened up.

After handing the dogs back to their owner, Mrs. Lönnberg, Faye hurried home. Her feet hadn't felt this tired in years.

She opened the door gently so as not to disturb Kerstin, who usually sat and read at this time of day, and went carefully up the stairs. When she reached the bathroom she discovered that the bath had already been run. There was a vase of handpicked flowers from the garden on the sink.

Kerstin appeared behind her.

"Thank you," Faye whispered.

"I thought you might need it," she said. "There's . . . I got you a little something. A present. It's on the kitchen table."

"How did you know?"

"That it's your birthday? It's in the rental agreement. I may be old, but I'm not blind. Now get yourself in that bath."

When Faye got out of the bath her stomach was howling with hunger. She crept down the stairs, opened the fridge and took out some boiled eggs, sliced them, and spread fish roe over them.

She sat down at the kitchen table with her crispbread sandwiches on a side plate and opened the green parcel.

It was a pair of black Nikes.

Tears welled up in Faye's eyes.

She put the shoes on and walked around the living room. They felt soft, perfectly molded to her feet. She stopped outside Kerstin's bedroom door. There was a crack of light beneath it, so she knocked.

Kerstin was lying in bed with a book. Faye sat down on the edge of the bed and lifted her feet so Kerstin could see the shoes.

"They're perfect—thank you!"

Kerstin closed her book and rested it on her stomach.

"Have I told you how I met Ragnar?"

Faye shook her head.

"I was his secretary. He was married. Ten years older than me, a company director, a millionaire, with a smile that made me feel faint. He took me out for fancy lunches, gave me flowers, deluged me with compliments."

She paused. Ran one hand over the covers.

"I fell in love. So did he. In the end he left his wife, she took the children and moved out of their house. And I moved in. I gave up my job. Spent my days playing tennis, running the household, looking after Ragnar. We went traveling each summer, Spain, Greece. One year we went to the United States. Four years passed. Five. Six. I didn't even have the sense to feel ashamed of what I'd done to his ex-wife. I didn't have the courage to protest when I saw the way he treated her and their children. On the contrary, I was happy not to have to share his attention with them. I persuaded myself that they deserved it. That they had never loved him like I did."

She ran her tongue across her bottom lip.

"All the rest of it . . . that sort of crept up on me. The darkness. The violence. The first few times I thought they were isolated incidents. He came up with excuses. Explanations. And I was only too happy to accept them. But gradually it increased. And I couldn't get out. Don't ask me why—I can't explain it to myself, let alone anyone else."

Kerstin coughed behind a clenched hand.

"I didn't have the courage to walk out," she went on. Her voice was simultaneously weak and strong. "Even though I grew to hate him with every fiber of my body. I could live with the affairs. That was nothing compared to the beatings my body was taking. To what he took from me. We . . . I was expecting a child. But he beat me up and I miscarried. Since then I've wished him dead. Every waking second I dream about him dying. Stopping breathing. When he had the stroke, at first I wasn't going to call an ambulance. I sat and looked at him lying there on the floor rolling about. His eyes were pleading for help. I enjoyed seeing him so weak, in need of my help. I was thinking of letting him lie there, but one of the neighbors had seen we were home and rang the bell. I had to go and answer, and in the end I had to call an ambulance. I played the role of shocked wife well, but when they were lifting Ragnar into the ambulance I could see in his eyes that he understood. And that he'd kill me if he ever got well again."

Faye didn't know if Kerstin was expecting her to be shocked, but nothing about male brutality surprised her anymore.

Kerstin adjusted a stray lock of white hair.

"I know who you are," she said. "And I understand what's happened. You were married to Jack Adelheim."

Faye nodded.

Kerstin picked at the bedspread. Then she looked up at Faye.

"I've figured out that you're up to something. I've seen you with your notebooks, your lists and sketches for the future. Let me know what I can do, and I'll help you any way I can."

Faye made herself more comfortable on the bed. Leaned back against the headboard and looked at her new landlady. What

Kerstin had told her was terrible, but it came as no surprise; Faye had already guessed as much. The fact that Kerstin was a fellow sufferer was beyond doubt, but could she trust her? Faye knew she was going to have to rely on other people's help, and she had made up her mind to trust the sisterhood. Though she wasn't so naïve as to believe she could trust every woman, in the older woman's voice she recognized the same darkness as her own. So she closed her eyes, took a deep breath, then explained how she was thinking of crushing Jack.

The plan had taken shape during all those hours of dog walking, where she was able to plot her strategy calmly and methodically.

Kerstin listened and nodded, occasionally smiling.

"I'm good at organization. I could be quite useful," she said.

Calm. Matter-of-fact. Then she picked up her book and carried on reading. Faye took that as a signal to leave the room.

Things had started to move. There was no way back. And she was no longer alone.

Faye developed her activities with Kerstin's help. The months flew by and the business grew. They brought in two women as part-time employees, expanded the area they operated in, and rearranged the basement so they could have dogs stay overnight.

Kerstin helped Faye with the administrative side of things, and anything she didn't know after so many years as a housewife she looked up on the internet. She was a marvel of efficiency, and with her help the figures were soon in the black. It took time to build up the capital that Faye needed, she had set herself a target of two hundred thousand, but forced herself to be patient. It would just have to take as long as it took.

Of course there was no way she could build up enough capital merely through walking dogs, but she invested every spare krona. She read the financial papers and followed all the major news media to keep herself up-to-date, and was able to use that knowledge in her investments. She had a natural gift for finance, but didn't take any great risks. She stuck at a level where her capital was slowly but surely growing larger.

She had lost thirty pounds since Jack said he wanted a divorce. Not because she cared anymore, but she knew Jack's weak points. Men's weak points. Getting thin was a necessary step to achieving the goal she had set herself.

Her old clothes were now too loose, and Kerstin had made a

couple of extra holes in her belt to keep her jeans up. Faye just laughed when Kerstin said she deserved some new clothes. Not a chance. Two hundred thousand. Until then she wasn't going to waste money on anything that wasn't essential.

Since Faye had moved in with Kerstin she was allowed to have Julienne every other week, but it was becoming increasingly obvious that Ylva Lehndorf had grown fed up with playing happy families over on Lidingö. And Faye already knew that Jack had no interest in having Julienne more than was strictly necessary. Making it difficult for Faye to see her daughter had merely been another way to hurt Faye. Jack called more and more often to ask if she could look after Julienne.

Kerstin was delighted to have a child in the house. She did everything Julienne asked, and was more than happy to drop her off at preschool in the morning.

Faye and Kerstin shared responsibility for Julienne, like a little family. Whenever Faye wondered if Julienne was taking up too much of her time, Kerstin would look at her as if she were mad.

"Your daughter is the little girl I've always dreamed of, and I'm so happy I don't have to be on my own anymore," she said, gesturing in the direction of the living room where Julienne was sprawled on the floor drawing. "She's a miracle, an angel, and I'm already dreading the day when you move out."

Faye was surprised to realize that she felt the same.

· · ·

The August sun was shining on Faye and Chris as they walked past the Enskede soccer field with three dogs: a miniature schnauzer and two golden retrievers. To their mutual surprise, Chris was holding the leash of the schnauzer, Ludde. Faye knew that Chris had always hated animals.

"I could actually imagine getting one of these," Chris said. "Then I wouldn't have to chase after a man to share my life with."

"That's not such a bad idea. Now that I've got something to compare them with, I have to say that I prefer dogs to men any day of the week."

"Speaking of Neanderthals, how's it all going? You're looking almost indecently happy."

Faye met her gaze. "I am."

"It's so good, seeing you like this. I realize that you don't want to spend the rest of your life dog-walking, but the past few months without that idiot have done you so much good."

Faye looked on as one of Mrs. Lönnberg's retrievers peed against a lamppost.

"I've got a business proposal for you," she said. "An investment opportunity."

"Really? Let's hear it!"

"Not here. Not like this."

She nodded toward the dribbling dog that was now frantically trying to hump the schnauzer. She jerked the leash to separate them.

"Have you got time for dinner this weekend? I'd like to show you my business plan."

"Sure. On one condition."

"Which is?"

"That we go out together afterward. Drink some wine, spend time together, talking, flirting with guys. I'll book a table. My treat. All you have to do is turn up with your business plan and that beautiful smile I've missed so much. Ideally with that body of yours squeezed into something super tight. If you haven't got anything suitable you're welcome to borrow one of my outfits. I'll send some things over later. It's time for you to shake the dust off. You'll soon need a can opener to get between your legs. You know it can seal up if you don't use it for a long time, don't you?"

Chris grinned and Faye couldn't help smiling. A night out with Chris sounded like something she'd be more than happy to go along with. At last she felt like starting to live again.

When Jack called, at the last minute as usual, to ask if she could have Julienne for the weekend, Faye said no for the first time. She hated to lose a moment with her daughter, but she had to think long term.

"Why not?"

"I'm going out with Chris."

"But Ylva and I are going away, we've booked a suite at the Yacht Hotel in Sandhamn."

"Good job, they do an excellent children's buffet there."

"But . . ."

"No buts, Jack. I'm sorry, but you can't call on Friday morning to ask something like this. Have a good time in Sandhamn."

She hung up before he had time to protest.

. . .

At Teatergrillen the maître d' gave her a friendly nod and showed her to the table. Faye felt people's eyes on her back as she strode through the room. She was wearing high heels and a short black dress that clung to her waist. All borrowed from Chris. She was wearing her hair down. It had been years since she felt this attractive.

Chris stood up and gave a theatrical round of applause. The

old blokes with their buttoned jackets and bulging waistlines stared at them as they gorged themselves on duck liver and oysters.

"Hell, you look good."

"You don't look so bad yourself," Faye said, running one hand over Chris's silvery sequined dress.

"Chanel," Chris said, sitting down. "Seeing as we're planning to mix business with pleasure, why don't we get down to work? Because I'm planning to get drunk later and I don't want to get dragged into any of your crazy ideas when I'm under the influence. I'm not good at making sensible decisions after too much drink. Entertaining decisions, sure, but not always very sensible."

Faye sat down opposite Chris on the curved, red velvet banquette.

A waiter filled Faye's glass as she fished out the sheet of paper containing her business plan.

"Here," she said, pushing it across the table.

Chris picked it up and read the single word that was written on it: *Revenge*. She burst out laughing.

"What . . . ?"

"Do you remember saying you wanted to offer me a job? You said I understood women. I've spent the past few months analyzing women's needs and desires. And do you know what almost all of them want? Revenge. For all our sisters who have been broken down by idiots, all the unfaithful husbands who have cast us off for a younger model. All the men, all the guys who have exploited us, patronized us, and deceived us."

Chris looked highly amused.

"And how are you going to get your revenge?" she said, sipping her champagne.

She looked smart and expensive. A lethal combination.

"I'm going to show Jack that I'm smarter than he is, and take over his company. And I'm going to do it by building up an empire. Together with other women. Have you ever thought about how many fantastic female entrepreneurs we've got in this country, women who own department stores, PR companies, financial businesses? There are far too few of them, but they're out there and they're starting to get noticed. I'm going to create a business model where I own fifty-one percent of the company and have forty-nine percent to sell to investors. I'm going to bring in forty-nine businesswomen and let them each have one percent of the company. I'm going to seek out each and every one of them, tell my story, listen to theirs—and get them to invest. Social media will play a crucial role. Every girl with a blog or an Instagram account is going to post links to Revenge, because they'll all want me to succeed. Getting this to go viral is going to be a piece of cake."

"So what is it you're going to be selling?"

Chris gestured to the waiter to top up their champagne. She'd emptied her glass in three mouthfuls. A group of businessmen in the next booth had started casting covetous glances at them, and Chris turned her back on them.

"Hair-care products and perfume," Faye said.

Chris nodded slowly, but still looked skeptical.

"Tough market," she said dryly. "Oversaturated. The competition's brutal. And it's a business that requires a lot of investment and capital, mostly for marketing and PR. It's a huge risk."

"Yes. I understand that. It could end up being a complete disaster. But I don't think it will. And what I want to ask is if you'll be my first one-percent investor."

"How much will it cost me?"

"One hundred thousand kronor."

"Where do I sign?"

Chris held her glass up for the waiter, who filled it to the brim. Faye held hers up as well. She knew Chris would get it. The first, and easiest, single percentage share was sold. Now there were only forty-eight hard ones to go.

When they'd finished eating they asked the maître d' to get

them a table at Riche. They were ushered through the kitchen, a shortcut that only a few initiates knew about. Bright light, the chef's orders warming under heat lamps, the sound of crockery and people dashing about.

As usual Riche was packed. Chris ordered a bottle of cava. By then they were too drunk to need champagne. That would be a waste of money, and Faye actually preferred cava and prosecco to champagne anyway. In a blind tasting she might well not have been able to tell the difference.

There was a swaying, intoxicated wall of flesh over by the bar. Most of them were a few years older than her. It was hardly surprising that Riche was known as the divorce ditch. It was a meat market for middle-aged divorcées, where the size of men's wallets mattered more than the size of their cocks. And where women who'd had far too much Botox clung desperately to the delusion that they could pass for twenty in the right lighting.

The bottle arrived in an ice bucket and Faye raised her glass to Chris.

"To freedom," she said, then realized it sounded more pompous than she had intended.

The alcohol had reduced her ability to filter out banalities.

But Chris looked her seriously in the eye.

"Well, it only took you thirteen years to realize," she said. "But now you're free. Cheers! To Jack! May the Lord have mercy on him!"

She giggled.

"Do you think I can succeed?" Faye said, putting her glass down. "With Revenge?"

"I think the first part, finding investors, will be the easy bit. Like you said, we've all been hurt. One way or another. We all want to get our own back, and can identify with your message. It's a stroke of genius from a PR and marketing perspective. Vengeance sells."

Chris grinned and emptied her glass. A waiter hurried over to refill it. They were used to thirsty women here.

"It'll take a few years. Is that crazy? That I'm prepared to devote so much time to getting my revenge?"

Faye felt a flicker of doubt.

"No. Not when you think about what he's done. Is your conscience starting to get at you?"

Before Faye had time to answer, Chris went on, her glass raised halfway to her mouth, "Don't forget that you helped build up Compare. Without you, Jack and Henrik would never have succeeded. Getting divorced is fine, it happens, but it's not fine to leave your previous life partner and the mother of your child out on the street. Not after all you've done, and everything you've had to put up with. All the shit he put you through. And by that I don't just mean after you split up."

"You're right. I know you're right."

"A man would never think the way you do. He'd press on without hesitation."

A figure appeared at the end of the table and Faye looked up. A guy in his mid-twenties met her gaze. He was wearing a tight black T-shirt and dark trousers. His arms were covered in tattoos. Close-cut hair, full lips. He was impossibly handsome. Like a young Jack.

"Sorry to bother you," he said, "but my friends and I are tired of standing at the bar being jostled by the other losers. We were wondering if we could seek asylum at your table? Or at least apply for a temporary visa?"

A few feet away two more guys raised their hands in greeting.

"Just one moment," Chris said.

"Sure, I'll be over there," he said, and went back to his friends. Chris laughed.

"What do you say?" she asked.

Faye shrugged.

"Why not?"

"Because only a few months ago you would have been embarrassed to sit here with three handsome young men."

"I was married then. Besides, men have always hung out with younger women without feeling embarrassed. It's high time we learned to do the same, and—"

She fell silent abruptly when she found herself looking directly into Alice's eyes. She was sitting with a group of people a few tables away. When she saw that Faye had seen her she turned away at once.

"Let them come, it'll be fun," she said, and drained her glass.

She could feel Alice's stare burning into her as she got her glass refilled, and noticed them sitting there whispering.

Chris ordered two more bottles of cava and made room for the young men. All three were wide-eyed, pleasant, and clearly impressed. Faye couldn't help thinking that this generation of men was very different from Jack's. To them, successful women weren't at all frightening. They treated them with friendly curiosity and asked about Chris's work. They showed nothing but admiration for what she had achieved.

She could understand the appeal of being surrounded by young, attractive people. It was intoxicating.

The conversation flowed easily, if very much on a superficial level. Nothing seemed complicated to these young men, who hadn't yet been weighed down by life. They flirted shamelessly. Faye's cheeks flushed, from both the wine and their compliments. The whole time she felt Alice and her table keeping an eye on proceedings. There wasn't enough Botox in the world to hide the looks of horror on their faces. The only question was whether they would be able to lower their eyebrows again afterward.

Jack would be furious, yell at her, but he couldn't hurt her. What she did was no longer any of his concern. Or who she did it with. The thought intoxicated her even more than the cava. And for the first time in many months she felt the stirrings of interest between her legs. She grabbed hold of the guy in the black T-shirt, the one who had approached them first, pulled him toward her, and kissed him. She started to get wet from the feel of his tongue against hers, his hands on her thighs. She kept her eyes on Alice the whole time.

The kiss only lasted a few seconds. When their faces parted she nodded toward Alice, reached for her glass, and raised it in a toast. Alice stared back at her, then turned demonstratively toward the person on the other side of her.

"What's your name?" Faye laughed, focusing her attention on the guy in the black T-shirt.

She could tell from his eyes that he wanted her, and when she glanced down she could see a bulge in his trousers. She had to stop herself from stroking his erection there and then, under the table at Riche. Instead she leaned toward him so he could get a better view of her cleavage. She knew her nipples were clearly visible, rock-hard against the fabric of the dress. Chris, as usual, had persuaded her not to wear a bra.

"Robin," he said, staring at her breasts. "My name's Robin."

"I'm Faye. And I'm planning to go home with you tonight."

She leaned forward and kissed him again.

. . .

Faye woke up with a thumping headache. Memories of the previous day flashed past as she stretched. Her hand bumped into a tattooed arm, hard with muscle. Faye got up from the bed, walked over to the window, and looked out. A parking lot and some apartment buildings. The sky was mottled and gray. Behind her the young man with the tattooed arm moved. Robert? Robin?

"What time is it?" he mumbled sleepily.

"No idea," Faye said. "But it's probably time for me to get going."

She felt uncomfortable in this small apartment in Solna.

"That's a shame."

He stretched out on the black bedclothes and looked at her with puppy-dog eyes. Faye's head was thudding out memories of last night. Hell, it had been a while since she'd had sex in a single bed in a cramped studio with all the usual accoutrements—glass table, black leather sofa, a yucca plant, and the obligatory collection of Absolut vodka bottles on a shelf on the wall. Young guys seemed able to withstand any changes in fashion.

"Really?" she said, looking around for her clothes. "What are you going to do today?"

"I thought I'd chill. Watch some soccer."

"Chill," she mimicked, unable to stop herself. "Sadly this old lady hasn't got time to chill today. I need to get home."

"You're no old lady . . ." He smiled in a way that was simultaneously cute and sexy. "Can I have your number?"

"Sorry, sweetie. It's been a lot of fun. But me and men aren't a good fit right now."

She heard how bitter she sounded. The previous evening had gone flat, her hangover was thudding against her skull and her tongue felt badly furred.

He laughed and threw the pillow at her. She jumped out of the way.

"You're very sexy, you know that?" he said.

He got up from the bed. Naked. His abs glistened as he turned to face her. She drank in the sight of him. She'd forgotten how quickly young men could recharge. The night was a blur, but she remembered losing count of the number of times he had taken her.

He walked toward her and she backed against the window with a smile. The glass felt cool on her backside. Robin kissed her. Pressed himself closer to her. She felt his erection against her thigh. Felt her body shouting for more. She sat on the windowsill. His face roamed over her body. Nipping, kissing, tickling. Her thighs, her crotch, her stomach. She groaned loudly, grabbed hold of his head, and pushed it down between her legs. Leaned back and allowed herself to simply enjoy it. Without feeling that she had to do anything in return. He was happy for the chance to satisfy her, taking pleasure from her pleasure. Which was something she hadn't experienced in a very long time.

When she came she stroked the back of his neck and let out a loud laugh.

This was a new phase of life, and it was her turn to enjoy it.

Faye looked out of the window at the trees rushing past. She was sitting on the train to Västerås with a bundle of sketches in her bag. She had left Kerstin in charge of the dog-walking business, and was on her way to meet a company that designed packaging.

Her products needed to be good, but there was something that was even more important if she was to be successful. Social media. It was all about reaching out, being visible in the torrent, going viral. And packaging was a simple way to create a must-have feel and make influencers advertise her products with their Instagram and Facebook accounts. The products needed to make the consumer feel special, and they needed to look good on pictures taken with phones.

Faye had decided that the pots of skin-cream should be black, and the round lid adorned with an ornate, gold-colored letter *R*. But the packaging wasn't only about the look of the jars. There had to be a story behind it all. All successful products these days had a story. Like Elizabeth Arden's Eight Hour Cream. It didn't matter whether she really had developed the cream to heal the leg of one of her injured horses, and that the wound healed in eight hours. The fact that customers *wanted* to believe the story was what counted. Everyone loved a good story. And Faye had one hell of a story.

As the train swept through the Mälaren Valley she felt nothing but pure, unadulterated joy. This was what she had been longing for: the chance to build a company from the ground up. Jack had taken that dream away from her. And she hadn't protested. When had he first been unfaithful to her? Had he ever been faithful? Even when she was sure he loved and desired her?

She had spent a lot of time wondering why Jack had replaced her with Ylva, a career woman, when he had wanted Faye to be at home, but she had come to realize that it was the chase that interested men like Jack. They always wanted something new to play with.

She had also realized that he liked having power. The power to turn her into someone that she wasn't.

She would never let a man own her again.

It was raining when she emerged from the station. She found a taxi, jumped in, and gave the driver the address. Västerås was an awful lot bigger than Fjällbacka, but for some reason the people made her think of her hometown. She always used to fend off those memories whenever they popped up. But something had changed after the turbulence of the past few months. People from her childhood and teenage years often came into her mind. The look on her father's face when something wasn't the way he wanted. The clenched expression on Sebastian's face. The accident that had affected the whole community. Her mom's pale arms and loud crying. The way her classmates had looked at her afterward. Sympathetic. Curious. Intrusive.

She had left all that behind. But would she ever be able to truly get away from it?

The car pulled up while she was lost in her memories. The driver turned to look at her. His mouth was moving but Faye didn't hear a word of what he was saying.

"Sorry?"

"Card or cash?"

"Card," she said, and dug in her handbag for her wallet.

She got out of the taxi, and a beige industrial building rose up in front of her. The rain had eased slightly, but small, cold drops were still falling. She pulled the door open and stepped into the entrance hall. A female receptionist with permed red hair looked up at her.

"Welcome," she said, but it sounded more like "please, get me out of here." She had been busy filing her nails when Faye walked in.

"Thanks—I'm here to see Louise Widerström Bergh."

The receptionist nodded. Tapped at her computer.

"Please, have a seat." She gestured toward some seats over by the window. "Coffee?"

Faye shook her head. There was a stack of magazines on the windowsill behind the sofa. She picked up a three-week-old celebrity magazine and leafed through it. There was an article announcing that John Descentis had broken up with his girl-friend. Faye studied the picture. It was the same woman he had been with at Riche, Suzanne Lund, apparently. The article claimed she was both a model and a singer.

"I'm not easy to live with," John explained in a quote. No, but who the hell is? Faye thought, remembering their desper-ate, pointless fuck in the cinema. How grubby and sordid it had been. That had been all she thought she deserved at the time. Now, in hindsight, she wished she'd told Jack about it, to rub his nose in it. She had been on the brink of telling him several times but never had. Largely for fear of being met with complete indif-ference.

She heard footsteps in the corridor. A woman in a blouse and suit trousers came toward her. She exuded a cool demeanor as she looked Faye up and down.

"Louise Widerström Bergh," she said, and held out a limp, slightly moist hand.

"Faye. Faye Adelheim."

The moment they walked into her office Faye's phone rang.

It was Jack. He probably wanted to shout at her about her

behavior in Riche. She dismissed the call and took out her sketches. She was no good at drawing herself, but Chris was helping until they could afford to bring in a professional. Louise settled down behind the desk as Faye sank into the visitor's chair.

"This shouldn't be a problem," Louise said, putting on a pair of reading glasses. "A little something to keep yourself busy?"

"Sorry?"

"Well, obviously I know who you are. I'm assuming this is for a party or something?"

Faye took a deep breath.

"I want thirty thousand of each of the three designs I've got sketched out here. Can you manage that, or should I look for someone else?"

Louise pursed her lips.

"Thirty thousand? Of these? I assume you can guarantee the order? The market for this type of product is already oversaturated, and obviously we can't afford to spend money on goods we don't end up getting paid for, as I'm sure you can appreciate. Of course if you were still married it would be a completely different matter. Jack Adelheim would be an excellent guarantor, but as I understand that you're now separated . . ."

"You haven't read the description of the concept? The one I emailed you? Don't you appreciate the unique aspects of what I'm going to be bringing to a very demanding market?"

Faye felt frustration burning her throat.

Louise Widerström Bergh snorted and took her glasses off. She shot Faye a patronizing smile.

"Yes, but like I said, I thought we were looking at some sort of themed party. Obviously I know the sort of life you Östermalm wives lead, and that isn't the reality for the rest of us. To be honest, I think the idea of launching a brand based on some sort of girl power suggests that you've got your head in the clouds. People in Stockholm are the only ones who can afford that sort of thing, out here in the rest of the country we let women be women and men be men. No, I'm not going to risk putting this packaging into production only to have to chase you for payment."

She started to laugh, and Faye stood up. Her temples were throbbing.

"I've got the capital to pay up front for the whole order. You could have had the money in your account tomorrow. And if this goes the way I think it will, this could have turned out to be a good, ongoing source of income for your company. Maybe it could have paid for a couple of extra holidays for you and your family. Or a nice summerhouse by the water. Or whatever it is you dream about. But I'll be taking my business elsewhere. And paying for someone else's holiday cottage or Christmas break in the Maldives. And believe me, I'll ask them to send you a postcard."

She turned on her heel and walked out. She could feel Louise's stare burning into her back.

...

She had missed twenty calls from Jack, but Faye waited until the train had pulled out of Västerås before she called him. After a long "What the hell do you think you're playing at?" harangue he launched into a diatribe about how inappropriate it was to be seen socializing with people on benefits.

"What are you so angry about?" Faye asked when he stopped to take a breath.

Anger and frustration at the failed meeting were still in her system.

Outside, the landscape was sweeping past faster and faster. Jack's anger didn't prompt any reaction in her at all. She shut her eyes and remembered her night with Robin. Against her better judgment she had ended up giving him her number, and had already received five text messages telling her all the things he wanted to do with her. Jack's voice broke through her fantasies and she opened her eyes in irritation. He was going on and on in a shrill, whiny voice. Like a child who had lost his favorite toy.

"Sitting in Riche making out with some boy who could have been your son. In public. That sort of shit rebounds onto me."

"Oh, you mean Robin? He's twenty-five. I'm thirty-two. I'd have to have had him when I was seven. You like numbers, Jack, so how about this one: there's a bigger age gap between you and Ylva Lehndorf than between me and Robin."

"For fuck's sake, that's not the same thing at all!"

"Why not? I'm genuinely curious now."

"I'm not behaving like some cheap whore in a club without a thought for this family's reputation."

"No, you just fucked her behind my back in our home, in our bed. And to be honest, I don't actually know which family you're talking about, Jack."

He spluttered. Then said in a more controlled voice, "Don't do it again."

"I shall do exactly what I want. You have no mandate to tell me how I should live my life, who I sleep with or where I sleep with them. Goodbye, Jack."

She ended the call. Shut her eyes. Felt Robin's tongue flitting across her clitoris. Her phone buzzed. Another text from Robin, telling her what he wanted to do to her. She hesitated, then sent a reply:

I'm on my way back from Västerås. Will be at yours in a couple of hours.

Who could turn down an offer like that?

Faye took another sip of wine. She could feel some of the other guests at Sturehof staring at her, but ignored them. Let them wonder what happened between me and Jack, she thought, let them whisper and gossip. One day I'll show them all.

She cast a quick glance at the time again. Sophie Duval was seriously late.

If Faye was going to find another partner now that Louise Widerström Bergh had turned her down, she needed to prove that she had financial backing, from investors who would not only contribute capital, but could also contribute to the mythology of Revenge.

She had met Sophie Duval on a number of occasions when she was with Jack. She had always been effusive in her praise of Faye, and would be the perfect next investor after Chris. She had a high profile in the business world, she was young, attractive, and was a media favorite. She was constantly in the headlines, always with a new man on her arm, always talking about her new investments.

Faye had never liked Sophie, but this was business, and she was convinced she could persuade Sophie to see the value of investing in Revenge.

Faye had finished her first glass by the time Sophie glided in.

"A glass of champagne, please. And I think I'm in the mood

for the shellfish platter today," Sophie said as she sat down, without looking at the waiter.

She tossed her dark hair back and turned her attention to Faye.

"How lovely that you got in touch! The last time we met was Oscar's fiftieth birthday party in Cannes, wasn't it?"

Before Faye had a chance to reply Sophie had turned and clapped her hands to get the waiter's attention.

"How can it take so long to get a glass of champagne?" She glared at the waiter, who came running over with a glass and a bottle. "It may not be champagne-o'clock yet, but I got back from Hong Kong yesterday, so I'm still on Hong Kong time."

Faye sighed silently to herself in response to Sophie's shrill laughter. But as long as she offered an investment Sophie could act as forced as she liked.

The shellfish platter arrived along with Faye's grilled char.

"God, this is *soooo* good," Sophie said, slurping happily from an oyster. "Better than sex, if you ask me."

She took a large gulp from her third glass of champagne, then looked at Faye.

"So tell me, darling, how are you? Have things settled down? Divorces are never fun, and I should know. I saw Jack and Ylva in Båstad last weekend—they're such a sweet couple. From what they were saying, little Julienne sounds completely adorable. Obviously they were sad it wasn't possible to come to an agreement with you, so that they could have taken her with them."

She dabbed at her mouth with the linen napkin.

"If you want my advice, you always have to think of what's best for the child in situations like that, no matter how sad and upset you might feel." Sophie put her hand on Faye's. "Our children's well-being is the most important thing of all, don't you think?"

Faye swallowed several times, she couldn't let Sophie see how irritated she felt. It had been Jack's weekend to have custody, but he had texted Faye at only three hours' notice to say that he couldn't possibly have Julienne because of a hastily arranged business trip.

She smiled at Sophie. For the time being the most important thing of all was the bigger picture: securing the money and investment she needed.

"Thank you, Sophie," she said, then bent down to take out the folder containing her prospectus for Revenge.

Sophie helped herself to half a lobster, then waved her hand dismissively.

"Let's eat first, we can deal with business afterward."

Faye let the folder slip back into her bag and reluctantly took a bite of the char. She had lost her appetite, but Sophie seemed to be starving. She licked her fingers noisily and occasionally let out a shrill "Hello, daaaarling!" when she caught sight of someone she knew.

She managed to get through another two glasses of champagne before she finished the platter and leaned back contentedly.

"So what do you say, shall we talk business now?" Faye said, reaching for her folder again.

"Of course, darling," Sophie said.

She glanced at her watch.

"Oh Lord, is that the time already? I'm late for my next meeting! Darling! This has been too lovely! We must do it again! Call my secretary and we'll fix another date. But it won't be for the next three or four weeks, I've got trips to Paris, London, New York, and Dubai lined up! I practically seem to have taken up residence in the VIP lounge at Arlanda these days!"

Another shrill laugh, then she was gone.

Faye sat there in mute astonishment. With a bill that was the equivalent of what she usually spent in an entire week.

At first Faye couldn't quite understand the sense of emptiness she felt. Then she realized. It was resignation. For the first time she was feeling a deep, overwhelming sense of resignation.

Julienne was snoring gently beside her. Her eyelashes looked like little fans above her cheeks, her face was calm and relaxed, and her nose was twitching slightly in her sleep. Exactly the same expression she had had as a baby, sleeping in her crib. Faye used to laugh at her back then, thinking she looked like a baby rabbit twitching its nose. But now all she could do was smile weakly. She felt utterly exhausted, her meetings with Louise and Sophie had sucked all the life out of her.

She wasn't sure what she had been expecting. Obviously she couldn't assume that every woman would automatically understand what she wanted to do, what she wanted to say, simply because they were women. But even if it was naïve, that was probably what she had been hoping. Now she wasn't at all sure how to recharge her batteries. The next would be make-or-break for the company. What if that one failed as well? The whole project would collapse if that happened. She wouldn't be able to achieve what she'd set out to accomplish. Jack would be able to carry on his life undisturbed, without having to pay any price at all. The thought made her skin crawl.

The sound of Kerstin working in the kitchen interrupted her

worrying. Kerstin had insisted on cooking that evening, and Faye was pretty sure she was making one of Faye's favorite dishes. Probably stuffed cabbage rolls.

Julienne had her dinner before she went to bed, Kerstin wanted to be able to have a quiet talk with Faye, just the two of them. When Faye walked in the door earlier that evening she had been aware that she must have looked deflated. Kerstin was usually able to cheer her up, but Faye wondered if that was going to work tonight. Doubts were clinging to her like sticky tar.

Julienne changed position in her sleep. She wasn't often allowed to sleep in Faye's bed, but tonight Faye wanted her daughter close to her. She would have dinner with Kerstin, talk through what had happened, then try to sneak back into bed beside Julienne again, and fall asleep to the sound of her breathing. She watched her daughter as she lay there in her thin white nightie, the one with the unicorn, then gently placed her free hand on her chest and felt her heart beating. Da-dum, da-dum, da-dum. Gradually her own heart started to fall into line and follow the same rhythm. That helped clear her thoughts. In the kitchen she could hear Kerstin clattering pans. The smell of food spread through the bedroom and Faye heard her stomach rumble. She felt her daughter's rhythmic heartbeat through her palm again. Da-dum, da-dum, da-dum. Her despair and frustration at the failed meetings began to fade. It wasn't over yet. She still had the most important meeting to come. And she wasn't going to let that one fail.

Faye was making her way across the cobblestones of Blasieholmen. She realized she was feeling nervous. Her meeting with Irene Ahrnell was particularly important. Through her investment company, Ahrnell Invest, she owned a large slice of the three largest chains of department stores in Sweden. Not only was she a potential investor in Revenge, but she could help to get the products into shops. Right from the start Faye had known that Irene could determine if Revenge was going to be a success or just another of the thousands of failed hair-care products and perfumes.

It was a crazy market to launch yourself at. One of the most difficult of all. Especially for someone like Faye who had no experience or platform in that area.

She was still seething after her recent failures, the meeting with Louise Widerström Bergh in Västerås and the lunch with Sophie Duval. The bill she'd been left with after the latter had stung, causing her to reevaluate her priorities when it came to potential investors. She'd gone through her list and struck off anyone like Sophie; they only had fool's gold to offer anyway.

Irene Ahrnell was infinitely more crucial when it came to Faye's chances of success. With Irene's backing anything would be possible, internationally as well as in the domestic market.

Faye had read up on Irene until she knew practically everything about her. Raised in an affluent family in Gothenburg, educated at Yale and Oxford. She was a generous donor to women's organizations, and supported female entrepreneurs. She had an impressive network, stretching right across Europe and the United States. The fact that Faye had been granted a meeting presumably meant that Irene was curious about her after everything that had been written about her divorce from Jack.

Faye didn't give a damn what the reason was, the thing that mattered was that she was being given a chance to enlist Irene's support. It was all up to her now.

Ahrnell Invest was based on the fifth floor of a handsome building dating back to the early 1800s. The view across the water was magnificent. Faye was given coffee and shown into a meeting room.

There were six chairs around the table. She remained standing, unsure where she should sit. She had been planning a rather daring opening move, but wasn't sure how Irene Ahrnell would react. There was a risk that it could be taken as unprofessional. But her meeting with Sophie had made her realize that she couldn't afford to let herself be easily dismissed. She needed to open with fireworks and demand the attention she deserved. Not wait politely until anyone deigned to give it to her.

Faye could feel her back sweating. She was starting to do the very thing she needed to avoid, doubting and questioning herself and the whole idea.

Irene came into the room wearing a navy-blue trouser suit. A cream silk blouse poked out of the top, Faye guessed it was one of Altuzarra's tied blouses. She'd been hankering after one just like it, but couldn't afford it until she had gotten her starting capital in place. She had borrowed the Stella McCartney suit she was wearing from Chris. A couple of months ago she wouldn't have gotten the trousers over her knees, but now they fit perfectly. She hadn't dared ask Chris what it had cost.

Irene put a similar mug to the one Faye had been given down on the table and held out her hand.

"Irene," she said in a neutral voice. "We've got ten minutes before I need to leave."

Chair legs scraped the floor as they sat down opposite each other.

Faye took a deep breath to calm her nerves. Reminded herself of why she was doing this. Conjured up the image of Jack thrusting between Ylva's legs in their home, in their bed.

"How many times in your life have you been betrayed by a man?" Faye asked, forcing herself to look Irene calmly in the eye.

The image of Jack was still etched onto her retina. Her pulse rate slowed down. Her uncertainty vanished. The first shot had been fired.

Irene looked unsettled at first but quickly composed herself. Her expression switched from surprised to affronted.

"I consider that too personal a question to answer in circumstances like this."

She looked like she was about to stand up.

Faye kept her eyes on her. Refused to let herself be put off by Irene's initial reaction. Her intention was to shock, and there was no doubt that she had caught the investment manager's attention. She leaned forward, folding her hands together on the conference table.

"The answer to that question is the basis of my business idea," Faye said. "But first, note that I didn't ask *if* you'd been betrayed by a man. I took it for granted that you had been. And why is that so shameful, prompting you to react the way you did? You weren't the one who did anything wrong."

Irene straightened her neck and leaned forward. She looked simultaneously amused and slightly unnerved. She seemed to make a decision.

"Twice," she murmured.

Her features relaxed for a moment before she composed herself again. Outside on Standvägen some cars were blowing their horns angrily.

Faye nodded.

"And you're hardly alone in that. As women, no matter what our standing in society, we will almost all of us have been betrayed by a man at least once. Yet we're the ones who feel the shame. Who are left wondering what *we* did wrong. Now, why is that the case?"

"I don't know. Do you?"

Irene's interest had definitely been piqued now. The door was ajar, and Faye needed to push through it. And be invited to stay.

"Well, I've certainly had good reason to think about that," she said. "Because it's humiliating to be abused and then rejected. Sometimes because our husbands find someone else they want to spend the rest of their lives with, sometimes because of a squalid fuck in a conference hotel in Örebro. All the love, children, time, and effort we've invested. All that can be thrown away for a drunken fuck in a conference center. We're replaceable. And they don't appear to show any remorse. Or have the grace to feel ashamed. It's as if it's their right to trample all over us. And they have an invisible network that we can't break into. Where they give each other advantages that aren't offered to us. Because they regard us as inferior."

Irene didn't speak when Faye paused for breath. But the hard expression on her face had softened. She looked curious.

"Have you ever dreamed of taking revenge on a man who betrayed you, walked all over you, treated you badly?" Faye asked.

"Of course, everyone has," Irene said, and her face suddenly looked naked and vulnerable.

Faye guessed she was seeing images in her mind. The sort of images you had to live with for the rest of your life, like war wounds, but in your heart rather than on your skin.

"And did you?"

"No."

"Why not?"

Irene reflected. "I don't actually know."

"My ex-husband, Jack Adelheim, was unfaithful to me for years. I have no idea how many women he slept with. This spring I walked in on him while he was having sex with his finance director, Ylva Lehndorf, in our bed. And that's only part of the betrayal. The less important part, really. I helped him build up his business empire. I can tell you the whole story some other time, over a few glasses of wine. But the short version is that he has me to thank for a lot of what he's got now. Yet he wasn't just unfaithful to me; when he discarded me, he left me high and dry. And you know what, Irene? I begged and pleaded with him to be allowed to forgive him so that everything could go back to normal. That was how desperate I was to save our family. Even though he had taken everything—my career, my home, my security, my self-respect. In the end, I decided that enough was enough."

"And now . . . ?"

"Now I'm going to take it all back. Plus a bit extra."

"How?"

They had switched roles. Suddenly, Irene was the one asking the questions. A sure sign that she was interested. She leaned closer to Faye, intrigued.

"By refusing to feel ashamed," Faye said, pushing a sketch of the Revenge packaging across the table. "And by tapping into an enormous target market. Smart marketing needs to press a button that no one has pressed before. Personalized marketing, taken to its extreme. Storytelling combined with good products."

Irene held the sketch up and inspected it carefully.

"What does the R stand for?"

"Revenge."

"I see," she said with a wry smile. "What do you need me for?"

"Distribution and advertising campaigns through the department stores you have shares in. I'll do the rest. I'm going to bring as many successful women into the project as I can, and I've worked out a campaign strategy that's unlike anything that's been done before. Particularly when it comes to this type of product. I'm not asking you to invest as some sort of ideological gesture. I'm explaining my thinking so that you appreciate the immense potential of this project. The target market for our products isn't just women, but women who are fed up with being let down by men."

There was a twinkle in Irene's eyes. She picked up the sketch again and looked at it thoughtfully.

Faye sat in silence. Let her think.

She had decided not to make Irene an offer but to let her raise the subject instead. Irene's share would be larger than the one percent she had been planning to offer the women who invested. Irene would get more. Faye had already given Kerstin five percent of the business. She had offered her ten, but Kerstin had refused, saying it was too much.

"I want ten percent," Irene said.

"Five," Faye said. Her heart was thudding in her chest.

"Seven."

"Deal."

She had to make a real effort not to let out a shriek and dance with joy. Instead she got to her feet and Irene did the same. They met in the middle of the room and shook hands.

Irene fished a card from her handbag.

"Call me whenever you need anything. This is my direct number. You don't have to go through my secretary."

When Faye emerged onto the street her mobile buzzed. She didn't want to be disturbed, she wanted to savor this moment, but when she saw it was Chris she answered.

"She's on board, Chris! Irene fucking Ahrnell is on board!"

"Brilliant!" Chris said enthusiastically. "So you're quite pleased, then?"

"Pleased?" Faye said as she set off toward Stureplan. "I'm over the moon! Revenge is going to be available in all her stores. And she's promised to use her international contacts if the Swedish launch is successful. Have you any idea how fantastic that is?"

"Yes, I have. But we'll have to celebrate later. Right now I've got two people who want to talk to you."

"Okay?" Faye said uncertainly.

"Hang on, I'll put you on speaker."

"Hi, Faye, my name is Paulina Dafman," a hoarse voice said. "I'm sitting here with my friend Olga Niklasson. Have you got a minute?"

Faye's heart skipped a beat. Olga Niklasson and Paulina Dafman were two of the biggest Instagram profiles in Sweden. Between them they had three million followers.

"Yes, absolutely."

"We're sitting in the Grand Hôtel drinking cava with Chris. And we loooove Chris! And she told us about what had happened to you, about that treacherous bastard, and about your business idea, and we're very interested. Is there any chance that we could get involved and help you with this?"

"You want to get involved?"

"Absolutely!" they said in chorus. "And I'm sure we can bring in a few more girls with good accounts. We know everyone who's anyone, you know."

"They really do," Chris said. "They know me, for instance . . ."

Faye stifled a giggle.

She was bursting with joy when she hung up. An older woman with a dachshund in her arms looked at her in surprise. Faye smiled broadly at her and the woman hurried on.

Faye paused to study her reflection in the plate-glass window of Svenskt Tenn, and knew she was looking at a winner.

PART THREE

A fan was whirring far too loudly somewhere, detracting from the luxurious impression the law firm was trying to convey.

Jack had asked to see her while he was in custody. Faye's lawyer snorted and shook her head when she told her.

"I can't understand how he's got the nerve to ask to see you. How can he possibly imagine that you'd want to, after what he's done?"

Faye didn't answer. She slowly stirred her tea as she sat in the meeting room. She stared almost hypnotized at the ripples in the red-bush tea, the maelstrom in the middle that seemed to swallow everything.

Her lawyer put a sympathetic hand on her shoulder.

"The prosecutor is going to press for life. There's no chance he'll get anything less, given the evidence. You'll never have to see him again after the trial."

"But is it going to be possible to prove anything? Without her . . ." Faye's voice cracked. "Without her body?"

"There's enough evidence besides that. And then there's his abuse of you. Believe me, he won't be getting out for a very long time."

Faye stopped stirring. She put the spoon on a white napkin and cautiously raised the cup to her lips. The tea burned her tongue but she welcomed the pain. These days it was her friend. The pain lived in the murky waters where she kept all her secrets.

Ingrid Hansson, the reporter from *Dagens Industri,* was picking at a Caesar salad. Faye was making do with green tea. The digital recorder was between them, its recording light flashing.

"It really is a remarkable journey that you've been on with Revenge," Ingrid Hansson said. "After your divorce from Jack Adelheim you went from being a housewife to the owner and CEO of a company that's expected to reach a turnover of one and a half billion kronor this year. What's the secret?"

Faye raised the cup to her lips and took a sip.

"Hard work, I'd say. And knowledgeable and engaged investors."

"But it all started with your divorce?"

Faye nodded.

"When Jack and I separated I hadn't a clue what to do with my life. I started a dog-walking business and spent my days doing that. In the evenings I worked on my business plan."

"Was it a messy divorce, given the name of your company? Revenge?"

The question was posed in a neutral way, but she knew it was a land mine. Faye was familiar with the whole media game by now. The worst ones were always the journalists who pretended to be your friend, who tried to play on sympathy. The ones who liked to hang around once they'd put the recorder away to chat "off the record."

In the world of the media there was no such thing as "off the record," nor "you mustn't use this." They were merciless. But Faye knew how to exploit them. She crossed her legs and clasped her hands together on her lap. She could afford an expensive wardrobe of her own now, she saw it as a uniform, armor. She used her clothes to signal power and success. Today she had chosen an Isabel Marant jacket and a Chanel skirt. But the blouse was a bargain from Zara. She liked mixing things up, not dressing from head to toe in expensive designer gear.

"Messy, no. But it was difficult. Like all divorces."

"How would you describe your relationship today?"

"We have a daughter, and we shared more than ten years of our lives. If Compare does end up going public, I'll probably buy a few shares."

"Really?"

"Yes, I was involved in the early years. Naturally I want to support the company now."

Ingrid Hansson wiped her mouth.

"So the name Revenge has nothing to do with your divorce?" she asked. "I've heard a lot of rumors about how you sold the idea to your backers."

Faye laughed.

"Every good product comes with a good story. Stories that take flight and spread across the internet and social media. I can't exactly claim that that's been a disadvantage. It's simply good business to find something that an awful lot of women have in common."

Ingrid nodded and changed the subject to performance indicators, the most recent accounts, international expansion, and the prestigious awards Revenge had won for its marketing. Also a fair number of questions about Faye's private investments, primarily in property, which had made such a significant contribution to her own personal fortune. Faye was happy to share information and advice. She had nothing to hide. Not when it came to her finances, anyway.

Half an hour later the interview was over. Ingrid Hansson left Faye's office in a prestigious building on Birger Jarlsgatan. Faye looked on thoughtfully as the reporter left, leaning against the wall in the window alcove as she granted herself a few rare minutes of peace.

Once the merry-go-round started to spin everything had happened at breakneck speed. The three years that had passed since the divorce had exceeded all expectations. Revenge was a huge success, bigger than she could ever have dreamed of. She had underestimated the impact her marketing campaign and products would have. Women had loved the company's angle and, after only six months, shops in France and Britain had bought licenses to sell her products. And they had recently signed a contract with one of the biggest retailers in the United States.

The big breakthrough had come about thanks to Instagram. The influence wielded by Paulina Dafman, Olga Niklasson, and their friends over a new, young generation of women turned out to be greater than she had ever dared hope. For hundreds of thousands of women in Sweden, they were the new ideal. The 2010s Sophia Loren, Marilyn Monroe, and Elizabeth Taylor. Whatever they wore, other women wanted to wear. Whatever they bought, other women wanted to buy. As ambassadors for Revenge they had written inspirational posts about female empowerment and had been happy to advertise products that fit in perfectly with the feminist winds that were blowing through Sweden. Revenge couldn't have been more perfectly timed.

In her more cynical moments Faye wondered where the feminist message lay in advertisements featuring well-toned women in bikinis turning their pert backsides to the camera to sell Revenge diet tea. But Chris had pointed out rather bluntly that you had to take whatever feminism was on offer, and that the path was never going to be perfectly straight. Besides, the internet was crawling with their male equivalents taking pictures of their bare torsos and advertising protein shakes. And was there any real difference, when it came to it?

The online store she had opened, with a special forum where women could share stories of how they had gotten their revenge on their husbands, had struggled to cope with demand. The forum was overflowing with stories. More poured in every day, they never seemed to stop. Another vital tool was Facebook. They had been able to target their advertising at the precise audience they were after: well-educated, aware women. Customers who also had money, which meant they could charge a higher price and make more of a margin on each item sold.

At first all sales were online. When it was time for Irene Ahrnell's department stores to introduce Revenge's products, Faye realized that something extra was needed to maintain the hype and mystique that had been built up online. She contacted a dozen female artists, authors, and actors and invited them each to design one piece of packaging, giving them full artistic freedom. Backed up by a huge campaign on social media. And all of it launched under the magical concept of the "limited edition."

Young women lined up outside stores to get hold of Revenge products bearing their idols' imprinted messages about the sisterhood. They suddenly found themselves reaching new target groups. Within their limited forum, they had managed to foster a spirit of revolution.

Kerstin cleared her throat in the doorway.

"You're picking Julienne up at four o'clock today."

"Any meetings booked before that?"

"No, you asked to keep this afternoon free."

"Of course, that's right. Thanks."

"See you at home this evening," Kerstin said, and closed the door.

She seemed tense today, and Faye wondered why. Then she remembered that Kerstin had been to visit Ragnar at lunchtime. She was always unsettled after seeing him. When Faye asked why she still visited him, Kerstin had replied: "I'm still his wife, in spite of everything. I only go to stop the staff phoning and nagging me. Besides, it gives me a certain satisfaction to see him lying there helpless. But I always fantasize about one day smothering him with a pillow."

Faye looked out of the window again. The traffic was rumbling by down below. It would soon be October, when Compare was going to be launched on the stock market, after years of speculation. And that meant that the second part of the plan could begin. After so much hard work, everything depended on whether she was successful in the coming months. She picked up her bag, containing the Dell computer she had bought earlier, and left the office. In Sturegallerian she found a café where most of the clientele were pupils playing truant from the private schools nearby.

She listened idly to their conversations, about which Gucci bag they'd like for their birthday, someone complaining about having to go on a family holiday to the Maldives because "there's, like, nothing to do there." She ordered coffee from an uninterested waitress, sat at one of the corner tables, opened the laptop, and connected to the Wi-Fi. Jack had had the same password since Julienne was born. During all their years together he hadn't changed it more than a couple of times. And he was a creature of habit.

Or at least he always used to be.

The very earliest documents relating to Compare were saved as PDF files in his Gmail account. But she could only access them if he was using the old password: *Julienne100730*. Faye raised the white coffee cup to her lips and took a sip. Her hand was shaking. Every step she'd taken over the last three years had been leading up to this. It all hinged on the supposition that Jack was too lazy to change his password.

She tapped in the letters and numbers, then clicked to log in.

Wrong password.

She tried again.

Wrong password.

She stifled a cry of frustration. The bastard had finally gotten around to changing it. She slammed the laptop shut and left the café.

What was she going to do now? She had to get into his emails.

Ten minutes later she was back in the office. As she reached the door the first raindrops had started to fall. Kerstin looked up at her expectantly.

Faye shook her head.

"Can you ask Nima to come and see me?" she said, and hurried into her office.

Nima, a skinny guy with pale skin and hairy arms, was Revenge's IT expert. Socially inept, but a genius when it came to computers.

Faye hung her coat up and waited for him behind her desk.

He appeared in the doorway a couple of minutes later.

"You needed help?" he said.

Faye smiled.

"Come in," she said, gesturing toward the visitor's chair.

He sat down, rubbing his hands anxiously.

"Is anything wrong?"

"Not at all," she said, flashing him a disarming smile. "Quite the contrary. I need your help with something. It's a bit embarrassing."

"Okay?"

"It's Julienne, my daughter. She's been given a computer, and I'm a bit worried she might be looking at unsuitable sites. I'd like to be able to keep an eye on what she's getting up to. I'm a real worrier, I just can't help it."

Nima nodded.

"I understand."

"Is it possible to do anything?"

"What sort of information do you want?"

"Her password for Facebook, that sort of thing. You can't help worrying these days, children will talk to anyone and they're so naïve."

Nima frowned.

"That can be sorted. I suggest you install a key logger on her computer. Then you'll be able to see everything without having to sign in to her social media."

"How would a . . ."

"Key logger . . . You just have to activate it on her computer. Then whenever you want you can download everything that's been typed in, in the form of an ordinary text file. Every keystroke gets registered, it's as simple as that. You can follow her every move without having to sign in to her Facebook or Snapchat accounts."

"And there's no way she'd know I was doing it?"

"No, not if it's hidden among all the other files. It would be buried in the background. And it would record everything without her knowing."

"Great. How do I get hold of one of these key loggers?"

"Give me a minute," Nima said, and stood up.

He was soon back, holding a black USB stick.

Faye pushed her chair back, and he inserted the stick into one of the ports on her computer and showed her how to install the program.

"I've got kids too, so I know what it's like," he said.

Faye looked at him in surprise. She would hardly have believed he had a girlfriend.

"I didn't know that."

"Astrid. Ten years old, and on the internet all the time. You can't help worrying as a parent."

"You must have been very young when you had her."

"Twenty. Planned, though, weirdly enough. I've always been old for my age."

"And you're still with . . . ?"

"Johanna." He lit up when he said her name. "Oh yes, we're married."

Faye raised her eyebrows. People never ceased to surprise her.

Money does something to people. Back when Faye was still Mrs. Adelheim the other children's parents used to call pretty much every weekend to invite Julienne to parties and playdates. They strained so hard that they practically shat themselves trying to pretend that it was their kids who wanted to see Julienne. The truth was that they wanted to cozy up to her and Jack. Or Jack, to be more precise. She was merely an accessory, a way to get at a successful man.

Julienne was their ticket to being invited to dinner, so they could bask in Jack and Faye's reflected glory in the hope that some of their success would rub off on them.

They stopped talking to her after the divorce. The phone stopped ringing. Enskede might as well have been Mogadishu or Baghdad as far as they were concerned. There wasn't a parent on Lidingö who was prepared to send their child there, not without a bodyguard and a load of vaccinations. They called Jack instead. And he in turn delegated the calls to Ylva, who had to spend a fair chunk of her time coordinating parties and playdates on the weekends they had Julienne. Not that that was ever more than one weekend per month.

Things couldn't have been more different after Faye's success with Revenge.

Julienne had started at Östermalm School. Jack had wanted her to go to the private school, Carlsson's, where the royal family's children went, or Fredrikshov Palace School, because there were rumors that was where the soccer player Zlatan Ibrahimović was planning to send his sons, but Faye had refused. She didn't want Julienne to grow up into the sort of teenager who complained loudly about having to go on trips to the Maldives.

Okay, so there weren't exactly a lot of kids on welfare at Östermalm School, but at least there were a few children who didn't take it for granted that the summer would be spent in Marbella or New York, Christmas in the Maldives, and half-term in their family's chalet in Verbier or Chamonix.

Julienne was having a great time. Faye and Kerstin were the cornerstones of her life. She looked forward to her weekends with Jack before they happened, but was always withdrawn when she came home. It seemed he made a habit of promising more than he could deliver.

Faye parked the car on Banérgatan. Julienne was waiting on a bench by the elevator with her face in her iPad. Faye sat down beside her without her noticing. She only looked up when Faye nudged her in the side.

Julienne laughed and gave Faye a hug.

"What are you playing?"

"Pokémon," Julienne said, tucking the iPad away in her backpack.

Faye took Julienne's hand.

"Have you had a good day?" she said as they walked to the car.

"Yes."

"You know you're going to Daddy's this weekend?"

"Mmh."

She opened the door for Julienne and fastened her seat belt.

"That'll be fun, won't it?"

"Kind of."

"Don't you like being there?"

"Sometimes. They argue a lot and that isn't nice. And Daddy's away working most of the time."

"Adults do argue sometimes, Julienne. Daddy and I used to as well. But it's absolutely nothing to do with you, though I can appreciate that it's not nice to hear. And it's for your sake that Daddy works so much."

She stroked Julienne's cheek.

"Do you want me to talk to Daddy?"

Julienne shook her head hard.

"He'd be angry."

"Why would he be angry?" Faye said, giving her a hug.

"Oh, nothing," Julienne said quietly.

"Are you sure?"

Julienne nodded against her chest.

· · ·

When Faye opened the door to the elevator Julienne rushed in ahead of her and ran into the kitchen.

The four-room apartment, spread out across eighteen hundred square feet on Karlavägen, right opposite the ICA Esplanad supermarket, had cost fifteen million. But it was hers. Hers and Julienne's.

"We're home, Kerstin!" Julienne cried. Faye followed her into the kitchen.

"Hello, my little one," Kerstin said, lifting Julienne into her arms.

Faye smiled. She had helped Kerstin buy the neighboring apartment, and they had dinner together most evenings. If Faye had to work, Kerstin was more than happy to sit with Julienne. There were no longer any au pairs in Faye and Julienne's life.

Kerstin spoiled Julienne far too much. Faye didn't really approve, but she didn't have the heart to make an issue out of it. Kerstin was her anchor, her rock.

While Faye put the kettle on and filled the dishwasher Julienne ran off into the living room.

"What went wrong?" Kerstin whispered.

"He's changed his password. I've found a way around it, but it's going to take more time than I expected."

The television went on in the living room.

"There's only one problem," Faye went on.

"And that is?"

"I'm going to need help from . . ."

She nodded in the direction of the noise from the television. Kerstin's eyes widened.

"You haven't said anything about . . . ?"

"Of course not. She's not going to be involved. Not knowingly, anyway."

"You know, Faye, I have no objection to almost anything you do, I admire you and am happy to support you, but I don't like this."

"Nor do I," Faye said. "But I haven't any other way of getting at his computer."

The kettle clicked. She took out two mugs and put them on the table.

"There are no guarantees here," she said quietly. "I don't even know if those documents are still there. But it's our best chance. The most important thing is not to get desperate and make any mistakes that can be traced back to me."

"To us," Kerstin said, blowing on her tea. "There are two of us in this. I'll back you all the way, regardless of whether I like it or not."

Faye nodded. She too felt distinctly uneasy about using Julienne. But she didn't have a choice.

. . .

They were lying on Julienne's bed reading *The Brothers Lionheart* out loud. The dishwasher was rumbling away out in the kitchen.

Before Julienne went to bed, Faye had shown her the USB stick.

"Darling, there's something I want to ask your help with," she had said when they were sitting at the kitchen table. "I'm planning a surprise for Daddy."

"What sort of surprise?"

Faye held up the USB stick.

"I can't tell you yet, but you know how Daddy usually leaves his computer on in his study when he watches the financial news? I'd like you to stick this into his computer. Then, when you've done that, I want you to press this button."

She pointed.

"And that's all. Then you can take it out."

"Why can't I say anything to Daddy? He's told me we mustn't have any secrets from each other. We only have secrets from you."

Faye frowned. What did she mean by that?

"Because that would spoil the surprise," she replied. "Then, when you've done it and I come and pick you up, I'll have a surprise for *you*!"

"What?"

"Something you've wanted for a long time."

"A mobile?"

"You're no fool, are you? Yes, your very own phone! So you won't have to keep borrowing mine."

"When can I have it?"

"On Sunday. It'll be here waiting for you, if you help me."

Faye felt terrible. But it couldn't be helped. She had to get hold of those files.

Now Julienne had fallen asleep beside her and Faye put the book down on the bedside table and kissed her daughter's warm hair. Her face looked so peaceful in her sleep, but a change had come over her recently. She had become more withdrawn, quieter. Faye could feel her anxiety growing, and couldn't help wondering what sort of secrets Jack was sharing with his daughter. Probably something trivial, like Julienne being given ice cream for breakfast. But what if they were hiding something important from her?

· · ·

Faye was lying on her back in her own bed—she'd found it hard to lie on her front since her breast enhancement. The air in the bedroom felt heavy, hard to breathe. She got up, grabbed her dressing gown and opened the door to the balcony. The autumn air felt fresh against her skin. She lit a cigarette and sank onto the wicker sofa. Every so often a car drove past on Karlavägen, but most of Stockholm was sleeping.

Three years had passed. Three fantastic, industrious, successful years. When she allowed herself a moment to stop and reflect over everything that had happened she always felt astonished.

She had built up a successful business, made successful investments, had bought an apartment for her and Julienne, another for Kerstin, and had gotten back on her feet again. But, ridiculously, she sometimes asked herself if she didn't still miss Jack. Or at least the fantasy of Jack.

Was that why her hatred had never faded? Was that why she was going ahead with a plan she had first thought up three years ago? Sure, there had been other men in that time, but before Jack was wiped out she didn't dare embark on anything serious. She mustn't lose focus. The goal was the whole point of it all.

Sometimes she wondered if she should be happy with what she had. After all, she had everything now. She had fought her way to success. She had money, social status, Julienne. But on some level she knew that wasn't enough. He had taken so much from her. He had walked all over her to the point where she had barely been able to get up again. She couldn't forgive that.

And her hatred had been nurtured by all the stories she had heard from other women over the years. Every day she went to the forum of Revenge's online store and Instagram account to read new stories. There was a huge need out there for restitution, to rebuild lost pride, to fight back, take control, take revenge.

There was something primitive in that desire. The Old Testament had a lot to say about revenge. An eye for an eye, a tooth for a tooth. A desire for justice. She was no longer driven purely by her own hatred, now it was reinforced by the voices of thousands and thousands of other women. She had awoken something that had been slumbering for far too long.

Their fury was hers. And her fury was theirs.

Faye blew off some ash that had landed on her dressing gown, reached for her mobile, and went into Spotify. Eldkvarn's "Alice" started to play quietly.

Her mom had always loved Eldkvarn. How many times had she told the story of the first time she saw them play live, and had been given Plura Jonsson's guitar pick? That was before she met Faye's father. After that the music had fallen silent.

The song, and the cigarette, cast Faye backward through a thirty-year journey. Back to her childhood, to Fjällbacka, to the house where they lived. Her, Sebastian, Mom, and Dad.

She had put the day's mail on the small table in front of her. At the top of the pile was another letter from her father. All the people she used to know were gone now. Only Dad was left. He had recognized her when the papers started writing about Revenge. And the letters had started up again, after so many years of silence. First one a week. Then two. Then three. Faye never opened them.

She had asked her lawyer to look into the legal situation. He mustn't be allowed to get out now. She knew how things were in

Sweden; in reality there was no such thing as a life sentence. Not even for her dad. Sooner or later he would be released. But not now. Absolutely not now. First she had to finish what she had set out to do.

She picked the letter up and held the cigarette against it. The relief when it started to burn was indescribable.

FJÄLLBACKA—THEN

THE ROAR OF THE SEA outside my bedroom window couldn't drown out the sounds from the kitchen. The voices getting louder and louder. Dad's full of rage, Mom's full of pleading. Still hoping that she might be able to fend off the inevitable. It was my fault they were fighting. I'd forgotten to clear up after the snack I made when I got home from school. How could I have done that? I knew Dad didn't like anything to be left out. Except when he had gotten himself something to eat. He never cleared up after himself, but the rest of us had to make sure that everything was kept clean, tidy, clinical. Me, Mom, and Sebastian.

Mom always took the blame. I loved her for that. And more than anything, I wished that I could grow big and tall and strong, so she didn't have to take the punishment for something I'd done. But as long as I was so small, he didn't dare punish me. He might clench his fists when I did something wrong, but he was afraid he'd break my brittle bones, hit me so hard that no one could save me. So he had to make do with Mom. She could bear more.

The first time I realized everyone was afraid of Dad was when I went to the supermarket with him when I was five years old. He had bought the usual things: a couple of packs of cigarettes, a large bar of chocolate, and a copy of *Expressen*. Sebastian and I rarely got to taste any of the chocolate.

As we approached the checkout a man jumped in front of Dad in the line. Just as Dad was about to put his things on the belt the man threw his shopping onto it. It was obvious from his clothes that he was one of the summer visitors. I was struck by the look of horror on the cashier's face. Her fear of Dad's anger.

Dad wasn't about to accept some *bastard tourist bastard,* as he called them, pushing in front of him. I found out later that the man ended up in Uddevalla Hospital with two broken ribs. I was only five when it happened, but the story lived on, and I heard it many times over the years, along with plenty of others.

My math book had been open at the same page in front of me ever since the first blows were dealt down in the kitchen. Division. Easy, really. I found math perfectly straightforward. But when the blows started I dropped my pen and covered my ears with my hands.

A hand on my shoulder made me start. I ignored Sebastian. Kept my hands over my ears. From the corner of my eye I saw him sit down on my bed. He leaned back against the wall with his eyes closed, trying, like me, to shut it all out.

I stayed inside my bubble. There was no room for anyone else in there.

Faye met up with Chris at the Grand Hôtel for dinner and a few drinks. She didn't feel like it—all she wanted was for the weekend to be over so she could find out if Julienne had succeeded. But she realized that it was a better idea to spend time with Chris, get drunk, maybe flirt a bit, rather than stay at home climbing the walls. The maître d' had prepared a table out on the veranda, with a view of the water and the Royal Palace. The noise level was slowly rising. At the piano bar at the far side of the room a beautiful woman was singing "Heal the World."

Chris ordered a hamburger while Faye made do with a Caesar salad. Just as their mojitos arrived two young women in their mid-twenties came over and asked if they could have a selfie with her.

"We love you!" they squealed excitedly before they disappeared. "You're such an awesome role model."

"Next time I'm going to have to book a private room so I can get a chance to talk to you," Chris said, highly amused, stirring her mojito.

"It's not like you're exactly unknown either," Faye said.

Chris gave her a wry smile.

"How are your tits?"

"Different," Faye said curtly.

She had been perfectly happy with her old ones, but had done what needed doing. Her body was a tool, something to help her reach her goal.

"Have you tried them out yet?"

Faye raised her eyebrows.

"With a guy, I mean."

"No, not yet."

"You need a good seeing to. It's food for the soul." Chris scanned the room. "That's going to be tricky here, though. Most of the men in this place haven't had an erection without pharmaceutical assistance since the fall of the Berlin Wall."

Faye laughed and looked at the clientele. Chris was right. Plenty of money, not much hair, and regular consumers of little blue pills—that pretty much summed things up.

Chris leaned forward.

"Where are we with Jack? It's not long until the IPO."

"There was a temporary problem, but we should be back on course now," she said, and told Chris what a key logger was. "Enough about me, though. What's going on in your life?"

Chris took a sip of her mojito, then smacked her lips softly.

"A couple of months ago I was seriously considering retiring and moving somewhere sunny. The whole Queen organization runs itself, and I don't exactly need any more money. But I've thought better of it now."

"Oh?"

"Yes," Chris said without meeting her gaze.

"Are you going to tell me or am I going to have to shake it out of you?"

"I am, embarrassingly enough, in love. Completely, hopelessly, fucking in love."

Faye almost choked on a mint leaf. She started coughing.

"In love?" she repeated lamely. "Who with?"

"You're not going to believe this, but his name is Johan and he's a high school Swedish teacher."

"That sounds very...normal," Faye said, who had been expecting a tattooed participant in *Paradise Hotel* with bulging biceps who was eligible for a student discount on flights.

"That's what's so weird about it," Chris said.

"How did you meet?"

"He came into our salon in Sturegallerian with his niece. He was wearing one of those ridiculous jackets with patches over the elbows. When his niece sat in the chair she said she wanted a Mohawk. That made me curious. How was he going to react? But he just nodded and said, 'I always wanted one of those, they're pretty cool.'"

Chris fell silent and looked out of the window.

"Shame he's already taken, I thought, because I assumed she was his daughter. But I stayed in the salon to talk to him. And when he was about to pay she asked when her dad was going to pick her up. My mood sank even lower then—I assumed he was gay."

"But?"

"She got picked up outside the salon by a bald guy whose face turned bright red when he saw his daughter's hair. They parted and I... fuck it, I might as well admit it—I canceled all my meetings and started to follow him."

"You *stalked* him?"

Faye was staring at her friend in amusement. This was crazy, even for Chris.

"Yes, just a bit, I guess."

"How much is just a bit?"

"To Farsta."

"You haven't ventured outside the city center since..."

"Since the Year of Our Lord 2006. I know. So, when we got to Farsta he finally turned around. I'm not exactly James Bond, so he'd noticed I'd been following him all the way from Stureplan."

"What did he say?"

"That he was very flattered, then he said I must be thirsty

after all that stalking. I said I was, so he asked if he could buy me coffee."

"Hell, Chris! I'm so happy for you."

Chris couldn't help smiling. "So am I."

"Then what?"

"He got me a coffee and I fell hopelessly in love. We went back to his place and I spent the next two days there."

She laughed, and Faye felt a warm glow spread through her.

"And now?"

"He's the one, Faye, the man I've been waiting for all my life."

For a fraction of a second her smile flickered into a grimace. Anyone who hadn't known Chris as long as Faye had wouldn't have noticed a thing.

Something was wrong.

"Chris, what is it?"

"What do you mean?" she said nonchalantly.

"I know you. What is it?"

Chris raised her glass and took a sip. Then she put it down.

"I've got cancer," she said in a thick voice.

Time stopped, the noises around them vanished, shapes blurred, sharp edges lost their focus.

Chris's voice sounded muffled and unfamiliar.

Faye couldn't take it in. Chris, so vital, so full of life, couldn't possibly have cancer. But she did. A rare type of endometrial cancer. As Chris pointed out, that was rather ironic given how little she'd used her womb. Glasses tinkled around them. The entrance to Stockholm harbor lay sunlit and smooth as a mirror before them, the Royal Palace loomed up on the other side of the water, looking as usual more like a municipal prison than a fairy-tale castle. It was an unusually beautiful autumn day, and it had drawn out the city's inhabitants in their hordes. At the tables around them people were enjoying their afternoon tea with clinking gold jewelry, and Faye wondered how they could be laughing when her own world had imploded.

"I wasn't going to say anything until I got rid of it. But it is what it is."

Chris shrugged. If the doctors didn't manage to stop it she'd be dead within twelve months. Faye kept looking for a sign that she was joking, kept waiting for Chris's loud, disarming laugh. But it didn't come.

"We have to get out of here," she said. She could barely breathe. "I can't sit here picking at a fucking Caesar salad while you tell me you've got cancer."

She regretted saying that at once. She realized Chris must be terrified and was struggling to hold everything together. This wasn't the right time for *her* to be saying what she wanted. And it wasn't the time for her to be feeling sorry for herself.

"Sorry. I'm just so incredibly sorry," she said.

Chris smiled. Sadly this time. An expression Faye had rarely, if ever, seen on her beloved friend's face. She forced herself to eat a piece of chicken. It felt like it was going to catch in her throat. She put her cutlery down, caught hold of a passing waiter, and ordered two gin and tonics.

"Doubles, please."

They sat in silence until the drinks appeared.

"Do you want to talk about it?" Faye asked when she'd taken a sip.

"I don't know. I think so. But I don't know how to."

"Me neither. So you have to get better."

"Well, obviously I'm going to. The timing's so fucking awful, though, with Johan and everything. At long last I'm in love, then a tumor pops up in my womb and wrecks everything. Someone up there has a sense of humor."

Chris's laugh didn't reach her eyes.

Faye nodded. She put her lips on the straw and sucked up more alcohol. She felt it spreading out, warming her up, making it easier to breathe.

"You mean you're worried he'll leave you?"

"I'd be surprised if he didn't. We've only been seeing each other a couple of weeks and if I'm going to beat this illness it's going to take all my strength. It's going to make me ugly, unattractive, I'll lose any desire to have sex, I'll be exhausted. Of . . . of course I'm worried. I really do love him, Faye, I love him so much."

"Are you worried about . . ."

". . . dying? Terrified. But I'm not going to die. I want to be with Johan, go traveling with him, get old. I've never wanted to live as much as I do right now."

Another grimace. Faye felt inadequate and uncertain. In the end she put her hand on Chris's. The hand that had been her strength during the abortion. It was trembling and felt ice-cold.

"Sooner or later you're going to have to tell him. Regardless of whether he leaves you or not."

Chris nodded and drank her gin and tonic in one gulp. Faye kept her hand on Chris's.

When Faye picked Julienne up on Sunday her daughter looked at her expectantly. Faye had forgotten all about what she'd asked her to do—Chris's illness had turned everything upside down.

"Where is it?" Julienne asked.

"What?"

"My mobile. I did what you said."

"That's good, darling. You'll get it tomorrow."

Julienne started to protest but Faye explained that she'd have to wait. Julienne went off to her room in a sulk, and Faye couldn't summon the energy to call her back.

Nor could she feel any enthusiasm for the fact that she would soon have Jack's password.

Chris had asked her not to tell anyone about the cancer. She didn't want anyone's sympathy, no stamp on her forehead announcing that she was being treated for cancer, as she put it. They had agreed that Faye would go with her for her first treatment session, and that they weren't going to talk about it again until then.

But it was impossible to think about anything else.

Life without Chris? She had always been there, she had been strong when Faye had just wanted to hide. Now their roles were reversed. Now Chris was going to need her. All of her.

Faye had money. She had a successful business. She had

shown Jack and the rest of the world that she could stand on her own two feet. Maybe she should let the key logger installed on his computer store his password, everything he wrote, and not do anything about it? Should she simply let go?

That was impossible. She felt sick at the thought of not following through on her revenge. She couldn't let go. Didn't want to let go. What sort of person did that make her? Her best friend was ill. Possibly terminally ill. And she was still thinking about how to crush Jack.

FJÄLLBACKA—THEN

I WAS TWELVE YEARS OLD the first time Dad hit me. Mom had gone to the supermarket, she'd left only moments before. I was sitting at the kitchen table, and Dad was next to me, at the head of the table, immersed in a crossword. I went to turn around but managed to hit the cup. In slow motion I saw it tip over, could feel the impact of my hand.

The hot chocolate spilled out across Dad's paper and the almost-solved crossword. It was as if fate had stepped in, letting me know it was my turn now.

Dad seemed almost nonchalant as his hand flew out and hit me above the ear. My eyes filled with tears. I heard Sebastian close the door to his room, he wouldn't dare come out again until Mom was home.

A second blow followed almost immediately. Dad stood up and this time his hand hit my right cheek. I closed my eyes and searched inside myself, making my way to the welcoming darkness. The way it welcomed me when I went to school and was able to shut out all the shouting and yelling.

Dad's palm hit my skin. I was almost shocked by how well I managed to withstand the pain.

When I heard Mom's footsteps in the hall I knew it was over. For the time being.

Faye met Chris at the Karolinska University Hospital. The city was shrouded in low cloud. Stockholm was gray and damp in that way it so often is in autumn. The leaves had started to fall, forming drifts of brown mush on the ground.

Chris was shivering outside the entrance.

"The worst thing is that I haven't been allowed to eat anything since yesterday, not even a cup of coffee," she muttered, glancing at Faye's 7-Eleven cup of bad latte.

Faye tossed it in a green trash can.

"You didn't have to do that," Chris said as they passed through the sliding doors.

"We're in this together, okay?"

"Okay," Chris said, and gave her a grateful look.

"If it had been me who was ill you'd have cut me open and removed the tumors yourself," Faye said. "Sadly I'm scared of the sight of blood so I'll have to make do with keeping you company and not drinking crap coffee. It isn't much of a price to pay for spending a few hours with my best friend."

She pulled Chris toward her. "How are you feeling?"

"Like a cancer patient. As for you . . ." Chris whispered in her ear, "you're not scared of anything. But thanks for pretending. For my sake."

Faye didn't say anything. Because the only thing she could have said was that she was actually scared. Scared that her best friend was going to die.

. . .

When they left the hospital Chris was so exhausted that Faye had to put her arm around her. Faye wasn't sure if it was mental or physical exhaustion. She didn't know anything about cancer. Or cancer treatment.

Chris would have taken a taxi, but Faye decided to drive her home and spend the night with her. She sent Kerstin a text, and she replied saying that she'd take Julienne to the cinema.

Chris leaned her head against the window with her eyes half-closed as the city rushed past outside.

"Is Johan at yours?" Faye asked.

"No, I told him . . . I told him I've got meetings all weekend and haven't got time to see him."

"You need to tell him."

"I know."

Chris picked at the car door with a red-varnished nail.

"But I'd like you to meet him first. In case he . . ."

"In case he what?"

"In case he leaves me."

"What sort of man would he be if he leaves you?"

"A typical man," Chris said with her eyes closed, smiling wearily. "You of all people ought to know how it works. Why should Johan be any different?"

Faye didn't know what to say, she had thousands of stories from the online forum lodged in her heart like lumps of ice. All the betrayals. All the lies. All the indifference and selfishness. She couldn't tell Chris she was wrong with anything approaching confidence. No matter how much she wanted to.

The short walk from the parking lot to the elevator felt endless. When they finally made it into the apartment Chris hurried into the bathroom and threw up. Faye held her hair back. Fifteen years had passed since they were last in that situation. It felt like a lifetime ago.

. . .

Naturally, after that brief flicker of doubt Faye decided to use the information from the USB stick. Now that the key logger was installed on Jack's computer she had gotten part of the way, but she had yet to find a way to collect it and copy the text file containing all the information. Then she had to hope that everything was still there in his Gmail account. The Jack she used to know was hopeless at getting rid of things. He always wanted to keep everything, just in case: "You never know when you might need it."

With a bit of luck she'd have an opportunity during Julienne's birthday party that weekend.

Then there was Ylva. Though it seemed Jack had already reduced her to a shadow of her former self, Faye couldn't forget the look of derision in Ylva's eyes when she had looked at her. In her bedroom. Naked and freshly fucked by Faye's husband. Slim, toned, and with perfect silicone tits.

Slowly but surely she had invaded Ylva's territory at the same time as Ylva had started to slide into hers. Faye's body was slim and toned. She had new breasts. And Jack had noticed the change. Each time they met to pick up or drop off Julienne his eyes would roam over her body. The way they used to back at the start. Back when she was the one he couldn't get enough of. Much as she hated him, the attraction she felt for him was as strong as ever. And she had never gotten used to seeing him with Ylva. She probably never would.

Her own love life was confined to short-term flings with younger men that she met in bars, slept with a few times, and then broke up with. No one was allowed to get too close. No one was allowed to stay. In her weaker moments she dreamed of crushing Jack, once and for all . . . and then taking him back. Another of her dirty, shameful secrets. The dark water kept replenishing itself.

No one could accuse Jack of restraint, Faye thought as she drove up to the house. Julienne had said she wanted her seventh birthday party to be a carnival, and Jack had brought in a company specializing in children's parties who had decorated the garden with pink balloons, party tents and stages, and a red carpet, although in this instance it was pink. And a professional photographer to take pictures of all the children as they arrived, then put their photographs up on a wall. There were tables laid in the garden, groaning under the weight of food and presents. Even by Lidingö standards, it was pretty over-the-top.

But then Jack had a greater need for self-justification than any of the other dads on the island.

Julienne let out a shriek, jumped out of the car, and ran up the drive. Jack and Ylva came out onto the steps to meet her. Faye got out and walked up the slope. She had chosen a tight, low-cut, short-sleeved dress, flesh-colored, from Hervé Léger, and she could feel Jack looking at her. Ylva seemed to notice him looking as well. She threw her arms open demonstratively to Julienne. Faye felt a pang in her gut when Julienne hugged her, but made an effort to go on smiling.

"How nice you've made it look," she said.

"We wanted to do something extra special for her today," Ylva said breezily as she air-kissed Faye.

She smelled pleasantly of shampoo and perfume. She too had begun to adopt an ingratiating, falsely familiar tone toward Faye once her success with Revenge had become too big and obvious to ignore.

Faye looked at Ylva as she disentangled herself from her embrace. Wasn't she starting to get the same bitter set to her mouth that Faye had noticed in herself during the latter part of her time with Jack? And a bit too much Botox in her forehead?

"If you run up to your room you'll see that we've organized an early surprise for you," Jack said, patting Julienne on the cheek.

Julienne ran into the house and her footsteps echoed up the stairs. Jack turned toward Faye.

"Ylva's organized a . . . what was it again?"

"A makeup artist," Ylva said. "The same girl who does Carola's makeup, actually."

A young man came over and introduced himself as a magician. He and Jack disappeared into the house, leaving Faye and Ylva to look out over the garden. Two men were carrying one of the tables between them.

"You really have made it look very nice," she said again, to fill the silence.

She wasn't lying. The house was beautiful, and the garden delightful. Their gardener deserved a bonus. They seemed to have gotten rid of the geese that used to shit all over the beach. There was a rumor that Jack had paid someone to shoot them at night.

Ylva smiled.

"Would you like to stay and join in? Juli would probably rather we kept out of the way as much as possible, but it could be nice, couldn't it?"

Faye's comments about her home seemed to have prompted a spontaneous show of generosity. She seemed to regret it at once, but it was out there now.

Faye felt like being sick when she heard Ylva call her daughter Juli. But instead of pointing out that she wasn't some damn pet guinea pig, she nodded. Partly because she hoped she might get a chance to access Jack's computer, but also because she had noticed Ylva's immediate regret about her spontaneous invitation.

"I'd love to."

"Great. Wonderful. Jack's managed to book Sean and Ville to come and sing a couple of songs."

Sean and Ville were a boy band Julienne and her friends were completely obsessed with. They knew all the songs and never missed their daily updates on YouTube. Some weekends she even forced Faye to take her to sit outside their studio, just for the chance to see the two wastrels throw themselves into a taxi without so much as a glance at the little girls waiting, first with shrieks of excitement, then tears of disappointment.

"That can't have been cheap," she said.

"No, their manager demanded eighty thousand kronor—for two songs. Plus a rider requesting champagne and chocolate truffles . . ."

"Dear Lord . . ."

"Jack wasn't sure at first, but I persuaded him. I so want this to be an unforgettable day for her. Would you like a glass of champagne? You can always leave the car here and get a taxi home. Or we can arrange to have someone drive you home in your car."

"That would be lovely."

"Let's go in."

There was a zinc bar in the living room. Ylva walked behind it and took out a bottle.

"Cava?" she asked. "I prefer it to champagne, I always have a few bottles in the house."

"Great, thanks."

Ylva took out a glass, opened the bottle, and poured some for Faye.

"Aren't you having any?"

Ylva shook her head.

"We've never talked about . . . well, what happened," she said.

She looked almost apologetic. Faye suddenly realized how much she hated her. She had slept with Faye's husband for months behind her back. And now she was standing here, in their fucking big house, cool and beautiful, if a little over-Botoxed, acting all sympathetic and imagining that everything could be forgiven. It would be more honest if she had continued to be as haughty and arrogant as she had been when she was standing naked in Faye's bedroom. Faye would have hated her less then.

Now all she wanted was to see her break apart in front of her eyes.

Ylva and Jack. They truly deserved each other. They deserved what was approaching on the horizon and would soon destroy their perfect life.

"There's no need," she said. "You and Jack are such a good match for each other. And things have turned out so well for all three of us."

She raised her glass.

"I'm very impressed with what you've managed to do with Revenge," Ylva said, sitting down in a large, flowery armchair.

A Josef Frank design from Svenskt Tenn. Jack had always loved their prints, but Faye couldn't help thinking they were better suited to retirees.

"Mm, thanks. And how are things going for you? Are you happy at Musify?"

"I'm actually going to leave. I . . . I've spent the last couple of years working part-time. Jack's work needs so much support, all the entertaining, this house, Julienne . . . well, you know."

Ylva waved one hand, but didn't look Faye in the eye. And Faye wondered how much time Julienne took up during the few hours each month that she was with them. But all she said was, "Oh?"

"We . . . well, er, Julienne's going to have a little brother or sister. And you know what Jack's like, he'd rather I stayed at home. I'm looking forward to it, because I haven't got a family of my own."

Faye stared at her. She had been wondering when this day would come. Had dreaded it. Even so, nothing could have prepared her for the kick in the solar plexus that the news delivered. But at the same time she realized that the end was fast approaching for Ylva. Part of Faye felt sorry for her, part of her wanted to punch her.

"That's great news. Congratulations."

Faye arranged her features into what she hoped looked like a smile, though her guts were twisting so badly that she wanted to bend double with pain.

Ylva put her hands on her nonexistent bulge and beamed at her. Faye returned the smile and took a large slurp of wine. Memories of the abortion forced their way into her head. Jack's cold indifference. And Julienne's birth. The hundreds of unreturned calls and texts to Jack, while she, immersed in panic and pain, gave birth to their daughter.

She looked out of the window. The garden was full of staff frantically preparing for the arrival of the party guests.

"When are you due?" she asked.

"Six months."

Ylva lit up when she saw Jack walking toward them. He poured himself a whiskey at the bar and sat down in the other armchair, some distance from Ylva, where he had a clear view of Faye's cleavage.

Ylva noticed.

"Is everything ready?" she asked. Her voice sounded tight.

"Pretty much. The other children will be here in forty-five minutes."

He held his watch up toward her. An Audemars Piguet, worth around half a million kronor. Not a Rolex, which Jack presumably considered too mainstream. Everyone had a Rolex these days. Anyone who was anyone had an Audemars Piguet. Or a Patek Philippe.

"The pop stars are coming at three. Don't say anything to Julienne, she doesn't know."

He nodded in Faye's direction.

"How's business?"

"Great, thanks. And things seem to be going well for you too. The stock-market launch is exciting."

"It's a lot of work. But it's worth it after everything I've been through."

Faye smiled at him and Ylva.

"Congratulations on the baby. Ylva told me."

She changed position, so that he could see a bit farther up her skirt. She wasn't wearing any underwear, she didn't want any lines spoiling her skin-tight dress.

Jack watched her movements.

He raised his glass to her. The crotch of his trousers looked tight.

"Mm, yes, great," Jack said in a thick voice.

He gave a strained smile. His eyes looked unfocused.

Ylva cleared her throat. "Jack's been a bit unsure. There's so much going on with his work right now, and you of all people know how seriously Jack takes being a parent."

Was that how she used to sound? *Jack thinks, Jack wants, Jack believes*? Christ, she must have been unbearable. And now Ylva was sitting there, a younger version of her, with her hands on her stomach and a stupid grin on her face, praising the same man. Blinded by love and admiration. And dependency.

Jack preferred his women like that, Faye realized now. But that only made her despise Ylva even more. Had she felt any qualms at all? During any of those no doubt countless times she had had sex with Jack at the office, in their home, in her own apartment while Faye sat at home waiting? Probably. But she had been blinded by her love for Jack. And looked down on his pathetic wife, drifting about the house all day with no career, no ambitions. No doubt Ylva thought herself far superior in comparison. And had concluded that Faye was unworthy of a man like Jack.

Faye drank the last of her wine. She looked sadly down at the bottom of the narrow glass. She didn't feel quite bold enough to go and refill her own glass at the bar.

"I think I might go and have a nap before everything gets going," Ylva said, and stood up with a last look at Faye.

A silence fell after she left the room. After a while Jack cleared his throat.

"You're looking incredible," he said quietly.

His eyes didn't leave her cleavage. She let him look at her. Tucked her hair back to uncover her neck and collarbone, no longer hidden under a protective layer of fat. She would be lying if she said she didn't enjoy him looking at her, but the fact that her body persisted in reacting to him didn't mean that he had control over her.

Part of her wanted to show him that she no longer needed him. Make him understand that she no longer saw herself in terms of him. But she mustn't give in to the temptation to show her superiority. Partly because she needed to get him to fall for her again, which would never happen if he didn't think he could control her. Partly because he—no matter how badly he had treated her—was still Jack. However much she might try to deny it, his words meant something to her.

"Thanks," she replied coolly.

His gaze moved down to her cleavage again and lingered there. She took out her mobile and pretended to send a text.

"Do you know, I still dream about you sometimes?" he said as he got up from the armchair, went over to the bar and fetched the bottles of cava and whiskey, and refilled both their glasses.

He sat down on the sofa next to her, coming far too close.

The smell of Jack's aftershave confused her. It was the same scent he had worn in Barcelona. She took a deep breath, told herself that she mustn't let herself be taken in by her memories, all the things she had believed to be true but which had turned out to be lies. She was going to have to reject his advances but maintain his interest. A precarious balancing act. Jack liked the chase. That was how she had caught him the first time, a long time ago in another life. She turned toward him and looked directly into those beautiful blue eyes, which were now focused solely on her.

Men like Jack always wanted what wasn't theirs. That was why he had been unfaithful to her. That was why she knew he was going to be unfaithful to Ylva as well, if he hadn't been already. That was why he would be unfaithful to any woman in his life for as long as he lived.

Hearing the sound of footsteps behind them, Faye and Jack turned at the same time and saw Julienne approaching. She was wearing a beautiful pink dress. She had makeup on, and it made her look very grown-up. Faye wasn't altogether sure what she thought about that.

"You look beautiful, darling," she said anyway. "Like a princess."

Julienne did a twirl.

"Jessica says I could be a model," she said.

"Jessica?" Faye repeated, searching her memory for the names of her daughter's school friends.

"The makeup artist," Jack said when he saw her confusion. "And she's right about that."

He swept Julienne up onto his lap and Faye felt a moment's doubt. As Julienne sat between them on the sofa it felt briefly as if they were a family again. It made Faye feel a bit lost, disoriented.

She reached for her glass and raised it to her lips as Jack stared greedily at her.

. . .

The sound of shrill voices could be heard in the garden. The girls had started to arrive. Luxury car after luxury car pulled up in the drive and out tumbled a deluge of six- and seven-year-olds in party outfits. Faye stayed in the background while Jack and Ylva chatted with the parents. The pile of presents on the table grew. Most of them were wrapped in white paper bearing the logo of NK department store. The magician got up onstage and the girls cheered. Waiters brought nibbles and fizzy drinks for the girls in their party dresses, who were sitting at round tables in the party tent, like some fancy evening reception. Julienne clapped her hands happily. A famous children's television presenter was acting as emcee, introducing the acts.

When Sean and Ville, last to perform, appeared onstage, the shrieks of excitement were deafening. Faye realized that this was her chance to scan the key logger. The girls left their tables and crowded around the edge of the stage. Ylva and Jack seemed completely absorbed in the girls' reactions as their idols appeared. She discreetly left the tent, went inside the house and upstairs to Jack's study. He still had the same desk he'd had when they were together, the one that once belonged to Ingmar Bergman. She felt a pang of nostalgia for the room in the tower. Its majestic stillness, hovering above the city, a memory from a distant time. She shook off the feeling and forced herself to focus. Those few moments on the sofa with Jack and Julienne had knocked her off balance. She couldn't afford that.

She put her handbag down on the desk and leaned over the computer. Beside the screen were two framed photographs. A black-and-white Polaroid picture of Ylva that must have been taken several years ago. She was staring seriously at the camera, her lips slightly parted. Fucking the camera, as Chris would have said. The other picture was of Jack, Ylva, and Julienne in a restaurant. Ylva and Julienne were wearing matching dresses. They looked like a happy little family. All three of them were laughing.

Faye took a deep breath. It was only an illusion, a façade that Jack had created. Nothing more.

She moved the mouse and the computer came to life, and she typed in Jack's old password. Held her breath. Good, he hadn't changed that one. An oversized picture of Jack and Ylva appeared. They were embracing on a Jet Ski. She forced herself to stop staring at the image, inserted the USB she was holding, and did what Nima had told her.

It took her a matter of seconds to find the hidden file that had logged his activity, and she clicked to transfer it to the memory stick. Then she went into My Documents and transferred the files she found there, even though she didn't anticipate finding anything useful in them.

She heard a scraping sound from the corridor outside. She quickly put the computer back into sleep mode and looked around desperately for somewhere to hide, but before she had time to do anything the door swung open. She turned around.

Jack was standing in the doorway. The expression on his face switched quickly from surprise to suspicion.

Faye thought quickly. She smiled at Jack. Submissively. Apologetically.

"I . . . I just wanted to see how you'd furnished your study. You know I always loved this desk. I suppose I was curious to know if you'd kept it."

He processed the information. Appeared to conclude that she was the same naïve, pathetic creature she had always been.

"Why?"

"Oh, this is so silly," she said, looking down at the floor. "Sorry, I know I shouldn't be in here, this is your home, it's not right, but I got a bit nostalgic . . ."

She took a step toward the door but when she was about to pass him he grabbed hold of her wrist. She almost dropped the USB stick from her hand.

"Why did you want to see how I'd furnished my study?" he asked with a smile as he pulled her toward him.

She smelled that familiar scent again. His hard penis pressed against her hip and against her will she felt herself getting wet.

"Do you miss me? Is that what this nostalgia of yours is all about?" Jack whispered hoarsely in her ear.

"Jack, stop it," she murmured.

But he ignored her protests. His eyes were blazing. He didn't like it when she objected. The old Faye had never said no, was more likely to beg and plead for him to touch her, to notice her.

His voice became scornful but he didn't let go of her.

"So little Faye has had her tits done to get more attention in bars. Have you missed getting fucked by a real man? Is that why you've come here, begging to be fucked? I've heard all about the way you've been behaving. Going home with one man after the other. No, not men. Boys. How many have you had sex with since we split up, Faye? Have any of their cocks been bigger than mine? I bet you've had more than one at a time as well."

His own words were making him pant, his cock grew harder against her hip, pressing against her. Faye's body responded, and she let it, so that she could protect the USB stick. She didn't protest when he unzipped her dress and pulled it down to her waist. He tore her bra off. Ran his fingers over her breasts. Squeezed them hard. They had healed well, but she didn't have any feeling in the scar tissue, so his touch felt rather odd.

"Little Faye, who just wants to be fucked."

Jack turned her around. Grabbed the hem of her dress and hoisted it up over her hips. Undid his trousers. He pushed her forward, over the desk that once belonged to Ingmar Bergman, and pressed into her. She gasped. Felt invaded.

"You like that, don't you?" he snarled. "Being fucked from behind like some horny secretary. You might be a CEO now, but you still like getting fucked like a whore. Is this what they do to you, Faye? Do they take you like this? Those young guys? Do they turn you around and fuck you from behind?"

He was panting harder now, and kicked her legs farther apart so he could push deeper, pressing her down on the desk with his right hand coiled hard in her hair.

His movements grew rougher. Faye held onto the desk with the hand that wasn't holding the USB stick. She groaned girlishly, she knew he liked that. With her left cheek pressed against the desk she stared at the photograph of Ylva's serious, black-and-white face.

He reached his climax. Faye felt a stab of pain as he pressed in farther. He groaned one last time, pulled out, took a step back, and fastened his trousers. She lay there for a few seconds before standing up and pulling her dress down.

"You've always been a first-class fuck," Jack said. "I've missed this."

He smiled at her, pointed at her breasts, which were still exposed, flushed, with large, swollen nipples.

"They've turned out really well, I like them."

Jack looked full of confidence. Order had been restored. He had conquered her, reclaimed what was his, at least for a while. She let him believe that.

Without letting go of the USB stick she slipped her arms back into the top half of the dress and pulled it up over her shoulders. Then she turned her back on Jack and held her hair up so he could fasten the zip. Seconds later he was gone.

When Faye walked back into the tent the girls in their expensive designer dresses were standing up and singing "Happy Birthday." Sean and Ville were leading the singing.

Ylva glanced over at her. She looked suspicious but resigned. Her skin had taken on a greenish pallor in the heat of the tent and she looked like she felt sick, her blond hair hanging limply. She pointed at Julienne, who was now wearing a sparkling crown.

When everyone in the tent had given three cheers Jack appeared beside Ylva, kissed her on the cheek, and put his arm around her. Ylva relaxed. Faye couldn't hold back a smirk. She could feel Jack's semen slowly trickling out of her, down the inside of her thighs.

FJÄLLBACKA—THEN

MOM WAS WHIMPERING down in the kitchen but I couldn't get up from my bed, couldn't stop Dad's blows from hitting their target. Instead I let the darkness envelop all my anxiety, shut out all my fear.

Autumn would soon be here and Dad would do worse things to Mom. To me and Sebastian. It felt like the stormy autumns never ended, with Dad like a raging animal trapped in a cage with his prey. We all circled around one another: a small, isolated unit in a small, isolated town.

Sometimes I dreamed that someone would come and save us. Everyone knew, after all. Even if they had no idea how bad it was, they knew enough. Why didn't anyone come and save us? Free us? But everyone sheepishly averted their gaze, blind to the bruises and cuts. None of the teachers ever said anything. None of the doctors at the clinic ever commented on the injuries Mom, Sebastian, and I showed up with. Last winter Mom had to get medical help eight times. A dislocated shoulder. A fractured wrist. A cracked jaw. No one questioned her stories about clumsy falls down cellar steps, the doors of kitchen cupboards suddenly flying open to attack her. Everyone shut their eyes.

What would this winter be like?

Mom's crying grew even louder when my door opened and closed. Sebastian padded over to my bed and curled up next to me. He fell asleep snuggled up beside me, like a dog seeking warmth. But I found no comfort in his presence. No one needed to tell me that the only person I could find comfort in was myself. I had found that out the hard way.

I was stronger than they were. Especially Sebastian.

Sebastian's breathing merged with the sound of the sea raging outside. The last of the summer visitors had left for the season. They all pretended not to hear the screams from our house, one of the few that was inhabited all year round. Presumably they didn't want anything unpleasant to disturb their summer holiday. In a way, I could understand that. But I couldn't help wondering if they ever spared a thought for the children in the next house when they shut their summer pleasures away and went back to their nice homes in Gothenburg. Probably not.

Once Faye had dropped Julienne off at school the next day, she shut herself away in her office, opened her laptop, and went through the file from the key logger. It took her ten minutes to find the new password for Jack's Gmail account: *venividivici3848*.

She hadn't told anyone about what had happened in his study. No matter how much she might have hated having to play the role of desperate little Faye, she hadn't had any choice. Jack mustn't be allowed to get suspicious, she'd had to go along with him to prevent him from finding the USB stick that had been scorching her hand. But she couldn't deny that she had enjoyed feeling Jack inside her again. That troubled her. Annoyed her. That was a chink in her armor that she couldn't afford.

Faye logged into his Gmail account, scrolled through the files, and found what she was looking for. She downloaded everything, calmly and methodically.

Everything she needed was there.

She spent the rest of the morning going through the text file in minute detail, tracking everything he'd been doing on his computer. His porn searches for "young girl," "teen," and "petite," banter with Henrik about the "slut" he'd had sex with in the office, and mockery of a female employee's weight. It could all come in useful one day.

Faye packed her new laptop away and told Kerstin she was going out. She went and sat in Starbucks at Stureplan and carried on looking through the documents. Compare was going to be put on the stock market on Tuesday the following week. That gave her plenty of time to work out a precise plan of how to use what she'd found. She'd probably be in a position to set everything in motion on Friday. Four days from now.

Her mobile buzzed. It was Jack. *Can't stop thinking how much fun we had. Do you want to meet up?* he wrote.

She considered how she should reply. Things had started to move faster than she had expected. She needed to keep him interested until it was time for the final step. She thought for a while longer, then tapped a quick message and pressed send.

. . .

Chris was drinking apple juice at a table on the upper floor of the Sture Bathhouse. The air was humid. Retirees wrapped in white bathrobes were eating two-hundred-kronor salads, all to the accompaniment of the water lapping in the pools below.

Faye pulled out the chair opposite her and sat down.

"Why did you want to meet here?" she asked.

Chris looked up in surprise.

"Oh, hi. I didn't see you. I don't know. The sound makes me feel calmer somehow. It's like being in a great big womb."

Faye looked at her as she hung her jacket on the back of the chair. There was a distant look in Chris's eyes.

"How are you feeling?"

"Today's a good day," she said. "But then I haven't had to go to the hospital. I'm having dinner with Johan tonight."

"What did he say when you told him?"

Chris looked down at the tabletop.

"I haven't told him. I . . . I can't do it. I can't lose him."

Her eyes filled with shame. And fear. That frightened Faye.

She had never seen Chris look ashamed before. Never seen her show any fear.

She took her friend's hand.

"Oh, sweetie, I understand. Would it be easier if I was there when you told him? Just . . . well, just in case."

Chris nodded slowly.

"Would you do that?"

"Of course I would, if it would make it easier for you."

"I hate to be a nuisance, but I feel so weak, so helpless. The few hours when I manage to be myself are so exhausting that all I can do when I'm not with Johan is sit around. Who'd have thought this was where I'd end up spending my last days. At the Sture Bathhouse."

And with that she smiled a real smile. A trace of the real Chris, Faye thought, and smiled back.

• • •

The school where Johan worked was a big red-brick building on Valhallavägen. A few boys and girls the same age as Julienne were hanging around the gates. They looked over as Faye and Chris got out of the taxi and walked into the schoolyard.

They entered a long corridor full of turquoise lockers. There was no one in sight.

"Do you know where he is?" Faye asked.

"No, but there should be some sort of lunch break now, shouldn't there?"

Faye looked at the time. Midday. At that moment the classroom doors ahead of them opened in a synchronized movement and the pupils streamed out. She grabbed a pimply teenager in a cap and padded jacket and asked if he knew where Johan the Swedish-language teacher was.

"Johan Sjölander," Chris added.

He shook his head and walked off.

They pushed up against the lockers to avoid being sent flying by a group of very noisy boys.

"Try calling him."

Chris put her mobile to her right ear and covered her left ear with the other hand. She turned away when he answered.

The corridor started to empty. Faye found being back in school unsettling. The height differences, the insecure, flitting eyes, the hierarchies. The tensions were all on the surface, ready to snap at the slightest provocation. Matilda had tried to move through corridors like this as invisibly as possible, but it had never worked. Everyone always knew who she was. Everyone knew what had happened.

Chris tapped her on the shoulder.

"He's meeting us outside."

"What did he say?"

"He seemed . . . surprised that I was here. And pleased."

She sounded nervous and excited at the same time. They followed the stream of pupils through a glass door, down the steps into the schoolyard again, and found a free bench close to some bushes.

"How are you feeling?" Faye asked.

"Nervous."

"It's going to be fine. Absolutely fine."

Chris nodded but didn't seem convinced. A door opened and a tall, thin man in jeans and a checked shirt came out. His blond hair was unkempt. He caught sight of them and headed in their direction with a broad smile on his lips. There was something very open, generous about him, Faye liked him immediately. He was nothing like the other men Faye had seen Chris with over the years. She took this as a definite plus. Chris had never been good at choosing men, but Faye had a feeling that Johan was very different.

"Chris," he said brightly. "Great to see you! What are you doing here?"

Chris leaped to her feet and hugged him. When they separated he turned to Faye.

"You must be the famous Faye. Lovely to meet you at last. I was starting to wonder if you were Chris's imaginary friend."

She shook his outstretched hand. He must have realized that their visit wasn't quite as cheerful as he had thought at first, because an anxious look appeared on his face.

"Is everything okay?" he asked.

"Perhaps we should sit down," Faye said, gesturing toward the bench.

Chris sat between them. She took a deep breath, hesitated, but Faye nudged her gently with her elbow. Chris glared at her, then took Johan's hand.

"Johan, there's something I need to tell you . . ." she began, and Faye nodded encouragingly. "I'm ill. I've got cancer. The sort it's hard to do anything about."

Her words came out quickly, and were almost unintelligible. But Johan's face revealed that he'd heard what she'd said. His mouth opened to say something, then closed again. He took a deep breath and nodded.

"I know," he said slowly.

"You do?" Faye and Chris exclaimed in unison.

"I saw the note about your chemotherapy appointment in your apartment."

"Why didn't you say?"

"Because . . . I thought it was up to you if you wanted to tell me or not. I assumed you would when you felt ready."

Chris wrapped her arms around him.

"And you . . . you don't want to leave me? If you did, I'd understand."

The fear in her eyes was so great that Faye broke into a cold sweat.

But Johan laughed and shook his head. A fractured, ragged laugh, but still a laugh.

"Hell, darling. It would take a hell of a lot more than cancer to make me leave you. I've never been with anyone who makes me as happy as you do."

"But I might die. I'm more likely to die than survive."

Johan nodded thoughtfully. "Yes, you might. And if you do, my ugly face will be the last thing you see."

Around them children were yelling and shouting, full of hope for the future, good and bad times alike ahead of them. Triumphs and mistakes. Chris ought to have plenty of mistakes left, she had always been world-class when it came to mistakes. She'd always said bad mistakes were what made life worth living.

Faye turned away so Chris wouldn't see her tears. From the corner of her eye she saw Chris lean against Johan as she explained the current situation. In spite of the terrible circumstances, it was the most beautiful conversation Faye had ever heard. And Chris smiled like a child whenever Johan so much as opened his mouth. Faye wondered how Jack would have reacted if she'd told him anything like this. Jack didn't like illness. Or weakness. He'd be gone before the end of the first sentence, on his way toward fresh adventures.

Faye got up to leave them alone but Johan asked her to stay. He turned to Chris.

"Okay, you've had your say, so now I want to say something that I've been holding back. And it's probably best if Faye stays, seeing as you might leave me after this, and then I'd need someone to give me a hug."

Chris looked worried, and Faye felt annoyed. Now wasn't the time to confess to any indiscretions or whatever else he was going to say. She got ready to drag Chris away from there.

But Johan put his hand in his pocket and pulled something out, then he got down on one knee in front of Chris and held both her hands. Something was glinting between his fingers, and Faye's heart started to thud. She glanced at Chris, who looked totally uncomprehending. Her anger faded as quickly as it had arisen, and she broke out in goose bumps all over. Johan only had eyes for Chris as he knelt there on the asphalt of the school-yard. Some of the children seemed to have realized something was going on, like dogs scenting a treat, and stopped to watch in small groups.

But in Johan's world there was no one but him and Chris. He cleared his throat. "Chris, you're the most wonderful person I've ever met, you're the kindest and smartest person I've ever encountered. I love you so, so much. Right from the very first time I saw you. If you hadn't followed me to Farsta I was planning to go back to the salon the next day, to get a Mohawk of my own, or God knows what. This ring . . ." He held out a sparkling engagement ring. "I bought this ring four days after we met. I've kept it on me ever since. I didn't want to look like a lunatic by getting it out too early, but for me there's never been any such thing as too early with you. So now I've kept hold of it for far too long. So I was wondering if you might consent to wear it on your finger? I guess what I'm asking is . . . will you marry me?"

The children around them started to whoop and cheer. A few let out wolf whistles. One girl yelled, "Come on, say yes! Mr. Sjölander's the best! Best teacher ever!"

Chris put her hands over her mouth and Johan looked suddenly nervous. Chris swallowed and held out her hand with tears streaming down her cheeks.

"Of course I will," she whispered. The schoolchildren cheered.

Johan grinned at them and gave them the thumbs-up, which prompted even louder cheering and applause until they slowly dispersed. He fumbled with the ring before he managed to slip it on to Chris's outstretched finger.

"I love you," she murmured, pulling him to his feet and kissing him.

Faye found a suitable café on Götgatan called Muggen, ordered coffee, opened her laptop, and connected to the Wi-Fi. She'd downloaded a VPN app to keep her IP address hidden and impossible to trace. She inserted the USB memory stick where she had arranged everything she had found in Jack's Gmail account, and looked through the material. She had organized it clearly and logically, a dream haul for any ambitious business reporter.

Faye had picked out a young journalist called Magdalena Jonsson at *Dagens Industri*. Faye had had her eye on her for a while. She was sharp and thorough, and she wrote well.

There's more if you're interested, she typed, and pressed send.

As simple as that. She was getting ready to leave when her inbox pinged.

Can we meet?

Faye thought for a moment. She was aware that reporters were careful to protect their sources, they were their most valuable assets. But at the same time they were only human. One loose word when they were drunk, a mislaid mobile, a confidential conversation with a boyfriend and everything would get out. She couldn't take the risk. Not yet.

No. Let me know if you'd like more.

The answer came instantly.

Okay, thanks! I need to get our experts to check the authenticity, so it might take a few days, but this is incredible—if it's true . . .

It is, she typed, then closed her laptop and left the café.

. . .

The front-page headline in *Dagens Industri* read: COMPARE CEO JACK ADELHEIM TOLD STAFF TO TARGET THE VULNERABLE AND ELDERLY. The article was accompanied by stills from the video Faye had sent Magdalena Jonsson.

Faye was drinking coffee at the island in the kitchen. The story of how Jack Adelheim, CEO of the recently IPOed Compare, encouraged his staff to lie to elderly customers to get their money was splashed across four pages. It included everything Faye had gathered from his emails and sent to Magdalena Jonsson, divided into juicy headlines. The most incriminating evidence was a video taken with a phone from the early days of Compare's rise that showed Jack instructing his staff at an internal sales conference in no uncertain terms to sell anything they could to "oldsters," using whatever means necessary. Results were the only thing that mattered. The video ran for ten minutes, ten minutes that completely destroyed Jack's moral credibility as a business leader. The film was the smoking gun that Faye had been hoping to find in his Gmail. The rest was merely the icing on the cake. The video alone would have been enough to sink Jack. And inflict serious damage on Compare. She had seen it before, and had been counting on the fact that he was arrogant enough to have saved it.

Now all she had to do was wait to see how much damage she had done. She was worried it wasn't going to be enough. The world was a cynical place. The media, the public, the business community—they were all very fickle. And self-interest was always the guiding principle. All she had been able to do was lay out the evidence.

Faye read on. Hungrily, greedily, full of schadenfreude. With a flutter of happiness in her chest at the realization that Jack was now the prey, the vulnerable one.

To her relief, the media were merciless. The angle *Dagens Industri* had taken was clear and consistent. Politicians, local councillors, relatives of the elderly customers who had been tricked—they all spoke out in the article. One of *DI*'s columnists called it the worst scandal of the past decade and declared that it was now impossible for Jack Adelheim to remain in his position. Faye read on eagerly. When she had finished she checked *Aftonbladet, Expressen,* and *Dagens Nyheter.* All three had the story as the lead article on their websites, with clips from the film. *Aftonbladet* even devoted its morning broadcast to a discussion of what the revelations might mean for Compare and its share value. They were competing with one another to seek out the harshest condemnation from the most heavyweight names. And the public joined in. How dare Jack? How dare Compare?

Faye tried to visualize Jack. What was he doing now? How would he react? Would he follow the advice of his critics and resign to save Compare and stop the share price from sinking any lower?

Maybe. If he felt sufficiently panicky, sufficiently skewered. With his background, he was more sensitive to public approbation than anything else. The heavy, damp burden of shame from his childhood might make him simply drop everything and run. That mustn't happen. That would go against everything she had planned. She had to encourage him to go into battle, to fight to the last to cling on. Massage his ego, tell him no one was better able to save and lead Compare than he was. She didn't think it would be particularly difficult. She knew exactly which buttons she needed to press.

She called Kerstin, who had gone in to the office early.

"Have you seen?"

"I'm reading it now. It's incredible. They're really going for it. Better than expected."

"I know. What . . . what do you think I should do?"

"Lie low. He'll come to you."

"You think so?"

"No, sweetheart, I *know*. In times of crisis we turn to people who can validate us. When Jack needs validation he comes to you. He'll ask for your advice. He's always needed you. He just hasn't had the sense to realize it."

"What's happened to the shares?"

Faye heard Kerstin tap at her computer.

"They're down from ninety-seven kronor to eighty-two since the market opened."

She cleared her throat. It was a big fall, but still a long way from her target. If they fell below fifty kronor she would instruct her stockbroker on the Isle of Man to buy every share he could get his hands on. That would probably be enough to give her a majority.

Jack and Henrik owned forty percent of Compare. They had needed a lot of investors at the start, and the investors had bought shares in the company. Jack and Henrik had made a big deal of the fact the people buying shares had the same vision for the business as them. But the fact that the two of them didn't have a majority made them vulnerable. As she had pointed out on many occasions. In vain.

"There's a way to go yet," she said.

"Don't worry. It's going to work. It might take a few days, but the more unhappy everyone gets with Jack, and the worse he handles it, the lower the share price will sink. All you have to do is persuade him to cling on, that it will all blow over."

"I'll try," Faye said.

A brief silence followed.

"When are you coming into the office?" Kerstin asked.

"I'm probably not coming in today, Chris needs me."

"Go to Chris," Kerstin said. "I'll hold the fort here."

. . .

Chris's doorbell echoed shrilly in the stairwell. Faye hadn't called ahead to say she'd be coming—she hardly ever did. Chris's door was always open for her, she still had her own key. She waited and listened. After a while she heard slow footsteps inside the apartment, the lock clicked, and the door swung open.

Chris looked tired. Her face was gray and she had big, dark bags under her eyes. When she saw it was Faye her face cracked into a weary smile.

"Oh, it's you. I thought it was a burglar."

"And yet you opened the door."

"I needed someone to take my frustration out on," Chris said as she bent down to unlock the white metal grille.

"Poor burglars. They wouldn't stand a chance. Have you eaten anything?"

"Not since yesterday. I haven't got any appetite, I don't even feel like drinking champagne. That gives you some idea of how bad it is. I was thinking of asking the hospital if I can take it intravenously instead."

Chris lay down on the sofa while Faye made coffee and looked through the fridge and pantry for something to force into her. All she could come up with were two crispbreads with cod roe. Chris took a few bites before pushing the plate away with a grimace.

"The cod roe is Johan's. I never liked it even when I was well."

She wiped her mouth with a napkin.

"Why didn't you say?" Faye said. "If you'd said you didn't like it I'd have gotten you something else."

Chris shrugged.

"The chemo seems to have killed my taste buds. I thought that might mean I could actually eat the stuff. But not even chemo can get my taste buds to accept it. I've tried telling Johan that it's horrible, but he refuses to listen."

"So what are your doctors saying?" Faye asked gently as she moved the plate.

"Do we have to talk about it?"

"No. But I'm worried."

Chris let out a deep sigh.

"It's not looking good, Faye. Not good at all, in fact."

The hairs on the back of Faye's neck stood up.

"What do you mean?"

"Exactly that. The treatment hasn't had any effect whatsoever. Well, apart from the fact that I feel sick the whole time, I keep throwing up and I've started to lose my hair. But at least I'm thin, so I don't have to go to the gym anymore."

"I don't know what to say."

Chris waved her hand dismissively.

"Can't we talk about something else? Act like you normally do. What's new?"

"You're not reading the papers anymore?"

Chris shook her head wearily. Faye went out into the hall, pulled the crumpled copy of *Dagens Industri* from her bag and returned with it. She put it down on Chris's lap.

After a quick glance at Faye, Chris opened the paper and leafed through the article.

Faye ate the rest of the crispbread while Chris read. She didn't share her friend's opinion of cod roe.

"This is incredible," Chris said, folding the paper. "Did you expect them to write this much?"

"No. And it gets better: the evening papers and *Dagens Nyheter* have joined in, along with the online media. There's pretty much a witch hunt on Facebook and social media."

"You must be delighted?"

"I don't want to count any chickens."

"You're more boring than me, and I'm the one who's dying! We need to celebrate this somehow. I wonder how quickly I can get hold of a drip full of cava?"

"There's no need, Chris. We can celebrate later, when it's over. When you're better." She forced herself to smile. "So how's life as a newly engaged woman?"

"Wonderful. Well, as wonderful as it can be when you're being sick three times an hour. Johan's brought me breakfast in bed every day."

"But you're not eating?"

"No, but he doesn't know that. And I haven't got the heart to tell him that if I ate it I'd be throwing up his lovely breakfast half an hour later."

"When's the wedding?"

"That's the problem. Johan wants to get married within a year and all that. I don't know what it is with young people today, they really are incredibly conservative. I don't think I can deal with that."

Faye refrained from pointing out that Johan, who was only five years younger than Chris, could hardly be described as young. She looked at Chris sternly instead.

"You need to tell him that," she said, in a stricter voice than she'd intended.

She didn't want Johan to put any pressure on her friend. Chris had time. She had to have time.

"The problem is that it might not happen otherwise. I've got some uninvited tumors that want to gate-crash the party."

"The treatment will help. It has to."

"We'll see," Chris said, and turned her face away from Faye. Soon after that she fell asleep.

Faye laid a blanket over her and patted her knees when she tucked her in. Then she crept quietly out of the apartment and locked it using her own key.

Faye felt deflated as she walked down the stairs. Chris had always been able to see the funny side of everything, but now she seemed to have resigned herself to dying.

The financial news on Swedish television was showing a downward graph to illustrate the collapse in Compare's share price during the day. Pictures of the entrance to Compare's head office on Blasieholmen were intercut with shots of the gates to the house on Lidingö. But no one had been able to get hold of Jack.

"Where could he be?" Kerstin murmured as she sat beside Faye, hunched toward the screen.

"He's probably locked away with frowning PR consultants who are trying to tell him how to deal with this."

"Will that do any good?"

"I doubt it. But the PR consultants will be able to send in some hefty invoices for all that wasted advice." She turned to look at Kerstin. "You went to see Ragnar today, didn't you? How was it?"

Kerstin shook her head. "You know I don't want to talk about him."

Faye nodded and did as Kerstin wanted. This time.

For every hour that Jack managed to evade the reporters, their frustration seemed to grow. When Julienne came into the living room, Faye discreetly changed the channel. She got ready to put her to bed, but Kerstin offered to do it instead. A special bond had grown up between Faye and Kerstin, with Julienne as the glue. These days Kerstin pretty much only used her apartment to sleep in, and Faye wouldn't have it any other way.

The sound of laughter was coming from Julienne's room and Faye smiled. She had Julienne and Kerstin in her life, couldn't she be happy with that? Did she have to crush Jack? Julienne had always worshipped her dad, and children needed both their parents. Even if Jack didn't always have time for his daughter, and even if Julienne sometimes cried before visits to her father. Faye knew that was natural for children with divorced parents. Eternal separation anxiety.

Faye honestly didn't know if Jack loved Julienne. He had always treated her like a princess, but sometimes it felt like she was primarily a beautiful accessory that he enjoyed showing off to the world. And a father's love wasn't necessarily unconditional, she was all too aware of that.

Faye allowed herself brief moments of doubt, but she knew there was no alternative. Jack had ground her down, humiliated and betrayed her. He had discarded the family that she had sacrificed everything for. Men had held power over her throughout her whole life. She couldn't let Jack get away with it.

She decided to skip the rest of the news bulletin and went out into the kitchen to get a glass of wine. When she returned to the living room and was reaching for her iPad, she got a message from Jack.

I need to see you, he wrote.

Where? she replied.

A minute passed before her mobile buzzed again.

Where we first met.

· · ·

Rain was falling steadily as Faye shut the door of the taxi and ran at a crouch to the door of the N'See Bar. There were three guys in their twenties nursing beers at one table. Jack was sitting right at the back. The same place she and Chris had been sitting sixteen years before.

Jack was sitting with his head bowed over his half-drunk beer.

The bartender nodded to her.

"Two beers, please." She guessed Jack's glass would soon be empty.

The bartender filled two glasses and Faye carried them over to Jack's table.

He looked up and she put one of the glasses down in front of him.

"Hi," he said with a sad smile.

He looked vulnerable. Small.

His dark hair was brushed back and one wet strand was hanging forlornly over his cheek. He was pale, his skin looked puffy. His eyes bloodshot. She had never seen him this dejected. Faye had to suppress a first instinct to put her arms around him, comfort him, tell him everything was going to be all right.

"How are you?"

He shook his head slowly.

"This . . . this is the worst thing that's ever happened to me."

Her last ounce of sympathy vanished when she realized just how sorry he felt for himself. He was absolutely wallowing in it. He hadn't spared a thought for how it must have felt for her to lose everything. Become a social pariah, isolated, rejected. She had experienced everything he was going through now and more besides. And he hadn't felt the slightest sympathy for her then. So why should she be any different?

But in order to get what she wanted she had to give him what he wanted.

"What are you going to do?" She made her voice soft.

"I don't know," he said quietly.

She wondered how to phrase it. He mustn't resign, because then everything would have been in vain. That would leave him as just another businessman who had turned out to be greedy. And there were plenty of those in the world. Jack's downfall needed to be far more spectacular than that.

She had to persuade him to stay on. She wanted him to have a long way to fall. And it was as if her mere presence made him more ready to fight. He looked at her with a fresh glint in his eye. In the background Carly Simon's "Coming Around Again" was playing. She'd always liked that song. That said, her own heart had felt smaller since Jack broke it. As if it had shrunk.

"That all happened over ten years ago," Jack said. "How can it even be news? I was young and hungry back then. You do what you have to, it's business. The only thing people care about is results. No one gives a damn about how you do it. But now? It must be envy. People hate anyone who's successful. They hate people like you and me, Faye. Because we're smarter than they are."

Faye didn't answer. Suddenly they were "we" again. And after all those years of telling her how stupid she was, here he was talking about how intelligent she was. Rage washed over her and she gripped her glass tightly. Jack went on with his tirade. His voice was whiny and he had flushes of red on his neck. She'd never seen that before.

"You can't get rich in this fucking country if you don't help yourself. Maybe our methods were a bit rough, but they weren't fucking illegal. Retirees ought to know how to hold on to their own money, I mean, we're talking about adults here. Responsible for their own decisions. In this fucking country everything's always someone else's fault, someone else has to clean up the mess, someone else has to take the blame. Then the witch hunt starts, even though the only thing you've done is build up a successful business, provided jobs for a shitload of people, and contributed to the country's GDP."

He shook his head in frustration.

"The big mistake is if you dare to make a few kronor for yourself, because that pisses people off. Communist bastards. Like fuck am I going to let them destroy everything I've built up!"

He gulped down the last of the beer Faye had bought him and

waved at the bartender for another. Faye looked at him. It was as if she was seeing him for the first time. He was behaving like a whiny child who'd had his favorite toy taken away. He wouldn't last long if he behaved like this in front of the media.

She had to find a way to calm him down. He was going to be roasted slowly, not burned out quickly like a firework.

"Jack," she said softly, putting her hand on top of his. "I agree with everything you're saying. But you need to present it in a less aggressive way. Tell them you were young, that you're different now. Maybe go to one of your old people's homes and spend a day doing volunteer work. Invite the media. Win back people's trust."

She imagined Jack visiting an old people's home. The reporters would see through him, obviously, and it would make the whole thing far worse. He'd be slaughtered.

But it would draw things out.

"Yes, maybe."

Jack looked thoughtful. The red blotches on his neck started to fade.

"Think about it, anyway. What is the board saying? Henrik?"

"Naturally they're worried. But I've explained that this will blow over. No one wants me to resign, there's no one better suited than me."

He stretched. Despite everything, he remained convinced of his own superiority, his invincibility. She resisted the urge to drive her Jimmy Choo heels into his Gucci shoes. Ugly Gucci shoes at that. He used to dress better when she was his wardrobe adviser. Ylva seemed to want Jack to dress like a Russian oligarch. For each year with Ylva he became less coordinated and more covered in labels.

"No, of course not," Faye said sweetly. "It's good that they appreciate that."

He met her gaze.

"I . . . I'm pleased you had time to meet me. I know I wasn't always easy to live with. What happened with Ylva . . . that's just the sort of thing that happens, the sort of thing you can't help . . ."

He was starting to get a bit drunk, and seemed to be having difficulty focusing.

"She doesn't understand me the way you do. No one does. No one ever has. I don't know what I was thinking . . ."

Faye looked down at their interwoven hands.

"I've grown up, Faye, I'm more mature. I don't think I was ready. But now I realize that I made a mistake. It didn't mean anything, not really. I just wanted . . . everything."

His voice was pathetic and pleading. He was slurring notice-ably. He was stroking the back of her hand with his thumb, and it took all of Faye's self-control not to snatch her hand away. She was so angry that there was a rushing sound in her ears. Why had she never realized how weak he was before now? Why had she refused to see it? And only seen what she wanted to see, filling in the gaps for herself? As if Jack was a huge paint-by-numbers project. An unfinished one.

"Try not to think about that," she said in a low voice. "It is what it is. The most important thing right now is for you to get through this."

He looked around.

"It looks the same as it did when we met here that first time. Do you remember?" His face brightened.

"Of course I do," she said. "I was sitting where you are now, Chris was sitting here."

Jack nodded. "Imagine if we'd known about all the things we'd go through, the way everything would turn out. I was crazy about you. God, those were the days. Everything was so . . ."

". . . uncomplicated," she concluded.

Anger was still roaring in her ears. Shutting out everything except Jack's saccharine, maudlin voice.

"Yes. Exactly. Uncomplicated."

A short silence followed, then she cleared her throat.

"What are you going to do?"

"I'm going to fight," Jack said. "I'm going to get through this."

He squeezed her hand one last time.

"Thanks."

"Don't mention it," Faye said. She only hoped Jack hadn't noticed the bitter undertone.

Three days had passed and Compare's share price had dropped to seventy-three kronor. A number of senior business figures had spoken out to say that Jack's position was becoming untenable. Shareholders were starting to sell their stocks. Jack's invitations to speak at two seminars were withdrawn. He had given an interview, not to *Dagens Industri*—the paper which had first released the video—but to *Dagens Nyheter*. Talking about how highly he valued the older generation. That the whole thing was a complete misunderstanding, the video had been taken out of context, it was so many years ago, it was all a failure of communication, someone was trying to sabotage a successful business.

Excuses, excuses, excuses.

The public hated it. And they hated Jack. The National Retirees' Association said it was impossible to understand why he hadn't accepted responsibility and left the company.

But the board declared that they still had confidence in him. As worried as they might be about what would happen if Jack remained CEO, they were even more frightened at the prospect of the company having to survive without him. Jack *was* Compare. Which was exactly what Faye had been counting on, knowing that would lead to his downfall.

While Chris was having one of her chemo sessions, Faye called her broker in the Isle of Man and asked him to buy ten million kronor worth of shares in Compare. The share price stabilized somewhat when it became clear that not all investors had lost faith in the company. While she was buying up a slice of Compare, she was also giving Jack some breathing space. The calm in the eye of the storm. Before she made her next move.

FJÄLLBACKA—THEN

I PRETENDED TO BE ASLEEP when Sebastian got out of my bed. He moved away cautiously and swung his feet onto the floor. He picked up his socks from the floor and put them on while I kept my eyes closed.

I heard Sebastian open the fridge and cupboards, then pull out a kitchen chair, which scraped gently on the wooden floor. A sudden crash made me start and open my eyes. He must have dropped a china dish; in my mind's eye I could see the fragments and yogurt spread across the kitchen floor. And imagined Sebastian's panic.

I sat up in bed, aware of what was coming. Dad was a light sleeper. It was a Saturday, and he didn't want to be woken early. Mom and Dad's room was on the ground floor, next to Sebastian's. They had been fighting late into the night and Dad was bound to be exhausted now. I had lain awake listening to the screams and thuds while Sebastian slept soundly with his arm over my chest.

Dad rushed into the kitchen with a roar. I pulled my knees up, wrapped my arms around them, and the darkness began to move inside me. Sebastian's shrill screams came through the floor, then Mom's pleading voice. But I knew Mom wouldn't be able to stop Dad. He needed to vent his anger, needed to hit something, needed the satisfaction of something breaking.

When the screams fell silent I lay down again and pulled the covers over me. The side where Sebastian had been sleeping was still warm.

Faye tucked Chris into bed and settled down on her sofa for a while. She didn't want to leave yet. She got her laptop out and checked her latest work emails. Chris's labored breathing in the next room made it hard to concentrate, it hurt so much to hear how her friend was suffering. When she was halfway through her inbox her mobile buzzed. A newsflash from *Dagens Industri*. It read: "Jack Adelheim speaks out!"

Her pulse was thudding in her temples as Faye clicked to open the interview. It was longer than she had feared, ingratiating and in fact might as well have been labeled as an advertisement. Jack was allowed to direct the conversation, and was described exclusively in superlatives. The journalist laid out the questions for him like teed balls on a golf course.

Faye scrolled down to find the journalist's name. Maria Westerberg. In the photo byline she was standing close to Jack at the entrance to one of the city's smartest hotels. They were both smiling broadly at the camera. Faye looked closer at the picture. Jack and Maria were standing in front of a shiny mirrored wall and the picture editor had evidently missed one particular detail when the image was selected: Jack's hand was on Maria's backside.

Faye snorted. She wasn't about to let Jack regain the advantage just because he'd seduced a journalist. She reached for her mobile and called his number. He answered with renewed vigor and enthusiasm in his voice.

"Things have started to turn around. People are buying shares in Compare," he crowed. "I knew it would come to rights!"

His tone was triumphant. Some of his old self-assurance had snuck back in.

"That's great, Jack. Not that I was ever really worried," she whispered. "I'm proud of you."

She looked up at the ceiling as she crept out of Chris's living room. Johan would be back soon.

"I was wondering if you'd like to meet to celebrate?" she said, enjoying her own acting skills. She needed more ammunition to neutralize what he'd managed to achieve by having sex with Maria Westerberg.

"Sure," Jack said. "I'm at the office. But I can sneak out if you've got time?"

Faye went into Chris's bathroom, opened the cabinet where she knew she kept her sleeping pills, and took out a blister pack of Ambien. Chris would never notice or mind that a few pills had gone missing.

"Are you still there?" Jack said. "Hello? Did the line cut out?"

"Yes, I'm here. That sounds good. Shall we meet at the Grand?"

"In the bar?"

"No. The suite."

. . .

Faye had texted Kerstin, and she had promised to look after Julienne. They were going to play Minecraft, like they did every evening these days. Kerstin had started to become something of a virtuoso at it, and Faye had even caught her playing it at work.

No price was too high when it came to getting revenge on Jack, Faye had reminded herself on the way to the hotel. And now she was lying in the big double bed looking at her ex-husband, who was high on newfound self-confidence.

"Christ, I can't get enough of you," Jack panted, looking down at Faye. He was on the edge of the bed licking her breasts, nibbling them, nipping them. And she was enjoying it—not the sex, but the fact that he thought he was the one exploiting her.

She didn't feel the same weakness for Jack, the same desire as when they fucked in his study, on Ingmar Bergman's desk. That had been a dream, a fantasy of something that had probably never been real in the first place.

When he kissed her she felt sick from his bad breath. He'd started to dye his hair to cover up the gray, but that only made it look more and more like a knitted hat. She also suspected he was using Botox.

The thought made her as dry as tinder between her legs. Jack merely grunted, wet his hand with his tongue, and lubricated her enough for him to go on thrusting until he came. Faye faked a few half-hearted groans and he was happy to let himself be fooled by them. He wasn't the sort of man who was all that bothered if a woman orgasmed or not. Other than for the sake of his own ego. She lay there after he got off and started strutting around the suite naked.

She found herself comparing his body with the men she had slept with since he left her. He might train at the gym five times a week, but not even Jack Adelheim could stop the passage of time. His buttocks were no longer as pert, and weren't those the beginnings of man boobs? It was as if she'd gotten a new pair of glasses after living with impaired vision for far too many years.

Had he been projecting his own image of himself onto her? She found herself missing Robin's firm body. Or Mike's. Or Vincent's. Or the guy with the Nirvana T-shirt she'd gone home with from the Spy Bar last weekend. Any of the men who had replaced Jack in her bed.

Jack went into the bathroom, whistling. Faye quickly got up and pulled on her bra and panties. She reached for her black Chanel Boy Bag. Inside was the powder she had made from crushing three Ambien tablets in Chris's kitchen. While Jack showered she poured him a shot of whiskey and opened a half-bottle of cava for herself. In the bathroom he was singing "Love Me Tender." She tipped the powder into his glass. When he had finished showering she drew herself a bath.

"God, I'm exhausted," he said, stretching out on the bed like a contented cat.

"It's just the tension easing after everything you've been through. Have a whiskey and relax for a while," she said, then closed the bathroom door.

She sank into the warm water and waited. Drank two glasses of cava. Then she called out, "Jack?"

No answer. She got out and cautiously opened the bathroom door. Jack was lying asleep with his mouth open, completely naked. His penis looked almost ridiculous in its limp state. It lay nestled against his thigh like a white grub. Faye giggled. Jack snored loudly and she flinched. But he merely rolled onto his side and sank deeper into the pillow.

She put on a dressing gown, took out his laptop, sat down at the desk, logged in, and connected to the Wi-Fi. How many hours did she have? She had been waiting for an opportunity like this, having laid the foundations by gradually letting Jack get closer, turning herself into someone he desired again. She had wanted to make him lower his guard, let her in, trust her. And now, this evening, she had finally gotten the chance. And she was going to make the most of it.

She read his most recent emails but found nothing of interest, except that he seemed to be having an affair with a young student at the School of Economics.

Faye looked her up on Facebook and discovered that she was twenty years old. Faye looked at her pictures. She was pretty.

Blonde, but she looked dull. Would the press be interested in something like that? No, they'd never publish it. A mobile buzzed in the bedroom. She jumped to her feet, padded in, and looked at the mobile lying by Jack's side. It wasn't that one that had received a text. Jack must have two mobiles. Of course he did. Presumably he used the secret one for his affairs. She felt the pockets of his coat and found a white iPhone.

It needed a password to unlock it. Or a fingerprint. Faye carefully lifted Jack's index finger and pressed the button with it. A moment later she was in. She checked that she hadn't turned the sound on by mistake.

The message was from Henrik.

Where are you?

She didn't bother to reply and looked through his messages instead. Jack was evidently completely mad, and in all likelihood a sex addict. She was astonished. Some days he appeared to have two or three sexual encounters booked in. She couldn't understand how he had any time to run his business. Women sent him naked pictures and videos of themselves showering and masturbating. Jack replied with pictures of his penis. She felt oddly indifferent, even though some of the messages and pictures were over three years old and had obviously been sent while they were married. She couldn't hate him more than she already did. But she was disappointed. Nothing she'd found on his phone could help her. Swedish newspapers didn't publish infidelity scandals unless they were a matter of national security. In Britain, on the other hand, news of Jack's penis pictures would have made it onto every front cover. Just to be on the safe side, she got her own phone out and filmed as she scrolled though the pictures. She even captured the text exchanges, making sure it was clear whose phone it was. There were also a few selfies among the dick pics.

There was nothing in the notes section but short, cryptic reminders. Times and locations of meetings. She checked a few of them with the texts and discovered that they didn't match.

What sort of meetings were they? Probably business meetings. So why weren't they noted in the diary?

She was about to put the mobile down when she spotted the voice memo icon. Without any great expectations, she opened it and discovered that there were around thirty-five saved sound recordings in there. She clicked on one, assuming that it was going to be something to do with sex, but to her surprise heard two men talking. One of them was Jack, but she couldn't identify the other man. They seemed to be sitting in a parked car. The sound quality was excellent. They sounded relaxed, as if they were good friends.

Was Jack having sex with men too? Nothing would surprise her anymore.

No, this was something different. Something worse than the video clip of Jack that had done such damage to Compare's share price. She felt like bursting into laughter but stopped herself. She mustn't wake Jack until she'd copied everything.

To make sure she didn't leave any electronic evidence she played the clips through the speaker and recorded them on her own phone. When she checked the sound quality she could hear Jack's snoring faintly in the background. She spent the next hour checking through his laptop, without finding anything else. But she was happy.

It had been a surprisingly lousy fuck. She pondered whether he had always been a useless lover. If that was yet another thing she had been deceiving herself about. Unless perhaps she simply hadn't had enough to compare him to. She thought about the guy in the Nirvana T-shirt and felt herself getting wet. He had given her three orgasms. In a row.

Faye tapped in the code to get into Chris's building without having to think about it. Chris had been so insistent on her coming that Faye was feeling nervous.

She got into the elevator and tried to think about anything but Chris.

She had sent the audio files to the same journalist who published the first leak. The new revelations that the CEO of Compare had known about and tried to hush up two deaths in their care homes that were the result of negligence had sent shock waves through Sweden, far beyond the confines of the business community.

Compare's share price sank like a stone. The business press and evening tabloids found plenty of politicians and business leaders ready to say that Jack had to resign, along with a number of anonymous sources on the board of Compare.

Today the share price had sunk to sixty-three kronor.

The elevator stopped and Faye had to make herself open the door. Johan had taken a leave of absence from work to be able to care for Chris full-time, so Faye's visits had become more sporadic. She was worried about intruding, worried about disturbing what she had started to realize was the last time Chris and Johan would have together. And sometimes it felt like she simply couldn't deal with it. Every time she saw Chris so sick it was as if a part of her died. When it came to Chris she wasn't the least bit brave. Just a cowardly shit who wanted to run away from the truth, from reality.

Johan opened the door.

"How are things?" Faye said.

Johan shrugged.

"It's . . . what can I say?"

"Do you want to pop out for a bit, get some fresh air?"

"Maybe. Chris wanted to talk to you on your own anyway."

Faye's stomach clenched.

When she walked into Chris's bedroom she had to stop herself from crying out. Chris was just skin and bones now, her ribs were sticking out, the skin of her shoulders stretched tight over her collarbones. Her eyes had sunk into their sockets, her cheeks were puffy, dry, and gray.

Outside life was carrying on as usual, buses driving this way and that, people arguing, loving, driving, getting married and divorced, but up in this loft apartment on Nybrogatan Chris was lying in bed, slowly fading away.

Faye sat down on the chair beside the bed and gently took Chris's hand.

"It's all over for me," Chris said.

"Don't say that."

"Someone has to. And you and Johan ought to be doing something more useful with your time than looking after me. I'm dying."

Faye squeezed her hand.

"But your doctors . . . ?"

"Oh, they can't do anything. They've stopped my treatment."

They had told her the cancer had spread. Chris's body was riddled with tumors and the treatment wasn't having any effect on them, they just kept spreading.

There was nothing more they could do except ease her pain. They had suggested an end-of-life plan, including moving into a hospice. But Chris had refused, as she explained to Faye in a hoarse voice.

"Does Johan know?" she asked tentatively.

"Not yet. I can't . . . that's why I asked you to come. I was wondering if you could tell him. I couldn't bear to see his face. I know I'm being a coward, but . . ."

"I'll do it," Faye said quickly. She couldn't handle another second of this discussion.

She patted Chris's hand softly, then rushed into the bathroom. Unable to hold back her feelings any longer, she wept quietly, curled up on the bathroom floor with her forehead pressed against the cold tiles.

She had no idea how long she lay there. She didn't get up until she heard Johan open the front door.

. . .

Faye and Johan were walking in silence along Nybrogatan. Faye had wanted some air, needed space to be able to talk to Johan. The walls in Chris's apartment felt like they were about to crush her.

They turned onto Karlavägen. She pointed at The Londoner.

"I think we're both going to need a drink."

She asked for two shots of vodka, and took a sip of hers as she headed toward the table where Johan was waiting. He was drumming his fingers on the table. His face looked taut.

She had to hold it together now, be the strong one.

"This . . . I don't know how to say this, Johan. The chemo's stopped working, the cancer's spread. They've stopped the treatment."

He nodded slowly.

"I know."

"You do?"

"My youngest brother's a doctor. An oncologist in Gothenburg. Chris had a copy of her notes in her bag. I copied them with my mobile and sent them to him. He helped me to understand what they said. I know it sounds terrible that I've been snooping like that, and I know it's her right to tell me as much as she wants, when she wants. But I . . . I couldn't bear not knowing . . . I can't help it, not when it comes to Chris. She's shutting me out when she doesn't need to."

Faye nodded. Put her hand on his. She understood exactly.

He looked up at her.

"I still want to marry her. I've booked a time in a church in two weeks. It was supposed to be a surprise."

Faye leaned back. She suddenly felt very uncomfortable. She thought she'd gotten to know Johan well by now, she liked him, and he didn't seem the sort, but she couldn't help herself, her own bitterness bled into her grief about Chris.

"If you're marrying her for her money," she said, leaning closer to him, "I'll kill you."

He flinched. Looked like he wasn't sure if she was joking.

"Understand? I'll kill you, with my bare hands."

She let him see a glimpse of the darkness she was constantly hiding, let it step forward for a moment.

"Why would I . . . ?" Johan was staring at her in shock.

"Because Chris is good for more than a hundred million, and I know what the scent of money can do to people. I've seen it. And I've seen what men can do. How ruthless they can be. I like you, Johan, I really do, you seem like a good man. But my best friend is going to die. The only person I've ever let get this close to me apart from Kerstin. And I'm not going to let anyone deceive or exploit her on her deathbed. So if there's any financial motive behind this decision to marry her before . . . before she dies . . . I suggest that you give up the whole idea of getting married and carry on playing the faithful fiancé with absolute conviction until . . ."

Faye took a sip of her vodka.

"But if your intentions are honorable, I'll help you arrange all the practicalities. And I'll be able to tell the difference. Don't make the mistake of underestimating me."

Johan met her gaze without being alarmed by her darkness. That made her feel calmer. Johan was genuine. He wasn't scared of her.

He slowly turned the glass in front of him. Eventually he said, "I like you. And I appreciate that you're looking out for her. I love Chris more than anyone I've ever met. That's my only motive. I want to be able to call her my wife."

They looked at each other.

"Good," Faye said, then drank a gulp of vodka and wiped her mouth with the back of her hand. "Let's get on with organizing the wedding of the century, then."

They drank a silent toast. But they both flinched at the chime of their glasses touching. For a fleeting moment it sounded almost like a bell tolling.

FJÄLLBACKA—THEN

THE DAY OF SEBASTIAN'S FUNERAL everyone got the day off school. Since his death, I had been left alone by the other kids. Too much had happened in too short a space of time. Shock lay like a blanket over the schoolyard, the classrooms, the metal lockers with their ugly, meaningless graffiti.

The church was full to bursting. Sebastian, who had never had any real friends, had suddenly filled a church. Several girls his age were crying and blowing their noses noisily. I wondered if they had even spoken to him.

Mom had chosen a white coffin. And yellow roses. The roses were pretty pointless, really. Sebastian never cared about that sort of thing. But I reasoned that stuff was purely for the people left behind. After all, Sebastian was lying cold and dead in the coffin. What did he care about anything now?

It was Dad who found him, hanged with a belt from the rail inside his closet. He yelled for Mom, then pulled Sebastian down and removed the belt from his neck. Then he shook him and screamed at him while Mom called for help.

It took a long time for the ambulance to arrive, but I knew it wouldn't make any difference if they got there quickly. Sebastian's lips were blue and his skin was white. I knew he was dead.

I could feel everyone staring at us as we sat in the front pew. Dad's suited arm was shaking against mine. Shaking with rage.

Because death was the only thing he couldn't control. The only thing he couldn't frighten into submission and obedience.

Death didn't give a damn about him, and that drove him mad as he sat there in the church staring at Sebastian's white coffin with the yellow roses Mom had chosen.

There was no coffee afterward. Who would we invite? None of the people who had packed the church to the rafters were our friends. Just vultures who were attracted to our grief and wanted to wallow in it.

Mom and I both knew that Dad would need to vent his anger when he got home. We'd sensed the fury within him for several weeks. Mom told me to go up to my room. I obeyed at first and went up the stairs. But at the top step I stopped and sat down. I leaned my cheek against the wooden post at the end of the banister and felt the cool white wood against my skin. From there I could see down into the kitchen. If they had turned around they would have been able to see me, but they just kept circling each other like two tigers in a cage. Dad with his head thrust forward, his fists clenching and unclenching. Mom with her head held high, wary, carefully watching every movement he made. Ready. Prepared.

When the first blow came she didn't try to dodge it. She didn't duck. Dad's fist hit her straight in the chin, making her head fly back, then bounce forward. Dad punched again. A light shower of blood sprayed from her mouth, peppering the white doors of the kitchen cupboards like an abstract painting. Something flew out of her mouth and skittered across the floor with a hard clatter. A tooth.

She fell to the floor but he went on hitting her. Over and over again.

I realized that Mom wasn't going to survive long in that house now that Sebastian was dead.

Two days later Compare's share price hit a new low. Faye was at a lunch meeting about a new collaboration between Revenge and the pop star Viola Gad—who was reeling from the shock of finding her husband in bed with an eighteen-year-old—when Kerstin texted: *49.95 kronor. Now!*

She put her cutlery down, apologized to Viola and her manager, and hurried off to the bathroom.

She locked the door and sat down on the toilet. Everything she had been fighting for was suddenly within reach. She had enough capital to buy fifty-one percent of the shares, take control of the board, and see to it that Jack got fired. It was a dizzying thought. She felt like yelling out loud. She called Steven, her Isle of Man stockbroker, and instructed him to buy every Compare share he could get his hands on. She told him to get in touch if he needed more money, and she'd transfer several million more from Revenge's account.

"No problem, boss. It will be yours before the end of the day," he said.

She waited another minute or so, then shook herself and went back to her table. Her pulse was racing. But as she sat down opposite Viola Gad at the table where the Taverna Brillo's famous whitefish roe pizza was waiting for her, none of the turmoil inside her was visible.

. . .

Faye walked across Stureplan, where the lunchtime rush was over and people were heading back to work. The air felt oppressively warm. She sat down on a bench, wondering how to spend the rest of the day. There wasn't much she could do while the process of acquiring Compare was underway. She called Chris but got no answer. She was probably resting. Johan wanted to organize the wedding himself, but had promised to get in touch if he needed help.

Her thoughts returned to the takeover. A man would have celebrated his success, his hard work, without feeling embarrassed, without having to apologize. She decided that was what she would do, so she sent a text to Robin, who she had thought she was finished with, asking him to meet her at Starbucks.

He wasn't far away, and they agreed to meet in fifteen minutes. No show of wounded male pride there. He knew what she wanted and wasn't particularly bothered that she hadn't been in touch for a while.

He had already ordered for them both by the time she walked into Starbucks.

"Great to see you. I didn't know if you wanted milk in your coffee," he said, gesturing toward the mug.

"We're not going to have coffee."

He laughed. His handsome face was open and cheerful and she found being in his presence oddly relaxing right now. He didn't need any explanations, there was no game playing, no subjects that had to be avoided, no excuses. He didn't require anything from life beyond his gym, food, water, and sex.

"No coffee?" His smile told her he understood what she meant.

"No, I don't want to drink coffee. I want to fuck you."

"Really?" he teased, but stood up at once. Like an obedient puppy.

"I've booked a room at Nobis."

He raised his eyebrows.

"We're treating ourselves today, then?" he said as he put his jacket on.

"I've just spent several million buying a company. I think I deserve it."

"I like you, you know that?"

Robin held the door open for her.

"Good. That'll make it easier to ask you to do the things I'm about to tell you to do."

"I'm your slave for the day."

"You're always my slave," Faye said with a smile.

Robin didn't protest.

Faye and Johan were sitting on either side of Chris's bed. Her chest was moving up and down, her face was ashen and the skin on her scalp looked tight. She was so small; she'd faded away so quickly.

Johan gestured toward the door. When they were out in the hallway he leaned back against the wall.

"I don't know what to do. She can't walk now. We're going to have to cancel the wedding."

"Out of the question."

"Really?"

"Absolutely. We'll do it here, at home. In the bedroom, if necessary. Chris is going to get married."

"But how . . . ?"

"We bring the reverend, makeup artist, and wedding dress here instead. There's no need to bother with any guests, apart from the most important ones. Chris doesn't like people much anyway."

She was fighting her own feelings. Suppressing the gales of grief raging through her. Chris had been strong for so long. She'd been like a big sister to Faye, had looked after her ever since she first arrived in Stockholm. Now it was time for Faye to step up. That was what sisters were for. Chris would get her wedding, and she would get her Johan.

"Tomorrow, two p.m.?" she said.

Johan swallowed several times.

"I'll call the people we want here, and the reverend. The wedding dress . . ."

"I'll pick it up on the way home this evening. And get hold of a makeup artist."

"What about food?"

"I'll sort it. Just make sure that you and Chris are ready to get married tomorrow. I'll be here first thing to help her get ready."

. . .

The next morning Faye was standing outside Chris's door with Kerstin. She took a deep breath and rang the bell. Johan opened the door, gave them both a hug, then stood aside.

"Everything's ready," he said. "Everyone's taken the day off, they understand that it has to happen like this if it's going to happen at all."

"How are you feeling?"

"I don't care if it's a big wedding or a tiny one. But before she . . . goes, I want to get married to her."

"Good. Then that's what we do."

He led them into the master bedroom.

Chris was sitting up in bed, propped up with pillows. In front of her was a tray of coffee, orange juice, and toast.

"How's the most beautiful bride in the world?" Faye asked, sitting down on the side of the bed.

"I know I wanted to be thin when I got married, but this might be taking it a bit far."

Faye couldn't bring herself to smile at the joke.

Chris looked up at Kerstin and Johan.

"Can you leave us alone for a minute?" she said. "I want to talk to my bridesmaid."

After they closed the door behind them Faye gently took hold of Chris's hand. It was so small and fragile, barely any bigger than Julienne's.

"I don't know what I'd have done without you," Chris said softly.

"Don't worry about that, weddings are always fun to organize, no matter what the circumstances."

"I don't just mean that, I mean everything. All these years, all the things we've done. All the shit we've been through together. Sure, there may have been the odd hiccup, with Jack and all that, but most of the time you've been the best friend anyone could ever wish for."

Faye couldn't hold back the tears.

"Do we . . . do we have to talk about this right now? You're getting married, after all."

"Yes, we do. I haven't got long. And I want to say this while my mind's still clear."

Faye nodded.

"I couldn't have asked for a better friend in life than you," Chris went on. "You bring out the best in me."

Faye brushed away the tears that were trickling nonstop down her cheeks. "You're the crack where the light gets in," she said. "The one Leonard Cohen sang about. I don't know . . . I have no idea how I'm going to manage without you."

"Oh, I'm not worried about that," Chris said. "I'm just so sorry I won't be able to join in."

"I slept with Robin again, by the way. Do you remember him? The guy I met when you forced me to go to Riche when I'd been feeling sorry for myself for far too long."

Chris burst out laughing. "See, you can manage fine without me."

She leaned back and took some deep breaths. The slightest movement seemed to exhaust her.

"Would you like me to leave you alone so you can get some rest?" Faye asked gently.

Chris shook her head. "No, not at all. I'm actually too weak to drink, but what the hell, it's my wedding day. In the bedside table you'll find a bottle of Jack Daniel's, let's have one last toast, just the two of us."

Faye leaned over and opened the cupboard, took out the bottle, unscrewed it, and passed the bottle to Chris.

"To us," Chris said, holding the bottle up. "And to the fact that I've never even come close to feeling bitter about it ending this way. How could I, when I've been able to live such a wonderful life?"

She drank a few sips.

"To you, Chris," Faye said. "The best, most beautiful sister a girl could have."

Chris blinked away some tears.

"I need to get myself sorted out, but first tell me how it's going with Jack."

"We've got fifty-one percent."

"So it's done?"

Faye nodded. "It's done."

Chris took hold of Faye's arms, her grip was surprisingly strong. "I love you so much."

"I love you too."

Chris swallowed several times. "I haven't got either of my parents here, and you mean the world to me, and even if it isn't a typical Swedish tradition, I was wondering if you . . . if you'd do me the honor of giving me away to Johan."

Faye wrapped her arms around Chris and hugged her as hard as she dared.

"Of course I will."

Faye looked out of the window, she could see people moving about on the street below. The city's nightlife had started to get going.

She turned back toward the screen again and went through the latest set of results. What was the best way to tell Jack he was being fired? And when? Jack was a liability to the company and needed to be gotten rid of. Part of her felt like letting Compare collapse, but there were a lot of employees to think about. She had already found a smart businessman who was prepared to buy all her shares at a knock-down price, on condition that the name was changed. That way Compare would still be history.

Despite all the scandals, Jack persisted in believing, with the obstinacy of a lunatic, that he could cling on regardless. That *he* was Compare. If only he knew what was coming.

• • •

It turned into a late night. On the way home Faye texted Kerstin and asked if she felt like coming over. They ended pretty much every evening with a glass of wine or two. They were probably borderline alcoholics, but told themselves they were only following the Mediterranean diet and that red wine every day was an integral part of that. Kerstin had said her grandmother used to have a large spoonful of whiskey every day, for a bad toe. After that they always joked that they needed a glass of red wine in each leg for the sake of their health.

"I can't help wondering how Jack's going to react when he finds out he's been fired," Faye called from the kitchen, where she was getting cheese and biscuits. A decent selection of cheeses was one of the essentials in her fridge.

Kerstin didn't answer, but Faye could hear her moving about in the living room. Faye put the cheese on a plate, added some grapes and digestive biscuits, and went out into the living room.

Kerstin was sitting on the sofa staring into space.

"What is it?"

Faye put the plate down. She sat down beside Kerstin and put her arm around her. She could feel the slender woman shaking.

"He . . . he . . ."

Kerstin couldn't get the words out, her teeth were chattering too much. Faye stroked her back as anxiety grabbed hold of her. Surely Kerstin wasn't sick as well? She couldn't bear to lose her too, not someone else, that would be unbearable. Sometimes she was so frightened of losing Chris that she could hardly breathe, even though the worst was yet to come.

"Ra . . . Ragnar . . ." Kerstin stammered.

Faye stiffened.

"Ragnar?"

"He . . . Things have changed. They called from the care home. He . . . his condition's improving. They think he might be able to come back home one day if things keep moving in the right direction." Kerstin laughed, a shrill, raw laugh. "The right direction! They actually said the 'right' direction! They have no idea that it's the wrong direction for me. How could they know that the useless lump they've been wiping shit and drool off is a hideous, sadistic bastard who'll make my life a misery if he ever comes home again? I wish I'd been brave enough, I wish I'd put a pillow over his face and smothered him while I still had the chance . . ."

Kerstin was rocking back and forth with her arms wrapped tightly around her. The scars on her back were visible through the thin fabric of her blouse.

The fury started as a warm glow in Faye's feet, then spread up through her body until it exploded in her head.

Kerstin was family to her and Julienne, she was their rock, their lifeline, their warm embrace. No one could be allowed to threaten that. No one could be allowed to threaten her.

Faye clutched Kerstin to her chest as she wept. The tears soaked up by her cashmere hoodie would soon dry. The darkness was moving inside Faye. There were no tears there.

The sun was shining, the sky was bright blue, people were laughing, talking, drinking coffee. The buses and metro were running as usual. But in a bed on the top floor of the Karolinska Hospital lay Faye's best friend, sustained by life-giving tubes and losing the fight she had been doomed to lose from the start.

Faye got out of the car outside the hospital only a few hours after she had last left it. During her visit the day before Chris had barely been able to speak, her voice had been so fragile, her eyes so tired, her body so weak. The wedding ring she had worn with such pride was far too big for her thin fingers. It fell onto the floor twice while Faye sat there telling her how much she loved her.

Faye had wept in the car on the way home, realizing that it would soon be over. And when Johan called an hour or so ago to say she should come straightaway, she rushed out of the apartment.

On arriving at the hospital, she hesitated in the entrance, wondering: How do you say goodbye to your best friend? How do you say goodbye to your sister? How the hell are you supposed to do that? She bought some cigarettes and a bar of chocolate and sat down on a bench. Some blue-clad nurses were eating lunch. Talking about their children. Two new parents were carefully carrying a baby toward the parking lot. They stopped every thirty feet, leaning over the stroller and smiling as they admired the little miracle.

Faye threw the pack away after two cigarettes, stuck the chocolate in her bag, and made her way to the elevator.

"Chris is going to die," she murmured to herself as the doors closed. "Chris is going to die."

The corridor was completely silent. Her footsteps echoed. She stopped outside room number eight and knocked before opening the door. Johan looked up as she walked in but didn't speak. He turned back toward Chris and stroked her hair.

Faye walked around the bed and stood next to him.

"There's not long left," he said. "She's not responsive at all now, she's in some sort of coma. It . . . she's never going to wake up again. I don't know what I'm going to do, how am I ever going . . . ?"

His face contorted. She pulled up a chair and sat down beside him.

"She's so small, so alone," he whispered, wiping his eyes.

Faye didn't know what to say. She just put her hand on top of Johan's and Chris's interwoven hands.

"At least she's not in any pain," Johan went on. The words came out jerkily. "What will they do with her when she's gone? I don't want her to be taken off to the basement like some dead animal and left there all on her own."

He fell silent.

Faye leaned back. Her chair creaked.

"Can I have a few minutes with her on my own?" she whispered.

Johan flinched. Then nodded.

He stood up, put his hand on her shoulder, then walked slowly out of the room. Carefully, as if she were worried about waking Chris, Faye moved to the chair he had been sitting on. The seat felt warm.

Faye leaned closer to Chris, her lips nudging her ear.

"It hurts so much, Chris," she said, fighting back tears. "It hurts so much that I'm going to get old without you. That all those dreams we had, of moving to the Mediterranean, opening a restaurant, sitting outside playing backgammon, getting blue-rinsed hair . . . that none of that's going to happen. Right now it feels like I'll never be happy again. But I promise you that I'll try. I know you'll be angry with me if I don't . . ."

She cleared her throat, breathed air into her lungs.

"What I want to say is that I'll never forget you. Being your friend for the past sixteen years has been the best thing that's ever happened to me. I'm sorry I've never told you the truth about who I am. About what I am. I was scared you wouldn't understand. I should have trusted you. I should have told you everything. But I'm going to tell you now, in case you can hear me . . ."

In a whisper she told Chris her secrets. About the accident, about Sebastian, about her mom and dad. About Matilda and the darkness. She didn't hold anything back.

When she had finished she stroked Chris's hair and touched her lips to her cheek. That was her last goodbye.

She fetched Johan. Then they sat in silence as life left Chris. Seven hours later she drew her last breath.

. . .

When Faye left Chris's room Johan was still sitting motionless with his forehead on his wife's cold hand. She took one of the big bouquets of flowers that had filled the room with her. She got in the car, googled an address, and started to drive. Her eyes were dry now. There were no tears left. She was empty, dried up. Her secrets were safe with Chris.

She parked under the shade of a large oak tree in the parking lot and walked toward the entrance. The door wasn't locked. She looked around warily. The lobby and corridor were empty.

She could hear voices from a room farther along the corridor, it sounded like the staff was on a coffee break.

She counted the doors. The third door on the right, Kerstin had said. Without asking why Faye wanted to know. She walked quickly toward it, pushed the door open firmly but silently, and stepped inside. She didn't feel scared. Just empty. She felt the loss of Chris as bluntly as if she'd had one of her arms amputated.

She had been hiding her face behind the bouquet of flowers in case anyone came into the corridor. She put it down on the chest of drawers to the side of the door. Yellow roses. Very apt. She knew yellow roses signified death, something their sender must not have been aware of.

She heard deep breathing from the bed. She crept toward the top end. The blinds were closed but faint light was filtering into the room. Ragnar looked weak. Pathetic. But Kerstin had told Faye enough about him for her not to be fooled. He was a bastard. A bastard who didn't deserve to live, not when Chris's body was growing cold in another hospital bed.

Faye reached carefully for a pillow lying a little way down the bed. The sound of loud laughter in the corridor made her start, but it soon faded away. The only sounds were Ragnar's breathing and the ticking of an old clock.

She looked around the room with the pillow in her hands. Impersonal. No photographs, no personal belongings. Sun-bleached walls and a tatty acrylic rug on the floor. The old man's smell hung in the air. That stale, slightly cloying smell of old people when they fell ill.

Slowly she raised the pillow and held it above Ragnar's face. She felt no uncertainty. No anxiety. He had reached the end of his time on earth. He was nothing but a lump of flesh, dead-weight, another evil man who had left women scarred and crying in his wake.

She leaned forward. Used her whole weight to press the pillow over his face, blocking his mouth and nose. Ragnar jerked a bit when he found he couldn't breathe. But there was no strength in his movements. Just some feeble twitching in his hands and feet. Faye barely had to exert herself in the end.

After a while he lay still. No more twitching. No movement. Faye held the pillow in place until she was quite certain Kerstin's husband was dead. Then she put the pillow down on the bed, picked up the bouquet of yellow roses, and crept cautiously out.

Only when she was in her car driving back to the city did her tears for Chris start to flow.

FJÄLLBACKA—THEN

I LOOKED AT THE FURROWS on the policeman's face. His expression was one of sympathy, but he wasn't seeing me, not the real me. He saw a gangly teenager who had lost her brother and now probably her mother as well. I could tell he wanted to put his hand on top of mine as we sat there at the kitchen table and was grateful that he didn't. I've never liked being touched by strangers.

I had called the police at five o'clock in the morning and they took Dad away an hour or so later. I was so tired I felt like laying my head on the tabletop and shutting my eyes.

"When did the noise stop?"

I forced myself to stay awake, to listen to his questions. To provide whatever answers I needed to.

"I don't know, sometime around three, maybe? I'm not sure, though."

"Why did you get up so early?"

I shrugged my shoulders.

"I always get up early. And I . . . I realized that something had happened . . . Mom would never leave the house as early as that."

He nodded seriously. Again with that look that told me he wanted to comfort me. I hoped he would continue to resist the urge.

I didn't need comforting. They had taken Dad away.

"We're still looking, but I'm afraid we're very concerned that something may have happened to your mom. There's some evidence to suggest that. And from what I understand, your dad has a history of . . . violence."

I had to make an effort not to laugh. Not because there was anything remotely funny about the situation, but because it was so absurd. *A history of violence.* Such a bloodless phrase, such a concise summary of the years of terror within these walls. *A history of violence.* Yes, that was one way of putting it.

I knew what they wanted, though, so I just nodded.

"There's still a chance that we might find her," the policeman said. "Unharmed."

And now it came. The hand on my hand. Sympathetic. Warm. How little he knew. How little he understood. I had to make a real effort not to snatch my hand away.

The weeks passed. The newspapers were told that Jack had been fired. The news that the company had a new owner who was promising to get to grips with things and conduct a thorough ethical review of the business meant that Compare's shares had risen to more normal levels again, while Jack sank ever deeper and seemed completely lost. It was as if time had suddenly decided to intervene in Jack's life: he aged, his hair turned gray quicker than he could dye it, and his movements became slower, wearier.

He tried to put a brave face on things. After all, he was still a multimillionaire. He assured the business press that he would soon be back. But he would call Faye at night, clearly drunk, babbling about the old days. About the people he had let down, about Chris, about all the sacrifices he'd made.

Faye managed to show sympathy but thought he was pathetic. She detested weakness, and he was the one who had taught her that. Jack's meltdown merely made it easier to crush him.

He broke off his friendship with Henrik because he believed his friend had betrayed him by remaining on the board of Compare. Neither Henrik, Jack, nor anyone else on the board had any idea that she was the new majority shareholder in Compare, because she only communicated with them via her British lawyers.

It was time to take the final step. It was Ylva's turn now.

Her tears for Chris were gone. It was strange how quickly things came to seem normal. She thought about her, missed her every day, every hour, but she had accepted the fact that she was gone. Accepted that nothing was going to bring Chris back.

Maybe Chris would have tried to stop her if she'd known what Faye was planning. Now she'd never know.

. . .

Jack was standing outside the door when Faye and Julienne came home with the groceries. When she texted that afternoon to ask if he'd like to come over he had accepted almost instantly.

"Hello, my darlings," Jack said, clumsily wrapping one arm around Julienne. "I thought you were two angels walking toward me."

"Flatterer," Faye said as he pecked her cheek.

Close up she could smell the drink on him.

He smiled dumbly at her.

"What have you got there, then?" He pointed at the bags.

"I thought I'd make my bolognese," she said.

"Great!" he exclaimed, taking the bags from her.

He slung Julienne's backpack over his shoulder and held the door open.

"How are you doing?" Faye asked as she unlocked the door to the apartment.

Jack was swaying slightly.

"Oh, fine."

"And Ylva? She must be due any day now? Are you looking forward to it?"

Faye knew he hated talking about Ylva.

"She's fine, I guess. She's gone to stay with her parents, so I'm footloose and fancy-free. Your text came at just the right time."

She started to unpack the bags on the island.

"You didn't say if you're looking forward to the baby's arrival."

"I think you know my feelings about that. I'll love the child, obviously, but I . . . I know who my family is. My real family."

She felt like hitting him, but instead took a deep breath and smiled coquettishly.

"So the grass wasn't greener on the other side?"

"No, that's one way of putting it."

"What are you going to do now?" she said as she started to brown the meat. "Now that you haven't got Compare?"

Jack opened the fridge, found a carrot, rinsed it, and stuck it in his mouth.

"No need to worry, people know what I'm capable of. By the way, that campaign you're running . . ."

"Oh?"

"I don't think that pop star's right for Revenge. I've had a look at your figures, and it seems to me . . ."

Her brain flared and her body tensed. Who did he think he was? But Jack didn't notice, he just kept going, coming out with one nugget of advice after the other.

"I'm sure you're right," she said once he had finished.

Breathe, she told herself. Maintain the façade. Stick to the plan.

When they sat down to eat Faye was struck by how unreal it all felt. They were sitting at the kitchen table talking in a way she used to dream about when they were married.

She had spent so many years hoping and longing for this.

"I've missed this dish, Faye," Jack said, helping himself to more. "No one makes bolognese like you."

He joked with Julienne and praised her for the things her teacher had said about her at the last parents' evening, telling her how proud he was of her.

Why couldn't we have had this, Jack? Faye wondered. Why couldn't you have been satisfied with us?

. . .

Julienne's eyes started to droop at half past nine. She protested at first when Jack picked her up, then let him carry her to her bedroom. When he returned he stood, looking slightly lost, between the sofa and the television.

"Well, I'd better get home."

"You can stay a bit longer, can't you?"

"Would you like me to?"

Faye shrugged and snuggled up against the arm of the sofa.

"It makes no difference to me. So if you've got other plans . . ."

He reacted to her nonchalance with the eagerness of a puppy.

"I'll stay," he said, and sat down. "Would you like more wine?"

"I'd love some," she said, pushing her glass across the table. "There's a bottle of whiskey, if you'd rather have that."

"In the kitchen?"

She nodded. Jack went out and she heard him rummaging about.

"In the cupboard above the freezer," Faye called.

Another door opened. A clink of bottles.

"This is a good one. Where did you get it?"

"I was given it by some foreign investors," she lied.

Robin had actually left it behind a few weeks ago when he stayed over. They had made love five or six times that night. Her crotch tingled at the memory.

When Jack returned to the sofa he sat down close to her, pulled her legs toward him, and laid her feet on his lap. He started to massage them. She closed her eyes as her feet warmed up.

"You know, it could be like this every night," Jack said after a while.

She shook her head.

"You'd get bored after a couple of weeks, Jack. Now go and turn the shower on instead of talking nonsense."

"The shower?"

"Yes, the shower. If we're going to have sex, I don't want you stinking of stale alcohol."

Jack's ears flushed red and Faye had to stifle a smile as he hurried off to the bathroom. While he showered Faye put her laptop on the shelf opposite the bed, and switched the camera on.

Jack was smiling when he came into the bedroom, but Faye felt nothing. Having sex with him was just a means to an end.

Afterward they lay panting side by side on the bed. His eyes twinkled hopefully.

"What do you say about me leaving Ylva and moving in here?"

"That's impossible, Jack."

"But you've forgiven me, haven't you?"

"The fact that I've forgiven you doesn't mean I want to live with you again."

"I could invest in Revenge, help you run everything. It's starting to get really big now, are you sure you can handle it? I mean, I've got far more experience of running a company than you have. There's a big difference between being an entrepreneur and setting up a company, and actually keeping it going. You've done a fantastic job, but I think it's probably time for you to let the professionals take over."

This little man, whom she had maneuvered out of his own company, believed he could still tell her what was best for her.

Faye forced herself to stay calm. To focus on the goal.

"I don't need any more investment," she said. "Don't worry about Revenge."

"I only want to protect you and Julienne. Look after you."

You should be worrying about protecting yourself, she thought. Keep an eye on what's happening behind your back. Sleep with one eye open. I've already crushed you. Now there's just Ylva left.

"It would be best if you left now, Jack," she said.

"Have I made you cross?"

Those puppy-dog eyes again, but they'd lost all their power.

"Not at all, but I've got an early meeting tomorrow and I don't want Julienne to see you here. You know it would only confuse her."

"It would do her good if we became a real family again."

"We were a family, Jack. The problem with you is that once you've got a family, you don't want it anymore. Go home to your pregnant girlfriend."

She turned her back on him and heard him gather his things and slink out.

When Jack had gone she took the computer down, looked through the recording, and picked out a scene in which Jack had his face between her legs. She made sure she was always waxed these days. Her breasts looked magnificent as she lay there groaning with pleasure. She took a few grainy screen-grabs where she couldn't be identified, set up an anonymous Gmail account, and sent three pictures to Ylva.

Your man knows how to satisfy a woman was all she wrote.

Faye was sitting in her office when Jack stormed in. His face was bright red and he was sweating profusely. He was shouting so loudly that he could be heard throughout the office, and curious heads started to peer around screens. Faye was smiling inside. Jack was so predictable.

"What the hell have you done?"

Saliva sprayed from his mouth as he yelled. She wasn't scared. It was a long time since she'd been scared of Jack. Or any man, come to that.

"Why the hell did you do that?"

"I don't know what you're referring to," she said, well aware that Jack wouldn't believe her.

But that was part of the game. She wanted him to know. That part of the charade was over now. Faye spun slowly back and forth on her office chair behind her beautiful desk. It was a designer piece by Arne Jacobsen, worth almost a hundred thousand kronor. Ingmar Bergman's moth-eaten old desk could fuck right off. Ingmar Bergman could fuck off too, for that matter. The male genius who surrounded himself with women to lord it over and put down. Such a fucking cliché.

Jack leaned over the desk. His palms left sweaty prints on the shiny surface. She didn't back down but moved her face closer to his. Looked at his puffy, tired face, smelled the stale wine and whiskey on his breath, and wondered what she had ever seen in him. He used to read Ulf Lundell's books when she first met him. She should have seen the warning signs right from the start.

"I don't know what you're up to, Faye. But I'm going to crush you. I'm going to take everything from you. You're a pathetic, crazy fucking bitch I picked up out of the gutter and turned into someone. Everyone's going to find out who you are and where you come from. I know more than you think, you fucking bitch!"

She felt his saliva on her face and slowly lifted her hand. She wiped it off with the back of her hand and from the corner of her eye saw two security guards approaching.

She jerked back.

"What are you doing?" she cried. "Jack, stop it! Help! Please, someone! Help me!"

When the guards rushed in she let out a loud sob and ran toward them. Jack stared at the men in Securitas uniforms, two guys in their twenties. For a moment it looked like he was going to take a swing at them. Then he took a deep breath, held his hands up disarmingly and fired off a broad smile.

"Just a bit of a misunderstanding. Nothing to worry about. A difference of opinion, that's all. I can find my own way out, I'm going now . . ."

He backed toward the door. Faye had retreated to her marketing director's office and was looking anxiously toward Jack as several of her staff gathered around her protectively. It couldn't have worked out better.

• • •

Faye was exhausted by the time she got home after Jack's scene in the office. The apartment was empty. Kerstin had picked Julienne up from school and they had gone on one of their endless museum visits.

Kerstin had been worried about Julienne recently. She had

gone from being open and bubbly to more and more withdrawn. Her teachers had said she tended to spend breaks on her own now. Faye was just as concerned as Kerstin. She recognized herself in Julienne, she had been a lone wolf too.

The letters from Faye's father were coming more and more frequently. She still wasn't opening them. She was only grateful that no one had discovered the connection between them. The case had drawn a lot of attention at the time, mostly because her father had been convicted, even though her mother's body had never been found. The court had decreed that there was enough evidence anyway. All the hospital records documenting her mother's injuries. The blood. The fact that all of her mom's personal belongings were still there. The verdict had been unanimous. A life sentence.

Faye poured a glass of wine, sat down in front of her computer, and opened her emails. Twenty new emails from Ylva. She deleted them all, she wasn't interested in anything she had to say. Faye opened the top drawer of her desk and took out the USB stick on which she had saved the key-logger file. It had served her well. She didn't know if she should save it as a memento or get rid of it.

As she was turning it around between her fingers it struck her that she had never checked the other folders she had copied on the off chance there'd be something useful in them, because it had turned out there was more than enough to compromise him. She inserted the stick into the computer and sipped the wine as the files appeared on screen. She clicked through them, but none of them caught her interest. Boring business documents, contracts, PowerPoint presentations. Boring, boring, boring. The last folder was entitled Household, and she clicked on it in spite of the uninteresting name. She realized what it contained with growing alarm, and the glass of Amarone fell from her hand.

She stared at the pieces on the floor. At the red stain spreading out. She knew she wasn't just going to have to crush Jack now, but make sure he was neutralized for good.

Faye let several days pass. Then she called Jack. She had a new plan now. She cried and begged for forgiveness. Even though she really felt like beating him to death, kicking his lifeless body, and spitting on his grave.

Jack fell for her weakness. He needed her submission, and she gave him what he needed.

Slowly she won his trust again. Jack wasn't a complicated man, and willingly let himself be taken in. She wished she had discovered that sooner.

Though she hadn't thought it would ever be necessary again, she allowed herself to be fucked by him. That was the hardest part. Trying to pretend she was enjoying it when her whole body felt sick with revulsion. When all she could see in her head were the pictures of what he had done.

Sometimes Jack cried in his sleep. His mobile lit up on the bedside table at regular intervals with Ylva's name on the screen; she hadn't thrown him out. Now she was the one begging and pleading. She would soon be giving birth to their daughter while Jack was sleeping with another woman. Just as he had done when Julienne was born.

Faye had managed to get a prescription for some more Ambien. While Jack was fast asleep she took out his laptop and conducted the necessary searches. Sometimes it felt like it was all too easy. But she knew that it would be far from easy. And that there would be a high price. Possibly too high. But she was who she was, and bearing in mind what Jack had done, no act of vengeance could be too brutal.

As darkness fell outside her bedroom she remembered the snowflakes falling outside the windows of the room in the tower. She remembered the feeling of floating. The feeling of being free and captive at the same time. Sometimes she missed the tower room. But she never missed the golden cage. Sometimes she thought about Alice, who was still trapped in hers. Of her own volition. But there were aspects of Alice's life that Henrik didn't know about. Such as the fact that Alice had been one of the investors in Revenge, and was now just as wealthy as he was. Or that Alice had asked for Robin's number, and met up with him once a week while Henrik thought she was at Pilates.

Faye didn't begrudge her that. If you were trapped in a gold cage, you needed the occasional distraction to make it bearable.

When dawn broke Faye watched as Jack slowly woke up, his head full of sleeping pills and whiskey.

"I'm going away on business next week," she said. "Could you help take care of Julienne?"

"Of course."

He smiled. Took the way she was looking at him as infatuation. But she was actually saying goodbye.

I PUT THE PHONE DOWN. The verdict had been announced and I was free. For the first time. I had never tasted that before, I didn't know what it felt like. But now it was as if my body was floating above the floor. I had never felt stronger.

I hadn't been allowed in court, they thought I was too young. But I could imagine Dad in front of me, sitting in the same suit he wore for Sebastian's funeral. His sweaty neck, the way he tugged at his shirt, uncomfortable, furious, captive in a way he had never been captive before. His imprisonment was my freedom.

A small part of me had been worried that they wouldn't find him guilty. That they wouldn't see the animal in him, just a pathetic, tragic little man. But the forensic evidence was over-whelming. Even without Mom's body.

He had been convicted, and he was going to be given a severe sentence.

I knew the whole town was delighted. Everyone had been fol-lowing the trial. Everyone had been horrified, they gossiped and whispered in the aisles of Eva's Groceries, standing in the square, stopping their cars and winding down the windows, lamenting and talking about the poor girl. I knew them all so well.

But I was no poor girl. I was stronger than all of them. I would have liked to stay in the house after Dad was arrested, but some-one decided I wasn't allowed to. In their eyes I was still a child. In the absence of any relatives or friends I was placed with an elderly couple who lived nearby. They let me go to the house as much as I liked, as long as I had dinner and slept at theirs.

The last few months had been nothing but one long wait. Everyone left me alone in school now. When I walked down the corridor they parted as if I were Moses approaching the Red Sea. They were fascinated by me, but avoided me. People only seemed to enjoy being close to sorrow and tragedy up to a certain limit. I had passed that limit a long time ago.

But now I was free at last. And he was going to rot in hell.

The rain was pouring down. Her eyes were stinging and her head throbbing. All Faye wanted was to get some sleep. She called Julienne's number twice, then Jack's. No answer. The hotel receptionist came over to tell her that the taxi was waiting. She thanked her, grabbed her suitcase, and started to tap in the number for the police.

"Emergency Operations Center."

"I want to report a missing person," she said.

"Okay," the woman at the other end said calmly. "Who's the missing person?"

"My seven-year-old daughter," Faye said with a catch in her voice.

"When were you last in touch with her?"

"Yesterday evening. I'm in a hotel in Västerås, I've been here on business. My ex-husband's looking after Julienne. I've been calling all morning but there's no answer."

"So you're not in the city?"

"No. Dear God, I don't know what to do."

"Is there any reason to think they may have gone off somewhere or otherwise be anywhere where they can't answer?"

"No. They're supposed to be at home. They were talking about maybe going to Skansen today. This really isn't like Jack."

"What's your name?"

"My name's Faye Adelheim. The apartment where they should be is in Östermalm, it's my apartment."

She gave the woman her address.

"We usually wait a few hours before filing an official report about a missing person."

"Please, I'm so horribly worried."

The voice at the other end softened slightly.

"It's really a bit too soon, but I'll ask a patrol to go over and check."

"Thanks, that would be great. Give them my mobile number so they can call me when they get there."

. . .

An hour and a half later the taxi turned off Odengatan and drove up Birger Jarlsgatan before turning onto Karlavägen.

There were two police cars parked in front of the door. A police officer was standing outside. She paid the driver, leaped out, and ran over to the policeman.

"I'm Faye," she said breathlessly. He looked at her seriously. "I don't understand, you said you'd found Jack. Why are you still here? And where's my daughter?"

"Can we go inside and talk?" he said, his eyes darting about.

"What do you mean? If you've spoken to Jack, then you must know where Julienne is?"

He tapped in the code and held the door open.

"Like I said, it's probably best if you come upstairs with me."

Faye followed him.

"Please, can you just tell me what's happened? Is Jack up there?"

The policeman held the elevator door open.

"Your ex-husband's up there," he said. "But your daughter's missing."

"But Jack must know where she is, surely? She's seven years

old, she can hardly have vanished on her own. He was responsible for her. She was with him. What does Jack say?"

"He says he can't remember anything."

"Can't remember anything?"

Her words bounced around the elevator.

The elevator stopped and they got out. The apartment door was open. Faye ran her hand over her face.

"We've found something that . . . there's blood in the hall."

"Blood. Oh, dear God . . ."

Faye stumbled and the policeman caught her and led her through the door. A white-clad forensics officer was crouched in the hall running some sort of instrument over the floor, where there was a patch of dark, congealed blood.

"Julienne?" she called out shrilly. "Julienne!"

Jack was sitting on a chair in the kitchen. Two police officers were speaking to him calmly. When Jack caught sight of Faye he started to get up but the officers stopped him. He sank back onto the chair.

"What's happened?" she cried. "Where is she, Jack? Where's Julienne?"

"I don't know," he said, sounding bewildered. "I woke up when the doorbell rang."

The policeman led her away.

"We're going to need something that belonged to your daughter."

Faye stared at him in confusion.

"What do you mean? What for?"

He led her gently but firmly away. She could hear footsteps and voices in the hall. More police officers had arrived.

"For identification purposes," he said. "Just in case."

She let out a gasp, then nodded.

"Such as?"

"Her toothbrush. Or a hairbrush?"

Faye nodded. Pointed toward the bathroom. The policeman took out a bag, pulled on a pair of thin disposable gloves, and led the way.

"That's hers."

He picked up the pink toothbrush with Elsa from *Frozen* on it and carefully put it in the bag. They got Julienne's hairbrush from her room. That too was pink, with Elsa on the back.

It had started to get dark outside the windows. Faye stood up when a policewoman came into the small room where she had been told to wait. She was tall and blond. Her hair was pulled up in a ponytail, and she had a friendly but focused look on her face.

"Is there any news?"

The policewoman shook her head.

"Please, sit down," she said, nodding toward the sofa. "My name is Yvonne Ingvarsson, I'm a police inspector."

Faye sat down and crossed her legs.

"I'm going to have to ask you a few questions, and I'd like you to answer them as carefully as you can."

"Of course."

"We still haven't found Julienne, but there are a number of things that we're concerned about. Extremely concerned."

Faye closed her eyes and swallowed.

"Is she . . . do you think something's happened to her?"

"We honestly don't know. But the blood in the hall is definitely human. Forensics are comparing it to the DNA on her toothbrush and hairbrush."

"Oh, God . . . I . . ."

"Your former husband, Jack, is unable to explain anything. His story doesn't make sense, to put it bluntly. He claims he can't remember what he was doing yesterday."

"But he couldn't possibly have harmed Julienne. You're wrong. Someone must have taken her, somehow. He loves her, there's no reason why he'd . . ."

"Who else could it be?"

She fell silent. The policewoman leaned forward and put her hand on her knee.

"According to his mobile phone and the satnav in his car, he went for a drive. At night."

"What do you mean?"

"He drove to Jönköping. And we've found traces of blood in the trunk of his car. We'll be comparing that with the blood found in the hall."

"Stop it . . . please, stop . . . I don't want to know." Faye shook her head.

"You need to be strong now, Faye. I know it's hard, but you're going to have to help us if we're to find Julienne."

She nodded slowly, and eventually looked up and met the policewoman's gaze.

"Our colleagues in Jönköping are examining the places Jack went last night. We've looked through both your computers, and I was wondering if you could explain what this is?"

Yvonne leafed through the file she had been holding on her lap and pulled out a sheet of paper. It was the email Faye had sent to Ylva. Faye opened her mouth to speak but Yvonne got there first.

"Is that you in the picture?"

She put the sheet of paper in Faye's hands. She cast a quick glance at it. Nodded.

"Yes, that's me."

"And you sent this to Jack's partner, Ylva Lehndorf?"

Faye nodded again.

"Why did you do that?"

"Because she was the one who took Jack away from me. I just wanted to . . ."

"Are you and Jack currently in a relationship?"

"What do you mean?"

"Have you and Jack slept with each other since you split up?"

"Yes. But not since he discovered I sent this to Ylva. Since then . . . he hates me."

"According to Jack, your relationship has continued."

"That's ridiculous. He stormed into my office, shouting and yelling at me a few weeks ago. The security guards had to throw him out. But our fight was about us, not Julienne, I know he'd never harm her." She shook her head.

"Do you know what else we've discovered? That you, via a foreign investment company, acquired a majority stake in Compare. The company Jack founded. And was fired from. Is Jack aware of that?"

Faye drummed her fingers nervously on the table. The expression on Yvonne Ingvarsson's face was hard to read.

"You're not under suspicion for anything," Yvonne went on. "But we need to know, so we can understand what's happened."

Faye nodded slowly. "Jack left me for Ylva. I found them in our bedroom . . . All I wanted was for them to feel the same pain I felt. I was humiliated, I lost everything. Of course I wanted revenge. And I did everything I could to crush Jack. Not without good reason. And he hated me—again, not without good reason. But it had nothing to do with Julienne, so I don't understand where she could be or why you think he's done something to her."

She twisted her hands in her lap.

Yvonne didn't answer her question. Instead she said tentatively, "Those injuries on your face. How did you get them? Was it Jack?"

Faye raised her hand to her cheek and flinched with pain. Then she nodded reluctantly.

"Jack was supposed to look after Julienne while I went to Västerås for a business meeting. I wasn't sure about it, I only did it for Julienne's sake. Jack . . . he's been so angry . . . He's been sending me terrible text messages recently. Threatening me when he's been drinking. That's not like him. He was angry when he arrived, and that was when he hit me. But he calmed down after that. We talked and things seemed fine when I left. He'd never lay a finger on Julienne, he was just so angry with me, I must have said something that set him off. I'd never have left Julienne with him if I thought . . ." Faye's voice broke.

There was a knock on the door. A policeman came in and introduced himself. He asked to speak to his colleague and Yvonne went out into the corridor with him. A few minutes later she came back in. She was carrying a cup of coffee which she put down on the table in front of Faye.

"Go on," she said.

"Is there any news about Julienne? Have you found her?"

"No."

"Can't you tell me? She's my daughter!"

The policewoman looked at Faye with a blank look in her eyes.

"We don't think Julienne could have survived losing the amount of blood that was found in the hall."

"Oh, God, so she's hurt? She's bleeding. My little girl's bleeding, all alone somewhere?" Faye cried.

Yvonne Ingvarsson put one hand on Faye's shoulder but said nothing. The unspoken thought echoed around the room.

Instead of sleeping in her own apartment Faye used her spare keys to Kerstin's apartment and moved in there. The newspapers were running big articles on Julienne's disappearance. The police had tracked Jack's car to an area of forest north of Jönköping. There was a small marina nearby. The following day they found traces of blood on one of the boats. But no body.

In the papers Faye read that they were working on the theory that "the ex-husband and millionaire," as they described Jack, barely concealing his identity, had dumped Julienne's body in Lake Vättern. Divers had tried to find the body, but the area was far too large. Julienne was never found.

A week later, with all the evidence pointing to Jack, and after the evening tabloids had found out from their police sources about the amount of blood found in the apartment, car, and boat, they published Jack's name. Crowds of reporters gathered outside his and Ylva's villa on Lidingö.

Yvonne Ingvarsson visited Faye and explained that they hadn't given up hope of finding Julienne alive, but that most of the evidence suggested that she was dead. She was offered psychological support and the services of a reverend. But Faye declined all offers of help. She locked herself away in Kerstin's apartment and watched as the gaggle of journalists outside the building diminished day by day. The cuts and bruises on her face had started to heal, and she tended to them scrupulously. She didn't want to be left with ugly scars. The charges against Jack also included his assault on Faye.

Jack hadn't made any kind of confession. But the evidence against him was growing steadily stronger. The detectives had found the most macabre Google searches in his internet history. And threatening texts sent to Faye were traced to Jack's mobile even though he'd deleted them. All of this was reported in the tabloids.

The findings on his computer tightened the noose around Jack's neck. He had investigated the depth of various Swedish lakes, downloaded maps of the area where he'd parked on the shore of Lake Vättern.

A month after Julienne disappeared Faye put the apartment on the market and informed Revenge's investors that she was planning to leave Sweden as soon as possible. She kept hold of ten percent of her shares, gave Kerstin another five percent on top of what she already had, and invited the existing investors to buy the rest. Yvonne Ingvarsson tried to persuade her to wait at least until Jack's trial was over before she moved, but Faye told her she couldn't face it.

"My life's in ruins, no matter what sentence he gets. I took his business away from him and destroyed his relationship with Ylva. And he responded by killing our only child. There's nothing left for me here."

"I do understand," Yvonne said. "You have to try to be strong. The pain will never disappear, but it will become easier to deal with over time."

She gave Faye a hug at the front door before buttoning her coat and walking out onto the landing.

"Where are you moving to?"

"I don't really know. A long way away, anyway. Somewhere nobody knows me."

When Yvonne texted her to say that the DNA analysis of the blood found in the hall, in the trunk of Jack's car, and on the boat matched the DNA on Julienne's toothbrush and hairbrush, Faye sent a message consisting of the single word: *Thanks*. She had nothing more to say.

Seven months had passed since Faye left Sweden. She gazed out across the green hills that rose up in front of the Mediterranean. She had a chilled frappé in front of her. Jack's trial was over and the verdict was expected any day now. The media and the Swedish public had already passed judgment: Jack Adelheim was the most hated man in Sweden. Naturally, Ylva had spoken out in *Expressen,* with Jack's daughter in her arms and a plentiful stock of condemnations. He had evidently subjected her to psychological abuse throughout their relationship. Ylva garnered plenty of sympathy from the public. Faye couldn't help laughing when she read about it.

Faye had finally had the hated breast implants removed, and had put on twenty pounds. But she was still exercising. She had never felt happier in her own skin.

She looked at the screen again as she dipped a *cantuccio* into her drink. The whole of Sweden had been following the sensational trial, and Faye could almost feel the country holding its breath from the terrace where she was sitting.

She wasn't worried. She had done her homework properly.

The anchor on *Aftonbladet*'s website was shuffling some papers as a veteran crime reporter frowned and pronounced somberly that there was no doubt that Jack would be found guilty.

Faye didn't even bother to smile. She already knew she'd won. The aftermath was merely a formality. She was done.

Julienne called to her from inside the house.

Faye nudged her sunglasses and squinted.

"What is it, darling?"

"Can we go to the beach?"

"In a little while. Mommy just needs to finish looking at this first."

Julienne appeared in the doorway. Her bare feet echoed on the terrace as she ran over to her. Suntanned and beautiful, her fair hair flying behind her.

JACK ADELHEIM FOUND GUILTY OF MURDERING HIS SEVEN-YEAR-OLD DAUGHTER.

Faye quickly closed her laptop as Julienne climbed up onto her.

"What were you looking at?"

"Oh, nothing," she said. "Shall we go to the beach, then?"

"Do you think Kerstin would like to come?"

"We'd better ask her."

Faye closed her eyes as Julienne hurried away. Her mind wandered back to those fateful days more than six months ago now.

. . .

She hadn't been afraid of the physical pain. It was nothing compared to the pain she had felt when she found the pictures of Julienne in the folder entitled "Household." Her beloved daughter. Terrified. Confused. Naked.

The initial shock had been replaced by a fury that almost consumed her, but she held it inside her, knowing she would need it later. Her rage would crash upon Jack like an avalanche, there wouldn't be anything left of him when she was finished.

Lulling Jack into a sense of security had been simple, but doing all the other things she needed to do hadn't been particularly difficult either. She only had to close her eyes and see Julienne's naked body in front of her. Exposed. Defiled. By the person who should have been protecting her.

She had taken some painkillers, then drained a liter of her own blood. That was twice the amount taken when you gave blood, but she had read that given the amount of blood a body contained, she could spare a liter of it.

Kerstin had protested at first when she explained what she wanted to do, but after she saw the pictures of Julienne she agreed that no punishment was harsh enough for a man like Jack.

Faye felt giddy, lightheaded, but kept going. She mustn't pass out now.

Kerstin and Julienne had gone on ahead of her. It had cost a lot to get hold of fake passports and arrange safe passage out of the country, but money can buy you anything. And Faye had plenty of money.

When the doorbell rang Faye took a deep breath, then went to let Jack in. It was time to destroy him. He wondered where Julienne was, he was supposed to be babysitting her, after all, and she said that Julienne was on her way home. Three whiskeys later she had managed to entice him into the bedroom with the promise of sex, but, just as she had hoped, he lost consciousness after a bit of clumsy fumbling inside her underpants.

She looked at herself in the big bedroom mirror. She could hear Jack breathing deeply on the bed. She had given him a double dose, so nothing was going to wake him. And when he did, his memory would be hazy.

She took a deep breath. Let the darkness pour forth, past all the barriers she had put in its way for so many years. She saw faces in the water. Heard the screams that rose shrilly toward the sky and made the gulls take off in fright. Saw the blood disperse in salt water. White fingers clawing for something, anything, anyone.

She saw Julienne again. Her frightened face.

Faye hit her forehead against the steel bedstead as hard as she dared.

Then she inspected her face clinically in the mirror. Would that be enough? She had cut her forehead and blood was gathering under her skin, she'd have a lot of bruises.

Faye fetched the little lifesaving dummy she had gotten hold of and laid it down in the hall. Then she poured the blood Kerstin had helped her to extract over the dummy, so that it spread out around the head and upper part of the torso. She hoped there was enough blood. She couldn't have given more and still have the energy to do anything. The smell was nauseating and she felt dizzy and weak, but forced herself to carry on. She left the dummy on the floor while she got on with the final preparations, in the hope that it would start to congeal around the outline of the figure.

She pulled on a pair of gloves and carefully took a ziplock bag containing a pink toothbrush and hairbrush from her bag. They were both decorated with pictures of Elsa from *Frozen*. Julienne had removed them from the packaging herself and put them in the plastic bag, so that her fingerprints would be the only ones found on them.

Faye began by brushing her hair. She and Julienne had the same honey-gold shade of blond hair, the same length. She made sure to brush hard enough to pull plenty of strands out by the root. Then she carefully put the hairbrush down and picked up the toothbrush. She brushed her teeth and mouth thoroughly, pressing hard so the brush would splay and look well-used. She put the brush in the glass in the bathroom next to her own toothbrush. Then she went into Julienne's bedroom and placed the hairbrush on her desk.

After that she washed the whiskey glass containing the sedative and refilled it with more whiskey. She took the glass and bottle of whiskey into the bedroom where Jack was still snoring loudly. Faye put the glass on the bedside table and laid the bottle down on its side next to the bed. The room really did reek of whiskey.

There wasn't much else to do inside the apartment.

Faye picked up Jack's mobile and went outside to his car. She quickly tossed the dummy into the trunk. It left traces of blood, just as she had been counting on.

The rest was simply a matter of logistics. Driving Jack's car to Lake Vättern and back. Smearing a bit of blood on one of the boats moored at a jetty. She washed the dummy and threw it in the water. There would be so much odd rubbish scattered across the bottom of the lake that no one would think to connect it to Julienne's disappearance.

As Faye drove back toward Stockholm she knew that both the satnav in the car and Jack's mobile could be tracked along that route. The satnav would provide more detail than the mobile, but they would back each other up. Together with the Google searches she had conducted recently on Jack's laptop, it ought to be enough. She hoped it would be. The devil, as ever, lay in the details.

. . .

Faye parked the car by the promenade. A warm breeze caught her dress as Kerstin helped Julienne out of the car. They found three free lounge chairs and paid the attendant. Julienne ran down to the water at once. Faye and Kerstin lay on the beds, not taking their eyes off her.

"He's been found guilty. They're saying he's going to get life."

"So I heard," Kerstin replied.

"We did it."

"Yes, we did. Not that I was ever really worried."

"No?"

Kerstin shook her head.

A woman was walking toward them. When she caught sight of them she stopped and waved.

"Room for one more?" she asked with a smile.

"Yes, as long as you don't mind sharing with Julienne," Faye replied.

"I'd be only too happy to."

She sat down on the chair covered with Julienne's turquoise towel and put on a pair of sunglasses.

"Are you coming over for dinner this evening?" Faye asked.

The woman nodded. Then she turned her face up to the sun.

The three women lay in silence together. When Faye shut her eyes and listened to the lapping of the waves and Julienne's happy shrieks she saw Sebastian before her. His death had led her to where she was today. In a strange way she felt grateful to him.

She turned her head and looked at the woman on the sun bed beside her. She slowly reached out her hand and caressed her mother's cheek.

ACKNOWLEDGMENTS

Writing a book isn't something you do on your own, even if a lot of people think that's the case. There are many who contribute, who make it possible, and who also make the work less lonely. First and foremost, I'd like to thank my husband, Simon, who never wavers in his love and support. My wonderful children are also a huge motivation: Wille, Meja, Charlie, and Polly. Thank you for being there, and for being the best kids in the world. Thanks, too, to my mom, Gunnel Läckberg, and my in-laws, Anette and Christer Sköld, for all the ways you make it possible for me to write. There are so many people to thank: everyone who pitches in when life gets complicated—I am eternally grateful.

Huge thanks to Christina Salabi, who works hard by my side every day, even when I'm not writing. You are my sister in all but name. Thanks, too, to Lina Hellqvist, who is an invaluable part of our work.

I wouldn't be half the author I am were it not for my wonderful publisher, Karin Linge Borgh, and my equally magnificent editor, John Häggblom. I don't have the words to thank you. Of course, there are many more people at my Swedish publishing house, Bokförlaget Forum, to thank, not least Sara Lindegren: *Thank you,* all of you!

The same goes for Nordin Agency: Joakim Hansson, Johanna Lindborg, Anna Frankl, and all your colleagues who have done such a wonderful job over the years helping my books reach a wider audience.

Among the many people who play an important role in the creation of a book are the experts who provide information the author doesn't know, among them in this instance Emmanuel Ergul, who contributed a wealth of invaluable knowledge about financial matters. And, as always, Anders Torewi, who provided information regarding Fjällbacka.

Thank you to Pascal Engman, a ridiculously talented colleague who gave invaluable input when I needed to discuss the characters in this book. As always, my colleague Denise Rudberg has been on hand whenever I've needed someone to talk to about writing. Or life.

Lastly, all the sisters, all the friends around us who love our family. There are too many of you to list, partly out of fear of accidentally omitting someone. But you know who you are. I love you.

And thank you, Dad, for giving me a love of books.

An excerpt from

CAMILLA LÄCKBERG'S

forthcoming novel

SILVER TEARS

AVAILABLE FROM ALFRED A. KNOPF, JULY 2021

PART ONE

Two inmates convicted of murder escaped early this morning from their prison transport. When their prison guard stopped at the Gränna motorway services on the E4, the men seized the opportunity and fled into the forest.

Several police patrol cars were summoned to the scene, but the search for the fugitives has as yet been fruitless.

According to the Swedish Prison and Probation Service's press spokesperson, Karin Malm, the men are not considered to pose a threat to the public.

Aftonbladet, *5 June*

Faye switched on the Nespresso machine. While it made her an espresso, she looked out the tall window in the kitchen. As always, the view blew her away.

The house in Ravi had become her paradise on earth. The village itself wasn't all that large—it was home to just two hundred permanent inhabitants. It took all of five minutes or so to walk around the entire village, if you dragged your heels a bit. But in the center of the small piazza there was a restaurant that served the best pizza and pasta she had ever eaten. And it was packed to the rafters every night. Sometimes a few tourists would trickle in, and now that the end of May was approaching, their numbers were increasing. Enthusiastic French cyclists, or American retirees who had rented a motor home and were now fulfilling their dream of seeing Italy, while their grown-up children wondered despairingly why their parents insisted on having their own lives instead of being on call as babysitters for the grandkids.

But no Swedes.

Faye hadn't seen a single Swede here since she had bought the house. That had been a deciding factor in the choice of location. In Sweden, she was famous the length and breadth of the country. In Italy, she wanted and needed to be anonymous.

The beautiful old house she had bought wasn't actually in

the village—it was some twenty minutes' walk beyond it. It was high on a hill with vines climbing the slope toward the house. Faye loved to stroll up and down the steep village streets buying bread, cheese, and air-dried prosciutto. It was the ultimate cliché of life in the Italian countryside, and she was enjoying it to the fullest. Over the last two years, while her ex-husband languished in a Swedish prison, she'd made a safe haven here for the two people she cared about most in the world: her daughter, Julienne, and her mother, Ingrid. This week they'd been joined by Faye's closest friend and business associate, Kerstin, who doted on Julienne as if she were her own and had spent her visit competing with Ingrid to spoil the child.

The espresso was ready. Faye picked up her cup and went into the living room at the rear of the house, where the sound of splashing and happy childish cries divulged that there was a pool before it came into view. She loved the living room. It had taken time to decorate the house, but her own patience and one of Italy's most talented interior designers meant it was exactly the way she wanted it. The house had thick stone walls that kept the heat out and made it cool even in the hottest summer months, but it was consequently rather dark indoors. They had remedied that with large light furniture and plenty of discreet lighting. The large windows at the back also helped to let in light. She loved how, almost imperceptibly, the living room faded into the terrace.

The white drapes caressed her as she stepped outside. She tasted the expresso and watched her daughter and her mother without them noticing her at first.

Julienne had grown so big, and her hair—bleached by the sun—was almost white. She got new freckles pretty much every day. She was beautiful, healthy, and happy. Everything that Faye wanted for her. Everything that had been made possible by life without Jack.

"Mommy, Mommy, look! I can swim without armbands!"

Faye smiled and made an expression of amazement to show her daughter how impressed she was. Julienne was swimming in the deep end of the pool, doing a tortuous dog paddle but completely independent of her Bamse the bear armbands, which were lying on the edge. Ingrid was watching her grandchild nervously, half sitting, half standing, ready to throw herself into the pool if need be.

"Relax, Mom. She's got this."

Faye took another sip of the espresso, which was almost all gone, and wandered farther out onto the terrace. She regretted not having made a cappuccino instead.

"She's insisting on staying in the deep end," said Faye's mother, looking despairingly at her.

"I think she takes after her mother."

"Thank you very much, I can see that!"

Ingrid laughed and Faye was struck—as she had been on so many occasions over these past two years—by how beautiful her mother was. Despite everything life had put her through.

The only people who knew that Ingrid and Julienne were alive were Faye and Kerstin. As far as the rest of the world was concerned, both were dead, Julienne murdered by her father—a crime for which Jack was now serving a life sentence in Sweden. He had come so close to crushing Faye. Her love for him had made her a victim, but in the end she'd seen to it that he paid the price.

Faye went to her mother and sat down next to her in a rattan armchair. Ingrid continued to watch Julienne, her body tense.

"Do you have to go away again?" she asked, without shifting her gaze from her granddaughter.

"This is a busy time for us. Expanding the Revenge brand into the American market means negotiating our way through a lot of red tape. And then there's the Italian acquisition, which will give us a foothold in Rome. Giovanni, the owner, wants to sell, but like all men, he seriously overestimates his own value. It's just a case of making him realize that my price is the best offer he'll get."

Her mother looked anxiously from Faye to Julienne.

"I don't understand why you're still working so much. You've only got a ten percent stake in Revenge now, and you'll never have to lift a finger again given the fortune you made selling your shares."

Faye shrugged, drained the last drops of espresso, and then placed the cup on the rattan table.

"Sure, there's part of me that would really like to hang out here with you two. But you know me. I'd die of boredom after a week. And no matter how many shares I have, Revenge is my baby. And I'm still chairman. What's more, I feel a tremendous responsibility for all those women who came on board and invested and are now shareholders in Revenge. They took a chance on me and the company, and I want to carry on repaying that. In fact, I've been thinking about buying a bigger stake, if there's anyone willing to sell. It would be a good exit for them, at any rate."

Ingrid sat up slightly as Julienne turned at the far side of the pool.

"The sisterhood," she huffed, then caught herself and apologized. "I'm afraid I don't have quite the same perspective on women's loyalty that you do."

"We're in new times, Mom. Women stick together. Anyway, Julienne is okay with me taking a quick jaunt to Rome—we talked about it yesterday."

"You know I think you're incredibly smart? You know that I'm proud of you?"

Faye took Ingrid's hand.

"Yes, Mom, I know. You take care of the kid and make sure she doesn't drown, and I'll be home again soon."

Faye went to the edge of the pool. Julienne was snorting,

switching between strokes and swallowing mouthfuls of cold water.

"Bye, sweetheart, I'm off now!"

"Bye-b—"

The rest was drowned out by another gulp of water as Julienne tried to wave while swimming. From the corner of her eye, Faye saw Ingrid hurrying toward the pool.

In the living room, her stylish Louis Vuitton case was packed and ready to go. The limousine to take her to Rome had probably already arrived. She lifted the case to make sure the wheels wouldn't scratch the dark wood floors and headed toward the front door. As she passed Kerstin's study, she spotted Kerstin absorbed in something on the computer screen, her glasses on the tip of her nose, as always.

"Knock knock—I'm off now . . ."

Kerstin didn't look up. There was a deep worry line between her eyes.

"Is everything okay?"

Faye took a step into the room and put down the bag.

"I don't know . . ." Kerstin said slowly without looking up.

"Now you're making me worried—is it something to do with the stock issue? Or America?"

Kerstin shook her head.

"I don't know yet."

"Do I need to worry?"

Kerstin took her time to reply.

"No . . . not yet."

A car honked outside, and Kerstin nodded toward the front door.

"Off you go. Seal the deal in Rome. Then we'll talk."

"But . . ."

"It's probably nothing."

Kerstin smiled reassuringly at her, but as Faye went toward the heavy wooden door, she couldn't shake the feeling that something was going on. Something threatening. But she would deal with it. She would have to. That was the person she was.

She got into the back seat, waved at the chauffeur to drive, and opened the minibottle awaiting her. As the car purred off toward Rome, she sipped the champagne thoughtfully.